THE SPELL'S THE THING. . . .

But casting one, especially if you're a novice, could be a total disaster. And so the Academy for Advanced Study was created as a place to train those special students who hold within them the gift of magic. Still, kids will be kids, and playing with magic can lead to some pretty unexpected situations, such as:

"Snake in the Class"—Their assignment was to find and learn from a totem animal. But when Matt and Janice both ended up with the rattlesnake for their totem, they never imagined where it would lead them. . . .

"Diary"—They told her her name was Anna, and perhaps it was. They told her to write everything down in the blank book they'd given her, but words were the hardest thing for her to master. Yet if she failed in her assignment, it might prove the entire school's undoing. . . .

"Freshman Mixer"—The first school dance had its own special magic. But when someone began casting unauthorized spells, the party really got going. . . .

The Sorcerer's Academy

edited by Denise Little

DAW BOOKS, INC.

DONALD A. WOLLHEIM, FOUNDER

375 Hudson Street, New York, NY 10014

ELIZABETH R. WOLLHEIM
SHEILA E. GILBERT
PUBLISHERS

http://www.dawbooks.com

First Printing, September 2003
1 2 3 4 5 6 7 8 9

DAW TRADEMARK REGISTERED
U.S. PAT. OFF. AND FOREIGN COUNTRIES
—MARCA REGISTRADA.
HECHO EN U.S.A.
PRINTED IN THE U.S.A.

ACKNOWLEDGMENTS

CONTENTS

INTRODUCTION

by Denise Little

EVERYBODY wants to be a sorcerer. After all, it would be wonderful to blast whoever's responsible for the telephone sales caller who just interrupted dinner for the third time this week, or to have the four elements at your beck and call when you need them. But I always wondered just how wizards and sorcerers managed to learn to use their talents. After all, a substantial body of literature indicates that it takes a lot of learning to become a good wizard. The Harry Potter books are just the latest in a long line of notable volumes on the subject. Hundreds of books, from T. H. White's *Once and Future King* to Diane Duane's *So You Want To Be A Wizard*, have speculated on this. It's clear sorcerers need to study their craft. That study, I've always imagined, would be a good bit riskier than learning to parse sentences and do algebra. In mundane learning situations, very few courses (with the notable exception of chemistry lab—I can personally attest to this) have the potential to explode in your face and kill you when you don't know what you are doing.

But wizardry does—and it seems quite likely that a school for wizards would be a fascinating place, especially a school with an American slant to it. As much fun as the Harry Potter books are, they are very, very British. So I started to think about what an *American* school for wizards would be like.

To begin with, it would have to be a melting pot, a place where all sorts of cultures and influences from around the world would meet and meld. And it would probably be heavily influenced by the native magics of the land. And, since boarding schools are hardly traditional for most American teenagers while a bit of rebellion is almost required, the teachers at the school would have their hands full.

So I dreamed up a school and a cast of characters and, with help from Josepha Sherman, a superb folklorist and writer, asked some of today's best authors to come and play in the world I had made. You hold in your hands the fruits of that labor. Welcome to the Sorcerer's Academy! I hope your stay there will be an exciting one!

WELCOME TO THE SORCERER'S ACADEMY

by Josepha Sherman

Josepha Sherman is a fantasy novelist and folk-lorist, whose latest titles include Son of Darkness, The Captive Soul, Xena: All I Need to Know I Learned from the Warrior Princess, by Gabrielle, as Translated by Josepha Sherman, the folklore title, Merlin's Kin and, together with Susan Shwartz, two STAR TREK novels, Vulcan's Forge and Vulcan's Heart. She is also a fan of the New York Mets, horses, aviation, and space science. Visit her at www.sff.net/people/Josepha.Sherman.

"THE Captain has turned on the FASTEN SEAT BELT sign, indicating our initial approach into the Phoenix area . . ."

The flight attendant's voice was as smooth and level as though she didn't have a care in the world. Why shouldn't it be smooth? It wasn't *her* life that was getting tossed upside down, after all.

Janice Rosa Redding, fourteen years old and determined to be cool about being so far from New York and her home, snuck another look out of the plane's window and tried not to wince. Geez. Still nothing much down there but . . . well, nothing, mile after mile of it. Yeah, with a few buildings directly below that had to be the city. She had known that Phoenix was smack in the middle of the flattest part of the Sonora Desert, but there had to be something other than all that brown and tan emptiness. Something more than what she guessed were golf courses, that was.

She ran a defiant hand through her curly, yellow-brown hair. *I'm just stopping in Phoenix. I'm going on to Sedona. That's supposed to be green and really gorgeous.*

Janice fumbled in her backpack, which was stowed properly under the seat in front of her, and managed to pull out the by-now grungy and dog-eared brochure. *Welcome to the Academy for Advanced Study*, it read above the glossy photograph of what looked like a movie set of gleaming white walls and red tile roofs surrounded by greenery and under a sky that was just too blue to be real. She knew the rest of the brochure almost by heart by now:

> *The Academy was founded by Dona Rafaela de Leon in 1848, in what was then Mexican Territory, but is now, of course, part of the State of Arizona. Legend has it that the mysterious and beautiful Dona Rafaela was also a powerful* bruja . . .

Yeah, Janice thought. *The old lady was a sorceress, all right.* With a Hispanic mother and an English father, Janice was thoroughly bilingual. Her mother had given her olive skin and dark eyes, and she'd gotten her curly yellow-brown hair from her father. Too bad her grandma had given her a, well, call it a stocky build.

With a sigh that this time had more to do with fashion and boys than being uprooted like this, Janice glanced back at the brochure.

> *The Academy took its official shape in the late 1880s, mostly through the work of the equally mysterious millionaire William Bryan Reynard, who relocated it in the lovely Arizona town of Sedona. It was*

he who gave it the official name of the Academy for Advanced Study.

Right. And we're not going to mention that he was a sorcerer, too. Just in case this "falls into the wrong hands," or something.

The Academy for Advanced Study. Boring name. Just an ordinary school—right. Ordinary, if you happened to be a weirdo who could start fires by looking at a candle too hard, or knock a book off a shelf without touching it.

Janice sat back in her seat, gritting her teeth, remembering an unfortunate incident with a candle and her mother's best tablecloth . . . no, she wasn't going to think about that one anymore.

A weirdo like me.

". . . indicating our final approach into the Phoenix area."

Final approach, Barry Silverhorse thought, fighting down a shiver. *Good choice of words. Really good. Grandfather would say it was some sort of bad omen.*

He wasn't going to think of Grandfather, down there somewhere on the dry desert lands of the Diné, or the Navajo Reservation, as the white people called it. That wasn't his life, hadn't been since he'd been sent to live with Aunt Lucy in Los Angeles when he was six. (His mind shied away from memories of Mother and Father, of that late-night fatal car crash that only he had survived . . .) Aunt Lucy was a modern woman, married to an Anglo, with a really booming art business. Barry had been helping her in the gallery lately, and had even been allowed, now that he was nearly fifteen, to attend a couple of gallery events. Hey, he'd met Stephen Spielberg once!

Grandfather still lived in an old-fashioned Diné hogan, even though the other people in his clan had moved to more modern homes.

Right. With no running water, most of them, no electricity. Modern, as in modern rural slum.

That was what Aunt Lucy said about them.

Barry stared out the window, but the sun's glare made him catch his reflection as well, showing him the Arizona desert and, superimposed over it, the face of a wiry fourteen-year-old boy with reddish-brown skin, black hair caught back in a ponytail, and really alarmed-looking brown eyes. Just for a second, they glinted an eerie green, and Barry looked sharply away and pretended to be reading the in-flight magazine. Again.

I can't be going to the Academy. They must have made a mistake. I mean, magic, sorcery—that's crazy stuff. No one believes in it anymore.

Except Grandfather. Grandfather with his stories of skin-walkers. Witches. All of them evil. No such thing as a good skin-walker.

Aunt Lucy thought those stories were stupid, stuff that no one in the modern world believed. And Barry wanted to agree with her. But . . . those stories had sounded awfully real, particularly when he was . . . what, maybe four? When there'd been nothing but the fire of Grandfather's hearth and outside, the heavy darkness of the night . . .

And then there'd been the weirdness. The night he'd awakened as a coyote pup and ran out into the desert. A dream, Aunt Lucy had called it. A vision, Grandfather had countered. Or could it actually have been . . . real? A skin-walking . . . ?

I'm not a witch. That's just plain crazy. I am not a witch!

"Have a good day in Phoenix, or wherever your final destination may be."

Fourteen-year-old Matt Johnson bit back a groan. Final destination. Gee, what a really cheerful way to put it.

He unsnapped his seat belt and retrieved his battered Stetson from where it had slid under the seat in front of him. Then, since he had the window seat, Matt just sat and waited, watching the inevitable rush of people scrambling to their feet in the narrow airplane aisle, as though they would be able to actually get off the plane before the door opened. This wasn't his first flight; he'd been traveling on his own to visit Grandma in Tucson for the last two years.

Yep, but this wasn't going to be just a nice, cheerful weekend visit.

Sedona. YEE-haw, Matt thought flatly. In his home city, Dallas, everyone called Sedona the Land of the Wild Woowoos. New Agers. Crystal Worshipers. Tree Huggers. And smack in the heart of that was the Academy for Advanced Study.

Matt ran a quick hand through his short brown hair, trying to get it to lie flat, then slammed the Stetson down on his head and got up. The brim brushed a woman's arm. As she turned to him, Matt gave her his patented Charming Smile, blue eyes wide, and won a smile from her.

That's me: Mr. Charming.

Charm, after all, was easier than magic, and less likely to rile folks. It had gotten him out of a lot of tight spots. He was short for his age, much to his disgust, and with his blue eyes and brown hair really stood out like a sore thumb—a short sore thumb—among the non-Anglos he seemed to keep running into in Dallas.

Sure, keep to the normal streets, keep to the safe people who look and act just like you. Only, you don't act like them. Matt refused to think about the one time he *had* used magic to defend himself, the time he'd gotten cornered by a gang (dumb, dumb, dumb, going into their territory), but he could still hear the horrid snap of their leader's leg breaking.

I could have killed him. I almost did.

Grimly, Matt pulled his duffel down from the overhead compartment, standing on tiptoe to do it, and started down the aisle after the others.

The Academy had promised to teach him control. It had better do just that.

Janice glanced about in confusion at the bustle of Phoenix International Airport. You'd think someone from the Academy would have been there to meet her as she got off the plane—no, wait, what with all the new security stuff, it would have been difficult for even a sorcerer to get to the actual gate.

Oh, duh. She'd been given the transfer information before she'd left home. Janice checked her ticket, found the right flight number, then asked one of the trimly uniformed, smiling agents where to make the connection. It was in another terminal. Of course. Janice set off at a good clip, trailing her wheeled carry-on. The last thing she wanted to do was to make a bad impression right from the start by missing her flight.

"Hey!"

"Whoa, watch it!"

Janice had nearly collided with a boy pulling his own carry-on bag. At first glance he looked real L.A.—sunglasses, name brand T-shirt, and all. But then Janice felt the tiniest prickle run up her spine, and saw from his start that he felt it, too. The two of them said almost simultaneously, "You're going to the Academy!"

They both burst into laughter. "Oh, kewl!" Janice exclaimed. "I thought I was the only one."

"Me, too. Hey, come on, there's supposed to be a shuttle bus to the other terminal."

"And here I thought I had to walk all the—Hey, yo, wait! We're coming!"

They caught the bus just as the driver was closing the doors, lugged their stuff on board, and sat panting, side by side. "I'm Barry," the boy said after a moment. "Barry Silverhorse."

"Neat name! Native American, right?"

"I'm from L.A.," he said flatly, the humor leaving his face.

"Hey, I didn't mean anything!"

Silence.

"I mean, look at me," Janice continued. "I'm Janice Rosa Redding. Mother from San Juan, Puerto Rico, father from London—I'm an All-American Mutt, and proud of it."

That got a laugh out of him, and melted his stony expression. "Sorry. I didn't mean anything either. It's just . . . well . . . I keep getting asked stupid questions, like, 'Got any scalps?' or 'You live in a teepee?'"

Janice gave a wry little laugh. "People can be such idiots. When they find out my mother's Puerto Rican, I get things like, 'My, you speak English so *well!*' I was born in New York, for Pete's sake!"

"Well, anyhow, my people are the Diné, you know, the Navajo, but—hey, we're here. Terminal X-the-Unknown."

"Next stop, Sedona . . . This is the right terminal, isn't it?"

"Private flight, number 1672," the driver said. "That's it, all right."

They were the only ones getting off. The terminal looked like an afterthought: no bright lights, no comfortable seats, nothing but bare walls.

A boy stood waiting anxiously for them, shifting his weight from foot to foot. He was smaller than Barry, almost exactly Janice's height, and his well-worn Stetson and cowboy boots all but screamed "Texas!"

"Hey!"

"Hey."

The boy gave them both a wide grin. "I *thought* there were two more Academy folks coming over on this shuttle." He shrugged. "You know how it is about hunches."

"You mean intuition," Janice said.

"Guesses," Barry cut in.

"Well, anyhow, whatever you call it, I thought I'd wait right here for you. We can all get lost together."

His grin was just too cheerful. Janice grinned back at him. "Trouble comes in threes, you mean. I'm Janice Redding from New York."

Putting down his duffel bag, the boy held out a friendly hand. "I'm Matt Johnson, Dallas."

"Barry Silverhorse, Los Angeles," Barry muttered, stressing the city over his name.

Matt didn't seem to notice. "Now, all we have to do is

find out where we're supposed to go. Not easy with a private flight, is it? I guess—"

"Forgive me," said a chill voice, and all three teens started and turned sharply. "I am late." The man who confronted them was tall and lean, with a bony face and grim gray eyes. "You are the three children bound for the Academy, are you not?"

Something wrong! Janice's mind screamed at her. Feeling suddenly like a bristling cat, she snapped in her best New Yorkese, "Who wants to know?"

The thin mouth tightened. "Child, your manners leave much to be desired."

"Tough."

"Manners can be corrected. Now come, I will take you to the plane."

"Not so fast," Matt said in a "let's be reasonable" voice. "First, let's see some ID, okay?"

All this while, Barry had been standing motionless. Now he said softly. "Look. He has no shadow."

The three teens acted as one—but in three different ways. The magic from three different spells glittered and blazed, engulfing the . . . man.

"Enough!" a new voice shouted.

With a boom like a plane breaking the sound barrier, the magic fire was gone instantly, and so was the . . . man. Along with all evidence that he had ever stood there.

"What—"

"Where—"

"Who—are you?"

Janice thought that the man who stood before them, neat in black suit, white shirt and blue tie, looked like any ordinary guy working in some New York office. But there was something more to him. He was an imposing man, and she imagined he could be terrifying if he wanted to. With that narrow face and his slightly slanted dark eyes, he was probably an "All-American Mutt" like herself. Something in those eyes was, well, far older than his face.

"I," the man said, "am Professor John Edwards. I teach

Comparative Enchantments, and it is my turn to shepherd the latest lot of newcomers to the Academy. You will note my ID and the school call list." He flashed an official-looking card at them, along with a list of their names on the school stationery. "I will eventually be teaching you three why you do *not* release three different spells at the same time." Not a trace of accent could be heard in his educated voice. "I trust that you already understand that you could have killed yourselves with backlash, maybe even have brought down the entire terminal. You were lucky I was here to keep things under control."

As the three teens stared at him in dismay, Professor Edwards continued, "Forgive me for not having gotten here in time to greet you the moment you stepped off the shuttle bus, but even the Academy can't predict what new airport security measures will be implemented at need, or what delays they may entail. And pray don't bother introducing yourselves to me. You are Janice Redding, you are Matt Johnson, and you are Barry Silverhorse. What you just faced down in so spectacular a fashion was a Sending."

"A Sending?" Janice asked warily.

"Who sent it?" Barry added.

"An excellent question," Professor Edwards said. "If you three had left me a scrap of evidence in that magical mess, I might have been able to answer that. But I doubt it was a friendly welcome greeting. Did you really think that the Academy and its students are without enemies? Now come. Our plane is waiting."

The teens were silent for a long time after that. Janice knew why. They were no longer in the nice, safe world they had known. And they probably weren't going to get back into it any time soon either.

With a sudden defiant surge of hope, Janice whispered to Barry and Matt, "We're going to find out who sent that. And we're going to make him, her, or it regret it. Agreed?"

Grimly, they nodded.

* * *

Sedona, Janice decided in the van from the small airport, might have its share of weird stuff and shops with names like "Crystal Creations," but they couldn't hide the fact that the land was really beautiful. She'd never seen anything like the stark red rocks—sandstone, she'd read—cut by the clear blue of streams and surrounded by all that startling green. It looked almost too vibrant to be real. "Power," she said suddenly. "That's why the Academy's here. Air, earth, wind, and—"

"And the desert fire," Barry finished. "That's the four elements, all in one place."

"Very perceptive," Professor Edwards commented. "There may be hope for you three."

"There," Matt said suddenly. "That's it, isn't it? Our new home."

The three teens stared at the white walls, at the red-tiled roofs, at the beautiful wrought-iron gates that were, all three of them could sense, much more Powerful than they seemed.

"There's a whole city in there!" Janice exclaimed.

Professor Edwards overheard, and gave the smallest, briefest of chuckles. "Not precisely. However, you will find that the Academy does, indeed, seem to be larger within the walls than is logical from without. It also is said to be impossible to accurately measure those walls, but that, I assure you, is mere story."

He pointed out some of the buildings. "Those structures are the Chemistry and Alchemy Labs. The thick walls are part of their necessary protections. We don't want any little mishaps in those buildings to get out of hand—so the structures are hardened sufficiently to survive almost any sort of blast. That's the Foreign Magics Building; that is the Library, and that is the Experimental Magics Lab. You may be sensing something just about now. The Lab, for reasons that should be obvious, has triple Wardings for the protection of everyone outside it."

"What about those inside . . . ?" Matt asked warily.

"We usually don't have to worry about them," Professor

Edwards said. After a deliberate pause, he added, "If an experiment fails, there generally isn't enough of them left to worry about. Ah, here are your dormitories. This, students, is where I leave you."

Luck of the draw, Janice thought. Of this year's newcomers, she, Barry, and Matt were the last to arrive. That meant Barry and Matt got to bunk together, while she, since there were an odd number of girls this term, had a room all to herself. But she barely had time to start unpacking—the rest of her luggage had actually arrived just as she did—before something glowing materialized before her eyes. Janice almost let out a shriek before she realized that it was a message. Evidently, the Academy believed in saving paper.

> *Welcome to the Academy for Advanced Study. We here hope that you will find your stay among us to be both educational and enjoyable.*

The message obligingly scrolled down as she read it. Janice hurried past the pat words of welcome, stopping short when she got to:

> *It is expressly forbidden for any student to work spells outside the Academy walls unless in the presence of a teacher. It is equally forbidden for any student to discuss the actual purpose or workings of the Academy with anyone not employed at or enrolled in the Academy. Penalties for breaking either rule will be severe.*

"Now go out and have fun," Janice muttered.

No time for that, even if she was still somehow in the mood. A new message was forming, and Janice found herself reading a list of courses. Some were purely mundane—the obligatory courses in writing and mathematics, though she suspected those would have a magical slant. Others: Wow!

ASTRAL PROJECTION 101: Open to First Term students. Comfortable clothing recommended.

ARCHAEOLOGY AND DOWSING FOR RUINS: Prior archaeological courses required. Natural dowsers may attend, pending professorial approval.

ADVANCED YUROK SHAMANISM—

Not for me, Janice decided. She was hardly advanced in any of this, even if she wasn't sure who the Yuroks were or had been.

When she tentatively reached out for the list, it obligingly turned itself into paper, and Janice, heart racing with what might have been excitement or sheer terror, hurried off to sign up for her first courses.

John Edwards glanced about at his fellow professors in the Teachers' Lounge with its vivid red-and-blue Southwestern hangings and comfortable leather chairs. "Yes, this year's new youngsters do show a fair amount of natural talent."

Vladimir Vasnov, Professor of Slavic Sorcery, raised an elegantly arched silver brow. "Enough talent, it seems, to destroy a Sending. Very interesting, that."

As always, the man gave Edwards pause: With that narrow face, those clear gray eyes that revealed nothing of his inner thoughts, and that long fall of prematurely silver hair, Vasnov looked too much like something out of Faerie. Not, Edwards mused, that there were any Doorways into or out of Faerie in Russia. "Talented, I'll grant you, Vladimir, like all of this year's new arrivals. But they are also dangerously reckless."

"They are young. No more than that. They vill learn."

Susan Nagata sighed. "If they have the chance." The

Professor of Oriental Sorcery was fashionably dressed as always, today wearing a dark blue suit that smacked of Designer. "John, who created that Sending? Have you any clue?"

He shook his head. "The youngsters did quite a job of demolishing the creature. Hopefully it was someone of the Dark merely testing the latest arrivals. Equally hopefully, that someone learned a harsh lesson."

Professor Vasnov shook his head. "And by the time there is another trial?"

"Why, they'll be trained and ready for it. Or . . ." But Edwards had no need to finish.

Matt plopped down on the chair next to Janice, his arms full of books. Janice glanced up at him from the index of the book she was studying and read off, "Sendings, aerial. Sendings, avian. Sendings, clairvoyant. Sendings, clay."

"That sounds more like the Golem," Barry said, looking up from his own book. "The guy was definitely not clay."

He rested his head on his hands with a weary sigh.

"Second that," Janice said.

They'd only been in school for a week, and already it felt as though they hadn't slept the whole time. So much information, so many spells to be memorized, so much just plain academic stuff—

"How does anyone survive to graduate?" Janice asked.

Matt shrugged. "It's not even as though they've let us do any magic yet."

Janice snorted. "Speak for yourself. In Pyromancy 101, Professor Sanders got me so confused over how to properly get a flame started that I exploded a candle all over both of us."

Matt winced. "Good thing the course is held outside."

"Good thing Professor Sanders has a sense of humor!"

"What about you, Barry?" she added. "I mean you haven't said Word One about any courses."

"Nothing to say," Barry muttered.

"Hey, look, it's okay. You've got the talent, I heard the professors say you did."

"Great."

"Barry, I told you, it's okay. You'll get the hang of it."

"Maybe I don't *want* to get the hang of it!" Barry snarled.

"My bad," Janice said after a startled moment. "Forgive me for trying to help."

Matt was busily leafing through the first book in his pile. "I don't think we're going to find what we want so easily," he said, a little too lightly. "I never realized there were so many types of Sendings. Too bad we can't just forget the whole—"

He stopped short at the twin glares from Janice and Barry.

"I know, I know. I've been getting the weird dreams, too."

Barry sighed. "Professor Edwards says most first-term students get weird dreams at first."

Janice nodded.. "All that stray magic wandering about. First-terms don't have the skill yet to keep it away."

"That's what Professor Vasnov says, too."

Matt closed his book with a thump. "And we know that's not the case here. Someone's very, very interested in us. And if the teachers don't believe it, it's up to us to do something about it."

"Tonight," Janice said suddenly. "Hey, don't look at me as if I've gone crazy. Tonight it's the dark of the moon."

Matt and Barry glanced at each other. "Okay," Matt said, "I'll bite. What about it?"

Janice leaned forward, voice almost at a whisper. "We can be pretty sure that whoever was behind the Sending is going to try something else. Besides dreams, I mean."

"Oh, boy," Matt said without enthusiasm. "And the dark of the moon is the best time for the dark arts."

"No one is going to try anything inside the Academy," Barry protested.

He stopped, staring at the other two. "Oh. Oh, no. I'm not going there. Outside the Academy? Are you two *nuts?*"

"Probably," Janice said. "But, hey, what could happen that Mr. Charming Texan can't talk us out of?"

"The mind," Barry said darkly, "boggles."

"Don't you want to get this matter settled?"

He glared at her. "Okay, let me see if I've got this right. You want to leave the Academy where we (A) are perfectly safe, and (B) which we are forbidden to leave without permission to (C) work magic we really aren't skilled enough to use yet."

"Barry, I don't know what's the matter with you, and maybe I don't want to know. But are you in on this or not?"

In a soft, intense voice, Barry hissed, "Look, you don't know what you're doing. This is dangerous, maybe even evil. Keep away from it."

"We can't just do nothing!"

"Then you're on your own! I don't want anything to do with this!"

Barry heard Matt rummaging around in the dark dorm room, but he said nothing, resolutely pretending to be asleep. Matt made a little more noise than seemed necessary, but Barry didn't move. Matt even attempted a few "ahems," but Barry still didn't move. At last Matt muttered, "Thanks for nothing," and left, closing the door with exaggerated care.

Of course. He didn't dare slam it the way he must have wanted to, because the noise would have alerted someone besides his roommate.

"Idiot," Barry said into his pillow, and curled up, determined to sleep.

Determined not to worry.

Wrong on both counts. At last Barry rolled over on his back, letting out his breath in a long sigh. Why couldn't the others understand? He *couldn't* use magic; he *couldn't* become a witch.

"Can't?" asked a voice that wasn't really a voice. *"Says who?"*

"Says whom," Barry corrected with his eyes shut—then came sharply awake.

A man of the People, long black hair trailing over dusky red shoulders and chest, was perched on the foot of his bed. The man's eyes were the laughing eyes of a coyote. *"Who, whom. Silly white-man words. What are you?"*

I get it. I'm asleep. This is a dream. "I'm Barry Silverhorse."

"White-man first name, Diné last name. But what are you?"

"I don't understand."

Without any shift having taken place, the man was coyote, no, no, Coyote, the Trickster himself, catching the terrified Barry by the throat with his jaws, not quite closing. *"What are you?"* the not-voice repeated, somewhat muffled.

Barry froze. "Diné."

"A name!" The jaws closed ever so slightly, pricking Barry's skin. *"What are you!"*

What did Coyote want? Boy? Human? The jaws were beginning to close, slowly, slowly. "I don't know!" Barry cried.

"Ahhhh!" Suddenly the coyote was man-shaped again, back at the foot of Barry's bed. *"Now there is something useful. We may build on it."*

"Build what?" Barry asked.

"Only a fool denies what he is or may be."

"No! I am not a witch!"

"Names! Names! This begins to bore me, and you do not wish me to be bored, child. Do you want your friends to live?"

"Of course!"

"Then see to it."

With that, Coyote was gone, and Barry—

—woke with a start.

No dream. He knew it as surely as any of his ancestors who had ever come back from a vision. No dream.

Coyote wasn't going to let him do nothing. In fact, Coyote, being both creator and destroyer, might very well destroy Matt and Janice just for the sake of change.

"Okay," Barry said, pulling on his clothes. "You win."

It was awfully easy to get out of the Academy, Janice thought. Too easy, as though it didn't matter who got out, so long as no one got *in*.

Including us?

"What d'you think we should do?" Matt whispered.

Janice reluctantly shrugged. "Haven't a clue. Wait, I guess."

"Till something goes—uh-oh."

Janice whirled. At first she thought these were just a couple of ordinary people, a man and a woman, two New Agers, maybe, out to try some silliness in the dead of night.

Oh, yeah. Right. And I root for the Boston Red Sox.

"Isn't it a little late for two young people to be out alone?" the man asked.

"None of your business," Janice snapped.

"Such rudeness," the woman crooned. "Ill manners can be corrected."

Matt settled himself squarely on both feet. "Sorry, ma'am, but I think we've heard this before."

"A pity you haven't learned from it," the man said, and his eyes blazed, twin cold blue flames.

"You ready?" Janice whispered to Matt.

"Ready as I can be."

Her not-quite controlled fire spell burst forth. Matt's more controlled protective spell came up in the next second, shielding them.

The woman blazed up into fire—

Then the fire was gone, leaving her smiling at them. Her eyes, like those of the man, were nothing but cold blue flames. "Did you think that would hurt *us*?" she purred. "And did you think we were alone?"

Uh-oh. More of the blue-flame-eyed freaks. "Matt . . . I think we're outnumbered."

"I . . . think I . . . can't hold this shield forever!" he gasped.

Where are the professors? Don't they sense what's going on? Don't they care? Janice gritted her teeth and threw up her own wobbling shield, hoping it wouldn't short out Matt's.

"Ah, the human children! They don't know that there must be three."

Three? Three what? Matt was gasping for breath, falling to his knees, and Janice knew she was going to collapse beside him any second now. Three—oh, Geez, they meant Barry, three of them united. But Barry was back in his room, sound asleep. Barry wasn't going to—

"We have three," Barry said, and slid into the faulty circle beside Janice.

She didn't waste breath asking what had made him change his mind. As Barry's Power flared up, Matt staggered back to his feet. Janice felt his Power, her Power, Barry's Power, blazing up into a perfect circle of force. The blue-eyed things hissed in fury, but they couldn't get through.

Someone shouted out a commanding Word. There was a surge of blinding white fire, and all three teens collapsed like so many dolls.

When they struggled back up again, the blue-flame–eyed creatures were gone.

"We're not out of the woods yet," Matt muttered.

"No," Professor Edwards told them, "indeed you are not. I do believe you recognize Professor David Reynard?"

"Uh . . . yes, sir," Janice said meekly.

"Sir," Matt echoed, and tried a charming smile.

"Never mind that, young man." Reynard's voice was cool, and though he looked like any Wall Street executive called to an unexpected board meeting, his eyes glinted with a power that made Janice shiver.

"Sir, we—"

"No."

"But we—"

"No!" Reynard shook his head in disgust. "Do you really think you are the first students to imagine they knew better than their professors? And do you really think you were out here without anyone knowing it?"

Janice, Barry, and Matt exchanged miserable glances. "It was a set-up, wasn't it?" Janice asked. "A test?"

No answer. Obviously they weren't going to be left with any clear answers.

"Are we, are we expelled?" Barry asked hesitantly.

Reynard raised a brow. "Why, Mr. Silverhorse! I thought you didn't want to be here."

"I. uh, didn't. I still don't. But, well, I don't think I have a choice. If we still *are* students . . . ?"

Reynard might almost have smiled. "For now," he said, and turned away.

The three teens exchanged quick, confused glances. "*Was* it a test?" Matt whispered.

"I don't know," Barry admitted.

"I know one thing," Janice cut in, glancing back to where the blue-flame–eyed things had been. "We three have a *lot* to learn. And I think we really had better start learning it. Quickly."

The room was featureless, with walls of plain adobe, reddish-brown in the near-darkness. There were neither windows nor doors, but none who sat there heeded that. None of the figures could be seen clearly, as though each wore its own shadows. And all listened without motion to the one who stood before them, featureless as the others in shadow, and whispered:

"They have come."

A hiss from another shadow: "They are but . . . children."

Another whisper from another shadow: "So were the others. These bear talent."

The standing figure whispered, "They all do. But these bear more. They may be useful—or a danger."

One shadow rose, looming over all. "We speak of children with talent. Interesting, yes, but not a peril. We are the Ancient Ones, not mere humans of the Third Existence. We are those who were there long before the humans came. Do we fear their infants? Watch, yes, act where it seems fit. Try them if it seems valuable. Then, if there is peril . . . why, simply destroy the peril."

THE PRODIGY

by Laura Resnick

Laura Resnick, a cum laude graduate of Georgetown University, won the 1993 John W. Campbell award for best new science fiction/fantasy writer. Since then she has never looked back, having written the best-selling novels In Legend Born and In Fire Forged, with more on the way. She has also written award-winning nonfiction, an account of her journey across Africa, entitled A Blonde in Africa. She has written several short travel pieces, as well as numerous articles about the publishing business. She also writes a monthly opinion column for Nink, the newsletter of Novelists, Inc. You can find her on the web at www.sff.net./people/laresnick.

I didn't *mean* to set the Alchemy Lab on fire," I said. "Honest!"

Professor Reynard's face was calm, but I could see the glint in his eyes that I'd heard some of the other kids talking about. The glint that they all said you definitely didn't want to see there. They said you especially didn't want to be the one who *caused* that glint to be there.

I bit my lip and hoped that by some wild coincidence, someone else had put that look in Reynard's eyes today, and my accidentally burning down nearly a whole floor of the Alchemy Lab was a minor distraction compared to whatever real problem was troubling him now.

"Your teacher can't understand how it happened," Reynard said to me.

"Me neither."

He tilted his head and studied me for a moment. "The lab is warded against incendiary anomalies."

"Huh?"

"Getting burned down."

"Oh."

There was kind of an uncomfortable silence.

Then he said, "I'm waiting for your explanation, Ms. Fitzgerald."

I didn't need anyone's advice to know that his addressing me formally like that, instead of just calling me Sheila, was a bad sign. It probably *was* me who was making that spooky glitter appear in his eyes.

I shrugged, wishing he would look at something besides *me.* "I just lost control of—"

"Yes, you lost control of your work. Many students do when they first start practicing pyromancy. That's why there are spells in place to protect all the buildings on campus." He paused. "So either you are, during your very first term here at the Academy, already so powerful that the strongest warding spells which our finest sorcerers have developed during more than a century of accumulated study and practice are completely ineffectual against the might of your totally unskilled pyromancy, or . . ."

"Or?" I repeated, getting the idea that he didn't think that first scenario was exactly likely.

"Or something happened to weaken the wards in the Alchemy Lab just in time for your pyromancy class today." He raised his brows. "As you may have heard, Barry Silverhorse lost control of his pyromancy spell this morning. No damage to the Lab. So the wards were working perfectly today. Until you entered the building."

"But Professor Reynard, I didn't do anything to weaken—"

"Interestingly enough, while you were waiting outside my office a few minutes ago. I got a call from Professor Vasnov. The wards in the Alchemy Lab are working perfectly again. Ever since you left the building." He paused. "You see my point?"

Oh, yeah. I saw. "You think I'm . . . I've caused . . ."

"It would be best," he said, "if you simply confessed."

"But I . . . *How* could I have weakened the wards?"

He folded his hands so that his forefingers formed a steeple. "Although you clearly have a long way to go in pyromancy," he said, sounding a little sarcastic, "you are quite gifted in certain other areas. It's why you're here."

When I didn't reply, he closed his eyes and sat motionless and silent for a long moment, as if communing with the forces of nature. Or possibly, as some of the rumors hinted, he was communicating with Doña Rafaela, the maybe-not-so-dead bruja who founded the Academy more than one hundred fifty years ago.

Jesus, Mary, and Joseph, I prayed, *please don't let him be communing with a dead bruja, or even a not-so-dead one.* I was scared enough already.

When I was at an ordinary school in Chicago, any kid who accidentally burned down the lab would have gotten suspended. At the military school where they sent my cousin after he got in one-too-many fights, maybe they'd beat a student for something like this. But here at the Sorcerer's Academy, we'd been warned during orientation that things "worse than death" could happen to us if we screwed up.

Reynard's eyes were still closed. He was concentrating so fiercely on something that he didn't even seem to be breathing. Meanwhile, I was finding that the words "worse than death" didn't seem like the melodramatic exaggeration I'd thought they were when I'd arrived here for orientation six weeks ago. I wondered if he was going to grow fangs, or sprout horns on his forehead, or conjure up a manifestation of Doña Rafaela to punish me for causing—let's face it—a whole lot of damage to the Alchemy Lab.

"Okay, I lost my concentration," I said, realizing maybe it would be better if I confessed, like Reynard had said. "I admit it. I'm sorry! I remember what you said last time I was in here . . . which was only last week, I realize, which makes me maybe a too-frequent visitor to your office . . . but I do remember what you told me then. You said that concentration is the most important thing, that it has to be our primary concern, that our talent is special and has to be treated with respect . . ."

"Quite," he said softly without opening his eyes.

"It's just that, well, I've been thinking I made a mistake taking pyromancy, because it's been six weeks, and I haven't even had a *glow,* never mind actual flames . . . And so I wasn't paying attention, really. Okay? There! I've confessed! I wasn't paying attention! Because, well, why would I? Not a single thing has happened in six weeks. I was bored. I was! I'm sorry. And then Janice . . . Janice Rosa Redding, the girl from New York who says Professor Sanchez has a weird accent in Spanish? Well, Janice was telling me about this diet she read about the other day—she doesn't say so, but I think she's a little worried about her figure—where you only eat foods that begin with the letter 'q.' Get it? You can hardly eat *anything,* because, after all, how many foods begin with a 'q,' right? So then we started trying to name some. You know, like . . . quinoa, quince, quamash, quail . . . And we sort of got stuck after that . . . Which was when I noticed that, um, I'd finally started a fire. And at that very same time, I noticed that I'd completely lost control of it."

He finally opened his eyes. "What part of the instruction didn't you understand when I said, 'Quiet,' Ms. Fitzgerald?"

"Huh?" I clapped a hand over my mouth. "You said *quiet?* Oh. I thought you said *quite.* As in, you know, agreeing with me."

Reynard sighed heavily.

"I'm sorry," I said. "About burning down the lab. Also about talking just now."

"Nonetheless, through the din of your heartfelt confession, I think I have detected some unauthorized Craft in the room, young lady."

"What? No!" I was *not* going to let him assign me a punishment "worse than death" for something I hadn't actually done. "I swear!"

"Nothing whatsoever?" he prodded sternly. "No amulets? No silent evocations?"

"No."

"No enchanted implements? No magical articles?"

"No!"

"No spells? No charms?"

"No, of course . . . *Oh.*" Oops.

"Have you remembered something, Ms. Fitzgerald?" he asked so courteously that my blood ran cold.

"Um, well, it's nothing, really, it's just, um . . ."

"Yes?"

Doña Rafaela would probably appear in a burst of swirling red smoke, cut out my heart, and feed it to the spawn of hell.

"I, uh . . ." I cleared my throat, waved good-bye to life as I had known it, and started unbuttoning my blouse.

"Sheila!" He sounded shocked.

I only undid two buttons, just enough to open the neckline so he could see.

Reynard looked at the small charm painted on my left collarbone with a substance that was a mixture of ground saffron, camphor oil, and my own menstrual blood. (Yes, I know: *gross!*)

"An evasion charm," he murmured, staring at it.

"Uh-huh."

He suddenly made a disgusted sound. "To slip in and out of your dorm undetected after curfew, of course."

"Yes, sir."

"I should have guessed." He rubbed his temples. "To meet a boy?"

If only. "I just meet some friends, sir."

"And do what?" he demanded.

"Homework," I answered.

"Lying will not help your situation, Ms. Fitzgerald."

"We, uh . . . Well, mostly we eat chocolate and talk about guys."

"Corrupt youth," Reynard said dryly.

"I'm sorry, sir." I frowned. "But I don't understand what this has to do with what happened in the lab."

"The wards which normally protect the building failed because your charm was so effective that your presence, even your pyromancy, were undetectable. To the wards, that is. I think there's no doubt whatsoever that every *person* in the building noticed the fire, and that the chairs, desks, and electrical system have also felt the effects. However, in magical terms, it was as if neither you nor your fire were actually there."

"Really? Wow. Cool!" I saw his expression. "Um, I mean I'm really, really sorry about that."

"There is a *reason* that all unauthorized magic is strictly forbidden to students here, Sheila. As you have learned today, your own power is extremely dangerous as long as you don't understand the ramifications of the things you do."

"Yes, sir. I get that now."

"People could have died. The whole building could have burned down, destroying years' worth of research."

Now I was really starting to feel like crap. "It won't happen again, sir. I swear. I'll wash off the charm as soon as I get back to my room, and I'll never disobey the rules again."

"How comforting."

I sort of had a sense that he didn't believe me one hundred per cent. But I really, really meant it. Well, at least at that moment.

I asked hesitantly, "Am I going to be kicked out of the Academy?"

"No."

"Am I going to be . . . killed?"

He blinked. "No. I don't think we'll start right off with killing. It's early days yet."

"So . . ." I took a deep breath. "This is going to be one of those 'worse than death' things, isn't it?"

He coughed a little. Probably he still had some smoke left in his lungs. He'd been one of the first people on the scene as we came running out of the burning building.

"For the rest of term," he said, "you're going to have to clean up after the shapeshifting class."

"What? *Me?* Shovel all that . . . *stuff* they leave on the floor when they're in animal form? No way! That's not fair!"

He didn't say anything, just gave me a dark end-of-conversation look.

I shifted in my chair and realized I was probably lucky to get off with just shoveling crap for the rest of the semester. After all, I had broken curfew *and* violated a fundamental Academy rule *and* set a building on fire. And that was just *this* week.

"Yes, sir," I mumbled.

"I will not waste time," he said, "asking for the names of the friends who also break curfew to meet with you at night. I trust you will explain the dangers of the charms you're using—"

"I will!"

"—and that you're smart enough to realize we will be up-grading our building wards and threshold enchantments to ensure that no one else succeeds with the same scheme after this."

"Yes, sir," I said morosely.

"You're a very gifted young woman, Sheila, and I would like to see you succeed here."

"Thank you, sir."

"I would hate to have to inflict something worse than death on you, so I sincerely hope you've taken this little chat to heart."

"I have, sir, I have!"

"Good. That will be all, Sheila."

I shot out of his office so fast, you would think I had tele-ported. Janice was waiting for me out by the fountain, along with Barry Silverhorse. My heart did a little flipflop thing. Barry is so cool. He's from L.A. *and* he's a Navajo. Could anything beat that?

"Heard you set the Alchemy Lab on fire just to get out of class early today," he said with a grin. "A little extreme."

"I was just so eager to start studying for tomorrow's midterm in Cuneiform Incantations," I said. "Where's Matt?" Matt Johnson, a really talented but not exactly fo-cused guy, was the fourth person in our study group. We had a ton of reviewing to do before tomorrow's exam.

Janice rolled her eyes. "Matt said something vague about meeting us later in the Foreign Magics Building."

Barry said, "Betcha he shows up five minutes before we're ready to quit for the night."

Studying isn't what you'd call a way of life for Matt.

"So what did Reynard say to you?" Janice asked. "What did he do to you?"

I told her what had happened.

"And you'd better get rid of your charm, too," I warned her. "You'll be in a lot of trouble now if they catch you with it on your skin."

Barry looked from me to Janice, and then back at me. "What charms? I haven't seen any charms."

"It's nothing," I said quickly. *He* was one of the guys we talked about late at night, so I figured it was best if we changed the subject now. "I'm just glad Reynard didn't turn my guts into snakes or suck my soul into some hell dimen-sion."

"Or expel you," Janice added.

"And send you home," Barry said.

"Home?" I repeated. I hadn't even thought about going home. "It's funny," I said after a moment. "I was so home-sick when I got here, I almost asked my parents if I could just go back home. Even after being so excited about com-ing here."

"I know what you mean," Janice said.

I looked at her in surprise, then met Barry's eyes. He looked a little surprised, too. Janice had never before told me she'd been homesick, and she was so tough that it had never occurred to me she'd felt the way I did when we first came here.

"But now," I said, "I don't want to go home."

"For one thing," Janice said, "your parents would probably ground you until you're thirty."

"Yeah, there's that," I admitted. "They'd be pretty pissed off at me if I got kicked out. But that's not it. I mean, I probably could've gotten expelled by refusing my punishment, but I definitely didn't want to. I want to be here now. So if I have to—ugh!—clean up after the shapeshifters for the rest of the semester in order to stay here, then that's what I'll do."

"I'm glad I'm not taking that class until next term," Barry said. "I'm pretty sure I'd rather not know the person who, you know, cleans up whatever we do when we're in animal form."

"The feeling is mutual," I said.

Barry straightened up all of a sudden, his whole body alert with interest. I followed his gaze and saw what—or, rather, *who* he was looking at now: Susan Nagata.

"Runway alert," I said to Janice.

"Oh, boy," Janice said morosely. "She's what, a size two?"

"Hi, Professor," Barry said eagerly as Nagata passed our way.

She wore a tight dress and little jacket that had hundreds of thin black and white stripes going off in all different eye-clashing directions. Her high heels and handbag matched the outfit, and her eye makeup was perfect. She looked like a Eurasian fashion model ready for a photo shoot in Paris, not like a teacher of Oriental Sorcery at a secretive magic academy deep in the heart of Arizona.

"Hi, Barry." She flashed her perfect teeth at him. "Hi, girls."

"Hi," I said, wondering how she got her straight black

hair to hold a *perfect* shape around her face every single day. Magic?

Barry turned around and walked backward so he could watch her as she walked away. Barry is into Professor Nagata. So are a lot of guys. I keep wondering if she'll ditch this magic gig and go become a supermodel.

"So, for the exam," Janice said, "we need to review units one through six, plus practice our group chanting."

Barry, who was still walking backward, tripped and fell.

"Are you paying attention?" Janice asked.

"Huh?" As he rose to his feet, he craned his neck, still trying to see Nagata in the distance.

Okay, so it made me a little jealous. Barry's a cool guy, but he should pay more attention to girls his own age instead of to a woman old enough to be his mother. Or at least his older sister. I, for example, am exactly the right age for Barry.

Maybe if Nagata's eyes turned red, her hair stood out like a hag's, and all her teeth fell out, Barry—and a few other guys we sometimes happen to mention over chocolate when we're breaking curfew—would forget about her and pay more attention to regular girls.

We went to our usual room in the Foreign Magics Building and started reviewing all the stuff we'd have to know for the exam the next day. We worked right through dinner, but luckily Janice had remembered to bring doughnuts, and since I ate a raspberry one, I had sort of a healthy meal. We got through all our material except the chanting, and Matt still hadn't shown up.

"If he passes this exam," said Barry, who always had to work harder than Matt, "I will be so bummed."

"This is so inconsiderate!" Janice said. "If we fail the group chanting portion of the test tomorrow because he didn't bother to show up to practice tonight . . ."

I looked at my watch. It was getting late, and I was taking curfew more seriously than I used to. "I think we should start without him."

Barry looked skeptical. "I can't do both guy parts."

"So just do your part. We'll leave out Matt's part."

"But then that whole guy-girl balance thing that we spent a week studying will be out of balance."

"He's right," Janice said. "We could overpower him and unbalance the chanting."

"Big deal."

"You know, you already set a building on fire today," Janice said, "so I would think you, of all people, would be worried about what might happen if we do this wrong."

"Look," I said, "it's late, Matt isn't here, we have to practice before tomorrow, and I have to make curfew tonight. So I say, let's just do it. Matt may not need the practice, but I sure do."

Barry looked at Janice. "I need it, too."

She frowned, staring down at her textbook for a minute, then finally said, "Okay. I guess you're right. Let's do it."

So we started chanting. The whole idea of the chanting is that, by our third year, we should be able to start using it for conjuration—a subject we wouldn't even be allowed to take until next year. This year, we were just learning how to decipher the symbols and explore the basic rhythms, pronunciations, and metaphysical properties we'd need to know later to use the chanting as a tool in more advanced sorcery.

The three of us stopped chanting as soon as we realized we had a serious problem.

"What's happening?" Barry said, rising from his sitting position on the floor.

Janice stayed where she was and gazed openmouthed at the whirling pillar of gray smoke that was taking shape in between the two of us.

"What the hell is that?" I said.

The smoke grew thicker, billowing violently and moving faster.

"Have you set something else on fire?" Barry asked, hauling me to my feet.

"No! I don't know . . ." My heart was pounding. "I didn't . . ." Oh, but I already knew that I *did*. This whirling, ever-thickening cloud of dark smoke, now slowly taking shape, as if solidifying . . . "I feel . . ."

"As if . . ." Janice said. "It's . . . connected to me."

"Me, too," I choked out.

"Like we've . . . made this thing," she said.

"We have." I could tell. It had come from me. From us.

"Whoa!" Barry said. "You guys *made* this?"

"I think so."

"What is it?"

"I don't know."

"What's it—gross!—becoming?"

"It looks like . . ." I thought I was going to throw up. "Is that a person?"

"Ohmigod!" Janice said. "You're right. It's becoming a person!"

"You've made a *person?*" Barry started backing toward the door. "I told you this was a bad idea!"

"No, you didn't!"

"I said the balance would be, uh, out of balance."

"I'm the one who didn't want to do this," Janice shouted. "You two insisted!"

"Maybe it'll go away now that we've stopped chanting," I said.

"Oh, right, like I'm just *imagining* that it's getting more solid by the second!" Barry snapped. "Oh, my God! It's . . . got . . ."

"Eyes."

"Eeyuuuw!"

It had bright red eyes. Horrible, evil, angry eyes.

"Oh, hell," Janice said. "We've conjured a demon."

"Let's get out of here!" I cried.

"Wait!" Barry stopped me.

"Let go of me!"

"Wait!" he repeated. "Why is it wearing Ms. Nagata's dress?"

"Huh?"

"Sheila, for God's sake, open your eyes!"

"What? Oh." I hadn't realized I'd closed them. I opened them and looked. "That's . . . Nagata's dress."

"It looks like something's been chewing on it." Janice backed up against the wall. "It's all in rags now."

"This thing has hurt Ms. Nagata!" Barry leaped for it.

The thing seized him by the shirt, flung him against the wall, and issued a horrible cackling laugh. As it laughed, all of its teeth fell out.

"And its hair . . ." I said. "Standing out like a hag's."

The body which was still forming out of the thick smoke was lumpy and pudgy. I turned to Janice and asked, "You pictured her fat?"

Her eyes widened as she realized what my question meant. "You're saying . . ." She looked at the creature again, then asked me, "You pictured her with bad hair and her teeth falling out?"

"Uh-huh. And red eyes."

Barry demanded, "What are you two talking about?"

"It's what you warned against," I said. "Our power—female power—overwhelmed you in the chanting. Somehow we've created the thing that was in our heads."

"*This* was in your heads? Jesus, what's wrong with the two of you? I thought you were nice, normal girls!"

"It wasn't exactly in our heads," I said. "More like . . ."

"It was a thought we'd had in common," Janice said. "At the same time about the same thing."

"Yes!" I agreed. "And when we started chanting together, singing the same phrases in the same way, it sort of . . ."

"Resonated with the same thoughts we'd had at the same time earlier today."

"And what the hell was that thought?" Barry shouted.

I looked at Janice. She flushed. "Oh, um, just some stuff about Nagata."

Barry stared at us both. "You're kidding me."

Janice shrugged. I cleared my throat.

"What do you two have against Professor Nagata?"

"What we have to worry about now," I said, "is how do we get rid of this thing?"

"Let's get a teacher to deal with it!"

"No!" Janice and I said simultaneously.

"You really are crazy!" Barry said. "We can't just—"

"Sheila has already been in big trouble once today for breaking the rules," Janice said.

"That's right!" I said. "And the teacher did say we should never chant with an imbalance of genders."

"So if they find out about this now," Janice said.

"I'll be expelled," I told Barry.

Besides which, if any of the teachers found out about this, Nagata would certainly learn about it. That would be *way* too embarrassing. And Janice and I might both fail her class, too, once she knew the things we thought about her.

"What makes you think you can get rid of this thing?" Barry asked. "You didn't even know you were conjuring it!"

"We'll figure it out," I said. "I am *not* getting kicked out of the Academy." And that's what might happen if Reynard found out I'd broken another rule so soon after our talk. Stupid, stupid, stupid!

"You better figure it out fast," Barry warned. "It's starting to grow legs!"

"We've got to get rid of it before it can start walking!" Janice said, burying her nose in her textbook and looking for an answer to our dilemma. "Lock the door! We've got to do everything we can to keep it in here until we can banish it!"

Barry locked the door. "I just *know* I'm making a terrible mistake."

The lights started flickering. "What's that?" I cried. "What's it doing?"

"That's not *it*," Barry said, "that's the signal that we're supposed to leave."

"Oh, of course." I tried to pull myself together. They always flicked the lights on and off to warn students to leave the academic buildings and get back to their dorms in time for . . . "Curfew!"

"If you can't get rid of this thing," Barry said, "missing curfew will be the least of your worries."

"Go away!" I shouted at the Nagata monster. "Begone!

Get thee back to wherever the hell you came from! Shoo! Shoo!"

"Very effective," Barry muttered.

"I'm sorry. I'm panicking."

"That does it, I'm getting help!"

"No, wait!" Janice waved her book at us. "I think I've found it!"

Barry squinted at the pages. "We haven't studied that. We're probably months away from studying that! I can't even understand the first line of this chant."

"Me, neither. But I do understand this word in the title." She pointed to it. "'Banishing.'"

I seized the book. "A banishing chant?"

"You don't know that for sure," Barry argued.

The lights flickered again. Final warning.

"Let's try it," I insisted. "How much worse could things get?"

"Now you're scaring me," Barry said.

"I don't know any of these words," I said to Janice.

"We'll just have to do this phonetically and hope for the best."

"I'm going to throw up," Barry announced.

"No," I said, "you're going to guard the door in case this doesn't work. If the creature grows legs and tries to get out of the room, you'll have to stop her."

"Stop her? Did you miss the part where she flung me against the wall?"

"We're wasting time!" I said. "Someone's going to start checking to make sure the building is cleared."

"All right, chant," Janice ordered.

I took a deep breath, timed my opening prayer to meld with hers, and we began chanting the text together while Barry—looking like he really *would* throw up any second—guarded the door.

The creature shrieked as it realized what we were attempting to do. It reached out for us, trying to attack us with clawing fingers and enraged blows. I flinched, briefly losing my place in the chanting. Janice clutched my hand, her eyes fixed on the creature. It wailed and began tearing out its hag hair. The teeth which had fallen from its mouth and onto the floor now began dissolving into smelly gray smoke.

"I think it's working!" Barry shouted above the noise of our chanting and the creature's shrieking.

It *was* working. Instead of forming out of smoke, Nagata's pudgy body was now dissolving into smoke. She was gradually disappearing. Unfortunately, as her body disintegrated, it gave off a terrible odor while she shrieked in protest.

There was a sudden pounding on the closed door. Barry yelled with surprised fright and leaped halfway across the room. The dissolving Nagata beast reached for him. He shrieked and leaped back toward the door again. Someone thudded on it once more.

"Open up! What's going on in there?"

"Um, nothing!" Barry called over the final screeches of the creature.

"Open this door at once!"

"Professor Reynard, is that you?" Barry asked, keeping his gaze fixed on the transformation.

"Yes! Open up!"

"Yes, sir!" He crossed the room to open the window, and said to us, "Let's see if we can get rid of some of the smoke. And the *smell*."

Janice was breathing hard as we finally stopped chanting. "She's gone. She's really gone!"

There was nothing left but smoke.

"Is someone hurt in there? Is everyone all right?" Reynard shouted from the other side of the door.

"We're fine, Professor!" I called back.

"Sheila Fitzgerald? Is that you?"

I winced at his tone. "Yes, sir."

"Open this door now!" he insisted.

I met Janice's eyes briefly, then went to the door, unlocked it, and opened it. "Professor Reynard! What brings you here?"

"Reports of a woman screaming her head off in this

room," he snapped, brushing past me. He immediately started choking on the remaining smoke. "What's going on in here? And, my God, what's that smell?"

"We're studying for our Cuneiform Incantations midterm," I said, "but we lost track of time. It's awfully late, sir, and I wouldn't want to miss curfew, so I'll just be leaving."

"*Just* a minute, young lady."

"Yes, sir?"

"What was all that shrieking?"

Janice spoke up. "Sheila and I disagreed on a passage in the text."

Reynard's brows rose. "That must have been some disagreement."

"I hold very passionate opinions," she told him sincerely.

"And all this . . ." Reynard coughed a little. "All this smoke?"

At a loss, I finally said, "I think we must be downwind of the Alchemy Lab, sir."

"The fire there was put out several hours ago," he pointed out.

"But all that smoke had to go somewhere, didn't it?"

"And this *smell* . . ." Reynard looked a little nauseated. "Even zombies don't smell this bad."

"I . . ." Barry's mouth worked for a moment. "I meant to shower. Forgot."

"Me, too," I said. "Sorry about that."

Reynard sighed and rubbed his temples. "Ms. Fitzgerald."

"Uh-oh," said Barry.

"I don't think you're malicious or wantonly destructive—"

"Thank you, sir."

"—but you are impetuous, and because you are so gifted, that makes you troublesome, even rather dangerous at this stage in your development."

"I'm trying to do better, sir," I said honestly.

"I'm a busy man, Ms. Fitzgerald. I have too many crucial

tasks to accomplish in too short a space of time. I therefore have no time to waste."

"No, sir."

He looked around at the dissipating smoke, the empty room, and the three of us. Finally, he shook his head. "I suppose I should be satisfied with the evidence that nothing is on fire this time, and leave it at that."

"That's very generous of you, Professor Reynard."

"More generous than you deserve."

"Yes, sir. Can I go now, sir?"

"I would like that very much, Ms. Fitzgerald."

I turned to leave.

"And, Sheila?"

"Yes?"

"I would also like to have no reason whatsoever to speak to you again this week. Understood?"

"Absolutely, sir."

As we left the building, Barry said, "You are soooo lucky, Sheila. I thought he would turn you into a lizard."

Janice said, "No way. I think he likes her."

Barry snorted. I tried not to take it personally.

We were outside on the sidewalk, in the clear desert night, when a familiar voice shouted our names.

"Oh, *now* he shows up," Barry grumbled.

"Hey! Where are y'all going'?" Matt asked in his Texas drawl as he trotted over to us. "I thought we were supposed to study for the midterm?"

Barry scowled at him. "We just *finished* studying, Matt."

"Sorry I'm late, I just—"

"No," Janice said, "'late' would have been two hours ago, Matt."

"I'm here now, though," he said cheerfully. "So if—"

"I'm going," I said, "I've got to make curfew. Good night."

"Hey!" Matt called after me. "Aren't we even going to practice our chanting?"

SILVA'S DREAM DATE

by P. N. Elrod

P. N. "Pat" Elrod is best known for her wisecracking undead detective, Jack Fleming, with her *Vampire Files* series and writing the I, *Strahd* novels. She's collaborated with Nigel Bennett on the James Bond-style *Richard Dun* vampire novels, and coedited two anthologies with Martin H. Greenberg. She's written stories in science fiction, fantasy, mystery, and romance genres and is a card-carrying chocoholic. If you see her anywhere near Hershey, PA, notify the state police.

"WHAT'S the point of learning magic if we can't practice it?" Silva asked her textbook. It was open to a blank page reserved for questions. After a moment the lettering seeming to float to the surface of the paper. It wavered, settling into normal print that looked like it had always been there.

Just because you know how to cast a spell doesn't mean it's a good idea to do so. Like being a surgeon. Knowing how to remove an appendix doesn't mean it's the right operation for every patient.

Silva found that to be an unsatisfactory reply. It read suspiciously like something one of her aunts from the so-called "weird" side of the family might have said. One of the aunts who had insisted Silva go to the Academy for Advanced Studies in the first place. You got to learn magic, then couldn't *use* it? It was—Silva struggled for the right word—patronizing. Adults talked like that when they didn't want you knowing anything really interesting. She slammed the book shut and tossed it toward the end of her bed. It smacked against the other texts piled there and slipped to the floor with a thud.

"It never tells you what you *want* to hear, only what it thinks you need," observed Cassie from her bed on her side of their dorm room. She read from the same book, *The Ethics of Magic,* but was on a different page, underlining passages with a highlighting marker. "And what you need more than playing with magic is a fix."

"Yes, a fix." Silva sighed, flopped back on the wrinkled spread, staring up. Tacked to the ceiling so his face was the first thing she saw in the morning was her treasured poster of Darian Daye, the greatest singer ever. "He's sooooo gorgeous."

"Yeah, gorgeous," Cassie muttered, distracted.

Silva had big plans for when she was free to cast spells outside class. There were so many limits on what the Academy allowed freshmen to do magically. It was like having a driving license, but no car keys. "I want a spell that will bring us together."

"Too vague. You could collide with Darian in a car wreck."

Silva *knew* that, nettled at Cassie for reminding her. "Oh, you know what I mean."

"Yeah, but the powers you'd draw on for castings have a very warped sense of humor. They *will* take you literally. If you finished Chapter One, you'd know that." She waggled the book slightly, still reading.

"I did Chapter One. I passed the six-weeks test and all the pop quizzes."

"It's one thing to memorize a fact, quite another to apply it."

"You sound just like Professor Sanchez, but without the accent."

"Thank you." Sanchez was Cassie's favorite teacher. "Get another fix, Silva. Please? I have to finish this."

Silva redirected her attention back to the divine Darian Daye as he smoldered at her from the poster. She never got tired of his deep blue eyes, the planes of his fashionably gaunt face, his artistic hands, which for this photo were wrapped possessively around his guitar. If she could just put herself there in its place . . . Maybe if she went to the computer lab and scanned in one of her photos, she could blend it with a scan of the poster. Then his wonderful strong—she assumed they were strong—arms would be around *her*. But that was a lot of work to make it look right. One of the seniors at the school could do the job magically and much better, but she didn't know any of them well enough to ask. They'd probably consider it a waste of magic or something lame like that. Obviously they just did *not* understand true love, which is what Silva had for Darian and his music, mostly for Darian.

Without a doubt, he was the best. Better than any of the male solo singers or boy groups that populated the videos of MTV. Darian was a real live prodigy, playing and composing since he was seven. Those other guys could *not* compare. Darian was just twenty and had gone to platinum twice since his debut on the rock scene a year ago.

He just sooooo deserves it, Silva thought, reaching for the headset to her CD player. It was programmed to endlessly repeat Darian's two albums. She couldn't wait until the release of his third masterpiece and had already pre-ordered it from a music store in Sedona.

Silva cranked the volume and let the first deep crashing chords sweep her off to Darian Daye Land. In her mind's eye—visualization was one of her best magical talents—she recalled every shot of his new video. Silva put herself in the place of his dream-girl costar. They flew hand in hand through clouds of dry ice fog over a fantasy landscape of crystalline mountains. Above them stars twinkled in time to the beat. But instead of rejecting Darian at the last minute and sweeping off, thus inspiring the song's theme of wistful loss, Silva *accepted* his heart's love, and they embraced and spun to farther heights toward a smiling moon. She looked wonderful as the endless train of her white silk gown undulated in their wake like white fire.

What a letdown to open her eyes on the ordinary dorm room. Cassie still crammed on the ethics book. No company at all. Fortunately, she was also a fan of Darian or life would have been impossible, but she wasn't up to Silva's level of appreciation. That was fine with Silva, for it put her in the position of being town crier for the latest news about him. She visited his website daily, and cruised the net for fresh word of his activities. The fan magazines were only good for outdated stuff. And pictures. Lots of pictures. Silva couldn't resist anything with his face on it, but she only bought ones with shots not already in her thick scrapbook. Her allowance from home wasn't enough to cover everything.

Silva stopped the player, seized with a need to check the message boards linked to Darian. She wanted to read her cyber-friends' reactions to her last posting. She'd rewritten the words to one of his songs, giving it a happy ending, and put it up. They'd probably love it. They always loved her work.

She bounced from the bed, pulled on a light jacket against the night air, and left Cassie to wrestle with magical ethics, Chapter Two. Silva went downstairs to the dorm lobby, presently populated by other fourteen-year-old girls talking or watching the communal television. It had cable and was tuned to MTV nearly all the time.

"Silva! It's your guy again!" one of her friends called.

She rushed over in time for the last moments of Darian's video, the one she'd just visualized. Too bad he sang to that frozen-faced anorexic supermodel. "What does he *see* in her?" she wondered.

"She's there so guys'll watch, too. It's not like those two are dating." This came from Janice Redding. Being from New York, she claimed more knowledge about show people than the other girls. "That one's got an actor boyfriend, so your guy is safe."

Silva didn't want to trust that assumption. Everyone knew that rock stars always married supermodels.

"She's so skinny," Janice observed, unable to keep a touch of envy from her tone. "How does she *get* that way?"

"Genetics and starving." This launched a debate about achieving weight loss, including the use of magic. Janice was always interested in the latter, but had no success in her research, which was really too bad. Lots of the girls were on a secret waiting list for tryouts should she turn up a useful spell.

The video ended and one of the more extreme-looking VJs appeared, sharing the screen with a picture of Darian. Silva came alert to a news flash.

The VJ smirked. "Teen thriller Darian Daye is taking a break after work on his new video, going underground to escape adoring fans. What *is* it this boy has? I don't know, but the baby-babes can't get enough of it. MTV just learned his Beverly Hills mansion was invaded by five devoted, under-age fem-fans who scaled the wall, setting off alarms. The cops found them having a skinny-dip party in his pool. Darian wasn't there, but hundreds of miles east, busy on a shoot at the Grand Canyon. Too bad, girls, but better you get arrested than double-D, right?"

"Oh, no!" Janice shrieked, bursting into laughter with the rest of the room. "Those simps! What were they *thinking?*"

"Hush!" said Silva, wanting to hear the rest, but a commercial replaced the VJ.

"Skinny-dipping? In *this* weather?" said Janice, laughing some more.

"It's warmer in Beverly Hills," Silva informed her. "Besides, he has a heated pool."

"What *don't* you know about that guy?"

"Not a lot. Did you hear that—he was at the Grand Canyon! If only I'd known, I could have gone!"

"How would you get there, fly?"

Silva snorted contempt at that possibility. Flying was

strictly for senior students. "Taken a bus, of course. They've got tours from the hotels in Sedona. It's not that far."

"You'd have been busted for cutting class."

"It'd have been sooooo worth it."

Janice made a snorting noise, too. "You're crazy. I bet you'd have been the first one over the wall into the pool with that bunch."

"I'd have so *not* been there! I'd have knocked on his door like a nice person should."

This garnered groans, but Silva knew she was right. One of the magazine articles about Darian's favs and raves had listed good manners at the top of his fav side. In fact, he had a reputation for being one of the most polite, easy-to-get-along-with stars in the business. Those swimming fans had been out of their freaking minds to think he'd be amused by such an intrusion. Everyone *knew* Darian was the private type. He only went to parties when it was a charity thing. The rest of the time he lived in solitary, isolated grandeur, working on his divine music.

The chief theme of his songs was loneliness, of searching for the right girl. *He should meet me,* she thought. *I'd be perfect for him. I sooooo totally understand him.* After all, hadn't she rewritten the most perfect lyrics into something just as good? If she'd only known about his Grand Canyon trip, she might have been able to speak to him or at least hand him a note with her new lyrics on it—along with her name and address, of course, in case he wanted to write back.

News of his Arizona visit might be on his web site. Silva still had time before freshman curfew. The campus was very safe from darkside magics, but the rules were firm, and after sunset you had to be indoors at certain set hours depending on your grade level and magical ability.

She pulled her jacket close and darted outside to greet the startlingly clean night air. The stars were so much brighter than those in the city, with lots more of them. Silva wondered if that was a magic effect cast by the Academy groundskeepers or reality. Either way, it made a perfect setting for a romantic walk in the dark, just like in one of Darian's songs. She rushed to the Cyber Lab, craving news.

Though within the thick white adobe walls that enclosed the Academy, the Computer Building was a distance from the others, swathed with wardings to protect the delicate machines inside. When Silva first glimpsed those heavy, shifting shadows with her magical sight, she thought it was some kind of Fort Knox. She later learned that computers were generally allergic to magic and needed the shielding. Students with laptops, cell phones, games, and the like had to have mobile protections cast by Professor Boreus, the Cyber-Magics teacher, on a regular basis. Once a week they all trooped in with their gear to renew the spells under her supervision.

Used to the shadows, Silva passed through, then pushed open the real-world doors. The first thing you saw going in was a yellow-and-red warning sign strictly forbidding all practice of magic here. It even had a picture of a wand in a circle with a slash over it, like a traffic caution. Powers help you if Professor Boreus caught you breaking that rule.

The huge, low-ceilinged room of the main lab was bright, warm, and filled with the hum of machines and the click of busy keyboards. Several upperclassmen were at work on mysterious projects, but stations were still open. Silva signed the log and a student monitor directed her to an empty slot. One personal, super-private, and very, *very* cool Darian-related password to her account and she was on the net at her favorite web site in seconds.

She scoured the latest news section, then the other places where fresh information might lurk, but to no avail. Computers could spread data quickly, but only if their human keepers bothered to do any input. Apparently MTV had scooped them all. Silva saved the message boards for last, and got what she expected, wild praise from her on-line friends for the new lyrics. Along with those postings were the usual flame wars. There was a really big one going on between "DariansDoll," "DariansDelight," and "DariansDream," feuding because of their similar names. They'd not made a lot of friends with the constant cross fire, but the creativity of the insults was amusing.

Silva checked her watch. Good grief, only ten minutes to freshman curfew. She had to move quick or get detention.

Just outside, on her way to the dorm, headlights coming up the road blinded her. One of the campus carts, she thought, until it passed her. It was the biggest, sleekest, whitest limousine she'd ever seen on or off TV.

A limo? Here?

Silva stopped flat-footed with surprise. What was going on?

It swung majestically around a curve, heading toward the VIP bungalows. Some kind of special guest of the Academy, but who would use a limo instead of a car? She followed, curious.

Standing before the first bungalow in the four-plex was the head of the Academy himself, Professor Reynard. Wow. Who'd blasted him from his office? And at this time of night? Silva wanted to move closer to see better, but she wouldn't be able to get there in time. Already the chauffeur was emerging to walk around and hold the door for the passenger.

Use of magic without teacher supervision was discouraged if not forbidden, but she saw no harm in casting a viewing spell on herself. She centered, shut her eyes, took a deep breath, then uttered the words that would give her a few moments of "eagle-sight."

When she opened her eyes, the distant tableau seemed to have jumped a hundred yards closer. It was like she was right next to Professor Reynard himself. The lights were brighter, with everything in very sharp focus, better than binoculars.

The chauffeur reached for the door, opened it, and out came . . .

Oh.

My.

God.

Silva's heart nearly stopped right then and there.

*   *   *

"No *way!*" said Cassie. "It couldn't have been him!" Her ethics book forgotten, she crouched on the edge of her bed, taking in every word, yet not quite believing.

"No way it wasn't him!" Silva countered. "I know his face better than my own."

"What would he be doing *here?*"

"I don't know! I did 'eagle-sight,' not 'elephant-hearing,' but I swear it's totally true. Darian Daye is with Professor Reynard this very moment. They shook hands and went into the guesthouse."

Cassie rocked back, overwhelmed. "I'm gonna die."

Silva felt the same. She dropped flat on her bed to look at the poster. She'd not been mistaken. *He* was here, breathing the same air, walking the same paths, only a short run across campus.

Of course she'd been late getting back to the dorm, but the monitor let her off the hook. It was a first offense, and she misinterpreted Silva's shaking excitement for sheer terror at breaking the rules. Silva shot up to her room and fairly burst out the news to Cassie. It required several repetitions to sink in.

"What do we do?" Cassie now asked.

"Do?" Silva didn't know they were supposed to *do* anything, she was still in shock.

"Yeah. We need a plan to get his autograph or something. Maybe he's here for a surprise concert. But why wasn't there an announcement?"

"Because half his fans and their cousins would swamp the place. Reynard would never allow that. I don't think Darian's here to sing, or his backup band and roadies would be getting the auditorium ready. I checked on the way back and it's dark."

Cassie's face screwed up with thought. "What other reason could he have?"

"Magical consultation? Reynard does that sometimes."

"I bet that's it! Darian needs magical help!"

"For what?" Silva couldn't imagine. Her mind instead raced on ways and means to meet him. If they just talked once, if he had just *one* look at her new song lyrics, he'd know they were destined to be soul mates. *That* was why he'd come. He had heard her call. Funny, but she'd not done any specific spell along those lines. Of course, there was a *slight* chance that things might be otherwise, but she shoved such a remote possibility aside.

"You know," Cassie said thoughtfully, "except for Reynard, we're the *only* ones who know about him."

Silva fairly glowed. "Yeah. Isn't it great? Don't you *dare* tall anyone else! He's allllll ours!"

"Ours," Cassie echoed.

They sighed in unison, then began forming a Plan.

Amazingly, the campus looked the same in the morning. The mountain air was as fresh and keen as always, the surrounding buttes the same rich red stone dotted with green scrub. As it was Saturday, students lazily milled the walks of the campus or lined up for a bus ride into Sedona and whatever activities lay there. No one, absolutely no one, seemed to have the least clue that the greatest superstar who ever lived was in their midst.

Silva was up and gone before dawn to stake out the bungalow. She knew he still had to be here; his limo had driven off leaving Darian, a small suitcase, and a guitar case behind. The implication was he'd be staying for at least a few days, maybe more.

Her heart thumped fast and hard every time she thought of it, and she had to clamp a hand over her mouth to keep from squealing with unsuppressed glee. Wait till the girls on the message board heard about *this*. But they'd want proof. A picture, just one picture, would do. Silva touched the disposable camera in her jacket pocket like a talisman. Then she touched a talisman in her other pocket for good luck.

Silva had the bungalow's front door under close watch, concealing herself behind some convenient scrub bushes that were part of the native plants landscaping. They made a prickly hunting blind but were only fifty feet from the yard. She'd be there until noon, when Cassie was to turn up to give her a break. Cassie had signed on for extra credit in the Charms Lab and couldn't get out of it.

It was a dreary wait without anyone to talk to, but at nine a car pulled up, partially blocking Silva's view. Professor Reynard was driving, in a much more mundane vehicle than the fabulous white limo. He tapped the horn.

Silva struggled to stand on numb legs, her camera ready.

The bungalow door opened and Darian emerged.

He's gorgeous! Silva snapped one delirious shot after another as he walked to the car and got in, acting just like a normal person. Instead of his concert clothes—skintight leather and a satin shirt that always managed to fall off—he wore a plain black T-shirt and faded jeans. With his hair unstyled and sunglasses in place he'd have blended anywhere, but not to *her*. Silva would have known him in any disguise.

The car drove away. Silva was shaking. Hopefully, none of that had transmitted to the camera. The images would be small, but unmistakable. This was wonderful; she had exclusive shots of *him*. No one else in the universe had these. As soon as Cassie arrived, Silva would dash to the Student Union Building and their photo drop for developing.

Another vehicle soon pulled up before the bungalow, one of the Academy staff transports, which were like overgrown golf carts. A woman got out, snagged up folded linens and a cleaning tote, keyed herself in, and shut the door. About fifteen minutes later she emerged with a bundle of what looked like used sheets and towels, dropped them into a hamper bin, and drove off.

Seized with inspiration, Silva quit her cover, sprinting after the cart. Its top speed was faster than her dead run, but it didn't go far, stopping at a faculty house just up the street. While the woman was busy inside, Silva raided the hamper, puffing hard as much from exhilaration as from exercise.

Cassie threw a fit when she arrived at their stakeout spot. "You're absolutely *sure* it's his?"

"Absolutely sure. The hamper didn't have anything else in it." Silva clutched the pillowcase like the priceless relic it was, flushed with her brilliant success. "Just think: mere hours ago his head was resting on *this*." Resting, sleeping, dreaming, perhaps dreaming up lyrics to another song.

Cassie touched the plain white fabric with reverence. "Oh, this is huge. Bigger than huge."

"And check this." She held it out. "It still *smells* of his shaving lotion or hair gel or something."

"I'm gonna die!" Cassie's eyes rolled up, and for a time she was not too coherent, bouncing in place and giggling. Silva had to hush her, lest their hunting blind be discovered.

Silva was better able to keep her composure, but then she'd had time to get used to the idea of possessing Darian's very own pillowcase. Tonight she would lay it gently over her own pillow and dream of him as never before. She'd keep it safe in plastic forever and ever, and when she died, she'd be buried with it—unless she decided to generously donate it to the Smithsonian Institution or someplace like that.

"Dibs on the next one!" Cassie cried, recovered from her fit. She seemed to have advanced geometrically in her devotion to Darian.

Silva wanted to be the *only* girl in the universe with Darian's pillowcase, but Cassie was her best friend, and without her along none of this would be nearly as much fun. Besides, having the first one made Silva's prize extra special. She hoped Cassie would stop at nabbing a case. It would be too freaky if she took a whole set of sheets.

They waited the rest of the day, taking turns as the need for food and bathroom breaks struck, but Darian never returned. They speculated why he would be gone for so long, but formed no conclusions, though they'd laughed themselves silly at the idea of Professor Reynard being in the next rock video, perhaps dancing in leather jeans, too.

The chill evening dark descending from the mountains forced them back to the dorm just before curfew. Saturday nights there were like a big noisy slumber party, but Silva went to bed hours earlier than usual, blissfully laying her head on the sacred pillowcase, her earphones on and Darian's music singing her to sleep. Just before she drifted off, she recited the words of a dream-drawing spell. If you worked it just right, you could have the most wonderful visions, though there was also the risk of having nightmares if you were upset or anxious about anything. Silva wasn't worried about that; she was in her best mood ever.

Her dreams were normally the usual kind, bits and flashes of intense imagery, some lasting a few seconds, some for hours, nearly all forgotten once she woke. But this night she dreamed of a reality as solid as waking life, and it looked exactly like the fantasy scape in Darian's video. She was truly there, breathing flowery air, caressed by wind off crystal peaks as she floated in thick white clouds.

She flew toward the highest peak where a young man sat, Darian himself. He was beyond gorgeous in his rocker clothes: black leather pants and red satin shirt. With his long legs in front of him, elbows resting on his knees, hands clasped, he watched an endless sunset or sunrise. The colors shifted so you couldn't tell, and time was quite suspended, so you'd never know. This was a forever place.

He looked up at Silva's approach, smiled, and waved her over. She touched lightly down next to him in as perfect a landing as any senior could have managed. Silva wore the silky white dress from the video, only she looked much, much better in it than the supermodel. The long train billowed about them like froth.

"This is a nice place, isn't it?" Darian observed.

Silva was too choked to respond. He acted as though they were longtime friends. They were past the awkward moments of a first meeting, being so in tune that talk was unnecessary.

This is what soul mates are all about, she thought.

"Yes," he whispered, putting a strong arm around her. "It is."

They watched the enormous sun and the shifting clouds for hours and hours, and Silva was so completely happy she thought she'd explode.

Then Cassie had to spoil it all by bellowing at her. "What's the matter? Silva? Come on!"

"Noooo . . ." Silva didn't want to leave her piece of

heaven, tried to dive back into it, hugging her pillow that still held *his* scent.

"Silva! Wake up now or I'm calling the dorm nurse!"

"Huh?" Groggily she tried to push Cassie away, but it was too late. The perfect place was gone. She groaned in anguish. "Why'd you do that?"

"Because you were having a screaming nightmare!"

"I was not, it was wonderful!"

But when Silva opened her eyes, she wanted to dive under the covers again. Girls from their hall were crowded into the room or peering through the door. They looked worried and scared.

"Is she all right?" Janice Redding wanted to know. She was barefoot and shivering in a dorm T-shirt with "I (heart) New York" on it.

"I'm *fine!*" Silva blurted. "What's the matter with everyone?"

"You scared us into next week with the screaming," said Janice.

Screaming? She'd been screaming? Not in *that* dream. "No way."

"Yes, way. It was a psychic attack."

Silva got annoyed. "Was not."

"Was to. And you better tell Professor Sanchez about it."

"You're paranoid!"

"If you don't do it, someone else will. You can't scream us awake at four in the morning and think no one'll notice. You know the rules. Sleep disturbances can be a sign of a darkside attack and must be reported."

Cassie came forward. "Everyone out. The show's over. We'll take care of it in the morning. Go on!"

Reluctantly, and with some grumbling, they left. Cassie rounded on her. "Well?"

"Well, what? I wasn't having nightmares, so I couldn't have been screaming."

"You got a sore throat?"

"Um . . ." It was a *little* sore. She felt really tired, too, like she'd been running for days, but lots of people felt like that when jolted from the middle of a dream.

"Right. Dr. Sanchez, first thing tomorrow." Cassie went to her nightstand and scrabbled for a stick of incense. She lighted it, muttering the words of a protection ward, then waved the smoke around the room, especially over Silva.

She wanted to say it was unnecessary, but was too tired. She fell instantly asleep again. Sadly, there was no return to her dream.

The story was all over the dorm when she dragged herself from bed in the morning, so there was no way to ditch seeing Sanchez. Cassie asked Janice to stay with Silva, who was in a very grouchy, growly mood from all the fuss. She was also jealous because Cassie would head straight to Darian's bungalow in search of her own pillowcase souvenir and possibly better photos of him with her own disposable camera.

Oh, it's just too lame, Silva fumed on her way to Sanchez's office with Janice along like a bodyguard. Or a keeper. She delivered Silva, then left, probably to lie in wait in the dorm lobby with other curious students. They'd want to know everything.

Sanchez projected concerned curiosity and gave Silva a Coke from her portable refrigerator, which was very nice of her.

"How do you feel?" was her first question.

Silva had to tell the truth. The academy's faculty had an uncanny ability to know a fib when they heard it. Whether it was to do with magic or long experience was up for debate. "Not so good," she admitted. "Tired. I don't think I eat right."

"That's something you have in common with the rest of the campus," Sanchez said with a smile. She took a hit off her own canned drink. "Janice provided a vivid description of how you woke everyone with your screaming. Now, the dream itself, tell me about it."

Silva did so. She admitted to the dream-drawing spell,

but said nothing about knowing Darian Daye was on campus. She emphasized the peaceful nature of the dream, at the same time hoping Sanchez wouldn't laugh. Adults often laughed or teased a person about their favorite things particularly if the fav happened to be a rock star. They got—what was that word?—patronizing. But Sanchez listened to Silva's narrative with a somber face and nodded.

"It doesn't sound very awful," she said. "I wouldn't mind having such a nice dream myself."

There were rumors that Sanchez often did horrendous battles with really skanky darkside monsters. If those were true, then what kind of nightmares might *she* have? Silva didn't want to know. "You gonna analyze me or something?" she asked, worried. She didn't want everyone clumping around in her subconscious thinking she was weird or worse.

"You had a sort of wish-fulfillment dream, nothing more, but at the same time another part of your mind wasn't happy. Any reason why?"

Well, technically the pillowcase was stolen. The Academy had hundreds of them, maybe thousands, and wouldn't miss just the one. But it was still theft. She'd been taught better than that. Darn. Making a face, she asked, "How much are the pillowcases here?"

That startled Sanchez. "Why do you want to know?"

"Well, I sort of took one that wasn't mine, and I want to pay for it."

Sanchez gave her a funny kind of blank look. "You took a pillowcase."

Oh, great going. Now she does think I'm crazy. "I can go into town and buy another one to replace it, only don't take away the one I took. Please? It's *really* important."

"What does a pillowcase have to do with anything?"

Silva wanted to *explain* it all, logically, coherently, so even an adult could understand, but everything rushed out at once. "Look, I took it and I shouldn't do stuff like that and I can pay for it and I will but please let me keep it, please?"

Sanchez fixed her dark gaze on Silva. "*Chica,* why don't

you start over again? I think I have only just come in on the middle of the feature."

Silva winced. Adults just never seemed to *get* it.

"How did it go?" Cassie asked. She was in their scrub bush hunting blind, and she had snagged a pillowcase, but not seen Darian, so Silva was still in the lead for being his greatest fan ever.

"Wasn't too bad." Silva had finally told all about Darian and being overcome by temptation to get the case. But she loyally excluded Cassie, which wasn't lying, just leaving out unnecessary details to keep things simple. "Sanchez listened and didn't drop the ceiling on me, then she said I could pay for the case later and cut me loose. I think she was surprised to learn Darian was here. Just as I closed her office door, I heard her on the phone asking to speak with Professor Reynard."

"Uh-oh. This isn't over, then."

"It is for me. I gotta blow three bucks of my allowance. That's how much housekeeping said the cases cost. I wanted to use that on a magazine."

"Focus, girl. You've got *his* pillowcase. That's worth a million magazines."

The sensible reminder helped restore Silva's good humor. "You're right. You wanna go in tomorrow after class and pay for them? Get it over with?"

"Okay."

That resolved, they settled in for another turn-on-turn vigil, but Darian never once showed. At sunset, they slowly returned to the dorm, where Janice was hanging with some of the other girls. They gathered around Silva.

"Where have you *been?* What did Sanchez say?"

Silva and Cassie had agreed to keep quiet about Darian. "She told me to eat more greens and less pizza. It's no big deal, people."

Rumbles of disappointment, but they'd get over it. Silva was dead tired and wanted a shower and early bed. She had a killer eight o'clock class.

*　　*　　*

Darian smiled at her, blue eyes like the heart of a candle flame. "I missed you."

"Missed you, too," she said, lighting next to him again.

"Hard day?"

"You've no idea."

"Then rest here. I love this place. I love it best when you're here." He put his arm around her.

Silva nestled against his chest, so close she could hear his heartbeat, feel his warm breath ruffling her hair. It was so peaceful and perfect.

Then Professor Sanchez spoiled the moment by swooping down from the blue. She floated directly before them, but Darian seemed not to see her. Sanchez stared at him, though, her dark eyes like chips of onyx, her overall expression that of supreme disgust. Before Silva could say anything, Sanchez vanished, there-and-not-there, faster than a ghost.

"What is it?" Darian asked as Silva sat up to look around.

"Did you see her?"

"Who?" His voice had gone odd, and his body was strangely taut.

"Nothing . . . I guess I saw a bird."

"A bird? What kind of bird?"

"I dunno." She sank back on him again. "Darian, tell me what it's like being a rock star."

His voice was normal again, husky and strong, with just a tinge of sadness. "It's lonely. You've no idea how lonely. Like a constant pain. But when you're with me, it goes away, and I'm happy."

Silva knew *exactly* how he felt. They were indeed soul mates. "Then I'll stay with you forever," she promised.

"Thank you," he whispered, holding her tight.

Silva barely heard the alarm. If Cassie hadn't given her a good shake, she'd have slept right through it.

"What's the deal now?" Cassie asked. "You look terrible."

"I feel worse. Maybe I've got the flu."

Cassie bit her lip, as though she wanted to say something. "Lemme see your neck."

"Huh?"

"The last time anyone looked like you do now was in a vampire movie. That character came to a bad end."

"I need to do my hair is all."

"I'm talking about your aura, girl. It's paled out with holes in it. Casper the ghost with a Swiss cheese sheet."

Silva groaned. "Just leave me alone, you know I'm allergic to mornings." The odds were Cassie would report this to Sanchez. Why was everyone so freaky? Silva sat up. The room spun, but she made herself get dressed. It was probably the altitude. She was used to it, but if she didn't drink lots of water, she got sick. It was not, absolutely, totally *not* anything to do with the pillowcase, which was now plastic-bagged and in her backpack for safekeeping for the day. Cassie did the same with hers.

"You have any dreams?" Silva asked before going down to breakfast.

"Not really. Wish I had. About *him*."

Classes were just the worst. She always enjoyed them, was a good student, but today nothing went right. She was all thumbs, fumbled easy answers, and fell asleep in the middle of Charms Lab, much to her embarrassment, because it was her favorite course. She dropped off again, this time during Cyber-Magic. Professor Boreus nudged her to consciousness just as the bell rang. She handed her a homework study sheet without a word and pointed toward the exit.

It was Silva's last class of the day, though, and close to the bungalows. To *the* bungalow. She headed for the blind. Cassie was stuck in Psionics Lab for another hour at least. Silva settled in, getting her camera ready, hoping Darian was still there. He could have left at any time during the day, and she'd never know.

Professor Sanchez came walking up the street. She went up to the door and knocked. It opened, and Silva gasped, catching a fleeting glimpse of Darian. Sanchez went in.

Good grief. What was *she* doing there? With *him?* Silva fought a surge of jealousy. She burned to know what was going on. Maybe she could find out, just march up and knock. She could say she'd had another dream—which was true—and had seen Sanchez and thought to tell her about it, and oh, hello, Darian. I'm Silva, so glad to finally meet you. . . . If she'd been dreaming about him, then he must also have dreamed of her. He'd know her at first sight. He would.

She started a dozen times to quit the blind, but kept chickening out. Finally, she decided against it. Yes, she and Darian *must* meet, but *not* while she was in school clothes grungy from hiding in bushes. She'd wash her hair and put on something nice. Janice had some really red lipstick she could borrow . . .

Then it ceased to be a consideration, for there was Darian now, sitting next to her, smiling. They were on the crystal mountain again. "You look wonderful to me with or without makeup," he said.

Silva melted. He was just the most perfect, perfect, *perfect* guy.

"Don't ever leave me again," he pleaded. "Today's been an agony without you."

"I promise," she breathed. "But . . . but won't you be leaving?" Sooner or later he'd have to go back to his music, the tours, the concerts, the videos. She wouldn't be allowed to follow, but if he'd wait for her to grow up . . .

"Never," said Darian solidly, with warm reassurance. "I'll stay with you for as long as it takes."

For what? she briefly wondered.

But he put his arm around her and held her close. "Let's just be together. Let's just *be.*"

She felt very tired. It came upon her, suddenly, like the first blast of winter wind when you know the season has finally changed for good. She clung to him for warmth. He murmured soft comfort over her, but it didn't seem to help. Perhaps they should go to another place in this dream-world. You can do anything in dreams, right? Silva wanted to talk with him, ask him things. Soul mates should be able to do that.

Without interruptions.

Professor Sanchez swooped down on them again, her dark eyes blazing like a Fury. This time Darian was able to see her. He stood, still holding Silva close, but too tightly. She tried to wriggle free, but he wouldn't let her. Why was he being like this?

"It's all right," Silva told him.

"Was this your 'bird?'" he demanded. His voice was funny again, deeper, less friendly.

"What's the problem? We'll just wish her someplace else."

Sanchez called to Silva. She hovered only yards away, but her voice seemed to be from out of a deep well. "Silva, you must break from him and come with me."

"I don't want to. You go away."

"I'm serious about this, *chica*. Just do it!"

"But why?"

"You're the only one who can help yourself here."

"I don't understand! I'm not doing anything wrong. Why are you bothering us?"

"It's important. Trust that. I'll explain later. Then, if you want to, you can return to him."

That sounded reasonable. She could always come back; all she had to do was fall asleep and she'd be there, unless it was in the Charms or Computer Lab. Didn't those rooms have a lot of magical shieldings . . . ?

"No!" Darian cried. His arms wrapped around her, harder than tree roots. Why was he freaking? What happened to his nice manners?

"Hey! Lighten up! I'll get this out of the way and—"

"NO!"

His arms seemed to sink into her, become a part of her flesh, holding her in place. She screamed against that, lashing at him, but she was so weak . . .

"Silva! Use a Protection spell!" Sanchez yelled.

Those were easy, the first ones they taught you, as basic

as water. Until now she'd never needed one. She tried to remember the words. As she began to utter them, Darian's
hold on her loosened, but he clamped a hand over her
mouth. No matter, just *thinking* the words was enough. She
thought them, a *loud* thought, over and over. Why was he
being such a jerk?

His turn to scream. He let go of her, falling away.

She floated clear, staring. He didn't look like Darian any
more. In his place was a shadowy mass, all dirty green and
black, writhing on the ground, a blot on the pure crystal of
the mountain.

Sanchez grabbed her and shoved her out of the way, then
rounded on the thing. She shouted Power Words, arms out.
A glow bright as the sun coalesced between her spread fingers. She was building an energy charge, a really big one.
Silva hurriedly retreated, flying backward so she could
watch.

The charge swelled until it was a good ten feet in diameter. Within its sphere gold fire snapped and blazed, as
though eager to burst forth. Sanchez pointed at the mass of
shadow, cried out a Word of Direction, then backed away at
top speed. She caught Silva's hand in passing, and they hurtled over the dreamscape like fighter jets.

Behind them the energy charge engulfed the shadow.
What had once been Darian boiled away into black steam
that roiled on the wind. Its last agonized shriek shot up and
up, louder and louder. Silva put her hands to her ears, but the
shock wave of noise tore through her. They tumbled help-
lessly in the turbulence, falling, out of control and
falling . . .

This time Silva woke on a couch in a dim room with a
low ceiling. It was very confusing, frightening, to have Professor Sanchez bending over her.

"Will she be all right?" a man asked.

Silva froze at the sound of that familiar husky voice.
She'd only ever heard it before in the music or her dream.
Never in real life.

Next to Sanchez was . . . *him?* Darian Daye himself. Smiling at her. He looked different from his dream-self, in a funny way less real. He was still beyond handsome, but not superhumanly gorgeous. He wore ordinary clothes: a dark T-shirt, faded jeans, and some very scuffed cowboy boots.

Silva tried to speak, to move, but had no breath. She felt like her lungs had been yanked out and carelessly slammed back into place again.

Sanchez spoke to Silva. "Don't you worry, *chica*. When you fell asleep out there, I sensed it. Darian brought you in so I could look after things. A little rest and you'll feel better."

She managed to point at Darian, her hand trembling from the effort. "Uhh?" she asked. It lost something in the translation, but Sanchez seemed to understand.

"This is the real-deal *hombre*, not that creature you saw."

Darian stepped forward, taking Silva's hand to shake it. "Pleased to meet you, Silva."

She felt like she was outside of herself, watching some other stricken, slack-jawed girl meeting him.

Sanchez made a wry face. "I think you've killed her, Darian."

He frowned. "I hope not."

Silva tried to sit up to prove she was just *fine* thank you, but was very wobbly.

"Easy now," said Darian. "It takes time to get over a darkside attack."

She finally found her voice. "But no one's attacked me."

"Not openly. What Sanchez took out was a creature that feeds off psychic energy. It set up the perfect dreamscape to get past your normal defenses, then had a feast on your aura."

She shook her head, but that made her dizzy again. "No way. You'd *never* do anything like that."

"It wasn't me, but a thing using my form to get to you."

"Was it caused by the pillowcase?" she asked in a small voice. She didn't want to give it back.

Darian looked confused. Sanchez stepped in. "Only indirectly. The case had a trace connection to Darian, and the creature sensed your dream-drawing spell, and followed a thin psychic trail to you. It expanded the dreamscape. One part of you embraced the fantasy, another part that the creature suppressed from your memory screamed her head off, seeing the danger."

"How many parts of me *are* there?"

Sanchez laughed. "We'll teach you all about it later, though I think a crash course in dream-defense will prevent additional occurrences. You'll recharge your aura pretty fast, though. You've got lots of good energy. That's how you were able to get away from it. In that plane only you could save yourself."

"How do *you* know about darkside stuff?" she asked Darian.

He made a wry face. "I used to be a student here."

"What?"

"A few years back, under a different name. My magic's in the music, always has been. My parents knew I'd need special training to learn how to control it. You've heard stories of wildly successful musicians and actors burning themselves up? Mom and Dad didn't want me to be consumed by my talent."

She looked to Sanchez for confirmation. She gave a grudging nod. "Not one of our best students, but he learned what he needed to survive and prosper."

Darian shrugged. "When the pressures get too much, I come to the academy for a refresher. Professor Reynard's been working with me this weekend, using the area energies to help me get grounded. I'm really sorry about that parasite latching on to you. The things are attracted to my kind of psychic energy. Lots of artists suffer from them and get depressed, but here I learned how to repel them."

"It's gone for good?"

"Until the next one. They're like a cold virus. Get rid of one, and another turns up sooner or later. You just happened to have caught my 'cold,' and I'm really sorry about that."

"I totally forgive you." Silva was strong enough now to

not only sit up but swing her legs off the couch. She couldn't *believe* she was talking to him like he was a real person. "Could . . . could I ask you for an autograph?"

He chuckled, looking exactly like one of his videos. "I think I can manage that. I've got some photos stashed for special occasions."

"And one for my friend Cassie? Please?"

"Sure. But wouldn't you two and Dr. Sanchez like to go out to dinner with me? I remember a really good restaurant in town . . ."

Silva really and truly, honest to everything, thought she would faint for sure. She had to hold herself together, though. She had to find Cassie. Then they had to get ready. It would be absolutely the greatest night of their lives, forever and ever, and they'd take a million pictures of it.

"She'll settle down," Sanchez said, observing Silva's reaction. "I'm the same way about Mel Gibson."

"I'd like to see that sometime." said Darian.

"Invite him to the Academy, why don't you?"

Silva practically floated out the front door. Sure enough, there was Cassie coming up the street to hide in the blind. Wait till she *heard*. . . .

SNAKE IN THE CLASS

by Diane A. S. Stuckart

Diane A. S. Stuckart is the author of five critically acclaimed historical romances written as Alexa Smart and Anna Gerard, as well as other short fantasy and romantic suspense pieces penned under her own name. Her stories have appeared in such DAW anthologies as A *Dangerous Magic* and A *Constellation of Cats*. She shares her Dallas area home with her husband, Gerry, and an amazing assortment of dogs, birds, and fish.

AND that concludes my lecture series on Totem Animals of North America." Professor John Edwards, dressed as always in an expensive pale gray suit of distinctly European cut, stepped from behind the ornate mahogany lectern and swept his cool gaze over the classroom. "Any questions?"

A dozen ninth graders were seated at the refectory tables that served as desks in this particular classroom in the Foreign Magics Building. They collectively squirmed in their carved, high-backed chairs but remained silent. From his own spot safely in the second row, Matt Johnson scrunched his skinny frame a little lower beneath the table and deliberately clamped his own mouth shut. If he hadn't done so, he might have been tempted to blurt some glib query.

Yo, Teach, can you tell us again how those totems got on those poles?

Back in public school, such a response would have been his duty as the acknowledged class clown . . . a role he had played since Grade One, Day One. It would have rated laughs from his fellow students back in Texas, and maybe even an unwilling smile from his teacher. But in the few short weeks he'd spent in Sedona, Arizona, at the Academy for Advanced Study—Sorcerer U, as its students dubbed it—Matt quickly had learned that the instructors there neither appreciated nor tolerated stand-up comedy in their classrooms.

Edwards' cool voice cut short Matt's musings. "Very well, I take it that everyone has a firm grasp on the material we have been discussing. Let us move on, then, to the matter uppermost in your minds, your midterm assignment."

Muffled groans arose from the students. Ignoring the despairing chorus, Edwards went on, "I have provided you with both traditional and anecdotal information regarding various totem animals, and how they serve as conduits between the mundane and magical worlds. You will be assigned one of these totem animal species as a research subject. Your task will be to communicate with a magical representative of its number. Once you have gathered sufficient field data, you will then author a thesis comparing your real-life experiences with that totem against existing opinion. Any questions regarding the scope of the project?"

"Uh, Professor Edwards?" a tentative voice spoke from the front row. It was Billy Winslow, whose mild manner and skill at the mystical healing arts both were at odds with his football player looks. "Where do we find these animals?"

"If you will recall my first lecture, Mr. Winslow, I explained that we do not find totem animals. Totem animals find us. Any other questions?"

Billy meekly shook his head, and Matt grimaced in sympathy. One major difference he'd immediately noticed between Sorcerer U and the Dallas public school system, from which he had come (beyond the obvious fact that the Academy's primary curriculum centered on magic) was that the former basically was a "no bullcrap allowed" kind of place. Ask a stupid question in Professor Edwards' class—a question that demonstrated you'd either not been listening to the lecture, or else had not taken time to try to puzzle out the answer yourself—and you'd soon find your self-esteem stomped all to pieces!

Edwards, meanwhile, had turned to the old-fashioned blackboard behind him. Upon it were listed in a chalked copperplate hand the names of twenty different animal species. He gave a careless gesture, and immediately all but six names—Eagle, Coyote, Cougar, Bear, Deer, and Rattlesnake—vanished from the board.

"These are the totems upon which we shall concentrate our efforts," he continued. "As we have twelve students, you will work in teams of two. The teams and the totem animals, I shall assign at random."

With that, Edwards reached into his jacket pocket and withdrew what appeared to be a slim deck of oversized playing cards. He gave them a shuffle, and then spread his palms wide.

Rather than scattering to the floor, the cards took flight. They circled him for a moment in a miniature whirlwind, before heading in formation up toward the high ceiling. There, they fluttered amid the wood beams for a few moments, whirring like doves released from their cote. Then, regrouping, they began executing various precision moves in a pasteboard version of the Blue Angels.

Matt and the other students grinned as they watched the demonstration. As far as magic went, this was strictly a parlor trick. Most of them could have replicated the feat, to some degree. None, however, could have sent those cards aloft with quite the easy grace of Edwards, nor have put them through such a complicated series of moves with seemingly no effort, as he now was doing.

And all of them knew that.

Which was the entire reason for their being at Sorcerer U, this opportunity to hone their respective skills in the magical arts. The students in his class had walked into the school just a few weeks earlier, possessed of little more than the raw aptitude for magic with which they'd been gifted at birth. With the guidance of the Academy's professors—each a master in his or her own particular field of magic—they'd begun the process of harnessing their talents into something manageable. By the time they graduated, four years hence, the majority of them would have grown into skilled practitioners of sorcery.

For Matt, the experience of being with others who had magical abilities was as unsettling as it was exciting. Back home, he'd always suppressed his talents, all too aware of the fear he would generate in the mundane world should anyone learn just what he could do. His father had encouraged that attitude, likening his sorcery skills to the black belt in tae kwon do that Matt had earned the year before.

Use your magic only as a last resort . . . only when you can't walk or talk your way out of a bad situation. Given Matt's glib tongue and swift feet—he might have been the shortest kid in his old class in Dallas, but he also was the fastest—he'd had little occasion to use his talents. Thus, only his immediate family knew that he was far different from most other teenagers.

And none of them, including him, had any idea just how powerful his magical skills might be.

Matt glanced about at his classmates and wondered if their experience outside Sorcerer U had been like his. He'd come to know most of them fairly well by now, and had a fair idea of their various magical skills. At the same table with Billy was Tyrone McNulty, a very broad and very silent African-American youth with an affinity for fire. Beside Matt sat Barry Silverhorse, the young Navajo from L.A. with a deep interest in Native American magic, who'd become his closest friend, so far, at the Academy. And, on the other side of Barry, sat Janice Redding . . . a loose cannon when it came to magic, and the biggest pain in the butt in the entire freshman class.

It was a distinction that she had earned big-time, in Matt's humble opinion. For starters, Janice persisted in playing the role of the street-smart kid. The problem was, everyone at school *knew* that she came from a rich family and could barely even see the street from her family's high-rise apartment. She dressed tough, too . . . usually in black jeans and T-shirt, both of which were just a tad too tight for her stocky figure, her curly yellow-brown hair held messily atop her head with one of those things that looked like a potato chip bag clip. What irritated him most about her, though, was the fact she always was complaining how much she hated living in Arizona, and proclaiming that the East Coast was the only place to be. Matt was homesick sometimes, too—heck, he'd never lived away from his family before, either—but he didn't yammer on about it like some people did.

The one time in the cafeteria that he'd finally told her off, she'd socked him with the psi equivalent of a right hook, dumping his soda into his lap. Since he was already late for his next class, he'd had to cover the big wet patch at the front of his jeans with his textbooks for a whole hour before he could make it back to his room to change. He'd not yet forgiven her for that one . . . wouldn't, until he'd paid her back, somehow.

As if hearing that thought, Janice turned in his direction just in time to catch his gaze. She sneered and mouthed the word, *dweeb.* He grinned in return, and she scowled even deeper, then whipped her attention back to the cards.

Satisfied that he'd won this round, he glanced up at the cards, as well. Each now broke away from the pasteboard flock to flutter gently down onto one of the polished tables below. By the time the final one made its landing, a single card lay facedown in front of every student.

His momentary lapse into showbiz concluded, Professor Edwards returned to the lectern and began gathering his lecture materials. "You will notice before you a playing card," he pointed out with cool understatement as he stacked his books. "On its reverse side, instead of the traditional suits and numbers, is one of the six totem animals. One other person in the class has the same card as do you. You may turn them over now, and discover the totem which you will research, and the person who will be your lab partner for this project."

A murmur of excitement arose as the teens began flipping over cards and comparing notes with their fellow students. Matt grabbed up his, hoping he'd lucked into one of the cooler totems . . . the Bear, or maybe the Cougar.

Rattlesnake.

He gave a philosophical shrug. At least he hadn't got stuck with the Deer, he told himself. Talk about wussie! Now, time to find out who his partner would be. Eagerly, he turned to Barry.

"Sorry, dude," Barry said with a shake of his ponytailed head, displaying his card, "but I got the Cougar."

"Me, too," Tyrone spoke up, swiveling his broad torso in his chair to grin and high-five his new partner.

A disappointed Matt glanced over at Carlie Barstock, considered the class hottie by most of the guys. Teaming up with her sure would make up for not being lab partners with Barry! Unfortunately, the petite redhead already was in eager conversation with the Winslow kid, and he could see they held matching Eagle totem cards. Everyone else seemed paired up, as well, leaning over tables or switching chairs to join up with their respective partners. Matt frowned. Professor Edward had said that there was two of each card, which meant a partner for everybody.

So who was left?

A leaden sensation—rather like the feeling he'd had the time he'd eaten five Big Macs in one sitting—settled in his gut. *No, no, no, no,* came the panicked thought as he shot a quick look past Barry. Alone of the other students, Janice was still frowning at her card, absently twirling a stray yellow-brown curl with one finger.

"Well, crud, " she announced to no one in particular, "I wonder who else got the friggin' Rattlesnake totem?"

Janice Rosa Redding sat outside Desert Creme, an up-scale ice cream parlor tucked between a couple of trendy art galleries in Uptown Sedona. She was spooning up the first of three scoops of rapidly melting Red Rocky Road, and ignoring the three teenage boys seated a couple of glass-topped tables away from hers. At least, she was trying to ignore them. It was hard not to overhear the sniggering comments that accompanied the laughing glances they shot over their shoulders at her.

Her brown eyes narrowed, and her nostrils flared. *Yeah, right, and you friggin' guys all give Brad Pitt a run for his money. Well, I'm not impressed.* She guessed them to be around sixteen . . . a couple of years older than she. One had red hair, the other two had brown, and all three were football players, by the size of them. Which also meant that, collectively, they probably were as smart as a box of rocks.

Nope, not impressed, at all.

She returned her attention to her ice cream, blinking back sudden, angry tears as she pretended not to hear the moos and barks that now came from that direction. So what if she didn't look like one of those anorexic TV actresses that all the boys seemed to think were so hot? She might weigh a couple of extra pounds more than she should, but she wasn't a dog!

Not to mention the fact that, if they truly ticked her off, she could zap them with a good old-fashioned magic spell guaranteed to give them either a) a nasty case of zits, b) jock itch, c) the runs, or d) all of the above. Unfortunately, that sort of retribution was expressly forbidden to Sorcerer U students. Heck, it was written out in boldfaced type in the handbook they'd received the first day.

Don't call undue attention to yourself or the school, was the first rule. *Don't use magic against the magic-less,* was the second.

That latter had been a hard habit for her to break. At her

old school, she'd not hesitated to zap her fellow classmates when they ragged on her. Usually, the insults had been about her weight; sometimes, because she was of mixed heritage . . . Hispanic and English. While no one had ever figured out she was using magic, the principle of negative reinforcement had worked, and they'd eventually left her alone. Here, she could use only her sharp tongue to deflect insults. Still, nothing in the code said she couldn't think about a little paranormal butt kicking!

So satisfactory was the contemplation of that fantasy vengeance, that Janice did not notice the florid green-and-white motorcycle until it was parked at the curb just a few feet from her table. Its short, skinny rider was clad in jeans and a denim jacket, his face hidden beneath a dark-visored helmet swirled with the same bright colors as the bike. He climbed off and, before she realized what was happening, had plunked himself in the chair opposite her.

"Hey!" she protested, as she shoved her own chair back. "You can't just sit—"

She broke off as the rider pulled off his helmet, revealing brown hair spiky with sweat above a familiar, if still not welcome, face.

"Hey, yourself," Matt said, his cocky grin making him look even younger than his fourteen years. "It's Saturday, so here I am, ready to go totem hunting."

He set his helmet on the table and looked at the bowl before her. By now, the remaining cherry ice cream mixed with marshmallows and chocolate chunks had melted into a rather unappetizing-looking soup. The grin faded, and he opened his blue eyes wide. "That was, um, a big bowl of ice cream.

"Yeah, well, it was a long wait," she shot back, momentarily contemplating the zit/jock itch/runs spell, as it could be applied to him. Unfortunately, she couldn't afford to put her lab partner out of commission, not when there was so much work on the project to be done. Instead, she contented herself with a snide, "You were supposed to be here half an hour ago."

"Sorry, I don't get to the fancy part of town much. It took me a while to find the place."

While Janice puzzled over whether or not this last was a veiled gibe directed at her, Matt reached into his jacket pocket. He pulled out a folded sheet of paper—also sweaty—that he smoothed open on the table. She craned her neck and saw it was the same vague rendition of the town and its outskirts that was handed out to tourists . . . main streets and landmarks only. A few areas outside town were circled in pencil.

"Okay, I have a couple of ideas for tracking down our totem," he began, not bothering with any preliminary chitchat. "You want a snake to come to you, you gotta hang out where they hang out. So, we head out to the desert."

"On what? That puny little thing?" she asked with a derisive nod toward his ride.

Matt bristled. "It's a 250 cc," he said, sounding offended. "It'll hold us both. And I even have an extra helmet. I know of some dirt roads off the main highways, and they go back pretty far into the rocks and canyons. If we're gonna find rattlesnakes, that's the place to look."

"Whatever," she replied, shrugging to cover up the shiver that threatened. If there was one thing that made her skin crawl . . . besides dweeby Matt, of course . . . it was snakes. Then another thought occurred to her, and she frowned.

"You're only fourteen. That's not old enough for a motorcycle license. How do you get away with it?"

"Good question. You see, I kind of have a deflecting spell attached to the bike. It, um, keeps the police from noticing me. Not that I'm not a good rider," he hurried to add, when Janice gave a snort. "I know all the rules, and I follow them. Once I turn fifteen in a couple of months, I'll get my provisional license. Of course, if you don't trust me, we could always walk our way out of town."

"Yeah, right, and march through acres of cactus and scorpions? No way." Then her frowned deepened. "You don't think we have to catch a snake, or anything, do you?"

"I think it has to catch *us*!" Matt assumed a stern, heavy-lidded gaze. "If you will recall Professor Edwards' *second* lecture, Miss Redding," he replied in a credible imitation of Professor Edwards' refined tones, "one communes with totem animals. One does not bag them and bring them home alive."

Despite herself, Janice grinned a little. Matt might be a dweeb, but he was kind of funny. Her amusement promptly faded, however, when a falsetto voice spoke up from the table of teenage boys.

"Oooh, look at the cute couple, eating ice cream together," cooed the redhead, flicking a mocking glance in her and Matt's direction.

Janice returned his look with a steely glare. It wasn't the first time she'd had an encounter with some of the local teens, all of whom seemed to have it in for any student who attended the Academy for Advanced Study. Not that this jerk, or any of the others, had a clue as to the school's true curriculum. Everyone simply assumed from its name that the students there all were gifted scholars . . . which usually translated into being geeks, which immediately put them at odds with the rich kids from the town's public high schools. And given that the town was small enough that all the kids seemed to know each other, it was easy for them to peg a Sorcerer U student and make him or her the butt of jokes, or worse.

"Isn't it nice they found each other?" the boy went on with mock sweetness. "The fat chick and the short, skinny dude . . . what a pair."

The other two joined in the heckling, as well, and Janice balled her hands into fists. Only the thought of being called up before Professor David Reynard kept her in her seat. Though well liked by both students and faculty, the Academy's longtime head was not the sort of man to cross. As heir to the legacy that his ancestor had established, the school was his life's work . . . which fact he made certain to reiterate during every student assembly at which he spoke. If that were not enough, she'd heard rumors of the sort of punishment meted out to students whose wayward actions

threatened Sorcerer U's carefully maintained facade of gen-
teel academia.

Detention did not quite cover it.

Matt, however, just gave a little shrug and shot her an encouraging grin. "Ignore them . . . they're just a bunch of red
rock hicks. Either of us could kick their butts with one
metaphysical hand tied behind us, so don't worry about it.
Okay?"

"Okay," she agreed through gritted teeth. She and Matt
had a mission to accomplish, and she shouldn't let a bunch
of losers distract her. Besides, if Matt was tough enough to
ignore rude comments, so was she. Unclenching her hands
just a little, she looked down at the map, where Matt was
tracing a finger along one penciled route.

"Let's try here first," he suggested, pointing to an area off
one of the main highways to the west. "If we don't find anything after an hour or so, we can head farther south."

At her nod, he grabbed up his helmet, and she followed
him over to the bike. As he'd promised, a second helmet was
bungeed onto the seat. She was pleased to see that it was
black, matching her T-shirt and jeans. She pulled off her hair
clip and bundled her frizzy curls beneath the helmet, then
caught a glimpse of her reflection in the restaurant window.

"You look like a Power Ranger," Matt said with a grin,
echoing her own chagrined thought as he climbed on the
bike and started it up. "All right, let's roll."

"Just a second." She turned back toward the football
players, who still were leering in their direction. She smiled
sweetly in return and raised one hand in what anyone watching would have interpreted as a friendly wave of farewell.

"Damn it, dude, you dumped my ice cream in my lap!"

The offended yelp came from the red-haired teen as he
leaped to his feet, displaying a wide streak of chocolate ice
cream down the front of his designer polo shirt. Grabbing up
a handful of napkins, he glared at one of his buddies.

The dude in question gave a violent shake of his head.
"No way, Jason, not me. Dave must have done it."

"Hell, no!" the beleaguered Dave shot back and pointed a finger at his accuser. "It was Ron. I swear it."

The argument continued as Janice smugly climbed onto the bike behind Matt. He glanced back at her, as if about to speak, then merely shook his head and flipped down his visor. "Hang on," she heard him say as the bike started forward.

She hung on . . . tightly . . . as he maneuvered the small bike through the tourist traffic. Given that it was the weekend, the streets were even more crowded than usual. Both vehicles and pedestrians inched their way along the main road, jockeying for their respective places with every change of traffic light.

Every third vehicle seemed to be one of those Pepto Bismol-hued sightseeing jeeps that took tourists out to the famous Red Rocks and to the various "power vortexes" rumored to dot the Sedona landscape. Once, when she'd first arrived in town, Janice had been bored enough to take one of those tours herself. She'd been greatly amused by her fellow passengers declaring they could feel the magic emanating from various rock circles formed on the ground along certain trails. She grinned a little at the memory. What she would have given to let loose with a little spell of her own, and see their faces when they saw firsthand what real magic was.

Then her grin faded. Most of the so-called power vortexes in and around Sedona were simply Chamber-of-Commerce-created photo ops for credulous tourists. Several, however, actually were genuine, and many more existed that never had been documented on any official visitor's map.

Janice knew from past class lectures that the vast majority of those legitimate vortexes were beneficial . . . the metaphysical equivalent of a natural spring. There, those with a genuine talent for sorcery could refresh their powers, rather like using a magical battery charger. Other vortexes, however, were far less benign.

Some sheltered bands of rogue Elementals, the supernatural equivalent of a street gang. Those Elementals, while usually merely a nuisance to a competent magic user, could still cause injury to the less experienced. But of far greater concern was the handful of vortexes that actually were conduits to alternate dimensions and nether regions. These vortexes harbored horrors and dangers likely to destroy an untrained practitioner, and which could undermine even the most skilled of sorcerers. Any student found near one of those particular vortexes was subject to immediate expulsion from the Academy.

Luckily, today's route took her and Matt away from those areas. Instead, Matt turned the bike southwest out of town. The area they rode through was mostly red dirt and tan rocks mixed in with spiky clumps of various grasses, and punctuated by the occasional scrubby oak or pine. Bleak, in Janice's opinion, but probably conducive to rattlesnakes.

Or not.

Over the course of two hours, they halted perhaps a dozen times at what appeared to be likely spots off the main road. At each stop, they climbed off the bike and grabbed up the notebooks they'd stashed in the bike's saddlebags, along with a few bottles of water. From there, they would wander gingerly off road and then wait for a totem snake to find them. Not even the garden-variety rattler paid them a call, however, let alone a serpent with actual magical powers.

Their last stop was at an abandoned picnic area. Matt pulled off the highway yet again and shut off the bike. He waited until Janice, with a great deal of grumbling, had climbed off. Then, dismounting, he pulled off his helmet and stuck it on one handlebar before reaching into the small saddlebag for what proved to be the last bottle of water.

Doffing her own helmet, Janet grabbed the water from him before he'd even popped up its spout. She took a long drink, spattering water down the front of her black T-shirt in the process. Her yellow-brown curls were flat now and, minus the clip, sagged to her shoulders in even greater disarray than usual. "Well, what next?" she asked as she handed over what was left of the water to Matt.

He finished it off, and stuck the empty in the bag. "Well,

we're pretty much off the beaten path here. Maybe we should walk around and see if we see anything."

"We've been off the beaten path since we started," she huffed, "and we haven't seen snake one yet. Maybe they only come out during the night."

"Nah, I'm pretty sure they like to sun themselves on the rocks during the day. But we do seem to be in a snake-free zone, don't we?" Then he brightened. "I know. We can do a serpent dance . . . kinda like a rain dance, except we'll ask for snakes instead of storms."

Grinning, Matt spread his arms wide and spun about, executing a couple of swift shuffling steps that Barry Silverhorse once had shown him when demonstrating how one began certain of the sacred Diné dances.

"Yo, rattlesnake gods," he called up, "how about sending some rattlesnakes our way?"

He began weaving his body in imitation of said serpents, even shaking his rear end like he was shaking a rattle. Janice rolled her eyes. Why couldn't she have ended up with the Deer totem . . . and with somebody for a partner other than the dweeb?

"Look!"

Matt had stopped dancing, and was frantically pointing to a spot behind her. Janice shrieked and swung about, certain that there was a snake slithering between her feet. Then she saw what he saw . . . a weather-beaten wooden placard crookedly nailed to a lone scrubby oak that grew on the highway shoulder. In faded red letters, the sign proclaimed, FOOD GAS 1 MILE. A smaller notation below read *Rattlesnake Farm . . . See LIVE Snakes*. A crudely rendered arrow in the shape of a serpent pointed down a dirt road leading off the highway and over a slight rise.

"All right!" Matt proclaimed with a wide grin. "Talk about luck. I might not have seen that sign if I hadn't been dancing around."

"I don't know," came her doubtful reply. "That sign looks pretty old. What if the snake farm isn't there anymore?"

"Hey, this is our one decent shot for communing with our

totem animal . . . at least, this weekend. So, I say we give it
a try. Besides, maybe they sell cold soda there."

That last decided Janice. She pulled on her helmet again
and climbed on the bike behind Matt, hanging on tightly as
he turned off the highway and began negotiating the rutted
dirt road. So intent was she on each jarring bump that sent
her teeth clacking together that it wasn't until Matt finally
halted the bike that she looked up.

They were parked in a sandy clearing in front of what appeared to be an abandoned service station. A single, glass-
domed gas pump . . . the kind that predated the "pay at the
pump" version by several decades . . . rose from a surrounding clump of grasses, looking as if it had been part of the
landscape from Day One. It sat not far from a crumbling
stucco building that sported a narrow covered porch and a
pair of filthy windows, one on either side of a sagging
screen door. Another sign, obviously painted by the same
person responsible for the one on the highway, was attached
to the structure's facade. This one read, FOOD GAS
RATTLESNAKES.

"One-stop shopping," Matt observed with a grin as he
pulled off his helmet and stuck it on his handlebars. "C'mon,
let's take a look."

"I don't know," Janice repeated as she dismounted and
pulled off her own helmet, propping it on the bike seat once
Matt had clambered off. Still on the alert for snakes underfoot, she shielded her eyes with both hands against the
bright sun and scanned the front of the building. "I don't
think anyone's home."

And, indeed, the place had an eerie silence about it that
seemed to indicate a total lack of both human and wildlife
habitation. No one called out a greeting from the building . . . no bird sang in a nearby scrub tree . . . no lizard rustled in a clump of grass. Not even a distant jet flew overhead
to break the hush and add a sense of normalcy to the scene.
Then, abruptly, a slight wind rose, bringing in its wake an
almost musical sound of metal against metal.

Wordlessly, Matt pointed to the far side of the gas station.

An old-fashioned pair of T-shaped clothesline poles were set perhaps ten feet apart, a trio of lines strung between them. But, rather than wet clothes, what hung from those wires were odd bits of metal . . . frying pans, wagon wheels, even what appeared to be the rusted frame of a child's bicycle . . . all doubtless scavenged from where they'd been lost or dumped in the surrounding desert. Each item was strung at a different height, and seemingly arranged with the greatest deliberation, so that the slightest breeze would set it clanking against its neighbor to create a giant set of wind chimes.

Matt broke into a soft humming of The Twilight Zone theme, and Janice glared at him. It was creepy enough out here, without the dweeb rubbing it in. "Funny. Now, let's go look for some friggin' rattlesnakes, and then get the heck out of here."

Before he could reply, the slamming of the sagging screen door as it flew open made them both jump. A shadowed figure stood in the doorway, its bearing faintly menacing. Janice edged closer to Matt . . . not that she needed his protection, she hurriedly reassured herself.

"You kids here to see the rattlesnakes?"

The high-pitched voice had a certain creakiness to it, as if its owner had not used it in some time. *Guess not many victims come out this way,* the thought flitted through her mind, before she gave her head a deliberate shake to dismiss it. Just because he lived out in the desert alone didn't mean he was some crazed killer. Besides, if he *did* try something, she'd zap him with a spell.

Then he stepped off the porch into the sunlight, letting the door slam closed behind him again, and Janice released a pent-up breath. Now, she could see the tangled white hair that flowed to his shoulders, and the old-man-style clothes that hung loosely on his frame. He had to be the same age as her grandfather, or even older . . . and, thus, most likely harmless. Doubtless, it had been the pronounced stoop to his shoulders that had given him such an ominous air.

"Well?" he prodded, sounding merely cranky now, instead of creaky.

Matt, who'd been uncharacteristically silent since the man's appearance, now took a step forward. "Uh, yessir, we are. Here to see the snakes, I mean. If you could just point the way—"

"That'll be five dollars . . . each," the old man cut him short and held out one hand.

Matt dug a hand into his jeans pocket and pulled out a bill, then looked up at Janice. "All I have is a five," he said in a worried undertone, "and I'll need to fill up the bike again before we head back."

"Well, crud," she muttered back as, digging into her own pocket, she pulled out a ten dollar bill. "I'll take care of it . . . but you owe me."

Tossing back her tangled yellow-brown curls, Janice marched up to where the man waited. She shoved the money into his hand. "Okay, here's the cash. Where are the s–snakes?"

She stammered over the last word just a little, caught as she was by surprise. Now that she stood but a few feet from the man, she saw that he wasn't as old as she first had thought. It had been the white hair and stoop that had deceived her. In fact, he looked quite young, no older than thirty years, perhaps . . . but rather odd, as well.

It was more than just the bleached-out hair and bent frame, she realized, trying not to stare at him. His face was remarkably pale and smooth for someone who apparently spent all his time in the desert. As for his eyes, they were an unusually bright shade of green, and so round as to appear almost lidless. And this was not to mention the two tiny, green-and-red feathers that had been tied into his hair.

Then he smiled, revealing two rows of small and very white teeth, and it was all she could do not to scamper back a few steps. Only the fact that she sensed that he knew just how unnerving she found his appearance kept her firmly in place.

"All right, let's see some rattlers," Matt declared in a hearty tone, breaking the momentary silence as he trotted up to join them.

Still smiling, the man tucked away the money. "Just follow me, children," he said, sounding suddenly cheerful, "and I'll show you all the rattlesnakes you'll ever want to see."

So saying, he stepped back onto the narrow porch and held open the screen door. Janice hesitated, glancing over at Matt and wondering if he had found the man to be quite as disconcerting as had she. Matt appeared unconcerned, however, as he trotted through the door and into the shadowed building. Shooting the strange man a mental warning . . . *don't you even think about messing with me* . . . Janice reluctantly stepped inside, too.

To her surprise, the structure consisted of but one gloomy room, which was completely empty. Not one stick of furniture remained; not a single newspaper lay forgotten in a corner. The air within the room was stale, as if the doors and windows were rarely opened. Beneath the staleness, however, lay the faintest hint of some musky scent that she couldn't quite identify. Maybe some sort of animal, she thought, wrinkling her nose.

The man joined them, and she and Matt followed him toward another door on the opposite wall. The faintest coating of red dust covered the sturdy wooden floor, just thick enough so that she could see the footprints the man left in his wake, and the ones they left as they walked after him. The only other marks in the dust were a series of faint lines that curved their way across the floor, almost as if someone had dragged a rope behind them.

You'd think he'd take a friggin' broom to the place, once in a while.

They reached the door, and the man pulled it open, letting in another blaze of sunlight. "Do step out into the garden," he said, and gestured them through the doorway.

Beyond lay the biggest surprise of all. Within a walled area twice as large as the building itself spread a colorful panorama that perfectly replicated the most flamboyant of the natural vistas that Sedona had to offer. Eyes wide, Janice and Matt took in every detail.

Miniature versions of the famed red rocks arose from the sandy soil, forming diminutive buttes and canyons. Janice even picked out tiny replicas of specific formations . . . Bell Rock, over here; Courthouse Rock, over there. Dotting the carefully hewn landscape were various half grown scrubby oaks and pines, interspersed with grasses in a gamut of sizes and shades of green. Cacti and the occasional wildflower added further color and texture to the garden, while a tiny stream trickled into a shallow pond tucked into the garden's far corner.

The single discordant note in this desert Eden was the diamondback rattlesnake sunning itself on a flat red rock little more than ten feet from where the trio stood.

Janice shrieked and grabbed hold of Matt, who let out an answering yelp. wildly, she looked around for an escape route, only to find that another rattlesnake had slithered its way onto the path that led back to the house. A third serpent poked a triangular head out from beneath the bush beside them, and Janice shrieked again.

The man, however, merely chuckled softly. "Don't worry, children. So long as you are with me, my snake friends will do you no harm."

"Yeah, right, whatever," came Matt's breathless reply as he tried unsuccessfully to pry Janice's fingers from his arm. "But maybe we can go back into the house now, anyhow?"

"And miss this opportunity to commune with rattlesnakes one-on-one? I thought that was what you desired. Besides, we must make certain that you each get your five dollars' worth."

Not waiting for a reply, he walked over to the flat rock where the large snake lay sunning and sat beside it. Janice grabbed Matt's arm with both hands now. "We're surrounded by friggin' rattlesnakes," she whispered as the rattler laid its head on the man's knee. "Do something."

"Like what? Sorry, but I left my handy spray can of "Snake-B-Gone" at school."

"Don't be such a dweeb! Can't you put a deflecting spell

on us, like you did on your bike, so we can walk past the snakes without their noticing us?"

Matt frowned, and then brightened somewhat. "I don't know . . . maybe. I'm not sure if it will work the same on people as it will on machines."

"Well, try. Otherwise, I'm gonna start zapping snakes, and I think that'll lose us points on our assignment . . . not to mention it'll probably tick off our new friend," she added with a glance in the man's direction. Now, the diamondback had slithered up into his arms, and he was calmly cradling it, just as he would a puppy. Damn, but she hated friggin' snakes!

Matt followed her gaze, and gulped audibly. "Okay, I'm convinced," he murmured. "I'll give the spell a shot."

He shut his eyes and scrunched his brow. Nothing happened for a moment, so that it was all Janice could do not to yell at him to hurry. Her patience had stretched to the breaking point, when she felt a warm breeze swirl about them, momentarily ruffling her curls.

Matt's eyes fluttered opened again, and he nodded. "That should do it. It's only temporary, though. We've got five minutes . . . maybe ten, tops."

"That's all the time I need," she muttered back, poking a curious finger forward. As she reached arm's length, she felt rather than saw a rubbery barrier, almost as if they were encased in an invisible bubble. "Not bad," she added, genuinely impressed with his skills.

Matt shrugged. "Wait until we make it back to the bike without any fang marks on our legs, and you can thank me. Now, let's make like a shepherd and get the flock out of here."

In unison, they turned and began a careful walk toward the door. Janice held her breath as they passed the snake in the bush, but it merely flicked a lightning fast tongue in their direction before returning to its hiding place among the leaves. The snake on the path paid them an equal lack of heed as they skirted it. Luckily, the door was still open, so that all they had to do was walk inside.

"Okay, run for it," she muttered, and gave Matt a none-too-gentle push. He needed no urging, but took off for the front door, Janice on his heels.

They reached the front screen without incident, stumbling out into the bright sunlight again. Janice shaded her eyes with one hand and clung to Matt with the other as they took off running. The bike was no more than twenty feet away . . . just a few seconds' sprint from the door.

And then, abruptly, Matt halted.

Janice smacked into him, her athletic shoes skittering in the coarse sand as she struggled not to fall on her butt. "You dweeb," she sputtered as she recovered her balance and started to push past him, "why in hell did you—"

"Stop!" Matt choked out and grabbed her arm. Pointing, he merely croaked, "Look!"

She blinked and gasped. To be sure, the bike was parked where they had left it. What was added to that scenario was a score of rattlesnakes, each coiled in what even Janice recognized as their striking pose, and forming a serpentine ring around the bike.

Turning to Matt, she made a fist and socked him in the shoulder. "This is all your fault, you and your friggin' snake dance. We're never going to get out of here."

"That dance thing was just a joke," he protested, nursing his bruised arm. "I didn't know it would work. And pounding on me isn't going to do us any good."

"Yeah? Then what will?"

Barely had the words left her mouth when the wind began to rise again. The almost tuneful clink of metal against metal resumed as the giant wind sculpture was once more set in motion. She glanced over at Matt, who met her gaze. "This isn't good," he declared, echoing her instinctive thought. "That was when things got weird the first time, when that noise started."

"I know." As casually as she could, Janice glanced back over her shoulder. "Uh, Matt," she managed in a shaking voice, "there's one big-ass rattler sitting right in front of the building, and I have a feeling it's about to come after us."

"Nope, not good." He poked at the invisible bubble and frowned. "We've got maybe a minute before this thing dissipates. Let's make a run for it, on the count of three. Once we're on the bike, we should be able to get away from the snakes . . . but if we can't, you start zapping them, and the hell with the assignment. Agreed?"

At her nod, he grabbed her hand and began the count, "One . . . two . . ."

"Three!" Janice finished for him and took off, dragging him alongside her. The snakes seemed not to notice as they rushed past, reaching the motorcycle without incident. Slapping on his helmet, Matt started the bike. "C'mon, " he urged over the sound of the ever-rising wind as she fumbled with the strap on hers. "You can fix it later. Get on and let's go!"

She needed no further encouragement but scrambled onto the bike and grabbed his waist. Matt gave the bike full throttle, gravel and sand churning behind them as they jounced down the rutted dirt road. She didn't dare glance back until they'd cleared the rise and reached the picnic area, where the dirt road T-ed into the highway.

"No snakes in sight," she called in relief, and Matt nodded. Still, he paused on the shoulder only long enough to make sure no oncoming traffic threatened, before whipping back onto the asphalt and pointing the bike back toward Sedona.

They did not stop again until they reached the Academy's high, whitewashed walls and made their way past the ornate front gate. Riding in on fumes, Matt had declared. Neither had voiced the reason behind their decision not to gas up on the way home again . . . the fear that, had they pulled over, they might find themselves surrounded by yet more rattlesnakes. Only when they were safely upon school grounds again, did either of them breathe easily.

Unfortunately, they had no time to compare notes on the day's events, for the afternoon was swiftly melting into evening. Soon the bell would ring for supper, and only an official excuse from one of the professors would allow them to miss that meal. With that in mind, they agreed to meet later that evening in the coziest place that Sorcerer U offered, the Library. There, they would discuss in greater detail their trip to the rattlesnake farm, and their encounter with its mysterious caretaker whom, for want of any better name, they had dubbed "Snake Man."

It was almost eight o'clock when Janice, the red dust brushed out of her yellow-brown curls, settled into one of the library's worn leather wingchairs to await Matt. Enough time had passed since their afternoon's adventure, that she had begun to feel a bit foolish over her panic at the rattlesnake farm. Still, those few hours also had given her time to review the past week's lecture notes, and to puzzle over a few less obvious details about the Snake Man.

A trip to the card catalog—holding with tradition, Sorcerer's U librarians did not track their books in a computer database—resulted in a slim, battered volume that she found filed under "Q." She was flipping through its pages, when the library's heavy double doors whispered open, and Matt finally walked in.

The soles of his running shoes squeaked against the black marble floor as he made his way to the alcove where she sat. He paused long enough to toss a cheery salute at the somber, life-sized portrait of the beautiful Doña Rafaela de Leon, the Academy's original founder. Janice frowned. Everyone knew that Doña Rafaela had been a *bruja* . . . a witch. Only a dweeb like Matt would be dumb enough to risk ticking off her spirit; that was, in the quite likely event that the woman still hung around the school in some form or another.

She forgot about Doña Rafaela, however, as Matt plopped into the matching leather wingchair beside her. Then, abruptly, he bent forward to peer between his legs at the expanse beneath his seat. Seemingly satisfied by what he saw—or didn't see—he straightened again.

"Snake check," he whispered by way of explanation, and with exaggerated care settled into a cross-legged position that left his feet tucked well above the marble floor.

Janice glared at him and resisted the urge to do the same, herself, though his antics set her feet twitching in sympathetic reflex. Then, she glanced about to see if the students she'd noticed in the library earlier were within earshot. A couple of senior girls sat at a far table, busily taking notes from a foot-thick volume bound in gold-stamped red leather. Another student perched on the heavy iron staircase that corkscrewed itself to the library's second floor. An unrolled antique parchment was propped upon that boy's skinny knees, and he appeared quite lost within its vellum sheets. None of the three seemed aware of her and Matt's presence.

"All right," she whispered back. "I've been thinking about what happened today, and I remembered a couple of weird things that happened."

"You mean, weirder than being surrounded by an army of snakes?"

Janice glared again. "Yeah, weirder. Remember when we went inside that building? There was a layer of sand on the floor, and I could see Snake Man's footprints and ours when we walked through the room."

"So, he's a crappy housekeeper. What's the big deal?"

"The big deal is that the footprints all went just one way, from the front door to the back."

When Matt merely shrugged at this revelation, she shook her head in disgust. "Think about it, you dweeb. There weren't any footprints leading to the front door. But the first time we saw Snake Man, he wasn't out on the porch. He had walked from the *inside* of the house to the *outside*. And that's not all. There were other marks in the dust, but they weren't footprints. They looked like someone had dragged a rope—or something like a rope—across the floor."

"Holy crud," Matt breathed, his eyes growing wide as he belatedly realized what she was saying. "Do you mean that you think Snake Man—"

"—really is a snake man," she finished for him, and settled triumphantly in her chair.

Matt let out a whooshing breath and sank back into his

own seat. "Wow, a dude who turns into a snake. That's pretty bizarre stuff."

"Not so bizarre, not in this part of the country . . . or did you sleep through Professor Sanchez's mythology class the other week?" Not waiting for a reply, she held up the book she'd been reading. "I think this might be a clue to that whole snake farm thing."

Matt looked at its title and frowned. "Uh, that's Spanish. You mind translating?"

"The book is called *The Legend of Quetzalcoatl*."

"Quetzal-who?"

"Quetzalcoatl," she repeated, rolling her eyes. She opened the book to where she'd been marking her place with one finger, and began to read. "His name means 'plumed serpent,' and he was the snake god of the Aztecs, symbolizing death and resurrection, wisdom, and so on. According to the book, he could change from a man into a snake, and vice versa. Some legends tie him into Cortez, since Quetzalcoatl was said to be blond with green eyes, like a European. Others saw him as a Christlike figure. And he had powers, specifically over the weather."

"You mean, like the wind?" His expression grew speculative, and she knew he was thinking about the giant wind sculpture. "Yeah, I think I did hear about Quetzal—er, this Q guy, in class. But I don't remember, was he a good god or a bad god?"

"He was a good god and fought against the bad ones," she replied, shutting the book again. "He also put a stop to human sacrifice among the Mayans and the Aztecs."

"Which makes him a hero in my book. Okay, let's get this straight." Matt held out one hand, and began ticking off each finger. "That Q guy has blond hair with green eyes; changes from snake to man, and back again; can control the wind; likes rattlesnakes; wears feathers in his hair. Ditto our buddy, the Snake Man. So, are you thinking what I'm thinking?"

"You mean, that the Snake Man is actually the Aztec god Quetzalcoatl?"

"Exactly!"

He leaped up from his seat and did a strutting little dance. "Man, we've got that 'A' for sure now," he exclaimed in an excited undertone. "Who else in class will have quotes from a god in their paper, huh?"

"Not so fast," Janice replied. "We don't have any sort of proof that he's a god, let alone Quetzalcoatl. Maybe he's an Elemental that's taken human form . . . or maybe he's just some crazy desert guy with a thing for rattlesnakes."

"Oh." He frowned and stopped his victory dance. "So what do we do to prove it, one way or another?"

"There's only one thing we can do." Janice took a deep breath. "I say we hop back on your bike again tomorrow, and pay another visit to the rattlesnake farm.

Sunday mornings tended to be quiet at the Academy. Students were free to attend the worship service of their choice . . . a traditional service at one of the churches in town, or a nondenominational earth-based service conducted within the school by one of the professors. Those students with less formal religious ties could simply opt to catch a few hours extra sleep. Thus, no one noticed or questioned when Matt and Janice left the Academy at midmorning.

Traffic was far lighter than it had been the day before, so that they traveled at a good pace. But by the time they reached the abandoned picnic area near the turnoff to the rattlesnake farm, Matt had begun to wonder if getting a top grade on this assignment was worth another meeting with the infamous "Q." Dealing with a desert creepo and his merry band of rattlesnakes was one thing. Mixing it up with a rattlesnake god was quite another . . . even if said god was supposed to be on the side of good.

He waited to say something, however, until after he'd parked the bike, and the two of them had wandered over to the lopsided concrete picnic table for a strategy session.

"You know, I've been thinking about our totem project," he began cheerfully, assuming his most disarming tone.

"Technically, all we have to do is commune with the totem animal—which we did—and then do one of those point by point comparisons with our lecture notes, maybe quote a research book or two. So what do you say we skip a second visit to Snakes 'R Us, and go do breakfast?"

Janice shot him an incredulous look. "Are you crazy? For one thing, we didn't commune with anything . . . we just ran away from a bunch of snakes. We're supposed to wait and let the totem animal impart some wisdom to us, which we did not, and they did not. We never even established that any of those rattlers were anything but your garden-variety snake. So no way we can finish the assignment."

"And for another thing," she went on, her tone growing more urgent, "suppose the Snake Man really is Quetzalcoatl? Why, that would be the chance of the lifetime, to talk to an actual god, find out which of the legends are true, ask him questions about Mayan and Aztec civilization. Imagine what we could learn from him!"

"Yeah, but think about it. Even if he admits to being that Q dude—"

"Quetzalcoatl," Janice interrupted with a shake of her head.

"—we'd just be taking his word for it. I mean, it's not like we can get a notarized statement to prove he's the real deal." He leaned forward, his manner as serious now as hers. "Here's another thought. Supposing he *is* for real, but he's just not Q. Remember what you said yesterday? Maybe he's an evil Elemental with an ax to grind. Who knows what kind of trouble we could get into . . . and no one from school knows we're here."

Janice had opened her mouth to reply, when the booming of a car stereo on steroids drifted to them. They both glanced up to see a gleaming black SUV rapidly approaching from the direction of town. It slowed as it approached the picnic area, rap music pouring from its open windows. Matt had a good enough look at its three occupants to realize he'd encountered them somewhere before. A sudden chorus of barks and moos from the vehicle confirmed that.

"It's those friggin' jerks from the ice cream place," Janice exclaimed as the SUV rolled past and began picking up speed once more. Before Matt could stop her, she stomped over to the edge of the shoulder and let loose with a few choice cuss words, even as she gave the retreating vehicle the universal middle finger salute.

A sudden flash of brake lights and the screech of tires indicated that her insult had not gone unnoticed. Then, abruptly, the driver began making a U-turn.

"Oh, man, they're coming after us," Matt said with a groan, snatching up his helmet and starting the bike. "C'mon, we'd better get out of here."

"You mean, try to outrun them?" she demanded, looking suddenly worried as she slapped on her own helmet and clambered on behind him. "No way we can go faster than they can."

No way in hell, Matt silently agreed, shooting a swift glance back up the highway. But, luck momentarily was with them. The SUV's wheelbase was far too long, and the road much too narrow, for the driver to make a U-turn in a single maneuver. The only way he could manage it was with that driver's ed specialty, the three-point turn . . . that, or he'd risk getting a wheel or two stuck in the sandy shoulder. Luckily, the youth's inexperience at handling a vehicle now showed, and the three points were becoming four, and then five.

"Let's head toward the rattlesnake farm," Matt decided. "Chances are this guy won't want to mess up his expensive truck on a road that bad."

"Okay," came her quick agreement, followed by a grudging, "Sorry," as he throttled the bike and whipped off the highway down the dirt path.

If yesterday's flight down this same road had been at a speed far faster than was safe, this ride was at a breakneck pace that left Matt struggling to keep the bike upright. The mirrors on his handlebars were vibrating with such ferocity that he couldn't tell by their reflection whether or not they were being followed. Instinct, however, told him that they were.

Matt gritted his teeth as they slammed across a particularly deep rut. If they could make it to the gas station quickly enough, they'd have time to conjure some sort of protection spell before their pursuers reached them. Or, if worse came to worst, maybe they could use their magic to rustle up a few of Q's rattlesnake buddies, and sic them on the trio.

A few moments later, they skidded into the familiar clearing, gravel spewing as Matt struggled to halt the bike. "Get off," he shouted at Janice as he hit the engine switch.

Once she'd jumped clear, he wasted no time, but scrambled off and let the bike slide to the ground. As he regained his balance and jerked off his helmet, letting it topple onto a grassy patch where hers lay, Janice met his gaze.

"The gas pump," she exclaimed, echoing his swift choice for a grounding place from which to cast their spell. Hand in hand, they raced toward it. Constructed as that equipment was of glass and metal, it would help keep their energy tightly centered and, thus, far more effective.

"Keep it simple. Let's try a blockade," he urged as the sound of rap music drew nearer.

Janice nodded in agreement. It was a technique they'd practiced in lab only the week before, and it had proved an effective spell.

Still clutching hands, they both shut their eyes and mentally began spinning the barrier that would hide them in plain view for as long as necessary. Unfortunately, it was a visual blockade only, and would not stifle sound . . . nor would it keep anything out. Any noise the pair of them might make could be heard, and anyone could walk past it to find them hiding within. Until the three boys had come and gone, he and Janice would have to communicate in whispers and gestures.

Matt opened his eyes again, satisfied from the rainbow sheen to the air within a six-foot diameter that the spell had taken hold. With luck, after a few minutes of fruitless search, the youths would give up and head back the way they'd come. Then he and Janice would conjure a more durable spell, one that would allow them to make the ride back to the school within a safe bubble of protection that only another sorcerer could possibly breach.

He glanced at Janice, who had opened her eyes, as well. She gave him a determined nod and then turned toward the burgeoning dust cloud that heralded the SUV's arrival. A moment later, the vehicle had screeched to a stop in the center of the clearing. The youths piled out, their stances aggressive as they swung about, looking for any sign of their prey.

"They've gotta be here somewhere," the red-haired boy named Jason growled. "Look, that's their puny little bike."

"Yeah, we oughta smash it up for them," Dave—or was it Ron?—answered him. Trotting over to the toppled motorcycle, he swung a booted foot, intent on destruction . . . and then yelped as his foot made contact. Spouting curses, he kicked it again, and then yelled even louder in pain.

Matt stifled a laugh. Not only did the deflecting spell he had on his bike protect against unwanted traffic stops, it warded off such hazards as stray nails and witless thugs. Even with boots on, kicking that bike would feel like kicking a steel-reinforced wall.

Ron—or was it Dave?—gave up trying to vandalize the bike and rejoined the other two, who were poking around the stucco building. "Hey, you two kids," Jason bellowed in the direction of the screen door, "you'd better get your asses out here right now! If we have to come looking for you, you're gonna be really sorry. I mean it, man!"

Yeah, right, Janice mouthed with a sneer, though the clamminess of her hand betrayed her nervousness. Matt gave her fingers an encouraging squeeze, feeling more than a bit nervous, himself. If it came down to a choice between using their magic, or getting the crap beat out of them, they'd have to opt for magic . . . and just hope that word never got back to Professor Reynard.

One of the dark-haired youths pulled open the screen

door to look inside. "Nothing in there, man. It's totally empty," he reported, and let the door slam shut again.

Jason uttered a curse. "Look around back, then. They've got to be here somewhere." But barely had his cohorts begun heading toward the back, when a sudden breeze arose. The wind chimes began their almost musical clanking, and the three halted, looking about to see what was responsible for that metallic chorus. And then, abruptly, the screen door slammed open, revealing a familiar stooped figure with flowing white hair.

"You kids here to see the rattlesnakes?"

"Damn it, Ron, you said the friggin' place was empty," the red-haired youth accused him. "So where the hell did this dude come from?"

"Hell, I don't know. Maybe he snuck in through the back."

The Snake Man, however, simply held out a hand. "That'll be five dollars . . . each."

Jason moved forward, his stance aggressive. "Look, man, we don't care about your friggin' rattlesnakes. Just tell us where those two kids went, and we'll leave you alone."

"What kids?" the Snake Man asked, his tone cranky as he started toward them. "You're the only kids that have been by today. If you don't want to see the snakes, you'd better leave."

"You're not listening, dude, " Ron spoke up, aping his friend's threatening manner. "A fat chick and a little skinny guy just rode up on that bike over there. No way they could have gotten away this fast . . . which means they're still here somewhere. We want to know where they are, and we want to know right now. Or else—"

"Or else you're gonna feel some pain," Dave piped up and rushed forward, giving the Snake Man a shove that sent him sprawling.

Janice and Matt exchanged quick, guilty glances as the Snake Man slowly dragged himself upright. "I don't know what you're talking about," the man insisted, his tone quavery now instead of cranky as he brushed dirt from his lanky frame. "I haven't seen any other kids."

"Maybe this'll jog your memory," Ron said, and gave him another, even harder push.

The Snake Man rose more haltingly the second time, and Matt frowned. "He's not doing very well for a god," he murmured in Janice's ear. "Even if he's just an Elemental, he should have been able to hit them with some sort of spell. But he's just standing there, taking it."

"He should have zapped them, by now, " she agreed in a worried undertone. "I don't know, maybe we were wrong. Maybe he's just some crazy snake guy, after all."

Jason balled up one beefy fist. ""Last chance," he declared, and stepped closer to the man. "Tell us where they're hiding, or we'll beat the crap out of you. Hell, you're so freaky looking, I think we'll beat the crap out of you, even if you do talk."

"S-Sorry," came that man's faltering reply, "I can't h-help you." With a shake of his head, he turned toward the house.

Jason grabbed him by the shoulder, jerking him back around again. "Wrong answer, dude," he declared as his fist connected with bone-shaking crack against the Snake Man's jaw.

The Snake Man crumpled, blood streaming from his lip. Matt and Janice stared in dismay, even as Jason yelled, "Hold him up so I can hit him again."

The other two gleefully scrambled to comply, dragging the injured man upright again. Jason cocked his arm, ready to punch again as soon as his victim was in place. Matt heaved a quick breath and shot a determined look at Janice, who nodded. No matter how crazy he might be, no way they could let the Snake Man take the punishment that was meant for them.

"Wait!"

"Stop!"

Their shouts came simultaneously, blasting away the visual barrier they'd created. The three youths swung around, surprise and confusion evident in their faces . . . and the Snake Man momentarily forgotten. Then Jason's expression twisted into a cruel little leer.

"Well, well, well . . . if it isn't the fat chick and the skinny little dude. Guess you're braver than we thought you were." Then his leer morphed into a look of mock concern. "What's the matter, you're all mad because I'm beating on your weird friend, here? Don't worry, it's your turn next," he exclaimed, and raised his fist again.

"Leave him alone," Matt warned in a calm voice, Janice beside him as they moved toward where the three youths surrounded the unsteady Snake Man.

If possible, he meant to settle this with words, not fists or magic. In a fair fight, he could hold his own if he fought them one at a time. But chances were the three would jump him as a group, and he'd likely end up on the bottom of the heap. As for magic, any number of spells would resolve the situation quite nicely. The problem was, he'd be breaking Academy rules One and Two, simultaneously. He wasn't going either place, not unless it was absolutely necessary.

He could only hope that Janice would stay with the game plan.

"You're not mad at the Snake M—, I mean, at this guy," he went on in a reasonable tone. "You're mad at us. So why don't you let him go, and then we can talk about the situation."

The three guffawed. "Man, he sounds like some kind of tree-hugging little peace dude," Ron exclaimed. "He wants to share his fe–e–e–lings with us."

"Yeah, well, we don't share feelings," Jason declared. "We beat the crap out of people. But, go on, little peace dude. Give me one good reason why I shouldn't beat up this weird dude, and then start on you."

"Because it's wrong," Janice spoke up before Matt could come up with an excuse. "It's wrong to hurt someone, just because you're bigger, and you can."

She shot a sympathetic look at the Snake Man, who was dabbing his bloodied lip. "And it's wrong to hate someone just because you think they're weird—" she paused and glanced over at Matt, "—or to call them a dweeb because they're short, and have a dopey sense of humor. Maybe if you'd try getting to know them, you'd find out that they're not so bad, after all. Maybe you'd even want to try being their friend."

Her words hung in the desert air for a moment, while Matt stared at her in surprise. Talk about tree-hugging peace dudes . . . or dude-ettes! He hadn't expected a *can't-we-all-just-get-along?* kind of sermon from Janice, of all people. As for the three youths, they had fallen silent as soon as she'd begun speaking. Now, they glanced back at the Snake Man, who nodded.

Abruptly, the air about the trio seemed to shimmer, as if they'd been caught up in one of those highway mirages so common in the desert. Then, almost faster than Matt could see it happen, their forms simultaneously thinned and lengthened. An instant later, in the same spot where the three boys had been, a trio of rattlesnakes sat coiled before the Snake Man's feet.

The Snake Man, meanwhile, no longer swayed, shoulders hunched and mouth bloody. Instead, he stood tall and straight, his white hair billowing about his pale, unmarked face like a nimbus. His emerald eyes glowed with tranquillity as he gave them a gentle smile.

"Well done, both of you," he said in a musical voice that was echoed by the rising wind and the clank of chimes. "I believe that you got your five dollars' worth . . . would you not agree?"

Before they could reply, the same shimmer wrapped him, as well. A heartbeat later, four rattlesnakes, one far larger than the rest, were coiled upon the rocky sand. The wind, meanwhile, had increased its intensity, whipping a broad ribbon of red sand around everything . . . rattlesnakes, building, gas pump, even the wind sculpture. Matt and Janice squinted against the onslaught and clutched each other, barely able to keep their balance as the blowing sand raked them. Then, just as abruptly, the gust subsided, leaving nothing but the sprawling desert landscape before them. The final notes of the clanking wind chimes drifted to them on the last breath of breeze, and then died away, as well.

A long minute later, Matt snapped his slack jaw shut again and looked over at Janice. "That was, er, interesting."

"Uh-huh," she agreed, her gaze fixed on the spot where the rattlesnakes had been. She took a deep breath and slowly turned to meet his gaze. "And I guess everything that happened kind of counts as wisdom imparting. But, do you think he was just a run-of-the-mill totem . . . or do you think he actually was Quetzalcoatl?"

Matt puzzled over the question a moment, then shook his head and grinned. "Beats me," he declared. "Maybe Professor Edwards will figure it out for us while he's penciling in that big old A+ on the front of our midterm paper."

"You are such a dweeb," Janice replied with shake of her head and a matching grin. She grabbed her helmet and headed toward the bike. "And, don't forget, you owe me five dollars."

Matt shrugged and followed after her. "How about I buy you a couple of scoops of Red Rocky Road over at Desert Creme, and we call it even?"

"Deal. But let's make it one scoop. Oh, and just one more thing," she added as she climbed onto the bike behind him. "If we see another sign for a rattlesnake farm on the way back to town . . . DON'T STOP!"

DIARY

by Michelle West

Michelle West is the author of a number of novels, including *The Sacred Hunt* duology and *The Sun Sword* series, published by DAW Books. She reviews books for the on-line column *First Contacts* and, less frequently, for *The Magazine of Fantasy & Science Fiction*. Other short fiction by her appears in *A Dangerous Magic*, *Black Cats and Broken Mirrors*, *Elf Magic*, *Olympus*, and *Alien Abductions*.

*T*HE *first day of school.* I survived.
   The second day of school. I survived.
The third day of school. I survived.
The fourth day of school. I survived.
The fifth day of school. Argh. The whole page looks the same. I don't like it.

I'm not good with words. I told the principal—or whatever he's called—that when I first walked through the doors of his office. To let him know.

He told me that, magic or no, words were the best way I had of communicating with people. With other people. He actually said that.

I shrugged. I'm not good with words.

"And names?"

Names are just more words.

So he stood up, ran his fingers through his hair as if I were already trouble. Walked to one of the shelves that lined the walls from floor to ceiling. Grabbed a ladder, dragged it over to the third shelf from the window. I didn't see the rest because I was too busy staring out of that window. It's above the ground, beneath the sky, open to the light. Not like me.

But I heard him land. He's light on his feet, but not that light.

He asked me if I was paying attention.

To what?

"To me."

No.

"Don't do that here," he said, but I hadn't done anything. Yet. "First, it won't work. Second, because it won't work, you'll have to carry a lot of the discharge internally, and if you're trying anything . . . big . . ."

He didn't finish.

Instead, he gave me a book. Great. A book. I told him, I'm not great with words.

And he told me, "Learn."

So I took the book. It's an old, old book. Leather, dust, spiderwebs, and inside, endpapers that are faded and grim with all that time. The first page had a picture of a lion. The second, a picture of an owl.

The third page had nothing on it at all.

"It's yours," he told me, and his voice made me look up.

"But there's nothing here."

"No?"

"I'm not good with words. I told you that."

He made that people-are-stupid face, but it was pretty subtle. "You're awfully familiar with those particular ones. You know how to use a pen?"

"Yes."

"Good. Pick one up. Write."

"On *this?*"

"Yes. You will write something every day. On those pages. In that book."

"But what if I make a mistake?"

"You make a mistake. It happens."

"But I—"

"You will write. Or you will leave."

So that's what happened on my first day here. Day zero of school. Before classes.

I'm new here. I live in a cage. The roof over my head, the walls around me, the stone beneath my feet. Pretty cage, and all, but *I don't like cages.*

I came here 'cause I thought it would be different. But it's not. It's the same; everyone on the inside and me here, beyond the glass wall.

There's one girl here, I think she'd be okay if she didn't talk so much. I like the sound of her voice, though. Her words are different. They dip in the wrong places. Sometimes she speaks words I don't recognize at all. She told me she was swearing. Offered to teach me.

I thought about it.

Anyway, her name is Janna, or Janice, or something. She has three names. I have two, sort of. But I don't really use 'em much. I answer to 'em if they're called; the teachers expect that.

Sixth day of school. I got lost.

Again.

Just like in the old places. The ones I hardly remember.

I came here so it would stop. Getting lost, I mean. It's better outside—I never get lost outside. But you don't get much outside time, and you don't get much time outside the cage. I don't like it. I think I already said that, though. But this place is like a big maze, a maze made of stone. You can turn a corner, and it's not the corner it was yesterday. I should never have come here.

I thought things would be different.

I was supposed to go to early Alchemy. Janice—her name is Janice, but I can't fix the other mistake—was walking beside me, but Barry Longhorse walked by us and she kinda turned her head in the wrong direction, and when I looked back, she wasn't with me, and I wasn't there.

I mean, I wasn't in the same hall. No one was.

I was in a long, long hall. A tall hall, with big windows. I like windows, but the glass parts started at the level of my armpits. As if I were a child again, in the big old place, as if it were a long time ago.

But I left all that behind.

I didn't want to look. I had to look. Sometimes it's like that.

The first window opened out on a red sky. The second, on a blue one, the third on a black one, as if I had spent a whole day just walking past them.

But there was a door at the end of the hall, and when I opened it and walked through it, I was back among the students, and Janice was standing there with her eyes getting wide in her face—and her eyes are pretty wide to begin with.

"Anna," she said, "where the hell have you been?"

"Just down the hall."

"What hall?"

I turned to point to the door, and it wasn't there. "Uh, that one."

She snorted and said something I didn't understand. "You know you're in a lot of trouble, don't you?"

"Why?"

"Well," she said, "you know how, if you piss your mother off, she shouts a lot, screams, maybe throws something?"

I shrugged.

"It's like that, except you made her *worry*."

"Worry?"

"You better come with me. Reynard has been looking for you for *three days*." She reached out to grab my arm.

And I kinda lost it. My grip, I mean, not my arm. My arm stayed where it was, except that it started to *shift*. Right in her hands, fingers splaying into flight feathers, arms into pinions. I don't know what my face looked like, but I can guess.

She shouted. A lot.

Professor Reynard came. And Professor Nagata. And they brought jesses, a hood, something dark.

I don't know what to call this day. Janice was right. I seem to have missed three days of school. Professor Reynard assumed I'd skipped curfew, and then skipped coming back to my room, and—oh, yeah—skipped all my meals as well. As if.

When I could see out of my own eyes again, I was in his big cavern of an office.

"Anna."

I nodded.

"What you did in the halls was unacceptable."

She shouldn't've touched me. I wanted to tell him that, but I couldn't say the words. Not while he was watching them.

He waited, and I nodded. His face formed up in frown lines. He stood up. "You've been writing."

I shrugged.

"Good." He walked over to the window—to the big window—and stopped in front of it. I thought it might be nice to see him fly, too. But I didn't say anything. After a few minutes, he came back to his desk. Big desk. Pretty old. At least, it *smells* old. Age scent in my nostrils. Hate it.

He picked up a few pieces of paper. "Do you know," he said, "that you're considered a flight risk?"

I laughed. A lot.

He didn't.

"Do you know why you're here?"

I shook my head.

"At the Academy, Anna, not in my office."

I shook my head again.

"Anna."

"No."

"You wanted to be here."

I shrugged. And then, because his face looked kinda stormy, I said, "I thought it would be different."

"Different? From what?"

"From all the other places."

"Go on."

"I thought I'd have my own room. My own space. I thought I would learn—"

"What?"

I shrugged. "Don't know."

"Anna," he said quietly. "You are gifted. You know it. We know it. But you and young Janice have something in common. Neither of you possesses the control necessary to utilize that gift."

Nothing to say to that.

"I want you to tell me," he continued, putting the papers down, "where you went."

"Down a hall."

"For three days?"

I shrugged.

"Describe the hall."

Words. I told him to read mine. He was quiet for a while, and then he told me go and get the book. I did.

I guess this is the eighth day of school.

Shapeshifting classes started yesterday, but I'm not allowed to attend them. So I have a spare.

But I did make it to Alchemy. Old buzzard was there, perched behind his glasses, waiting for me, his beard all grizzled, his eyebrows like unruly wings. He gave me a slate. And chalk, white chalk.

"Anna," he said. Actually he said another word as well. A name, my name this time, but I can't remember what it was. The other girls in the class were speaking; two of them were exchanging pieces of paper, and one of them, golden-haired and tawny like a lion, turned her eyes on me. I don't like her much. I don't know her name.

I looked at the teacher instead.

"You've been excused from shapeshifting," he said, so the whole class would know.

Except he didn't do it to let them know—he did it so that

I'd know he knew. More words in the background, like the din of traffic, like the great machines.

"I understand there was some difficulty yesterday."

I shrugged.

"Understand," he continued, "that Alchemy is not just about lead and gold; it is not simply about the essential element and the transformation of dead things, of things that know no life."

A lot of words. It took me a while to put them all together so they made sense. He waited. And waited. Not glowering, not angry, not really impatient. Just . . . waiting.

"In order to apprehend—to comprehend—the rites of transformation, you have to understand that these things are imbued with a spirit." He paused for another minute, and it was a long one. Then he placed both his hands on the surface of my desk. "All spirits have names," he said, and his voice was so quiet it was like he wasn't using words at all, and I could hear him so clearly I knew what he meant.

I touched his hands then.

Because I wanted to.

"Names are the hardest things to learn." He didn't pull his hands away. He didn't move. But he wasn't like Professor Nagata; he was *there.* "I know what you're called—Anna Sevenson—but I don't know what it *means.* I'll learn it, the way I learned the seven names for gold, the three names for moon, the thirteen names for night.

"And you," he continued, "will learn the names of the elements. Fire's heart, that turns gold into liquid. Water's heart, that purifies all elements. Earth's heart, that hides all secrets, all the buried, ancient things."

"I don't want to know Earth," I told him.

"I know. I know, Anna. But in the Earth, and the stone, you'll find your name."

"What about Air?" The golden-haired girl asked.

"She knows the name of Air, " he replied, without turning. "And we will not speak it here."

I sit alone at meals.

That's what I've always done.

But Janice Redding brought her tray from the cafeteria line, and she said, "Mind if I join you?" And I didn't know how to say no. So she sat down beside me.

After a few minutes, Barry Darkhorse joined us.

"Do you know Barry?" Janice asked me.

I shook my head.

"Barry, this is Anna Sevenson. Anna, this is Barry Silverhorse."

I didn't know what to say. After a minute, I said, "You don't look like a silver horse."

He rolled his eyes, as if I was making a joke. But I don't make jokes. I don't understand them. "You look like a Dark horse."

He didn't say anything, but he looked at Janice. She shook her head.

"I used to live not far from here, " he said. "On a reservation, with my family. They . . . aren't happy about the magic. Or the Academy. It's too white. And it's . . . wrong. To them." But the way he said it, I knew he meant that it was wrong for him, somehow.

"I used to live in New York, the center of the universe," Janice added, with a broad smile. White teeth, lips lined a minute with her smile.

I kept eating, and they waited. Finally Janice jogged my elbow and said something in the other tongue. "Anna?"

"What?"

"Where are you from?"

I shrugged. "Everywhere. Nowhere. I don't remember."

"You must have come from somewhere."

It's true. Everyone comes from somewhere.

"What about your family?"

"Don't have one."

She was quiet, then. I mean, her eyes were quiet; no crinkles around their edges, no shininess. I like those crinkles, even though they smooth away when her face straightens. "I'm sorry to hear that. I—when we go home for Christmas—if we're allowed to go home for Christmas—you should come with me. I've got enough family to spare."

But Barry Silverhorse—Silverhorse, Silverhorse, Silverhorse—said, "Where were you living?"

Too many questions. "I—I lived in the Beckwith Orphanage." Too many words.

"The Beckwith Orphanage? Sounds like something out of a Frances Hodgson-Burnett novel."

"A what?"

"A book, Anna."

"Oh. She wrote about Beckwith?"

"No. Are you going to eat that muffin?"

"This one?"

"There's only one, Anna."

"No." I pushed it across the tray; it fell over the edge and she picked it up. She eats a lot. But I like it when she eats, because eating makes her happy. She isn't like Susan Nagata, or like the golden-haired girl, or like the redhead—any of the other ones. She eats, and she sings, and she speaks her other language, and she laughs, and she—she's like a whole life. I don't think she's afraid of anything.

"Where was Beckwith?"

"Someplace else."

"Was there a school there?"

I nod. "A school."

He looked at me then, and shook his head. "Sorry. When did you—look, if you want us to stop asking questions, we can stop."

I shrugged.

"When did you lose your parents?"

Just like that. As if he understands. "I lost 'em a long time ago. They were there, and then they weren't there." I don't want to tell him the truth.

I don't remember my parents. It's as if I never had them.

He nods quietly. His eyes look gray, like cloud or storm. I would like to see Barry fly, and I know that he can. That he does. That he doesn't like it.

*   *   *

Ninth day of school.

Classes. More classes. Oriental magic is too smelly; Professor Nagata burns incense in braziers, captured fire, something offered to flame. Makes me think of Alchemy. What is the name of fire?

Breakfast, and I eat alone. At lunch, there's Janice again, and she's in the middle of a whole bunch of people, and her hands are flying like hummingbird wings, and her eyes are light and crinkled.

"Oh, look, it's mute girl," the golden-haired girl says. Janice says something in Spanish. It's swearing. I can tell. The golden-haired girl shrugs. "Sorry."

I don't care for her. I don't know her name.

But that's not what I'm writing about.

Tonight, I found my wings. Not flight wings, though; wings I've never taken. Or maybe I have; maybe it was a long time ago, in the dark place. But these are thin wings, supple and veined, and I am small and hollow-boned, and I find little nesting spaces in the beams of the old, old ceiling. I can sit in the shadows and watch.

I fly.

I like to fly. I know the air, and its currents, and air is the only thing I trust. It carries me.

Even with these wings, even with these rotten eyes, these huge ears.

I flew to the dean's office. The principal's office. No, never mind, the Reynard's office, his cave. His place. And I sat up, on top of the shelves, behind the lip of wood that keeps the dust in place.

Breathing dust, breathing age, I listened.

He wasn't alone. Susan Nagata was with him. And another man, with a funny accent. The Alchemy teacher was there as well. And someone else, someone I had never seen before—a woman, a pale, pale woman. She stood behind Reynard's shoulder and she didn't speak a word.

"That's how she must have done it," Reynard said.

"Three days walking down one hall?"

"Three days. And we can't find the hall."

"You don't think she's lying."

"She's not."

"Did you even do a background on her, David?" Susan Nagata's voice. Cool.

"Yes."

"Tell us why she's here. She's a shifter—we've all seen evidence of that. But she falls asleep every time she walks into my classroom, and she's not doing well in pyromancy. She says she doesn't know the fire's name."

"Water delving," the other man says, "is the same. She says she doesn't know the name of water. The word for it."

Reynard nods. "She probably doesn't. She can remember, word for word, anything that's said to her—but the memory is superficial; she's describing the surface of the thing, and not the meaning."

"Makes her kind of difficult to teach."

Old buzzard cleared his throat and adjusted his glasses. "She's not difficult to teach if you understand her."

"And you've become an expert in human nature, Alexander?" Nagata again.

"Not precisely. But I used to keep birds in the old country. I used to hunt them. She's like a bird. If she consents to it, you can jess her, hood her; if she consents to it, she'll fly. But you let her fly, and she hunts what she hunts; kills what she kills."

"Let's not speak of killing," Reynard said, but his voice was cool.

"A figure of speech."

"A poor one."

"With birds, the only control you have is the control they give you. They come back, or they fly free."

"She's flown free a number of times, judging by the history we've managed to cobble together. She's been in and out of foster homes—the last home she was in, the foster mother said she never once spoke their names."

"She probably hadn't learned them."

"Alexander."

"If you're aware of the problem, David, why did you

admit her? We turn away a large number of possible candidates, and we have strict rules regarding control."

He shrugged. "Janice Rosa Redding has some problems with that. So does the young pyromancer who destroyed the test lab this morning. If control were our only measure, Susan, we'd only have you."

She smiled, but only a shadow smile.

There was a silence, and then Reynard said, "I think she's an alternate temporal."

There was a lot of silence then.

Susan Nagata said, "That's a large leap. You're speaking of the three days?"

He nodded.

"If she's accurate."

"She doesn't lie."

"And if there are no other forces involved here."

At that, they were very, very quiet. Reynard rose. "You've felt it, then?"

She nodded. "It's an old, old magic," she said quietly. As if that were answer enough.

"Cabalistic?"

"I think so."

She shock her head. "She's a risk, Reynard."

"I know."

"And?"

"I think we need her."

"It's too risky."

He went back to his desk. "Has she made any friends here?"

"Not really."

"Ah. But she does have two people who seem to watch over her. Janice and Barry. Doesn't that suggest anything to you?"

"That Janice is the universal Mother, and that Barry understands wild creatures."

"Yes. Exactly."

The old buzzard rose. "She has my vote, if you need it, Reynard."

"Why?"

"Because I think she understands the true names of things, when she can find them at all."

"And how is she going to find them if she can't even find her own?"

No one answered.

I am Anna.

I am called Anna.

These aren't the same. I was called other names before. Mary, I think. Margaret. Beth. Shadow names. I don't remember them all. It's hard enough to remember Anna.

But when Reynard spoke of other forces, I heard a name in the words, a name he didn't say, and I didn't like it. I flew out of the room when the door opened, and I could swear I felt his eyes on my back, on the back of thin membrane wings and fur.

I want to escape this. I want to be someplace else.

I just stood up to leave the room, the Academy. I had packed almost nothing. Weight is hard to carry when you're flying, and I can always find other things.

But there was a knock at the door, and I hesitated, and then I answered it. I don't know why. But Barry stood at the door. Barry *Silver*horse. He didn't look very comfortable. I waited for him to say something.

He waited for me to say something.

Both of us can wait when we have to.

Lucky for us that Janice was right behind him. Sort of. She shoved him into the room and shut the door, and he ran into me. But he didn't touch me; he kind of bounced with his hands held wide to either side, palms out. No danger, no danger there.

"We need to talk," Janice said.

I like her because she talks. When she says we, she doesn't mean us, she means her.

"Be careful, Janice."

"I'm always careful."

He snorted. Like a horse.

She walked over to my desk and rolled the top up. Stuff fell out. Mostly my clothing. "Don't you use drawers for this?"

I didn't answer, and she swept the rest of it onto the floor. I noticed then that she was carrying a big tube. "We need more room. What about the bed?"

He didn't say anything. I didn't. But she heard something because she turned and stripped the bed to its bottom sheet, and then she took something out of the tube and she put it down.

It was a drawing of some sort. Lots of squares and rectangles, with little lines, tiny words, lots of numbers.

"Do you know what this is, Anna?"

"No."

"This is one of the early plans for the Academy."

I looked at it.

"And this," she said, pointing at one long, long rectangle, "is where you disappeared the other day." She waited for me to catch up. I didn't.

She said, "this one was a preliminary plan. Look, when buildings get made—any building, but especially one like this—there are always different plans drawn up. This is one of them. It's *not* the plan they went with."

"I don't understand."

"Clearly. Look, that hall—the one you said you were in—it doesn't exist. But if the bruja had decided on *this* plan, instead of the one she did decide on, it *would* have."

"But the hall—"

"Yes. I don't think you're a liar, Anna. Frankly, I don't think you're capable of lying. You were in this hall. And it doesn't exist. Not . . . here. Not in our now."

Barry whistled.

She looked at me. "You understand, don't you? You walked straight into another place, a different possibility."

"But—"

"No damn wonder they admitted you," she added.

I stared at the drawing for a long time. "What's that?"

"What?"

"That big round circle?"

"I don't know."

"What does it say it is?"

She frowned. "It's in Latin," she said. "My Latin is *really* rusty. Hold on a sec." She gestured at Barry and he handed her a flashlight. Beam bright and round, light circle inside a paler one. Like the heart of a target.

She really frowned. "It says it's the battle circle."

"The what?" Barry frowned.

"The battle circle." Before he could ask another question, she lifted her hand. "And that room, the one just beside it? It says it's the charnel house."

"What's a charnel house?"

"A place for bodies."

Lot of silence then.

David Reynard wasn't surprised to see us. It was almost as if he was waiting for us. He opened the door and he stepped out of the way, and he let us into his office, his great library, his own space.

"Janice. Barry. Anna. Please come in."

Janice closed the door behind her. She would have leaned against it, and that made me feel strange. Comfortable. Safe, even. I don't know why.

Reynard looked at her. After a minute, he said, "Is something wrong, Janice?"

"This," she answered, and threw him the tube. He caught it.

His room, his room has tables big enough for her drawing. And he cleared one, moving a stack of books to a chair, and another to the edge of his desk.

"Where did you get this, Janice?"

"The library," she answered.

"Which library?"

She shrugged. "The teacher's library."

"Which is strictly forbidden to students."

"If it was strictly forbidden, I wouldn't have the blueprint now, would I?"

I'm not good with words, but even I wouldn't have said that.

"Ms. Redding."

She dipped her head. "Yes, sir."

He looked at the drawing. She left the door and walked over to his side. Put her fingers on the paper. "That's the hall," she said.

"I am aware of where your interest lies. Yes. That is the hall."

"She was gone for three days, sir."

"Yes."

"She was there."

He frowned. "I am not in the habit of discussing the progress of students with other students."

"And she asked me what this room was," Janice continued, unfazed. "It says it's a battle circle, and it has a charnel house attached to it." Then she folded her hands into fists and dropped them on her hips. "Sir."

"You are aware that there is no such room in the Academy."

"Yes."

"Good." He let the map curl up at the edges. Put his hands behind his back. "You are aware that the Academy has its history," he said at last.

"Yes."

"This map is part of that history, and it is not a history we teach. Not to the students."

"I think we need to know this."

"Sadly, I think you may be right." He walked away from the map. Walked in circles. I thought he was pacing until light flared up along the path he'd traced. Bright light, red and green, sharp and harsh.

"I am loath to discuss this with you, Ms. Redding, because you have a tendency to let your mouth run away with you."

She didn't say anything.

"But Anna appears to know your name. And she appears to have also managed to learn Mr. Silverhorse's name as well."

"This is significant?"

"For Anna, yes."

"She knows Professor Nagata's name."

"I believe, for the time, we will leave Professor Nagata in peace."

"Yes, sir."

"The Academy's history—the history that is taught—speaks of our founding by Doña Rafaela de Leon. This is true. It is not all of the truth, of course. But it is the truth that matters.

"When the Academy was founded, there were difficulties. People of a religious bent were likely to react poorly to the use of magic. Witch hunts had ended, but the memory of old ghosts lingers, and it's not a kind one. Many of the . . . mages . . . who found their way here, answering the founder's summons, were people who had cause to know the truth of that very personally."

He looked at me.

"They were convinced that the only way to survive was to wage a war against those of a less magical persuasion. Things were very different then," he added quietly. "And I ask you not to judge the early practitioners."

Janice shrugged. "I don't have a problem with self-defense."

"Of course not. Nor do we. But the definition used by some of the leaders was broader than ours, and the penalties for use of magic outside of the Academy were . . . lax." He bowed his head.

"Doñ Rafaela was a fierce woman, in a time when women were allowed little ferocity. You would have liked her, Janice. But although she had had some dealings with people who took exception to her gifts, she was able to separate them from the vast numbers of people who either did not know, or did not care. She felt that our best hope lay not in destruction but in something entirely different.

"There were arguments," he added quietly. "And there were deaths. Something of this nature is seldom founded without bloodshed; the men who came to her were proud and scarred.

"This, this plan, was one that was drawn by a militant faction." He was quiet.

"And what happened to that faction?"

"It lost the struggle to take over the Academy."

"And?"

"It left."

"Alive?"

He closed his eyes. Opened them. "Janice, you understand that we have rigorous admission procedures, yes?"

She snorted.

"But you assume that we choose on the basis of power and the ability to control it."

"I assume it because that's what we're told at every single interview we have to talk through."

"Fair enough. It is not untrue."

"Let me guess. It's not *all* of the truth."

"It is not, indeed, the whole truth."

"And the whole truth?"

"We choose candidates based on disposition as well as ability."

"Meaning?"

"We like nice people."

She really snorted then. *"Nice?"*

"Some exceptions are made."

"Good to know."

"Anna is an exception."

Barry and Janice turned to look at me. I waited.

"Anna knows so little about her past that her motivations were unclear. But the master of the dark arts deemed her untainted, and we decided to take a risk. Anna?"

I nodded.

"Who were your parents?"

And frowned. "I don't remember my parents."

"Do you remember your foster parents?"

"I lived in an orphanage."

"Ah." He walked over to his desk and picked up more of his papers. As if that were where his real magic lay. "You did not mention this in any of your interviews."

"I did."

"No," he said softly, "you didn't."

I thought about that.

"When were you in this orphanage?"

"When I was young."

"When was that, Anna?"

I didn't like the question.

"Professor Reynard," Barry said, lifting a hand.

He closed his eyes for a minute. When he opened them, they were silver. "Anna, what did you learn in the orphanage?"

"How to use a knife and a fork."

"Ah. And?"

"How to dress. I think. How to read. And write. How to—"

"Yes?" Soft word.

"How to fly."

"How to fly?"

"Sir—" Barry said, his voice more urgent.

But it was too late. The wings I found earlier weren't the wings I found this time. This time, they were wide, and white, and they stretched longer and thicker than the reach of my arms. And my neck, my face elongated, my feet becoming webbed and wide, my face black; I reared up, and up again.

They were speaking, but they didn't speak a language I understood. Janice was shouting. Reynard was shouting. The door to the office was closed, but the windows—the windows were there, glass thin enough to let all the light in. Thin windows. Too thin for pinions.

But Barry Silverhorse—Silverhorse, I *remember* his name—walked away from them, toward me. He had to look up to meet my eyes, had to draw close. My wings were wide. I knew I could kill him if I hit him with their pinions.

"Anna," he said, turning the word around, using it the same way I use fire. And then he laughed. I understood him.

Reynard said something, and Janice, words over words over words, squawking, terrible.

"*Anatidae*," Barry said. "It's a . . . bird family. It's not a . . . name . . . at all."

They spoke again. He shook his head. "Swan is the form she's taken," he said again, "but it's not her name. It's not what she *is*. Yes, I know that, sir. But it would really help if you got Mr. Alcom." He approached. Held out his hand. There was something in it, in the flat of the palm.

Something for me.

The door opened and closed. There was noise. But Barry Silverhorse had dropped to one knee, and his eyes, his dark perfect eyes, never wavered. His hand didn't either. I bent down, slowly, and picked up what lay there, holding it gently in my beak.

"I can't teach you to fly," he told me, his voice so gentle it was almost like a song. "But I can help you learn how *not* to fly."

Something dangled in the air between us, something made of string and grass, of small flowers and something wild with rain and dew, of fur and feathers.

The door opened again and old buzzard came in. His eyes were as round as his glasses, and dark; his brows rose up, and up again, as if they had pinions. "David," he said, in a voice he reserved for bad behavior in class.

Reynard said something.

"No, I'd prefer that you *shut up*."

He joined Barry Silverhorse.

"I don't know her name," Barry said.

"No. Neither does she. It's been hidden from her," he added, and for the first time, I heard real anger in his words. "And she's been taught to flee it."

"But why?"

"I don't know."

"How do you know so much about anima, anyway? Aren't you the Alchemy expert?"

Old buzzard snorted. "In the old days," he said, looked at me, spreading his hands as wide as Barry's, although they were older and they shook more, "Alchemy was not about turning lead into gold. It was not a hunt for the philosopher's stone. It was about things more precious than mere metal. A transformation of a different kind. Not that I expect you to understand that."

He stood up, and walked toward me. "Come back, child," he said softly. "There is food here, and water. The skies are open, but the storm is upon the horizon. Come back and we will shelter you." He reached out with his hands.

I had touched his hands. I remembered the feel of them beneath my palms. I touched his hands and he didn't pull them back, and he didn't hurt me.

I remembered his hands, even if I didn't remember his name, and that was important.

"She's coming back," Janice said, and I looked down, down, to see that my wings were shrinking. My hands were growing out of them, shedding feathers, and weight, and the vast stretch of muscle that lay behind them.

"Beckwith," Janice said quietly.

Barry kicked her, but I looked up at him. "It's . . . okay." I reached out, and the old buzzard gently stroked the back of my hands. My hands were shaking.

But David Reynard had once again fled the surroundings; was scrambling up the ladder to where his books—his millions and millions of words—lay bound in leather.

"Yes," he said, as he flipped a book open, inhaling a cloud of dust. "You're right, Janice. Beckwith was one of the founding members." He closed the book. "And that blueprint was his."

I think it is the tenth day of school.

Barry helped me fasten his charm around my wrist. He says he wears his around his neck, but he didn't ask me if I'd do the same. I wouldn't. He knows.

I like Barry Silverhorse. I like his eyes. I like the way he is quiet with me, even if he is not quiet with the other girls. They all watch him. I wonder what they see.

"Anna," he said, after dinner was over, "Beckwith Orphanage doesn't exist."

"Is it gone?"

He nodded. "It is gone."

"Is it part of the history that we aren't supposed to talk about?"

"No. It's—"

"I won't fly, Barry." I lifted his charm. "I mean, I'll try not to."

"Good. Good, Anna. Beckwith Orphanage never existed."

"Not even in the history?"

"Not even there."

"Is it like—is it like Janice's drawing? Is it a maybe place?"

He nodded slowly. "I think, yes, it's a maybe place."

"But I was there."

"I know. Do you know why?"

"They took me in. When my parents were . . . killed. I think they were killed."

He is afraid I will fly again.

"Why did they teach you how to fly?"

"I don't know."

"Did you always return to them?"

I was afraid. "I can never escape."

"Did Beckwith die?"

"Not recorded, Janice."

"Could he have founded an orphanage?"

"No. Not—not one that specializes in magic. We'd know."

"This place is pretty hidden."

"It is not hidden to anyone with magic and skill. We would *know*, Redding. Leave it be."

"Then—then—"

"Yes," he said quietly. "I think that she has crossed a continuum of some sort. She lies at the heart of a nexus of possibility."

"But—but do you think—she came from *there?*"

"I don't believe that's possible," he said quietly. "At least I do not believe that she was born in an alternate reality."

"And how can you be so certain?"

"*This* is reality, Janice."

She snorted. "Yeah. Where magic works. And people turn into birds or bears or wolves. And set whole labs on fire because they're thinking of something else. And—"

"Janice, if you're worried, why don't you just tell us all what it is that's bothering you?"

"If she came from here, someone must have figured out how to send her *there.*"

Professor Reynard nodded bleakly. "Yes."

"But why?"

"Because," he said softly, "not everyone is happy with the way things are; especially not those who believe that things should have come out very, very differently."

He turned to me. "Anna," he said quietly.

I nodded.

"You got lost today, didn't you?"

I nodded again. "I didn't write it down," I told him.

"I know. Why didn't you write it down?"

"I—"

"Because, sir," Barry said quietly. "I was with her."

I asked Barry to write this part, but the pen didn't work for him. So I have to write it, too, and I don't want to write it. It's a bad thing.

We found the battle circle. We walked down a hall that was suddenly empty, and the windows were wrong. I would have gone alone, but the charm that Barry gave me—I never take it off—started to smoke, and he grabbed my hand, the back of my hand. Just as he had seen old buzzard do. So when the other students vanished, he was there, and he didn't let go, and I didn't want to.

We heard the sounds of fighting. Shouting, and scream-

ing. I heard fire, the voice of the fire, and I almost knew its
name, but it was a name I didn't want to know. We stopped
in the hall—I stopped—and Barry stopped with me, and the
doors at the end swung open.

And I could see the round walls of the big room, and they
were charred black in places, and covered in blood, and a
man lay on his front across the floor. He smelled of death,
even this far away.

"The victory is awarded," a voice said.

It was a bad voice.

"Take the body out. Will any challenge the victor?"

No one spoke. And then the doors opened wider, and
wider still, until we could see the whole of the room, as if it
were moving toward us. And I wanted to fly.

But I couldn't. Not with Barry.

"Ah, there she is." A man in dark robes stepped into the
hall. "Margali, we have been waiting for you. Will you not
join us?"

He stepped out into the hall, and Barry Silverhorse
stepped in front of me.

I wanted to tell him how wrong that was, how dangerous,
but I couldn't speak.

"Can it be that you don't remember us, Margali? After all
that we have taught you? Come. It is almost *time*."

"Not your time," Barry muttered.

"Oh, but it is, little boy. Because you—you are out of
place here, and if you can arrive here, with her, she has finally progressed enough to take *us* back."

And Barry Silverhorse shook his head. "Anna," he whispered, and I heard just a faint hint of a strange fear in his
voice, *"Fly."*

I found my wings. Short wings, brown wings, wings
made for soaring the thermals and diving out of their
warmth on a whim. I rose, and then I realized that the charm
he had given me was still caught in my flight feathers.

Barry Longhorse.

No, no, Barry Silverhorse. Barry.

Fly, I told him.

He was afraid. To fly. *Fly,* I said, *or I won't.*

I don't know why I said this.

But he looked at me, at the charm, at the man in robes who had suddenly gotten much, much closer, and then— then he took his form. I will never forget his name again.

Barry Silverhorse.

His wings were darker than mine, and larger; his beak was an eagle's beak to the falcon. His eyes were golden. He *was* the bird, the spirit of all of the Falconiae. He rose, in the great hall, and I rose with him, drawn to him; when he shattered the glass, the shards nestled in our wings as we took to the open sky.

And in the sky, a third shape joined us, but it was no bird's shape, no transformation, no true form: it was shadow, cloud, thunder; it was a power that had no place in the air.

I fled, and Barry fled. with me, and as we circled in the air, the sky changed, the color of it deepening. The building beneath us was a building I recognized, the courtyards full of people in funny uniforms, moving up and down at the boom of a loud voice.

We were home.

The twelfth day of school.

No classes for me, and people are happy because Alchemy was canceled. Old buzzard came to Reynard's cave.

Barry was with me, but he was very quiet. Wings gone, he was quiet.

"Barry, don't you like to fly?"

He shook his head. "If we were meant to be birds," he said softly, "we would have been born to egg. There is a natural order."

"You cannot understand a thing without becoming it."

"Say that about the darkness," Barry shot back.

"It is also true of the darkness, but perhaps there are some things that do not bear understanding. When you leave the air, Barry Silverhorse, you leave the form; the memory stays with you. But when you become the darkness, there is no escape; it lingers in any form you choose, defiling it, clouding the truth of transformation."

"He called me Margali," I said.

They both looked at me. "Is that your name, Anna?"

"I don't know. Where is Janice?"

"In Pyromancy."

"Is she burning things?"

"Yes. Unfortunately, not on purpose."

"Oh."

"I have been asked to teach a special class today," he said, sitting on the table and crossing his legs beneath his robes.

"To us?"

"To you."

"Oh."

"You are not good with words," he said quietly, "because you understand their power. But you understand only one facet of it. The other has left you. Anna," he continued, speaking in the quiet voice, the voice I like, "do you know what people are?"

"No."

"They are words," he said quietly. "More than words, but words remain at their core. Some people cannot speak them aloud; they use hands and gestures, they use computers, they use technologies that seem like magic to these old eyes. But there is a reason that babies must be both touched and spoken to, else they perish. Words are a gate. They are things that exist between two people."

He rose. "Memories are often made of words. We speak them, we give them roots. We build our lives, day after day, and each day is a little anchor, something that we cling to, some part of what we become. If you walked these halls and spoke no word to anyone, ever, you would not become a part of the Academy, although you dwell within it.

"Someone has taken these words from you, as much as they can ever be taken. You are writing, yes?"

I nodded.

"*Those* are your words, child. The words you hear, the

words you say, the words you think. Yours. Every word you write brings you closer to us, to this reality, to this place. And it is only when you are fully here, when you know our names and understand how your own fits in, that it will be safe for you to . . . fly . . . again."

The thirteenth day of school.
I woke up this morning.
Before classes. Before breakfast. I woke up screaming. My throat was too small for the whole scream, and it had no words.
But I remember the dream.
I was in a dark place. Not a night dark, but a dark dark. Like a closet, like a room with no windows. There was a door, and it was open, and someone was standing inside its frame, and he held fire in his hands as if it were a bird.
He spoke. He spoke to me. I am trying not to remember his words. I was crying. There are no words when you cry, even if you want to say them. He seemed so large, in the room, in the door of the small room.
But I wanted to run away. I kept hitting the walls, and my hands hurt, and there was no way out. So I tried to fly. It was a dream. I tried and I couldn't.
I woke up because Janice and Barry were grabbing my shoulders, and my skin was full of feathers, and my legs were scaly, like large, bird legs, and I was trapped there, not human, not bird.
Janice spoke to me. Barry spoke to me. I couldn't understand them. I knew them, but I couldn't say their names. I couldn't say anything; my throat was caught between.
And then Barry let go, and I squawked. But he shook his head, and he closed his eyes, and then *he* changed.
He wasn't a bird. He wasn't a horse, although that would make sense. He was a small, large-eared red fox, with great, golden eyes, small paws. He leaped up on the bed like a cat, and he put his paws on my shoulder, and he said, "What am I?"
And I heard him, and he said, "You're Anna. You're

Anna. Become your name. Make it mean whatever it is that you *are*."

The feathers vanished. I sat up slowly, and I reached out to touch his kit's face, and his fur was soft beneath my fingers. Then he leaped back from the bed and ran out the open door, leaving me with Janice.

"Wow," she said softly.

"What?"

"He must like you, Anna." She looked at the swinging door.

"Why?"

"Because he hates doing that. He thinks it makes him cousin to Coyote, and that's not a good thing to be, where he comes from. But he did it."

I didn't ask why. I knew.

I caught her hand. "Janice?"

"Yes?"

"Thank you."

When I went to Alchemy class, I got lost.

I got lost because I was thinking of Barry Silverhorse. The fox Barry, the totem Barry.

I opened the door into a different class, and I froze there. Beckwith. Beckwith Orphanage.

And Beckwith was standing before the blackboard in an empty room. He smiled when I walked in. "Good afternoon, Margali. Please, take a seat."

I did what he told me. I did it without thinking. Without speaking.

"We're pleased," he said, "to see that you've finally arrived at our destination. I think it's time to finish the lesson that began so long ago. Do you remember it?"

I shook my head.

"Ah. I see that you still haven't recovered your speech. A pity." His smile was a lie. "But you have an important role to play in the future of the Academy—a future that starts now." He shook his head, smiling.

"Do you know that your grandparents were part of the

founding of this place? They were a strange couple. I almost miss them, but they chose the wrong side." He looked a little like old buzzard, but only to the eyes.

"And your parents could have corrected that mistake, but they were too old, and too grounded. You," he added quietly, "were such a jewel. They hated to part with you. Do you recognize this room?"

I said nothing.

"Margali." Fire, fire in his hands.

I nodded.

"Good. I believe it is used for Alchemy now. But had we attained our proper position in the Academy, it would have been used to greater purpose. Come. It is time to change the world."

He opened his hands and the fire fell from them like blood, scouring the desk, charring the wood in a circle that began and ended with his palms.

"Magic," he said quietly, "is about possibility. All of the possibilities that we *lost*. You can bridge the gap. You had a brother; he failed us. But you were young enough to be . . . unanchored." The fire grew brighter, its heart white.

"Do you know what you will do when you graduate from the Academy? This one? You will *serve*. You will serve the interests not of your brethren, not of your equals, but of those without the power and the will to serve *themselves*. This is wrong," he continued. "And together we might right it. This room is real now. There are other rooms that need to be made real."

He walked toward me, and the fire followed, circling him. "Come," he said again. "We go to Reynard's office."

The halls were different. There were paintings across the stone. No rules on plaques, no lists, no teams, no *words*. I wanted to fly, but the fire followed me, and I knew it would burn my flight feathers forever.

Nothing was the same as I remembered it, as I thought I remembered it. The floors were slightly different. The markings on closed doors were symbols, burned in wood. No names. Nothing I recognized.

But I felt as if I knew this place, knew it better than I knew the Sorcerer's Academy. We walked up stairs, and the doors that happened to be in the way parted before Beckwith, just as I had. And at last we stopped in front of a set of doors that seemed almost familiar.

"This room, " he said quietly. "Give me this room, and I will give you back your name."

Words. His words.

But I nodded. I couldn't do anything else. I walked past him, and I touched the doors, and they opened into an empty room.

But it was a room I recognized.

Beckwith frowned. I could feel it in the heat of the fire at my back. "So this," he said, with disdain, "is the heart of the Academy. A library. How quaint."

He walked past me, to the desk that looked exactly like Reynard's desk. Forgot about me, and why wouldn't he? I couldn't remember myself.

But I remembered this room, this place. I remembered the books and the ladder. I remembered *David Reynard*, standing a little to the left of where Beckwith stood, asking me his questions, offering me words, and more words, and demanding that I give him words in return.

I walked over to the ladder; Beckwith was going through the drawers, and there seemed to be a lot of them. I hadn't known that; I'd never seen the part of the desk that faced the window before.

"Don't think of flight, Margali," Beckwith said, not looking up.

I didn't answer. Instead, I touched the ladder, the great brass thing that rode on a rail and a set of funny, round wheels. I pushed it, and it glided across the floor without making a sound.

It stopped just as quietly, and I walked over to it. Climbed it carefully. There were books here, row upon row of them, words on leather spines in languages that I could never hope to read.

But there was one book that I did know. I reached out to touch it, and as I did, something caught my eye, dangling on string in the air. Feather, fur, leaf, flower.

Barry. Barry's charm.

"Barry," I whispered.

The charm began to smoke, as if it were on fire. But the smoke was sweat. I looked over my shoulder. Beckwith had paused in his search; the contents of the desk were all over the floor. I didn't know what he was looking for, but I knew—I knew that I didn't want him to find it.

I reached out and grabbed the book.

My book. The book that I'd been told to write in.

I opened it. Saw the picture of the lion, with its mane, its wide eyes, its crossed forepaws. Turned the page, met the gaze of the owl. Something that old buzzard said came back to me: Lion for strength. Owl for wisdom.

I had neither.

Hands shaking, I turned the page.

First day of school. I survived.

I touched the paper, and my fingers left a mark. An ink mark, wider than pen.

I turned the pages quickly, then, flipping them forward.

Beckwith looked up. I felt it; the hairs on the back of my neck rose. I couldn't look back. I was afraid to look, afraid to lose sight of the words.

I found blank page, blank paper. Without a pen, I wrote a name.

Barry Silverhorse.

"What are you doing, Margali?"

Another name. Janice Rosa Redding.

"Margali, come down from the ladder before you fall."

And another. David Reynard. Alexander Alcom. Susan Nagata.

Help me.

The doors flew open. The ladder jerked free of my feet. I lost the book as my fingers started the curve of another letter, and it fell, its old, old covers splayed wide, its pages facedown against the floor.

Beckwith's fire lapped across the covers.

And a voice I recognized said, softly, *Fly. Fly, Anna, if that is what you desire.*

I looked up, my hands clutching the brass rungs of the ladder, as a wind entered the room. Behind it stood David Reynard. To his left stood Susan Nagata; to his right, the old buzzard. And behind them, like shadows, Barry and Janice.

I had called them and they had come.

Beckwith called fire, and the fire was a dark fire, and I knew—I *knew*—what it would do. It would burn away . . . the words. All their words. Their names.

My arms became wings, white wings, wide wings, and my neck became long and slender. I looked past Beckwith to the glass of the window.

And then looked toward the door.

"You," Reynard said, speaking to Beckwith.

"You recognize me. How gratifying. I'm afraid, however, that you are late."

I had learned their names. I didn't want to lose them.

"Margali," Beckwith said, in a voice made of that fire, that terrible forgetting, "come here."

"I am not Margali," I said, and the words were a trumpeting, terrible sound.

His eyes widened as I leaped off the ladder, widened as I passed over his circle of fire. It burned me. It burned me as it had burned me before, once before.

"Anna!" Barry shouted. He pushed his way between Reynard and the old buzzard; the old buzzard hadn't moved an inch.

I flew at Beckwith, my wings spread wide: swan wings, powerful wings, all white. I felt his bones snap as they met mine.

Reynard and the old buzzard came running then, and stopped just short of my shadow. And then Barry inched toward me, and closing his eyes as if he were in pain, he slipped into his fox skin, his small fur.

"Don't kill him, Anna," he said.

"He killed me."

"No."

"He did. I don't remember anything clearly. I don't remember—"

"You remember me," Barry said. "You remember Janice. You remember Professor Alcom."

"It's not enough!"

"No," he continued, speaking quietly. "It never is. But . . . this is important, Anna. You've claimed yourself, you've made yourself free. You *have* a choice."

"He's right," the old buzzard said, and I turned toward him. "Choose your name, Anna. Choose what you *will* be. Be aware that this first act will anchor you in a way that no other act can.

"Will killing be the thing that you come back to, time and again? You will lose your way," he added softly. "because you are human, and we all do, from time to time."

"But he's dangerous!"

"He is," the old buzzard said. "But look at him."

I did. I looked down. He lay at my feet, groaning.

Barry scampered up and across his body. His great ears were twitching. He looked up at me, way, way up, his little neck craning.

I looked at him, at Beckwith, at him.

I heard old buzzard's words, and I saw something in them, something that he hadn't said: that if I killed Beckwith, Barry would see it, and know it, and it would be something that he would never forget, something that words couldn't change.

I would lose him. I would remember his name, and he would remember mine—but when he thought of my name, he would see only Beckwith, dead, and me, his killer.

A killer.

He was waiting. I lowered my head slowly, and I touched his nose with the tip of my beak.

And then I let go, and we were both sitting on the ground just beside Beckwith, our noses touching. Barry coughed and stumbled backward, making Beckwith scream as he trampled his arms.

My nose was tingling.

It's still tingling, as I write these words.

Tomorrow I will find out the name of the golden-haired girl, who is a little like a lion, and I will find out the names of the rest of the teachers, and I will write them down everywhere I have paper and pen.

More stuff happened. More talking, Reynard and Nagata arguing, her with her icy voice and he with his careful one. But the most important thing is that my nose still feels warm where his nose touched it, and I remember his name, and I will never, ever forget it.

FRESHMAN MIXER

by Rosemary Edghill

Rosemary Edghill's first professional sales were to the black & white comics of the late 1970s, so she can truthfully state on her resumé that she has killed vampires for a living. She is also the author of over thirty novels and several dozen short stories in genres ranging from Regency romance to space opera, making all local stops in between. She has collaborated with authors such as the late Marion Zimmer Bradley and SF Grand Master Andre Norton, worked as an SF editor for a major New York publisher and as a freelance book designer, and is currently an Associate Editor for Swordsmith Books and a professional reviewer, as well as a full-time writer. Her hobbies include sleep, research for forthcoming projects, and her Cavalier King Charles spaniels. Her web site can be found at: http://www.sff.net/people/eluki

S O, who are you asking?" Davetta Brightlaw asked idly, killing time until the bell that would release them from the cafeteria rang.

Though classes had already been in session for almost a month—counting Orientation—the Freshman Mixer would be the first chance the students would get to meet many of their classmates, and since—except with special permission—they were restricted completely to campus during the first semester, it provided a welcome respite from classes as well. Those who came from "party hearty" surroundings, like Kaylin, had been complaining about the lack of social activity since Day One, and those from stricter households had been eager to sample the fruits of their new freedom.

And although the event had been specifically designed as a "mixer," nearly everyone had decided to "couple up." Whether it was a case of True Love At First Sight, like Oliver and Amanda (who were popularly expected to *still* be dating in their Senior Year—and for that matter, their Golden Years), or an alliance of convenience, like Matt and Davetta (Matt swore he needed Davetta to protect him from the "hordes of lovelies" who would seek to carry him off the moment he appeared on the dance floor, while Davetta said that what he needed was a keeper, period), everybody was going with somebody.

"That's my secret." David Huygens grinned nastily. David—or "Weej"—as he had been early and inevitably labeled—was (like all the rest of them) a freshman at the Academy For Advanced Study in Sedona, so, as Janice frequently reminded the others, he must have some redeeming qualities, but since they'd gotten here, nobody had seen any sign of them. He wasn't the youngest member of the freshman class, or the smartest, or the weirdest—that honor certainly belonged to Shadow Moonboy—and he certainly wasn't the most good-looking guy here. Weej was short, pudgy, and had a really stupid pair of glasses; in fact, he bore a really strong resemblance to, well, a pig. And not in a cute way.

None of that would have mattered—after all, Oliver Mason was short, had glasses thicker than Coke bottle lenses, and the world's worst acne, but he had plenty of friends and in fact was taking Amanda Spiegel (short-listed for Prettiest Freshman) to the Freshman Mixer—but the thing with Weej was that even more than the other things he didn't have, he twice didn't have any of what Janice Redding's dad, an immigration lawyer back in New York, referred to as "social engineering skills." Weej wasn't just a nerd—and face it, most of them here at Professor Xavier's School for Gifted Wizards were nerds of one kind or another; it went with the magic powers—Weej was a *lame*, rude, nasty nerd. In fact, if they hadn't been assigned to the same table in the cafeteria, Davetta and Janice and Barry and Matt and the others would never have spoken to him twice. Weej had a way of making you feel like he was playing a vicious joke on you every time he talked to you—and from the looks he gave them, he *liked* making people feel that way.

But being stuck with each other for a minimum of two hours a day, three meals a day, they'd all gotten to know each other more quickly—and more thoroughly—than might otherwise have chosen to. Which was, Janice supposed, part of the point of having assigned seats and assigned tables, and having to stay in them for the whole lunch period. It was part of "getting to know their fellow students," which was one of the things the Academy brochure had assured them they'd be doing . . . along with learning to cast spells and control their innate magical abilities.

They'd all come to the Academy from different parts of the country. Matt Johnson, Barry Silverhorse, and Janice Redding all came from big cities: Dallas, L. A., and New York, respectively, where each of them had fit into the mainstream as well as possible with Freakylinks happening all around them, while Weej came from a small town in Indiana, and Davetta came from an equally small village in Connecticut. Kaylin Trent was a total Valley Girl, Amanda was a Disney Princess in Training from Ohio, and Oliver was from Boston, from a famous old literary family more likely to *be* ghosts than see them. Each of them, like all of the students here, had grown up knowing they were different from the other kids their own age—that somehow, around them, strange things tended to happen, and some of them were their own fault.

Then, just a few months ago, each one of them, along with almost a hundred other kids from all over the world, had received a letter of enrollment to the Academy for Advanced Studies in Sedona, Arizona, bringing with it an admission into a world few of them had suspected existed. But despite its amazing unbelievable unworldly promise, once they had arrived at the sedately named Academy, life settled down into . . . well, not quite a *rut* exactly, but into something as ordinary as life could get at a school where the required freshman subjects included Unnatural History, Introduction to Divination, and Pyromancy.

In fact, being at the Academy was only as strange as attending any boarding school might be, and some of them—like Kaylin and Oliver—were already familiar with that. The strangest thing of all was the city of Sedona itself, a mix of glorious Southwestern scenery and the flakiest sort of New Age woo-woo, most of the latter centered around the so-called "energy vortices" that supposedly dotted the landscape around the small touristy town. Since freshman students were only allowed to leave the campus for field trips and class assignments, no one had yet had any opportunity to discover whether the "energy vortices" were anything more than what Barry disdainfully called "bliss-ninny psychobabble."

"So, speaking of secrets, where's Moonboy?" Janice said. If Weej wanted them all to tease him about his date—not that anybody really had dates for the Mixer, or not exactly—then she was definitely changing the subject.

"Tray in his room, as usual. It's daytime." Matt jerked a thumb at the windows. The noon sunlight poured down out of a cloudless sky, so intense you almost expected it to make noise when it hit the ground. Matt was from Dallas and Barry was from Los Angeles, so Janice supposed this must look sort of normal to both of them, but she was from Brooklyn Heights, and all the colors here appeared too harsh and too bright to her, almost disorienting. It was even worse for some of the others. She'd heard some of the Irish students marveling at the brightness of the sunlight here in the

American Southwest. The Academy had a fair number of foreign students from all over, and she supposed that Shadow Moonboy must be from someplace that got even less sun than Ireland.

Wherever that might be.

Antarctica?

He was certainly pale enough for that. Shadow Moonboy made even the Danish kids look positively dusky. And he hadn't gotten that shoulder-length silver hair of his out of a peroxide bottle. But he wasn't albino. Human albinos usually had pale blue eyes with a reddish tint, not dark green with a gold ring around the pupil, and a kind of washed-out look besides, and when Moonboy *did* venture out of his room (unlike everybody else, he had a room to himself; another weird thing), once the sun was down, he was certainly healthy enough.

Really healthy.

Pinup-billboard-in-Times-Square wouldn't-you-like-be-a-male-model healthy.

Janice sighed.

"Lucky Moonboy," Kaylin said, poking at her tray as if she thought the food might be hiding under what was on it. Kaylin was beach-bunny blonde and did her best to live up to every single cliché about Southern California girls. Her parents both did something in The Industry, which, as Janice had quickly learned, meant movies. "I wonder if he ever eats anything on those trays?"

"Of course he does," Davetta said, sounding puzzled. "What else is he going to do—send out for Chicken Delight?" She sounded wistful; fast-food deliveries from off-campus were another thing that was banned during the first semester, and the cafeteria pizza just didn't measure up.

"What if he doesn't eat at all?" Kaylin said, sounding mysterious.

"Well *that's* stupid," Janice said roundly. "Of course he has to eat." In every group, somebody always had to be the voice of reason, and she and Matt were splitting the duties there.

"But not cafeteria food," Kaylin said, lowering her voice to a dramatic hush. "Not if he *isn't human.*"

Barry stared at her for a moment, then exploded in whoops of laughter, making Kaylin blush furiously. Janice suspected that Kaylin had a bit of a crush on Barry. Well, crushes were easy to come by—especially when you were in a place where you could finally be yourself for the first time in your life. And she had to admit that Barry was quite the piece of eye candy: long dark hair, flawless skin that seemed to echo the tones of the red rocks outside, deep brown eyes that flashed green at disconcerting moments. Janice already knew (but had heard it again from Kaylin, who was shameless at fishing for gossip and efficient at presenting her finds) that he was Diné and had family in the area. Yet to other people, Barry presented himself as the complete Angeleno, with nothing the least bit Tribal about him.

Only sometimes she wondered. From her reading, Janice knew that Tribal peoples were absolute death on witches, thinking all of them were evil. If none of the students here at the Academy were actual witches, they were the next best thing, weren't they? That had to bug Mr. Barry I'm-So-Anglo Silverhorse just a little, didn't it?

Not my problem, she told herself firmly. An honest look in the mirror was enough to tell her that. Janice was plump, plain, and short, except for her yellow-brown hair taking more after her Puerto Rican mother than her Anglo father—not homely by any means, but not dazzling like Kaylin, or inconceivably cute like Davetta, or even Snow White perfect like Amanda (who made up for being beautiful by being incredibly sweet as well)—and facts being facts, she'd have as much luck roping the moon as she would of getting someone who looked like Barry to ever look at her twice. Her lot in life was obviously to be the comic relief, the gal pal that everybody depended on without thinking *she* might ever want to be the fairy princess. . . .

She sighed, and darted a sideways glance at Weej. Having lost the group's attention, he'd buried his nose in a book again. *I wonder just who IS dumb enough to be Weej's date for the Mixer?* Janice wondered idly.

"Hey, did you hear? I'm taking Barry to the dance!" Kaylin announced, twirling into the lounge a few days later.

Each floor of the dorm had a study lounge—with, for no reason Janice could see, an enormous fireplace at one end. Even in September, Janice couldn't imagine this place ever getting cold enough for a fire. It was large enough to roast a whole ox in, too, and looked like something out of a Zorro movie. In fact, most of the campus looked like something out of a Zorro movie—the buildings had been built in the 1880s by a mysterious millionaire (and sorcerer) named William Bryan Reynard who had relocated the school from its original home and given it its current name. According to the school brochure, the Academy was originally founded by Doña Rafaela de Leon in the late 1840s. According to the students, Doña Rafaela might still be around here somewhere. . . .

"Does Barry know you're taking him to the dance?" Janice said to cover the quick lurch of her stomach. It wasn't that she was in love with Barry—she liked Barry and Kaylin both and was glad to have both of them as friends—and at fourteen, she really wasn't interested in getting into the heavy romance thing just yet. But Kaylin was tall and blonde and slender, and Barry was exotic and devastatingly handsome, and sometimes it seemed that things like this were just one more proof that she'd always be included out, never fitting in anywhere.

"I asked him. He said yes." Another twirl, and finally Kaylin came to rest on one of the couches. "Well, at least that's taken care of. What are you doing?"

"Studying. Biology. Cryptozoology, actually." Janice stared down at the page. *Chapter Seven: Freshwater magical creatures.*

She'd come in here to find a quiet place to study during her free period—the lounge didn't get much traffic during the day. "I wonder if we'll ever *see* any of these things?"

"I'd die," Kaylin said frankly. "It's one thing to, well, you know . . . start fires. Find things. Tell what people are thinking or make somebody feel better. I think anybody can do that, really. My grandmother could."

"That's because sorcerous talent runs in families," Janice explained patiently, knowing she sounded stuffy and pedantic, like one of their teachers. "Healing, telepathy, pyromancy, and psychometry are *not* gifts everybody has. They're indications of magical talent that can be trained."

Kaylin wrinkled her nose. "You sound like Professor Reynard. Isn't he awful? I don't think he was ever our age—and I *don't* want to grow up to be Harry Potter, thank you so much!"

Janice had actually rather liked Professor David Reynard, the Academy's headmaster, though she supposed he could seem rather ominous. Especially if you had a guilty conscience.

"*All* I want is to—oh, well, never mind! It's only four years—and then I can go to a real school!" Kaylin bounced to her feet again—she was never still for long—and rushed out again, leaving Janice alone with her books.

"*A real school.*" Not for the first time, Janice wondered what came next. Her father had always talked about her becoming a lawyer like him; her mother had hoped she'd follow her into medicine—that was before they'd found out she was a student wizard. At least she had years to worry about that. Other matters were more urgent. *The Mixer's tomorrow. I wonder if I'm going to be the only one going alone?*

"Is it too late?"

Janice jumped and squeaked at the sound of the voice behind her in the hall.

For some reason, tonight she'd felt unaccountably shy about anyone seeing her preparations for the dance—though everybody was going to see her outfit once she got there, of course—so she'd hung back, making excuses, until Kaylin and Latisha had dressed and left. As a result, she was the last one here on the girls' floor. Everyone else would already be there when she arrived, but no biggie—it was just a stupid party, right?

She spun around. Shadow Moonboy was standing in the hallway, regarding her uncertainly. He looked like a Gap ad—everything a little too perfect.

"Too late?" she asked breathlessly.

"To ask you for the dance. *To* the dance. It is the custom here, is it not? I do not wish to offend."

"You want to go to the Freshman Dance with me?" Janice asked, just making sure she had it straight. English was the official language of the Academy, but it was a second—or even third—language for some of the students, and mishaps were common. "Is this some kind of a joke?"

"It is only a dance," he said, sounding a little discouraged. "It is meaningless. Not like . . . not as if I asked you to dance where I come from," he finished, smiling. "That would mean more."

Janice had never seen him smile before. She was willing to bet that nobody here had. Certainly, if Kaylin had ever seen Moonboy smile, Barry would still be waiting for his invitation. She smiled back. "Don't say nobody else asked you?"

There was a pause while Moonboy worked out what she meant.

"No one did ask me to dance. To *the* dance. And I did not know if I— If it was permitted— There are rules here. Professor Reynard has explained to me what I may and may not do, but I am not always sure. And I wished to ask you, Janice Rosa Redding, but I did not wish to do it in front of others, in case I am in error."

"Me? You wanted to ask me?" Janice felt herself blushing, sure for one horrible moment that this was some kind of nasty trick that somebody had put him up to. But she was good at reading people, and if Moonboy was weird, there was no nastiness in him. He was just one more confused exchange student. And maybe they *liked* frumpy half-breeds where he came from.

"Yes. You. Is it too late?" he repeated.

"No," Janice said, feeling a big silly grin she couldn't suppress break out all over her face. "It isn't too late. Yes, I will go to the meaningless dance with you."

Anywhere but the Academy, a school dance would be held in the school gymnasium, but as far as Janice had been able to tell in her explorations so far, that was one building the Academy for Advanced Studies didn't possess. *No football team either,* she supposed.

So the dance was being held in the school cafeteria . . . at least, she and Moonboy had come through the same door that usually led to the school cafeteria. A wave of music greeted them . . . somebody had a sound-system up and running, and people were already dancing.

The room inside, however, was completely different.

For one thing, it was twice as big. For another, everything *cafeteria-ish* had somehow been removed. The only thing that was still the same was the long row of windows on the south side looking out into the quadrangle.

"Very nice," Moonboy said, an undertone of laughter in his voice.

"What did they do, push the walls back?" Janice said.

"Might have," Matt said, strolling up, as if he'd been watching for her to arrive. He had a paper cup of punch in his hand and was wearing a positively lurid shirt—black, Western-style (of course.) with pearl buttons, gold piping, and embroidered roses all along the yoke and down both sleeves. "The senior students did the decorating—with the professors to help, of course." He looked hard at Moonboy, and then shot a questioning look at Janice.

"Good evening, Master Johnson. *Mister,*" Moonboy corrected himself firmly.

"Shucks, plain 'Matt' is good enough for me," Matt said, laying on his country-cowpoke act with a trowel. "And what do your folks call you?"

Again—because she was looking for it now—Janice caught the faint hesitation. It wasn't because he was all that bad at English, she was coming to think, but more because Moonboy was trying to figure out the *appropriate* response, as if wherever he came from, things were so different there that he had to work really hard at fitting in.

"Moonboy," he said at last. "Moonboy is good. Or Shadow. Shadow is good, too, Matt." He smiled, and Matt was no more immune to that smile than Janice had been. He thrust out his hand, grinning.

"Well, Shadow Moonboy, I've seen you around, but I'm right pleased to get to know you better. C'mon, let's get some punch before it's all gone."

As the three of them crossed the floor, Janice saw that things that wouldn't have been worth a look back home were worth a second and even a third look here.

There was the inevitable mirrored disco ball, suspended from the ceiling. Only it wasn't. It was just hanging in midair, revolving gently, and it didn't seem to be attached to anything at. all. The strings of party lights weren't—they were lights, but they weren't strung on anything; they just sort of seemed to be scattered around the upper walls and ceiling.

But the banners that said things like "Welcome Freshmen" and "AAS salutes the Class of '07" looked mundane enough. Like everything else since she'd gotten here, the dance was a mixture of the breathtakingly bizarre and the numbingly normal.

"So. Where do you hail from?" Matt asked Moonboy.

Janice would have liked to hear his answer, but suddenly someone grabbed her by the elbow and yanked her violently away from the two boys. She staggered backward, off-balance, and almost fell into Kaylin and Davetta.

"I cannot believe you're dating a vampire!" Kaylin hissed furiously.

"What date?" Janice hissed back, hoping their voices didn't carry to the others. "He asked me to the dance!"

"That's because he couldn't get in here without an invitation!" Kaylin whispered excitedly.

"Kaylin, grow a brain," Janice groaned feelingly. "He

eats *dinner* in the cafeteria! Besides, why would Professor Reynard admit a vampire to the Academy? Why would a vampire want to come?"

"So he could—I don't know! But—oh, he's staring at us!" Kaylin whirled away and disappeared, ducking behind a knot of other students.

Janice glared feelingly at Davetta, who shrugged apologetically and followed Kaylin.

He must think I'm nuts. Bracing herself, she turned around, but Moonboy wasn't even looking at her, despite what Kaylin had said. He was standing at the edge of a group of boys—no one she knew particularly—clustered around one of the punch bowls, watching them curiously. She forced herself to walk back over to him, smiling nonchalantly. Just as she got there, the boys went hurrying off, laughing.

"They put something in it," Moonboy said, frowning at the punch.

"It's only 8:30. A little early for that," Janice said. She leaned over the bowl and sniffed, but couldn't smell anything. She wondered where they'd gotten alcohol—and for that matter, if it was alcohol they'd poured into it. The things they were learning to make in Alchemy—not to mention Philters—were not things that would improve a fruit punch. And if some moron had managed to smuggle some drugs from home—Ecstasy, say, or roofies . . .

"I will fix it."

Before she could stop him, Moonboy reached out, and passed his hand slowly over the punch bowl. *"Épurent,"* he whispered.

The contents seemed to shimmer, for just a moment, and then the dark-red liquid inside went clear. Even the ice was gone.

Janice sniffed again, then stuck her finger in it and tasted. Water.

"Oops," Moonboy said gravely, regarding his handiwork.

"Yeah. Oops. Let's get out of here before anyone spots

that—no, *don't* try to fix it again! C'mon." She tucked her arm through his and dragged him out onto the dance floor.

Water? He'd turned it into *water?*

She wasn't going to think about that right now. With any luck, what had just happened would be blamed on the kids who had spiked the punch in the first place.

She'd always been a good dancer, and back home there'd been plenty of chances to polish her stuff. Moonboy didn't seem to be familiar with the moves, but he caught on quick, and soon enough was teaching *her* some new chops. Dancing with him was *fun*—enough fun to make her forget about the punch, about Kaylin, about everything else but the music and the two of them mirroring each other and the beat. She made sure they stayed in the middle of the floor for at least half an hour, until somebody else had a chance to discover the contents of the punch bowl. By then she was hot and breathless, but Moonboy hadn't even popped a sweat. He was willing to follow her to the edge of the room when she signaled a halt, though—*far* away from the food.

"What did you do?" she asked, looking around to make sure there were no teachers in earshot. She'd already spotted Sanchez and Nagata, as well as half a dozen more of their teachers on patrol. Even Dr. Taverner, the school librarian, and Nurse Claremont were keeping an eye on things here tonight.

Moonboy sighed, looking exactly like someone who was already in so much trouble that a little more wouldn't matter. "I purified it. Perhaps a little too well?"

Yeah, just maybe.

"But there are wards—dampers—all over the place here so nobody can try out any of the stuff they've learned, even if they get tempted. But I *saw* you do it!" she protested.

"All you must do is work inside them," Moonboy said. "If your magic does not touch them, the wards do not see it. It is simple."

Simple for Merlin the Magician, maybe!

"So you're not here to learn magic," she said bluntly.

"I am," Moonboy protested instantly. "Not the magic I

know, but my . . . mother's magic. She was a witch. My father . . . was not. Now they both feel it's time for me to learn to fit in here. So I am here. And I am most strictly forbidden by Headmaster Reynard to use . . . the magic I know."

Mixed marriage, huh? And you don't fit in either place. Well, I guess I know how that feels, don't I?

"Like you did tonight. Don't worry, I won't tell. It was in a good cause, anyway. C'mon. Let's go see if they've fixed the punch-bowl and get something to eat, okay?"

Moonboy quickly agreed, and it was only after they started back through the dancers that Janice realized she hadn't taken the chance to find out where he was *from*.

"Hey, look—there's Weej . . . and his date." Barry gestured, the half full cup of punch in his hand sloshing dangerously.

It was a little after ten, and some of the kids had already left. The mixer shut down at eleven, so that nobody would still be here when the spells that held the lights floating in the air—and the other illusions—dispelled at midnight. There'd been an announcement a few minutes ago—Professor Reynard had made it personally—and he'd hinted at "severe penalties" for any freshmen caught hanging around the cafeteria at the Witching Hour.

But the five of them—six if you counted Moonboy, and eight if you added Oliver and Amanda—were having too much fun to even think of leaving before the last minute, so they lingered around the (now-empty) buffet table, while the DJ played slow dances that none of them (except maybe Oliver and Amanda) really felt like dancing.

Janice glanced toward Barry before looking where he was pointing. Barry was looking spectacular, in a tight turquoise T-shirt and even tighter white jeans, but Janice didn't feel any particular envy at Kaylin for having scored the trophy-escort. It might have been different if Kaylin looked smug about things—or if Barry had actually seemed to notice he was supposed to be anybody's trophy—but Kaylin just looked wound especially tight: too much makeup, enough Giorgio to stop a charging rhino, and everything on "fast-forward."

She looks scared, Janice realized, and wondered why. Kaylin couldn't still believe that idiocy about Moonboy being a vampire—and Janice was going to have a long talk with her tonight about that anyway—and besides, he was nowhere near her. No, whatever Kaylin was scared of was inside Kaylin. She'd brought it with her.

Everybody looked.

Weej was dancing with a girl in a long pink ball gown. She wasn't dressed like anyone else here—in fact, she looked like she'd stepped off the box of the Disney Sleeping Beauty video. Her expression, as she looked up—up!—at Weej was cloyingly adoring.

"Did he bring a townie?" Oliver asked in tones of well-bred horror. "He'll get so kicked out for that."

"Who is that?" Matt asked. "Does anybody know?"

There was a murmur of confused disclaimer. Among the four of them, Kaylin, Davetta, Janice, and Amanda knew most of the freshman girls at least by sight, and the girl dancing with Weej didn't look at all familiar to any of them.

"Who is that?" Moonboy asked, in a completely different tone, putting a hand on Janice's arm.

She turned, and looked where he was pointing.

At first she saw nothing at all, and. then, like a slow fade-in in a movie, there was someone there, in the shadows by the door—a man, wearing a weather-beaten denim jacket, jeans, and snakeskin boots, with a red scarf tied around his neck. His unruly dark hair was streaked with gray—not as if he were old, but as if there were something feral about him. Not wolf, but *like* a wolf.

He glanced up and saw her watching him. His eyes flashed red, like an animal's in the dark, and he smiled. It was a charming smile, utterly untrustworthy and dangerous, and she felt him assessing her. All her Urban Survival instincts kicked in—this guy was Trouble, and if he took even one step toward her, she was going to scream, run, make a *big* fuss!

She felt Moonboy's hand tighten—hard—on her arm, willing her to be still, to do nothing to bring any more of the interloper's attention to her than she had already attracted.

Janice stood utterly still, not even daring to breathe, as that coldly playful assessment continued. Who was he? What was he doing here? She knew he wasn't one of the teachers, and he didn't look like one of the custodians, not really. Then the stranger lost interest, turning away and continuing to slink—there was really no other word to describe how he moved—along the wall.

Janice turned back to the others. None of them had noticed anything.

"What—?" she gasped.

"Who—?" Moonboy asked.

There was a scream from the dance floor. The girl in the pink ball gown was screaming—a high, thin squeal of horror like fingernails on a chalkboard. And she wasn't the only one squealing.

Where Weej had been a moment before, was a pig. A very nice, small, pink *Babe in the City* pig, but . . . a pig.

The ripples of transformation spread to the other dancers, and in seconds the cafeteria was filled with goats, cats, dogs, chickens, pigeons—flying wildly around the room—hamsters, guinea pigs, llamas, wolves . . .

Moonboy dragged Janice back toward the windows as the ripple of magic spread to engulf her friends—horse, monkey, cougar, crane, parrot . . . The song was still going, but you could barely hear it for all the barks and squeals as all the animals started going crazy, and in the middle of it all, looking like some crazy Circe, stood the girl in the pink dress, the only one untouched by the transformations. The kids who hadn't been touched yet were backing away. Some were screaming as they stared at their friends. In a moment Janice and Moonboy would be transformed as well.

"Dissipent!" Moonboy shouted at the top of his lungs.

He threw both hands into the air, making a *flinging* motion, as if he were tossing something away from him. Both hands were spread wide, and Janice could see his fingers glow, as if someone had switched a light on inside him.

"Ohmigod!" she gasped.

The two waves of magic—one from this world, one most emphatically *not*—crashed into each other, stopping the tide of transformation just before it reached them. Suddenly there was a squeal and a pop. The music stopped, and the lights in the cafeteria went out, but there was a full moon tonight, shining in through the wall of windows, and between that and the still-functioning lights on the quad, it wasn't completely dark. Janice wasn't sure how it was that silence could be so loud, or how something you couldn't see could hurt your eyes. But it seemed that she *could* see it—and hear it, too, making a sound like frying bacon as it spread over the other magic, eating it up. She flinched away from it, closing her eyes tightly, but she could still sense what was going on, even without seeing it. Whatever Moonboy had done was still spreading, expanding to fill the entire room.

She heard a crash, and opened her eyes quickly. The disco ball had fallen to the floor, shattering into a zillion mirrored tile pieces. Fortunately, nobody had been directly under it. The little colored lights were falling, too, hitting the ground with soft plops and winking out. The room was half the size it had been a second before, and the steam tables and the kitchen were back where they'd been at dinnertime.

And everybody was back the way they ought to be.

Except for the small white mouse—formerly Weej's date—determinedly clawing its way out of the billows of pink fabric that had been its party dress.

There were some more screams—not frightened ones, this time—and everybody started talking at once. Janice stared around wildly, trying to spot the stranger in the faded denims, but couldn't see him anywhere. Beside her, Moonboy leaned back against the window, breathing hard.

"You two. My office. Now." Without waiting to see if he was obeyed, David Reynard strode past them and out onto the quad.

"Oops," Moonboy said softly, looking down at her.

"Double oops," Janice said glumly. "We are so busted."
She looked around, but didn't spot the rest of her friends
anywhere in the confusion. It was probably better this way.
"C'mon. Let's get out of here before anybody notices us. We
can figure out what just happened on the way to our execu-
tion."

Neither of them really felt like talking on the way to the
Headmaster's Office, though. It had all happened so fast that
Janice was only now coming to realize just how scared
she'd been. First that freaky looking guy with the red eyes
had showed up—and smiled at her (and if Kaylin wanted a
candidate for vampire guy, Janice was willing to nominate
him, whoever he was), and then Weej had turned into a pig,
and then everybody had turned into animals.

And then Moonboy had put them all back—only he
hadn't just put them back, he'd put *everything* back.

"What just happened?" she said in a shaky voice as they
reached the steps of the Administration Office.

"I don't know," Moonboy said, and, from the sound of
his voice he sounded just as scared and frustrated as she felt.
"I don't know who that was—one of the Land Powers, I
fear, and now I have offended it, and there will be war—"

"War?" Janice was startled. She shook her head. "I don't
think so. Maybe where you come from, but not here."

"Where I come from, there is always war," Moonboy
said glumly. "Over an insult, over cattle . . . they last for
centuries, and we sing of them." He sounded bitter.

"Freaky," Janice said. It was on the tip of her tongue to
ask where he was from—it didn't sound exactly like any
place she'd ever heard of, even Bosnia—but this didn't
seem to be quite the right time. She shrugged. They were
probably both going to get kicked out over this anyway.
"C'mon."

They went inside. There were a lot of people here for—
she checked her watch, and was mildly boggled to see that
it was running backward, and fast—well, for late on a Fri-

day, anyway. Professor Reynard's receptionist was even here; Mrs. McGonnagal told them both to take a seat on the long oak bench outside the office, where they both sat until 11:15 (the wall clock was working just fine) in glum silence, while several teachers went in and out, and they could hear the muted sound of Professor Reynard on the telephone.

Three guesses what all this is about, and the first two don't count, Janice thought. She only hoped he wasn't calling her parents, even if it was only a little after seven back East, and probably neither of the 'rents would be home yet.

"Redding? Moonboy? You can go in now," Mrs. McGonnagal said at last.

Janice had been in Professor Reynard's office before, and though she liked him, she'd really hoped she wouldn't be seeing it again so soon. He was sitting behind his desk. He regarded them both in silence for a long minute before he spoke.

"I had really hoped we could get through the first month of term without something like this happening," he said at last. "Perhaps you would both care to give me your version of this evening's events. Lord Underhill, you may begin."

Moonboy winced, and Janice's eyes widened. A lord? Well, that explained a lot. Or maybe it didn't.

"Weej had brought the bespelled mouse to the Freshman Mixer," he began hesitantly, looking to Janice for confirmation. She stared at him blankly. A mouse?

"Yes, yes; the Theriomorphic Transmogrification spell is a fairly simple one for some of the students, especially lycanthropes, and naturally the wards would not affect magic that was done elsewhere and then brought into a warded building. I see I shall have to arrange for Mr. Huygens to receive additional tutoring in Magical Ethics. Go on."

"Then the Land Power entered the building," Moonboy said. "I did not know what it intended, save that it was powerful, and old. It saw Janice and me, and then it saw Weej."

"And seeing as Mr. Huygens had already played a trick on all of you, Coyote decided that it was all right for him to play one as well." Professor Reynard looked angry.

"I know I promised I would not use the Seleighe magic here," Moonboy burst out, "but I did not know what else to do!"

Professor Reynard regarded him in grim silence for a long moment before turning to Janice.

"And what do you have to say for yourself, young lady?" he said.

"That you should buy that thing a flea collar," she snapped without thinking. She gasped, horrified, but Professor Reynard actually smiled. "Yeah. What he said," she added, when it became clear that Professor Reynaz'd was waiting for her to continue. "Except I didn't see any mouse—just a blonde girl nobody knew. And a scary guy with red eyes. He looked right at me. And he kind of . . . slunk right in."

"Unfortunately, this land was Coyote's before it was ours," Professor Reynard said. "I suggest you read up on him in your Comparative Theogony text—he's discussed in Chapter Nineteen. Coyote is a trickster, with a strong sense of fairness. If Mr. Huygens hadn't been meddling with spells far beyond his appropriate curriculum, in all probability Coyote would simply have taken a look around and left. But Mr. Huygens gave him an opening, and so Coyote took it, and so I suggest that you also read Chapters Five through Eight in *Theory of Magical Defenses* and prepare a five-thousand-word essay, due on my desk one week from today, on why it is a bad idea to conduct yourself in such a fashion that the Greater Powers take notice.

"By the way, I wouldn't bother to mention any of this to your friends. Having been twice-bespelled, none of them remembers anything about the way the evening ended but the two of you. And Lord Underhill? Do try to be more careful in the future?"

"Yes. Yes, my l—Yes."

Moonboy was already on his feet, and it looked like the interview was over and they were both still enrolled. The two of them wasted no time in getting out of there.

"I don't know which was worse," Janice said, when they were safely outside the building again. "Coyote—or him."

"I do not think you need to ask," Moonboy said. Side by side, the two of them walked back toward the freshman dorms. The cafeteria was lit up again and still full of students—was it really true that nobody else would remember anything? Janice wondered what kind of explanation Kaylin would come up with for the sudden reversion of the cafeteria to its original format, and what kind of wild rumors would be flying by breakfast time tomorrow. Nothing as good as the truth, that was for sure.

"Five-thousand-word essay. In a week," she groaned, suddenly remembering that part of their interview. It wasn't like the course load was a walk in the park to begin with, either. Another thought struck her, and she stopped suddenly. "He called you *Lord* Underhill?"

"Don't tell anyone," Moonboy begged her. "My father . . ." He took a deep breath, as if preparing to tell her something horrible. "My father is King Under the Hill."

It took Janice a moment to figure it out, together with the hints and half-explanations he'd let slip all evening.

"You're from Elfland?" she blurted.

He winced. "We call it Under the Hill, and yes. He married a woman from here, and here I am. Only the sun is so *very* bright here, and the food is so strange . . . Professor Reynard says I will adjust, with time."

"Well, hey, cafeteria food," Janice said. "Nobody gets used to that. Look, I won't tell anybody, okay? We'll just stick with the story about you being a vampire. Every high school needs a vampire; it's like a requirement. Now c'mon, we better get back to the dorm if we don't want to run into anybody."

"Very well," Moonboy agreed. "But first, what is a 'vampire'?"

Janice giggled, relieved that they'd gotten off so lightly; all things considered. "Boy, have you got a lot of catching up to do! Got a DVD player? I'll see if I can borrow Kaylin's *Buffys*. . . ."

*   *   *

She was still the first one back to her dorm room, and decided that cowardice was the better part of valor. If she could at least pretend to be asleep when the rest of them got back, maybe she wouldn't have to answer too many awkward questions about the end of the dance.

She quickly washed and undressed and got into bed, and as she pulled up the covers, one last thought occurred to her.

I can't believe Weej brought a mouse as his date to the Freshman Mixer!

And unfortunately, she was never going to be able to tell anyone.

HARD KNOCKS

by John Helfers

John Helfers is a writer and editor currently living in Green Bay, Wisconsin. A graduate of the University of Wisconsin-Green Bay, his fiction appears in more than twenty-five anthologies and magazines. His first anthology, *Black Cats and Broken Mirrors*, was published by DAW Books in 1998 and has been followed by several more, including *Alien Abductions*, *Star Colonies*, *Warrior Fantastic*, *Knight Fantastic*, *The Mutant Files* and *Villains Victorious*. His most recent nonfiction project was coediting *The Valdemar Companion*, a guide to the fantasy world of Mercedes Lackey. Future projects include editing even more anthologies as well as a novel in progress.

ALEXANDR Ivanovich Dragunov stood on the edge of the rock butte, his breath a white plume in the chill morning air. The sun was just beginning to rise over the vast Arizona desert far beneath him. The sparse landscape was deserted, an occasional clump of yucca and flat-leafed cactus the only visible signs of life. There wasn't even a road here, six miles northwest of Sedona, Arizona, and four miles from the unusual school Alexei attended. *Peace and quiet*, he thought. *The perfect place to concentrate.*

"You know, people come to the desert expecting that 'dry heat' you always hear about," a clipped male voice said. "*This* is not what I had in mind."

Well, almost. Smiling, Alexei turned to the three people behind him. Two of them, a boy and girl, were huddled together, bundled up in parkas with heavy hoods. The third person, a dark-haired girl in a cropped T-shirt and jean shorts, was wearing even less than Alexei, who had on a long-sleeved black shirt and jeans. The girl in the shorts stood on the butte's edge, enjoying the view, apparently unaffected by the cold.

The first girl, who was a striking blonde, though nobody could tell it today, buried as she was beneath her layers of clothing, said, "Why don't you just write up a subroutine to keep us warm, Mr. Whiz-kid?"

"Like I told you about a thousand times before, virtual arcana is still in its theoretical stage," the tall boy said, trying to contain his shivering. "We haven't been able to create anything stable on a reality platform for more than 3.8 seconds. Look, you're the elementalist, why don't you whip up a fire or something?"

"Duh, take a look around. If you can find a fire elemental out here, I'd be happy to," the slim girl next to him said. "We're in the middle of the desert, doofus. You want twenty buttes like this one, no problem. Trying to alter the heat index is another story. And don't forget about that *efreet* that got both of us up here on that air carpet. I think I've done enough today."

Shaking his head, Alexei turned back to the desert vista. The three teens behind him were the first friends he had made here at "Sorcerer U," as the students called the Academy of Advanced Study. After six weeks of settling in at the school and being swamped by the introductory magic classes that were a part of every freshman's curriculum, he'd felt a strong urge to take a look around this new country he had arrived in. The local desert on this brisk Saturday morning in October had seemed a great place to begin.

I've come a long way from Novgorod for this, he thought,

inhaling the crisp dry air. *I like it. It is so unlike Russia and yet . . . it has a beauty all its own.*

Alexei could trace his heritage back through more than 1400 years of European history to the sixth century, when his distant ancestors, known as the Sclavini, had settled in the region that was now modern-day Poland, near the Dniester River. Once in every generation, a child was born with the powers of the *oboroten*, or sorcerer. Now it was Alexei's turn to master the magical gift that was his family's birthright. To this end, his family had sent him from Russia to the Academy for Advanced Study in Arizona. In other words, he'd come to attend a school for sorcerers, along with his three friends and many other similarly gifted children from around the world.

Ryan Running Fox's ancestry was no less noble than Alexei's. Hailing from the Tsimshian tribe, located on the Pacific Coast of Canada, his family had not been medicine men, but hunters and fur trappers. His ancestors had survived the Native American persecutions to become the primary spokespeople for their tribe in recent years, as well as working in the forefront of the conservation movement in North America. But Ryan wasn't following in his parents' footsteps. When he was four years old, he had gotten his hands on an old TRS-80 computer and programmed a picture of his teddy bear (he *had* been only four) that looked real enough to touch. For the next twelve years, he had gone through every hardware and software upgrade he could get his hands on, working in the wondrous world that had been created by computers until his freshman year in high school, when he had opened a portal into what the uninitiated called "cyberspace." It was actually something much more interesting. Thirty-six hours later, the headmaster of the Academy was knocking on his parents' door, offering Ryan a full scholarship to Sorcerer U to research "virtual arcana."

The third girl glanced at the squabbling pair, then walked over to Alexei. "Are you sure you don't want any—"

Alexei held up one finger. "I told you all before—you

could come with me as long as you didn't try to help with this."

"Yes, but . . ." the girl peeked over the edge of the butte again, "Getting up here was one thing. How you're going to get down is something else. You're planning to cover that four hundred feet in a little under five seconds, and that's too fast for anybody." She grinned. "Even me."

"Well, I've got a few tricks up my sleeve, too. By the way, just how did you beat me up here?" Alexei asked. "I've never seen anyone climb like that before."

The girl flashed a dazzling smile. "Trade secret."

Alexei frowned at her comment, but said nothing. When the four of them had arrived at the base of the butte, Alexei had told the others he would meet them at the top. Myuki Samuelson had smiled, and challenged, "Race you."

And she had, climbing the sheer cliff face with amazing agility and speed. For all intents and purposes, it had looked like she'd run up the side of the cliff. Ryan had nudged Alexei. "Physical Adept, you gotta admire that," he had said, watching Myuki's lithe body flow up the cliff wall as though she were jogging through a park. "You better get going if you're gonna win, sport." Although he had used every trick he knew, Alexei hadn't come close to catching her.

Alexei knew of a field of study at the Academy that covered magic and its effects on the human body. Its practitioners were known as Physical Adepts, fusing mysticism, martial arts, and mental powers into a perfect discipline for the body, mind, and spirit. *Judging by her climb, Myuki must be progressing in her studies quite well,* Alexei thought. *Maybe I'll ask her how that works later.*

"Hey, not to be rude or anything, but would it be possible to get on with this sometime today?" said the fourth member of the group. Samantha Armitage huddled in her Hilfiger jacket and pulled the hood of her FUBU sweatshirt tighter around her head. Although she looked like a Nordic princess with her white-blonde hair, fair skin, aquiline nose, and sky-blue eyes, Alexei knew Sam was a distant relative of his, kin to the Slavic tribes that had lived in Central Europe for two millennia. She was a different kind of *oboroten*, a mage with the power to control the elements. Samantha was already in her own advanced class, where she was learning how to bargain with natural spirits, such as the *efreet* that had brought them all here. Later, she would learn how to control the elements by herself. At the highest level of study, she would be able to transform herself into one of the primary elements. Alexei knew he wouldn't want to be around when she was practicing, having already heard horror stories about students losing control of their elemental forms and causing havoc on the campus. Once she got the hang of it, it would be a different story, of course.

"All right, all right, just a second," Alexei said. The sun was up in full force now, slanting through the canyons, the surrounding mesas, and the dry wash where flash floods roared down from the mountains. *Now.*

"Watch this," he said, stepping to the very edge of the butte. Alexei heard whispering behind him, but focused instead on what he was doing. He sensed the power lying coiled at the base of his skull, waiting for him to shape it to his will. Closing his eyes, Alexei opened his other senses. He felt the cold wind brush across his face, heard the lonely cry of a hunting hawk echo across the desolate land. *Soon enough, my brother,* he thought, concentrating on the form he wanted.

Taking a deep breath, Alexei spread his arms and dove off the cliff.

The wind increased to a roar around him, whistling past his ears and buffeting his face. Alexei didn't even notice, already feeling the magic that was as much a part of him as breathing. He clutched the special amulet his grandfather had given him before he left.

The gentle buzz began in his mind, and he felt himself changing. His clothes disappeared, melding into his body. His legs shrank down to three claw-tipped digits, the skin on them hardening, turning a dull yellow . . . his rib cage and torso condensed even as his bones lightened and shifted within him . . . his arms dwindled down to one-sixth their former size, his fingers fused together as one . . . his neck, shoulders, and back sprouted downy feathers, then a stiffer layer of flight feathers over those . . . continuing down to parts south, where larger tail feathers fanned out . . . his head reduced in size, his eyes shifting, one to either side of his newly streamlined face . . . his nose and mouth elongated into a hooked, pointed beak . . . the feathers solidified into a glossy gray, and the primary flight feathers at the tips of his wings spread out to channel the air currents surrounding him.

Seventy feet from the ground, Alexei caught an updraft and soared into the air, his new body riding the wind. The kestrel hawk form was the second one Alexei had mastered, after a common house cat. Flying had been tricky at first, but after several years of practice, it felt almost as natural as walking to him.

Circling back to the butte, he watched his shadow pass over his three friends, all of them watching him with their mouths open. *This is what it's all about,* Alexei thought. *The wind in my feathers, the open sky all around me . . . hey, was that a gopher down there?* That was the problem with shapeshifting. When an *oboroten* shifted, he felt some measure of what the animal he'd changed into would feel. The longer a sorcerer stayed in animal form, the more pronounced those animal instincts became. Alexei remembered stories of relatives who disappeared forever into the deep forest. They had just gone off into the wild, never to return. His family referred to it as "going feral."

Speaking of feral, I wonder what raw gopher tastes like, Alexei pondered, spying a large coyote far below that appeared to be tracking the rodent. *He can have it, I'm not that hungry,* he thought. *Maybe those instincts are kicking in already . . . hey, what was that?*

Turning on his wing, Alexei wheeled over and dove toward the bright reflection of sunlight on glass. *Huh, I didn't think you could hunt out here. Wait, is that . . . Pyotr? I haven't felt that presence since—*

Without warning, Alexei took a sharp blow on his left wing. It folded like a broken accordion, a puff of feathers spraying into the air. Pain lanced through his body, and he began plummeting to the ground. The booming vibration of a gunshot reverberated around him.

Can't . . . fly, Alexei thought as he fought for his life. Although he beat desperately at the air with his good wing, the wounded one dangled limp and useless. He plunged toward the ground, completely out of control. The last thing Alexei saw was the hard-packed desert rushing up to meet him . . . then darkness.

An odd series of images and sensations accompanied Alexei on his journey back to consciousness. Glowing golden eyes coming out of darkness, staring at him . . . a feeling of floating, marred only by an occasional shock of pain in his arm, or was that his wing? He could feel a piercing gaze on his skin, looking him over, a warm hand pressing against his forehead. Cool whiteness . . . followed by the most intense agony he had ever known, as though he were being broken on a medieval rack, tortured like his ancestors. His limbs felt stretched and pulled past the point of pain, even past the point that should shatter them. They seemed to flap bonelessly at his sides. Alexei's eyes fluttered open. A tall man bent over him, scrutinizing him. Alexei remembered feeling that gaze even while unconscious. The man's suit was so carefully tailored it made London's best look slightly tawdry. The man could have been any age from thirty to fifty. Other than a light dusting of silver at the temples, Alexei had no way to guess how old he was. But he'd seen this man once before, at the welcoming ceremony for the new students.

"Professor Reynard . . . ?" Alexei rasped, his voice as dry as the desert he had crash-landed on earlier. "What are you doing here?"

"When one of my students gets injured, I take a personal interest. Here, drink." Raynard held a straw to his lips, and Alexei sipped. It was the best water he'd ever had, not just because he was thirsty, but because he was still alive. He drained the glass.

"I crashed in the desert," Alexei said. "How . . . how did I get here?"

"Your friends brought you. You were still in your . . . other form. You needed immediate medical attention, and a bit of magical assistance as well." Alexei became more aware of the dull throbbing pain in his left arm. Looking down, he saw it was encased in a cast and sling. "Well, that frags the volleyball tryouts."

"Perhaps not." A smile appeared and vanished on Reynard's face so fast Alexei thought he had imagined it. "You're young. You'll probably be up and around in no time. However, the state of your health is not the only reason I'm here. The circumstances of the accident concern me as well. I want to know what happened out there this morning, and why you were casting on open ground."

Oh. Not good. Well, time to 'fess up . . . Alexei stammered out a fair description of the events at the butte, though he omitted Samantha's bargaining with the *efreet. No sense in getting us all in more trouble*, he thought. He told Reynard everything he remembered, up to and including crashing into the ground passing out.

"Professor Reynard, among the *oboroten* of my people, shapeshifting is as natural as breathing. Once we learn to do it, we must use the power often, or it becomes harder to summon the next time. If we go long enough without shifting, the power may even become dormant. I know I'm not supposed to practice magic except under controlled conditions, but I know my own limitations and needs. I needed to shift, and I chose that spot because I thought no one would be around, and I could practice in peace. The school grounds are really no place for a hawk."

Reynard's face was impassive, but he nodded at Alexei's words. "I'm sure you thought you were taking the appropriate precautions, Alexei, but it was a very foolish thing to do. These rules against unsupervised magic aren't in place just for your own protection. They're for the safety of everyone here. We have enough problems with hostile mages and other . . . creatures trying to find the Academy. Our reputation alone draws them like nectar draws hummingbirds. Not to mention the energies here—all of the magic auras coming together are like a beacon to anything supernatural. We have to stay one step ahead of them at all times. If someone or something gained access to our campus through one of our students, the results could be catastrophic. You can understand that, can't you?"

Alexei nodded.

"So what happened to you could be a random accident, an attack on the school, or something much more personal. I need to know which of these it is before I react to it. My question to you, Alexei, and think about this carefully before you answer, is: do you have any idea why someone would want to harm you?"

Alexei looked the headmaster of Sorcerer U straight in the eyes.

"No," he lied.

Reynard turned his gaze up full blast, but Alexei held his own, not wavering or looking away. After a few seconds, the tall man relaxed. "So far, I'm thinking this might fall into the category of random accident. I've asked the local authorities to look into the matter. It looks to me as if a poacher was hoping to bag himself a raptor, and you got in his sights instead. Does that sound likely to you?"

Alexei kept his voice steady as he replied. "Professor Reynard, that is exactly what it looked like."

Reynard nodded. "Well, until we come up with something else, that's the trail we're pursuing. I'm going to ask that you be more careful where and when you practice your skills. If you require space, I can arrange for an appropriate private area within school grounds."

Alexei hid his grimace, knowing that Reynard meant well. *I'm sure my wolf form would love pacing in a small white room and climbing the walls for exercise.* No, there were some things that were just better done in natural surroundings.

"Give it some thought, all right? That's what we're here for, to help," Reynard said. "I'm sure your friends want to see you now."

He walked to the door, then paused. "I'll be talking with Ms. Armitage and Ms. Samuelson later about your little 'field trip.' You know, I don't recall you mentioning how all of you traversed that cliff wall so easily. Perhaps one of them will be able to enlighten me."

Alexei shook his head. *That guy doesn't miss a thing.* "Yes, sir."

"Good night, Alexei." Reynard said as he left. The door didn't even have time to close behind him before his three friends trooped in, all trying to talk at the same time.

"I can't believe the head man was in here. Tell me we're not in trouble—"

"Are you all right, Alex? When we saw you go down—"

"Dude, look at that busted wing—arm, I mean. Uh, no offense, man—"

Alexei raised his voice to be heard over the din. "Please, please, one at a time. Yes, that was Headmaster Reynard I was speaking with, and we're not in trouble, at least not yet. I'm all right, except for the 'busted wing,' as you put it, Ryan," Alexei said. "Maybe one of you can fill me in about everything . . . well, after I hit the ground."

The three teenagers exchanged glances, then Myuki nodded. "When we saw you go down, I leaped off the butte to get to you as soon as possible—"

"Luckily, the *efreet* I had asked for a ride was still hanging around, so Ryan and I hopped on the air carpet and took off after her," Samantha interrupted.

"Yeah, and when we got there, we saw this huge coyote, I mean, almost wolf-size," Ryan began. "We were afraid it was going to eat you."

"Wait a minute. You said a coyote?" Alexei asked.

"Yeah, big, like Ryan said, with those creepy golden eyes. Anyway, it didn't seem to be hungry. In fact, it didn't act like a normal animal at all. It looked more like it was—

well—guarding you would be the best way to put it," Samantha continued.

"I reached you first, and it growled at me," Myuki said. "Whatever it was, it wasn't a natural animal, that's for sure."

"When we got to the scene, it backed off, but hung around, watching us, like it wanted to make sure of our intentions," Ryan said. "I wrapped you in my jacket, and we took off for Sedona—"

"Landing a bit outside of town, so we could hoof it back in. What a great idea that was," Samantha said.

"Hey, it was better than soaring over to the local hospital—or veterinarian. We almost got into an argument over that, too. Myuki finally said we should just take you back to the Academy, and we thought that sounded like the right thing to do, and so here we all are," Ryan said.

"When they brought you into this room, I thought I was going to throw up," Samantha said. "You changed back, like, right in front of us, and that arm . . . or wing . . . or whatever it was did not look pretty."

"Reynard told us that this room is warded against magic, so any active magical effects are dispelled upon entering," Myuki said. "It was funny seeing your clothes appear out of nowhere."

"Speaking of the big man, what'd he want?" Ryan asked.

"He wanted to make sure I was all right, and to reinforce the rules about keeping magic under wraps when outside the Academy," Alexei said.

"Out there? The only things watching us were the other birds. I could have sworn we were the only ones in the area," Samantha said. "Well, except for Creepy Coyote."

"There was somebody out there. I have conclusive proof we weren't alone." Alexei pointed to his wounded shoulder. "Reynard thinks I took a stray shot from a poacher. At least, that's what he's telling the local authorities."

"Do you agree?" Myuki asked.

"Sure, what else could it have been?" Alexei asked, hating to lie to his friends too, but knowing he had no other choice. "No one knew we were going out there, and there hasn't been any other unusual magic activity in the area for the past few months, or it would have been off limits."

"I guess it's possible. I mean, we were all warned about the Others trying to capture or kidnap us, not shoot us. Taking a potshot at one of us just doesn't seem to be their style," Ryan said.

"Yeah, it was probably some hunting wacko out for blood, and the Birdman here just got in his sights," Samantha said.

"A mistake I do not intend to repeat," Alexei said.

The foursome were interrupted by a nurse entering the room, who informed them that visiting hours were over.

"Hey, Sam, Myuki, before you go," Alexei said as the nurse hustled the other three toward the door. "Expect a visit from Reynard. He's curious about how we got way out there and up the cliff face."

"Great," Samantha muttered. "I knew this was a bad idea. But no, I had to listen to you three—"

The door to the room closed, cutting off the blonde girl's complaints in mid-sentence. The nurse checked Alexei's chart, and asked if he needed anything. Finally, she departed, leaving Alexei alone with his thoughts.

He's found me. Nine thousand miles away, and, I thought, completely hidden, and Pyotr's found me here. Alexei couldn't believe it. *I should have known he was in the desert this morning. That shot was just a warning, a challenge, so to speak. And now that's he's announced his presence, he'll want to face me. I don't know what I'm supposed to do. But I know I have to fight him, eventually.*

Lying so that his broken arm wasn't causing him too much pain, Alexei stared at the rising moon. He had to make a plan, prepare for what was to come. But the stress and shock of the day caused his mind to wander, and soon he was fast asleep.

"Buenas noches, amigo."

The rasping voice in a corner of Alexei's room snapped his eyes open. He stared at the ceiling for a moment, trying to figure out whether the words had come from his dreams, or if—

"*Dios mio!* You look worse than I did after I decided death should be forever for everyone. Seemed like the whole world had a bone to pick with me about that, and they made sure I knew it."

Alexei pushed himself back against the wall, staring hard at the dark corner where he'd heard the voice come from. The rest of the room was bathed in moonlight, but that particular area was wreathed in an unnatural darkness, an obsidian lack of light at odds with the space around it.

"Who's there?" Alexei asked, grabbing the nurse's call button and wondering if he could press it before whatever was over there got to him. *It isn't Pyotr. That much I know.*

"Relax, *niño*. I'm not here to give you a hard time," the smiling voice said. A pair of golden eyes appeared in the middle of that cloud of darkness, seeming to float in midair. "In fact, I'm gonna give you a hand."

That's definitely not Pyotr, Alexei thought. "Who are you?"

The eyes retreated back into the darkness, then Alexei heard a strange *whoosh* of air. A black shadow hurtled toward him. Before he could even twitch, it landed on the far end of his bed without a sound.

The man in front of him crouched at the end of the hospital bed like a large dog, legs cocked underneath his body, ready to leap at a moment's notice, his arms straight, his hands curled into fists pressed into the mattress. He was dressed in worn blue jeans that looked as if they might have been made by Levi himself, a matching dusty, beat-up denim jacket, and battered cowboy boots. Windblown brown hair curled down to his shoulders, but Alexei couldn't make out the rest of his face. All he could focus on were those gleaming golden eyes. He sensed that this guy could tear his throat out in a heartbeat and not blink twice, if he chose to.

"What you staring at, *amigo*? Oh, I see." The man

blinked, and when his eyelids lifted, the eyes behind them were a normal hazel. "Better?"

"Maybe." Alexei watched the man with a mix of fascination and dread. "I thought—I thought magic couldn't happen in here."

The man grinned, reminding Alexei of how his family's dogs looked after they'd killed a stag back home. "First lesson, Alexei—there is magic and there is *magic*. I happen to fall into the latter category."

"So you were the—one out in the desert yesterday morning?"

"Well, that depends on which one you mean. Are you referring to the guy doing the shooting or the guy hanging around your unconscious carcass until your friends showed up?"

"Uh, the second one," Alexei said. "The coyote, right?"

"Hmm, all that talent and brains, too. Dang, I sure picked me a winner," the man said. "Now, come on. This whole, 'roof and four walls' thing is starting to chap my ass, know what I'm saying?"

"Come on? What do you mean? I'm not going anywhere," Alexei replied. "I'm hurt. I'm supposed to stay here until tomorrow morning, so the doctor can check my arm."

The man was at the window by the time Alexei had finished speaking. He lifted the latch and swung the double panes open. "Now that's more like it," he said, breathing in the autumn wind.

He turned back toward Alexei. "Don't get me wrong, I like Reynard. His heart's in the right place. This crib is a little too structured for me, you know, but I do admire what he's doing here. However, there are times when he can be a bit too narrow-minded."

"What are you talking about?" Alexei asked, more intrigued by his guest than fearful now. *I can't describe it, but I feel as if I . . . know him from somewhere, although I'm sure we've never met.*

"That's because we haven't, but you still know who and what I am," the man said, although Alexei hadn't said a word. "A bit of my essence flows through your veins, as it does through every shapeshifter on this planet."

"But that would mean you're a coy—the Coyote, or Changer, or Trickster, the First One among us all," Alexei said.

The man sketched a mocking bow. "Guilty as charged. Well, perhaps that was an unfortunate choice of words, given everything I've been accused of causing in this world. Now, come on, we've got a lot to do, and only a few days to do it."

"I still don't understand," Alexei said. "What do you want with me? Why are you doing this?"

Coyote regarded him for a second. "I know what happened out there in the desert this morning. I practically invented the concept. Let's just say I know what it's like to be in your shoes. As for why I'm here, I just want to show you a few fine points of shifting, that's all," Coyote said, that bright, dangerous grin reappearing on his face. "Look, all of this hoopla and rigamarole and 'cast here but not here,' and 'no spells between the hours of eight and five' may be fine for the rest of these focus-clinging, crystal-polishing, book-learning feebs, but for people like us, who have the magic *inside*, it's a whole different story. *Hay de qué,* you don't need to wait for some doctor to set your arm, you can do it yourself."

"I can?" Alexei asked. "How?"

"The same way you shift. Look, think of it this way. Everything in your body, bones, veins, muscles, skin, all of it has a counterpart in animal form. Well, almost everything. Anyway, you got a broken arm, right? What's the first form you mastered?"

"House cat," Alexei said.

"Okay, good, nothing too complex. So, imagine your broken arm as an uninjured forepaw of a cat. Then make the change. After all, it's not like you don't know how."

Alex flexed his broken arm, feeling pain shoot up into his shoulder. He looked at Coyote, who nodded. Taking a deep breath, he visualized the change, one he had been able to do

since he was eight years old. Alexei's vision blurred, then
sharpened. Coyote's features became more distinct as his eyes
gathered all of the weak light available. Alexei's hands and
fingers shortened into blunt stubby paws, the nails sharpening
and retracting into the spaces between his toes . . . soft gray
fur sprouted all over his body. His arms re-formed into agile
feline legs.

In a few seconds, Alexei was a gray tabby cat, licking his
left paw, which felt as though he'd never broken it. *This is
amazing,* he thought. *Jeez, this means that, as long as I can
still change into my animal form, I can't be hurt.*

"Not exactly. There are certain limitations, which can be
overcome in time," Coyote said, then cocked his head.
"Wait a minute. No one's taught you partial transformation
yet?"

Alexei looked at him with a puzzled expression, then
shook his head back and forth.

"Well, that is something we'll have to remedy," Coyote
said. "How's that foreleg?"

"Meow," Alexei replied. Tensing, he sprang from where
he was sitting to the end of the bed, then to the chair in the
corner of the room and back, all without a hint of a limp.

"Since that form seems to be one you're most comfortable in, let's see how well you use it," Coyote said. In a
twinkling, a large coyote was sitting in his place. *"Follow
me, amigo, and try to keep up."*

With one bound Coyote leaped out of the second-story
window to land silently on the grass below.

Alexei jumped to the windowsill, looked back one more
time. *Nothing ventured, nothing gained,* he thought, then
gathered his legs under him and sailed out into the night, his
eyes fixed on the coyote shape flitting away from the Academy into the dark desert beyond.

"Mr. Dragunov!"

Alexei jerked awake and looked around, blinking in confusion. He rubbed his face, aware of how haggard he must
have looked. It had been several days since his first noctur-

nal meeting with Coyote, and since then he had entered a state where time didn't hold much meaning for him. Day and night blended together in an exhausting blur of learning and practice. He was paying the price for his adventures with Coyote here in his classes.

He heard snickers of derision around him. The tall Asian woman dressed in a traditional Eastern silk sheath dress embroidered with a cheerful cherry blossom pattern was staring at him. Professor Susan Nagata's expression was anything but cheerful.

"Unless you're getting a head start on meditation practice, Alexei, I would advise you to attend class with your eyes open. Now, give me the three basic forms of power available to a mage in today's society."

"Um . . . power intrinsic to the mage himself . . . power derived from natural sources, such as crystals or ley lines . . . and . . ."

"Who can help Mr. Dragunov out?" Susan Nagata said, her laser-sharp gaze sweeping the room. Several students raised their hands. "Yes, Ms. Armitage."

"Power granted by or bargained for from otherworldly spirits," Samantha said without a trace of her usual superior smile. In fact, she shot a concerned look at Alexei as she answered.

"Correct." The elegant Asian woman leaned closer to Alexei as she strolled by. "Two out of three isn't bad, but that isn't going to cut it in the real world."

Alexei nodded and managed an embarrassed smile. *If it's Friday, this must be Beginning Comparative Magic Theory. The one thing you don't want is to get Professor "Dragon Lady" Nagata on your case, and I've managed it without even trying. Great. With Coyote running me ragged every night, and classes every day, I'm amazed I could even come up with two examples.*

For the rest of the class he sat up straight, doing his best to fight off the bone-deep weariness in every inch of his body. When the bell rang, he struggled to gather his books and trudge toward the door.

"Hey, Alexei, wait up," he heard Sam call from behind him. Alexei slowed down even further, which wasn't hard, since he was barely moving to begin with.

"Dude, you look terrible!" Sam said. "Aren't you supposed to still be in the infirmary? And what happened to your sling?"

"Uh, we shifters heal fast. I've just been burning the midnight oil keeping up with my classes," he said.

"Well, I think your flame is close to sputtering out. I hate to ask this, seeing how you look and everything, but remember that assignment I told you about for my Fundamental Laws of Magic class, about observing a magical effect on someone or something without my involvement?"

"Uhh . . . no."

"Shoot, I could have sworn I told you about it," Sam said. "Anyway, I need to do the observation like before tomorrow, so I can record my findings, and I was wondering if you'd mind—if I could observe you transform?"

"Why didn't you watch more closely at the butte last weekend?" Alexei asked. "I would have been happy to show you in more detail then."

"Yeah, well, I was going to bring it up there, but you jumped off the cliff and then got shot, so I didn't think that would be the best time," Samantha replied. "It would only take a few minutes, and I'd be eternally grateful. Could we—you know—take care of it now?"

I owe her, Alexei thought. *If I get it over with fast, I can grab some sleep.* "Okay. My next class isn't for a couple of hours, so we'll do it now."

"Great! Let's head over to my dorm room, and I can get set up."

Alexei followed Samantha, clumsy with exhaustion. They soon arrived at one of the Spanish-style dormitories all freshmen were required to live in for their first year at the Academy, to minimize the chances of accidental magical interaction with the locals in Sedona.

Alexei plodded up the steps to Sam's third-floor room. Inside, he collapsed into the chair she pulled out for him.

Sam bounded around the room, checked her answering machine for messages, then got a notepad and pen and sat down cross-legged on the bed.

"Now, what I'd like you to do is just change into something as different from your normal human body type as possible. Please keep it small, given our limited space, and preferably mammalian. No bugs or stuff. Don't let me know what you're doing. I need to record my observations of your transformation as it happens. Whatever form you take, please stay on the chair so I can observe you more easily. When I'm ready, I'll signal you to change back, and ask you a few questions, okay?"

Alexei nodded, just wanting to get this whole thing over with. He closed his eyes and focused his flagging energy on the form he desired.

Coyote has made my transformations happen more smoothly and quickly, that's for sure, he thought. When he opened his eyes a few seconds later, Samantha was looming over him, and the chair was now several dozen times his height. Alexei's arms and legs had become stubby, fur-covered limbs with short claws at the end, his torso was short and round, and the rest of him looked like a common North American mouse.

A shadow fell over him, and he heard Sam say, "Sorry about this, Alex," before something fell over him. The room suddenly distorted around him, the walls and ceiling becoming oddly curved, and Alexei realized that he was surrounded on all sides by glass.

What the— Hey, this isn't funny—he thought before being bowled over as Samantha scraped the jar across the chair seat, knocking Alexei off his feet. In one deft motion, Samantha scooped the jar up and turned it over, sending Alexei skidding to the bottom of the container. He righted himself with angry squeaks, stretching to try to touch the rim of the jar, which was a few inches out of reach.

What does she think she's doing? Dammit, let me out of here! Alexei sat back on his haunches and thought for a moment. *I could try to transform, break my way out of here, but*

I've never done that before, and I don't know if it'd work. I'll wait and find out what she's up to, but if this is a joke, she'll find out we Dragunovs are not people to be crossed.

Sam set the jar on the desk and went to the door. Opening it revealed Ryan and Myuki outside, both with worried looks on their faces. The pair came in and Ryan picked up the jar with Alexei furiously squeaking inside.

"On behalf of all of us, I apologize. You were so busy in the past couple of days that we weren't sure just how to handle this, but finding some way to detain you seemed to be the best way to talk to you," Ryan said.

"Alexei, we're all worried about you," Myuki continued. "You disappear every night, and you come back exhausted in the morning, so tired that you fall asleep in every class we're in together. None of us know what's going on, but whatever's happening, it's wearing you out. We just want to help, that's all, but first you gotta tell us what's going on. I know we haven't known each other for very long, but we are your friends, and if something's going on, we want to know about it."

Alexei had stopped squeaking, and was sitting in the jar with a distinctly human look on his face. As soon as Ryan and Myuki had come in, he had sensed what was going on, and their words had only confirmed his suspicions.

And it's not like I don't want to talk about it, he thought. Lately, what he had been going through was weighing on him like a boulder on his chest. Coyote, while a stern and thorough instructor, was not one given to small talk or any conversation of an emotional nature. Alexei had kept his feelings about what was happening bottled up inside, focusing instead on what he had to do. Now, seeing the lengths his friends had gone to just to try and talk to him, he felt a flush of embarrassment redden his furry cheeks for not trusting them sooner. With a resigned look on his face, or as least as resigned as a mouse can look, he nodded.

Sam tipped the jar over on the bed and took it away. In seconds, Alexei was back to human form.

"That never would have worked if I hadn't been so tired," he said.

Samantha wiped a skeptical lock off her face. "Yeah, sure it wouldn't. Look, we are really sorry, but it did seem like the best way to get you to talk for more than a few seconds."

"All right, all right, you got me," Alexei said. "I can't tell you all of it, but I can let you know some of what's been going on. Have a seat."

When everyone was settled, Ryan next to Sam on the bed and Myuki gliding into a graceful lotus position on the floor, Alexei continued.

"There is a tradition among *oboroten*, disallowed in most modern places now, that a sorcerer may challenge another to a duel, with the prize being the loser's magical ability, which is absorbed by the victor. The guy who shot me in the desert is one of these, an *oboroten* who duels for power. He has come from my homeland to fight me."

"Okay, no problem, we just let Reynard know, and keep an eye out for him. I'm sure the wards around the campus are strong enough to keep him out," Ryan said.

Alexei shock his head. "It is not that easy. In my family, it is a matter of honor. He has challenged me, and I must accept."

"Honor?" Samantha snorted. "Alex, you're in America now. Believe me, honor is a concept that is in relatively short supply around here, despite our fearless headmaster. Your best bet is to avoid this guy, and sooner or later he'll get bored and go find some other target—"

"None of you understand!" Alexei said, rising with such force that he tipped his chair over. "I cannot just run and hide. That is exactly what—" He stopped, breathing hard.

"You know him, don't you?" Myuki said from the floor.

Alexei's shoulders slumped. "Yes, I know him, I've known him all my life. He is my older brother, Pyotr."

There was shocked silence in the room for a few seconds. Alexei was the first to speak. "Once a generation a child is born with my power. But in this case, nature favored my family with two children, an occurrence that only happens once every, oh, thousand years or so.

"Unfortunately, Pyotr saw the magic as a tool to gain power, not as a gift. Once he learned of its potential, his only desire was to gain more. He was banished from our family for practicing the duel, for attacking *oboroten* and stripping them of their powers. I have not seen him for several years, had no idea where he'd gone. But I felt him that day in the desert, as one *oboroten* can sense another.

"Who knows what he has learned since then. But if he is not stopped, then he will not stop with me." Alexei swept the room with his gaze. "If he learns about this place, no one would be safe from him."

Ryan, Samantha, and Myuki exchanged glances, each knowing what the others were thinking, how, although their abilities could be troublesome sometimes, they wouldn't want to give them up—wouldn't want to be just like everyone else—for anything.

"So, he must be stopped," Alexei said. "And I must do it."

"Uh, okay, but how's that going to happen?" Sam asked.

"That I can't tell you, but trust me, where I've been for the past few nights should even up the odds. Let's just say I've been getting a crash course in the art of dueling."

"All right. When is the duel going down?" Ryan asked.

"Tomorrow evening," Alexei said. "In the desert where he first found me."

"That settles it, then. We'll be there, right beside you," Ryan said, locking to Sam and Myuki for agreement.

"What? No, Ryan, Myuki, Sam, I cannot ask you—" Alexei began.

"You don't need to ask, Alexei," Myuki said. "You would do the same for any of us in the same situation, right?"

"Well . . . of course I would . . ." Alexei said. "But it could be dangerous—"

"Hey, danger is our middle names," Ryan said. "Well, Sam's might be Princess, but two out of three ain't bad. Besides, having a Physical Adept and an Elementalist by your side can't be a bad thing, right?"

"Yeah, so the question is, why will you be there, VR freak?" Sam asked.

"Um, moral support?" Ryan said with a grin. "Don't worry, I'll have a few digital tricks up my sleeve, just in case."

"Thank you, my friends," Alexei said. *I just hope I know what we're all getting ourselves into*, he thought.

Saturday passed with agonizing slowness, the sun creeping inch by painful inch toward the horizon. Night fell at last, and the four teenagers met outside the main gate of the Academy. They walked a few blocks away from the school, where Samantha summoned her *efreet* again, and the four of them took off.

As fast as they were going, the trip took only a few minutes, even though no one felt anything more than a slight breeze on their faces. Alexei tapped Sam's shoulder and pointed towards a cluster of flickering dots on the desert floor.

"Head down toward the lights," he said. Sam nodded and concentrated. A few seconds later, they began to descend.

As they approached, the lights resolved into lit torches, their flames snapping in the light breeze, set atop poles thrust into the ground, marking a square about ten meters long and wide. In the center was a man sitting cross-legged, his eyes closed.

The *effreet* deposited the four teens on the ground, and Alexei got up and approached the square.

"Um, Coyote?" Alexei said.

"I hear and smell more than one here. You've brought friends?" the man asked without opening his eyes.

"Uh, they kind of insisted," Alexei replied.

Coyote opened his eyes, then rocked back and rose to his feet in one fluid movement. "No skin off my nose, kid. Besides," he said, looking the other three over, all of whom were trying to mask their amazement, "good friends are hard to find. Speaking of friends, I've asked an impartial observer to attend this little tete-a-tete."

"Oh?" Alexei asked.

"Well, you all know him," Coyote answered with his trademark grin, gesturing with a nod behind them.

"I can't say that I condone this kind of activity," said a familiar voice. "But Coyote has convinced me that this is the best way to handle the situation."

The four whirled around to see David Reynard walk into the firelight, his suit freshly pressed and razor-sharp, not a hair out of place. He looked as if he had just stepped out of his office into the Arizona desert.

"However, one thing I did not expect is to see you three here," he said, indicating Ryan, Sam, and Myuki. "I'd think it would be best if you headed—"

"Aw, come on, Dave, let 'em stay," Coyote said, the hint of a real smile crooking the corner of his mouth. "Call it a field trip, let 'em see how things are done—what's the phrase nowadays?—old school."

Reynard sighed. "Only because you and I are here will I permit them to observe." He turned to the three students. "I think you know that anything you see here tonight will *not* be discussed at the Academy, are we clear?"

They all nodded, and Ryan managed a shaky, "As crystal, sir."

Coyote raised his head and looked to the north, sniffing the air. "Company coming."

Everyone looked in that direction just in time to see two forms appear out of the darkness, one tall, one shorter. They stopped just outside the northern boundary line of the torches.

"Pyotr," Alexei breathed.

"Yeah, but who's that with him?" Ryan asked.

"I don't know, but is it just my imagination, or did the temperature around here just drop twenty degrees?" Sam asked, shivering inside her cashmere long coat.

The solid, shorter form was unmistakably male, with eyes only for Alexei. The other figure loomed several inches over the young man, and was wrapped in a long flowing black garment that obscured it from head to ankles. All four youths sensed an almost palpable field of malevolent evil radiating from the shrouded form. The wind, which had died down, now swirled around the area, bringing a new, faint scent of decay and rot with it.

Coyote was the first to break the silence. "Baba Yaga, I didn't think you traveled outside the old country anymore."

The tall figure stepped forward into the firelight, then reached up and unwrapped the long scarf covering its head, revealing a woman unlike any of them had ever seen. Her face was wrinkled iron, with parchmentlike skin clinging to the skull, her ancient visage gnarled and twisted by the centuries. Only her eyes contained any life, resembling icy blue diamonds, hard and cold. Looking at the four children, she licked her withered lips, revealing pointed teeth.

Ryan, Sam, and Myuki huddled closer together, their eyes fixed on the gaunt woman like baby birds hypnotized by a weaving cobra. None of them noticed David Reynard, his eyes gleaming with summoned power, interposing himself between the teens and the square.

"And you, Coyote, the last time we met you were still wearing a breechcloth and squatting on the ground to take a crap," she replied, her voice rasping like a handful of nails dragged over broken glass.

Coyote shrugged. "Well, you know, when in America—"

"Sink to the level of an ignorant savage. Yes, that's something you were always quite good at," she said.

"Is your oven still hot, Old Iron Tooth?" Coyote said, grinning. "Perhaps you should go home and check it again?"

"Pah, enough of your useless prattle," Baba Yaga said. "My protégé has called for a duel. Who will face him?"

Alexei stepped forward. "I will, but before I do, I ask of him one question."

Stepping into the square, Alexei faced his sibling. "Please, Pyotr, I beg you to reconsider. There is no need for this."

Pyotr stepped inside the square as well, stripping off his

heavy jacket and tossing it aside. He was about twenty years old, a taller, stronger version of his younger brother. "You always were weak, Alexei," he said. "You don't deserve the gift our blood has given you."

"I am no more worthy than you, for I am content with what nature has given me, and don't lust after more than my fair share," Alexei said.

"Enough!" Pyotr said. "Already I am sick of this. Name your term as challenged."

"First blood only," Alexei said. "I will not commit fratricide."

Pyotr turned to Baba Yaga. "As I said, he is weak. First blood it is. My term will be to use partial shifting magic, that is, if you even can."

Alexei smiled, even though the fear was visible on his pale features. "Surely you don't feel threatened by me? I agree."

"The area for the duel has been set," Pyotr said. "At least you remembered that much."

"Have a care with your words, cub," Coyote said. "You travel in dangerous company."

"After tonight, I will travel as an equal," Pyotr said. He shrugged his shoulders, and there was a sound like tearing cloth. "Let's go."

Alexei approached his opponent one step at a time, hands at his sides. Pyotr tensed in anticipation, not moving, waiting for the boy to come to him. Alexei came closer, until he was three steps away, then two . . .

Something shiny and dark blurred into sight over Pyotr's shoulder, aiming for Alexei's chest. Alexei crouched and seemed to shrink as he did so, batting the thing aside with a raised arm. He leaped away, covering fifteen feet in a single bound, and landing near one of the torches, bobbing and hopping on his feet, which were now crooked beneath him, like a kangaroo rat's.

"You have been studying the animals of the desert as well," Pyotr said. "I thought it fitting, considering where we are." He relaxed, and a scorpion's tail, complete with stinger, rose into view above his head, the pointed tip stabbing through the air as he approached Alexei.

"Professor Reynard, can't you do something!" Myuki said, grabbing his arm in her excitement. "If that stinger is poisoned, it could kill him."

"There's nothing I can do here, Myuki," Reynard said, his eyes still locked on the circling pair. "I have no power here, neither as a mage or as your headmaster. I just hope Alexei knew what he was doing when he agreed to this. If Coyote has been tutoring him, then most likely he's got a better chance of coming out on top than any of us think."

"You mean you knew?" Sam asked.

"I know everything that goes on with my students," Reynard replied. "Now keep still and watch."

Back in the ring, Alexei launched himself at Pyotr, aiming not for his opponent, but for the lethal scorpion tail. Clearing his brother's head, he grabbed just below the stinger and dragged it to the ground with him, slamming it into the dirt. Pyotr growled in pain and whirled around, his hands raised high, fingers curled so that the first knuckles stuck out.

As soon as Alexei hit the ground, he rolled out of the way, but not fast enough. Pyotr lashed downward, and everyone heard cloth tear again. When Alexei scrambled to his feet, he looked down where his flannel shirt hung off him in several ragged strips. Pyotr raised his arm again, revealing wicked curving claws between his fingers, much like a mountain lion's. Bringing his hand/paw down to his nose, he sniffed it.

"No blood, a mistake that shall not happen again," he snarled, his features becoming more feline as he spoke, the nose ridge growing more prominent, and his eyes turning an eerie golden yellow. Both his hands were transformed now, and there was still the seeking scorpion's tail, making Pyotr look like a creature straight out of a Japanese *anime*.

"Why the hell isn't Alexei transforming or something?" Ryan muttered to Sam and Myuki. "Eventually he's gonna get tagged."

"He must know what he's doing," Myuki said. "Goddess, I hope so."

"I just wish there were some way we could help," Ryan said.

"Professor Reynard said even he can't do anything about this, just watch," Myuki said. "Oh, Alex, look out!"

Pyotr had feinted an attack high with his clawed hands, then whipped his tail around and tried to trip Alexei. The boy had only been partially fooled, however, but he failed to completely avoid the heavy tail, which slammed into his shin, causing him to cry out and stagger away, limping heavily. From the sidelines, Baba Yaga watched every move the combatants made, her eyes flicking from one to the other.

Sensing victory, Pyotr moved in, both hand/paws held high, like a kickboxer, the scorpion tail arched high in between them. Alexei backed away from him, then his injured leg gave out and he fell to the ground. Snarling with pleasure, the elder Dragunov stood over him and lashed out with his tail, aiming straight for his brother's chest.

There was a hollow thud, and Sam looked away, burying her face in Ryan's chest. For a moment, nobody moved. Coyote, Baba Yaga, and Reynard all leaned forward, eyes locked on the two warriors.

A puzzled look crossed Pyotr's face as he stared down at his brother. Alexei reached up with one hand, undoing his shirt buttons and pulling it open to reveal his chest.

Instead of skin, there was a large square of odd, pebbled hide streaked with red and black covering his stomach and rib cage. Pyotr's stinger had struck home, but he had failed to penetrate the tough, leathery hide. His eyes widened in shock, and that's when Alexei brought up his other hand.

Or rather, wing. Scooping up a wingspan of dirt, he flung it in Pyotr's face. At that range, he couldn't miss.

Shrieking in pain and fear, Pyotr staggered backward, pawing at his blinded eyes. Alexei leaped up and ran at Pyotr, moving as if he hadn't been injured at all. Dodging the scorpion tail, which was lashing wildly around the older boy, Alex bided his time, then grabbed the tail again as it whipped by him and raked it across Pyotr's cheek, drawing a bright red line of blood.

"Hold!" both Coyote and Baba Yaga cried out together. Alexei and Pyotr both froze where they were.

"Ah, an oldie but a goodie," Coyote said. "That always was the problem with you Europeans; you're all too damned overconfident."

Her fleshless lips pursed, Baba Yaga drew herself up to her full height. "Alexandr Ivanovich Dragunov, you have won the *oboroten's* duel, and as such, you are accorded the right to name your victory price."

"Uh . . ." Alexei said, releasing his hold on Pyotr's tail and straightening up. "I don't want anything from this, just to be left alone."

Coyote held up his hand. "Perhaps I can help here," he said, entering the square and whispering in the boy's ear. Alexei listened, then winced and nodded.

He turned to face his brother. "Pyotr, I am sorry, but it is obvious you cannot be entrusted with our family's power."

He turned to Baba Yaga. "I want my brother to live, but to have his magic ability stripped from him for the rest of his life."

Baba Yaga smiled, an even more chilling grin than Coyote's. "It shall be done." She advanced on the elder Dragunov, who had gone slack-jawed with terror upon hearing his sentence.

"I tried to warn you, cub," Coyote said. "Some folks aren't as forgiving as I am."

"Come, little one, this won't hurt—much," Baba Yaga reached out with a clawed hand and drew Pyotr to her, enfolding him in the multiple layers of her garment. An agonized cry split the air for a brief moment, then a figure crumpled to the ground, and a tall, gaunt shadow drew away from him, forming a column of coal-black darkness that swirled around like a shadowy dust devil, and dissipated into the night.

Alexei looked around to make sure she was gone, then let his guard down, his shoulders slumping as he sat in the middle of the square. With a whoop of joy, Ryan ran over to him, followed by Myuki and Sam, all of them talking at the same time.

"Wow, I can't believe you pulled that off! What was that stuff, gila monster skin? That was incredib—"

"We just saw *the* Baba Yaga, here in the freakin' desert! I'm not going to sleep for a week—"

"Alex, are you all right? How's your leg? Are you hurt at all?"

Alexei had dusted himself off by now and was helped up by his friends. Behind them all he could see Reynard and Coyote conferring together. "I'm all right, guys. I just feel like I could sleep for a week, that's all."

"I thought Coyote was teaching you shapeshifting, but you hardly did anything during the fight," Ryan said. "What was that about?"

"Coyote was teaching me—teaching me how to fight dirty," Alexei replied. "He said that Pyotr would be expecting me to fight using shifting, so we worked out a strategy that allowed me to surprise him instead."

He tried to look past his friends again, only to see Reynard walking toward them, alone.

"Where'd Coyote go?" Alexei asked the headmaster. "I wanted to thank him for his help."

"Oh, I wouldn't worry about that," Reynard said. "He hinted that he'd be checking up on you from time to time. Something about more night classes, I believe." He looked the boy over from head to toe. "Are you all right?"

"Yes, I think so. "I hope I did the right thing, that's all," Alexei said. "It seemed like the best thing to do at the time."

"Trust me, you did." Reynard leaned over Pyotr's still form. "He's just unconscious, and," his eyes glowed a lambent green for a moment, "there's not a trace of magical power left in him."

Reynard straightened up. "I think the best thing to do would be to modify his memory so that he doesn't even remember being a sorcerer. If you'd like, we can take care of that back at the Academy," he said, hoisting the unconscious man up and slinging him over his shoulder.

"It'd probably be for the best," Alexei said. "I don't know about the rest of you, but I think I've had enough of the desert for a while."

"Hear, hear," Ryan, Sam, and Myuki all chorused.

"Come on, I'll get us all back to the Academy together," Reynard said. "That way, you can all begin your reports on tonight's events."

The four students stared at the headmaster, their mouths hanging open.

"I think—oh, about ten pages should be sufficient, wouldn't you?" he continued. "Approach it any way you'd like, a history of Slavic magic, a mythic biography of Baba Yaga—good luck on that one—or the comparative differences observed between innate abilities and spell-casting, it's up to you. Let's say papers are due two weeks from tonight, okay?" Reynard turned and began walking south, then paused. "Oh, and in case you feel like protesting, remember that your punishment for leaving campus without permission *again*, and unauthorized summoning of an *efreet* could be a lot worse." With that, the tall man continued walking toward the lights of Sedona.

Alexei turned to his three friends, a weak smile on his face. "What are you all looking at me like that for? I *told* you it probably wasn't a good idea to come along."

FAMILIARITY BREEDS CONTEMPT

by Bill McCay

Bill McCay is a seasoned author in multiple genres, with over fifty published books to his credit, including five books carrying on what happened after the movie *Stargate* ended, and three novels written with Marvel Comics' Stan Lee. His *Star Trek* novel *Chains of Command*, written with Eloise Flood, spent several weeks on the *New York Times* Paperback Bestseller list.

Young protagonists have been a specialty for Bill McCay, who has written the adventures of Young Indiana Jones, the teenaged Net Force Explorers, The Three Investigators, and even the Mighty Morphin Power Rangers, to name a few.

In this story, he tackles the notion of the traditional sorcerer's familiar, with a bit of an offbeat twist . . .

*S*TUDENT *Profile Notes:*
Developing this student's Talent has proved more challenging than anticipated, due in part to culture shock. I recommend teaming Ms. Redding with the first articulate familiar who becomes available . . .

* * *

Janice Redding pushed open the Lab building's door, stepping into the brilliant Southwest sunshine—and heat like a breeze off a blast furnace. "Back in New York, they told me the high temperatures out here were okay because it was a dry heat." She glared over at Matt Johnson, her eyes snapping. "They freaking lied."

"You call this hot?" Matt scoffed, brushing away a bead of sweat trickling down the side of his face. "If you want hot, you've got to try August in the Panhandle."

"Right," Janice said with heavy irony. "Because if you want the biggest, the best, the hottest, the most, you've got to go to Texas. Everything but the most humility."

Matt shrugged. "For that, you have to go to the Big Apple. They're big on humble there, I hear—along with big buildings and big mouths."

Janice hissed a single-syllable word of Power, and Matt yelped. "Fire elemental!"

He responded with a Word of his own, giving her a dirty look. "We're not supposed to be fooling with stuff like this outside the lab."

"I don't know why not," Janice said. "A couple of water elementals might cool things off."

"The buildings are air-conditioned," Matt pointed out.

"I'm talking about out here," Janice complained.

"We're not supposed to use the Talent where we can be seen."

She gestured around the deserted quadrangle. "And who's going to see—except for Academy types?"

Matt shrugged. "I dunno—delivery people, maybe?"

Before Janice could come up with a sufficiently scathing retort, she was interrupted by a most unlikely delivery person.

"Ms. Redding."

Those two words were enough to identify Professor D'Estaing, their instructor for Elementary Spellcasting. The professor's voice was as quiet as always—with its usual odd, metallic undertone, as if each word were coming off an anvil instead of his tongue. While the two students stood wilting in the sun, the teacher wore a black suit over a buttoned-up black tunic-neck shirt. His silver hair was brushed back impeccably from a pale, bloodless, strangely youthful face, unlined by age, life . . . or emotion.

"Yes, Professor?" The man's pale, cool visage made Janice all the more aware of the glow of sweat on her dark, sharp-featured face.

"Dean Kerwin asked me to pass this along to you." Professor D'Estaing extended an envelope. "You finished your lab work early."

"Um—yes. Thanks, Professor."

D'Estaing nodded curtly, turning away the moment Jan took the envelope.

She shot a glance at Matt. "The Vampire D'Estaing," she muttered, using a popular student nickname for the professor. "You don't think he's using something to beat this heat?" She held out the envelope, watching the faculty member stride off. "It's still chilly. What's his specialty, anyway? Necromancy?"

Matt looked a little nervous. Sorcerer's Academy wasn't the place to crack wise about the faculty—unless you were comfortable about the possibility of spending the rest of your life as a toad.

"Maybe you shouldn't be so interested in the temperature of that envelope as what's inside."

Jan tore the edge off the envelope and extracted the enclosed note. "It's an appointment to meet the dean in about an hour."

"Oh—uh—"

She cut off Matt's stammering. "You can knock off the 'it's been nice to know you' stuff." Janice gave him a smug smile. "A familiar has become available, and the dean thinks that I'd make a good match."

Doubt struck only when she was actually sitting in the reception area outside the dean's office. She'd tried tapping into the student grapevine but had turned up no news about available familiars. A crash research session in the library had unearthed a lot of hard facts about familiars, their use as a focus of Talent and reservoirs of psychic energy. What Janice wanted, however, was softer info—how did a mage and familiar develop their relationship? How did it feel?

In his *Life of a Thaumaturge*, Finnbar of Tara had some amusing anecdotes about settling in with Graymalkin, the cat who came to share his researches and spells. But the usually voluble Finnbar was silent about how he'd met Graymalkin and how they'd bonded.

Janice knew she had a prickly disposition and didn't make friends easily. She and Matt had ended up hanging around because Matt's personality was pretty well impervious to insults short of an invoked fire elemental. And, growing up in a crowded New York City apartment, Janice had never had a pet. Allowing someone else to share her life was difficult enough. But an animal?

By the time Dean Kerwin came out of the office, Janice was a nervous wreck. She vividly remembered the single previous time she'd been in the room—the "sink or swim" interview each student had with the dean. Unlike other institutions of higher learning, the Academy for Advanced Study was not interested in issuing degrees—"education tickets," as Kerwin had dismissed them.

The job of the Academy was to take a small minority of the population—those with the inborn gift for magic—and to develop that Talent. Such development wasn't achieved merely through lectures, tests, and the occasional term paper. Students worked in the labs, worked in the world, and, sometimes worked at the very edges of the field of knowledge. Failure to meet unanticipated challenges could have serious consequences on the body, mind . . . and soul. Janice couldn't repress a shiver as she rose from her seat. She hoped this particular meeting would be a bit cheerier.

Dean Kerwin smiled in greeting, calming a bit of her nervousness. "I hope I didn't let you work up a full head of worry."

He waved away Janice's reply before she could even speak. "No doubt, you tried to get in a little reading on the subject of familiars, and found out that there are no records of first meetings." The dean's smile became reminiscent. "That's because the first meeting has a magic all its own."

One hand opened the office door, while the other made a curiously formal gesture. "Your familiar awaits. I'll let you go in and get acquainted, then I'll join you."

Timorously, Janice entered the large, cluttered room, the door swinging closed behind her. She scanned the floor, the desk, the chairs, the books piled on tables . . .

A piercing whistle brought her attention to the top shelf of a bookcase— and something she'd initially dismissed as an ancient, tattered Zuni doll.

It wasn't—it was a parrot.

Beady little eyes regarded her from this perch above Jan's head level. Facts from her recent data search whispered through her brain. Parrots were indeed included among the ranks of familiar creatures, sometimes serving for decades. Parrots could live to age sixty. This particular specimen looked about sixty-seven years old. Its feathers had a peculiarly patchy look—molting? Had the bird been plucked?

Facts cut out, and emotion cut in. The dean—the Academy—was going to team her with a bird?

The parrot suddenly squawked. "Not very impressive."

"That's just what I was thinking," Janice shot back. "Maybe I should have asked the dean before coming in here. But I sort of expected—"

"A cat," the parrot finished for her, its harsh voice dripping with scorn. "All you newbies want a cat. I suppose you think cats are cool."

The bird flapped its wings in annoyance. "Ever seen a cat hack up a hairball? That might change your mind on cool. Myself, I don't like 'em. Never trust anything with retractable claws, that's what I say. Cats have eaten relatives of mine."

Things went downhill from there. As Dean Kerwin reentered, he found Janice swearing at the parrot in Spanish.

"—*su Madre!*" she screamed.

"I've encountered classical Spanish, Castilian, Latin American, and the variety they speak around here," the parrot replied. "But yours has to be the ugliest accent I've ever heard."

Janice subsided, sputtering.

The dean cleared his throat. "So, Janice, I see you and Cosmo have had a chance to get to know one another."

"A real treat, so far," the parrot rasped.

Janice looked from Cosmo to Kerwin. "Dean Kerwin? Could we talk—outside?"

In the reception area, Janice had to ask. "How exactly did Cosmo—er—become available?"

Her suspicion was that the familiar's former partner had simply had enough.

"Cosmogenes, son of Hermia, had worked with Dr. Gattopardo." Dean Kerwin looked a little grim. "Perhaps it was too soon. The memorial service will be on Tuesday."

Janice stared at the dean. Memorial service? "I don't think I've seen Dr. Gattopardo." What she wanted to ask was whether the need for the memorial service was due to a long disease . . . or something else.

"Dr. Gattopardo was on sabbatical," the dean replied.

Since that could mean anything from "a long-needed vacation" to "off fighting unspeakable evil," Janice was still left wondering.

"It's been very difficult for Cosmo," Kerwin said. "He's taken the loss quite hard."

Yeah, he looked pretty broken up. But Jan kept her thoughts to herself. "He seems a little—bald. Is he sick?"

The dean shook his head. "No, that was part of the . . . incident."

Well, there was a partial answer—something Sorcerer's Academy specialized in. Janice also realized that this was about the best she was likely to get.

"I know the atmosphere was pretty—acrimonious—as I came in," Dean Kerwin said. "But I hope that you—both of you—don't rush to a decision."

"Erm—" Janice frowned in the direction of the office door. Somehow, this interview had slipped from her control. She'd actually gotten the Dean out of his own office to discuss the parrot. With an advantage like that, she should have been able to reject Cosmo and make it stick. Instead, the dean had sneakily let her ask questions . . . and calm down. Maybe she should have started this conversation with a resounding "No parrot—no way!"

Looking at Kerwin's bland but determined expression, Janice suspected that wouldn't have flown either. "You mean a trial period?" she said. "How long? A day? Two days?"

"Two weeks, minimum," Kerwin said in reasonable—and implacable—tones.

Janice opened her mouth to protest, then shut it. She wasn't going to like the coming two weeks. But if she stuck it out and then vetoed the parrot, what could the dean say?

With that much time, she should be able to come up with a more politic reason for getting Cosmo out of her life.

Something good. Maybe she could fake an allergy to feathers.

"It's only been three days," Matt Johnson said as he followed Janice through the back streets of Sedona.

"Three very loooooooong days," Janice replied. "It's bad enough the animated dust mop is still dropping feathers everywhere. But he's pushing his beak into everything, and he never gives his tongue a rest."

From the start, Janice knew a birdcage was out of the question. She thought Cosmo would reside on a perch someplace out of the way, maybe a ring dangling from the ceiling like she'd seen in old-time movies. Instead, the parrot had staked a claim on the lowest, most accessible bookshelf overlooking her desk. He'd scattered birdseed around until Janice had moved her computer, fearful he'd clog up its internal workings.

Cosmo's specialty was cracking nuts—loudly—while she was trying to think. When she complained about the litter, he humped his wings in a good impersonation of a shrug. "You're the one with the thumbs. You want to clean, clean."

At least he flew outside when nature called.

After a couple of days, Janice wound up putting newspapers down in his lair. Cosmo immediately demanded each day's special section from the *New York Times* her parents sent her.

"Hey," the bird squawked. "At least it gives me some intelligent company."

That's what was driving her crazy. She could tolerate some extra mess, even the loss of her privacy. But the constant drumbeat of comment and criticism had Janice dreaming of Cosmo, roasted to a golden brown.

She'd even take him without cranberry sauce.

The only time the damned parrot had been quiet was when he was sleeping . . . and during the memorial service for Dr. Gattopardo. At Dean Kerwin's strong "suggestion," Janice had taken Cosmo to the small gathering.

Small—but definitely A-list. The heaviest hitters from the faculty had attended, plus some of the most formidable of the Academy's advanced students. Whatever Dr. Gattopardo had taught, it had apparently been some pretty powerful stuff. Even Janice, who had more self-confidence than some people considered healthy, had felt herself severely outclassed in this company and done her best to keep in the background. Thank heavens Cosmo had not been his usual loudmouthed self.

While no direct mention was made as to the cause of the doctor's demise, Janice quickly gathered that her familiar's former partner had come to a heroic end. Students praised Gattopardo's brilliance, colleagues praised her rigor. And in the end, Cosmo had surprised Janice by flying to the front of the room to say that he'd miss his former partner.

It was the nicest thing Janice had heard come out of his mouth in seventy-two hours.

"Hey, this was your idea, you know," Janice said as she and Matt approached one of the town's main shopping drags. As one of the New Age capitals of the world, Sedona

ran heavily to shops featuring Tarot decks and various crystals . . . and vegetarian restaurants.

What Janice and her friend were searching for was a
block with several joints that featured meat on the menu. Or
rather, their interest was the rear end of such establishments,
where they would find dumpsters—and, hopefully, cats.

"I was kind of joking," Matt mumbled as they turned
onto an alley illuminated mainly by light escaping from half
open kitchen doors.

Delicious smells of roasting meat and baking bread
mixed with the stink of decomposing garbage, making Janice's stomach roil.

She spotted movement at the edge of one pool of light.
"There."

"What?"

"It's either a cat or the Rat King of Sedona," she said im-
patiently.

After three days of listening to Janice's and Cosmo's
bickering—not to mention Janice complaints—Matt had finally made a suggestion. "Maybe you should figure some
way to put the fear of God into that parrot."

"Like what?" Janice demanded.

"Well, he's always going on about cats," Matt began.

Janice shook her head. "I don't think the Dean would
take kindly to having a familiar get eaten."

"Well, you don't want it to get that far," Matt said. "Picture it this way. Cosmo's in your room. A cat gets in. Cosmo
enjoys a nice, brisk chase around the place. Then you come
in and rescue him. He should be able to take the hint."

Janice nodded, liking the idea. "So where do we get a
cat?"

The search for a hungry, untraceable stray had led them
to this dingy locale.

"There he goes." She pointed.

"Where?"

"Just have the bag ready." She held up the piece of paper
with the cantrip written on it. The old grimoire she'd copied
it from in the library had belonged to a hedge-wizard—a

small-time practitioner with small-time spells. This was supposed to make guard animals drowsy for a sort period of time—hopefully, long enough to get an alley cat into a gym bag.

Janice recited the short spell, feeling the now-familiar sensation of power crawling along her skin like a slow-moving static electricity charge.

The prowling shadow slowed and stumbled. Janice dragged Matt and his bag over. The cat was breathing in loud, stertorous rasps as Matt bunged him in.

This got a frown from Janice. The spell was supposed to leave its target dreamy, not fast asleep. Of course, it was meant for true watch-animals, big guys like mastiffs and bears.

Maybe size counted here.

As she and Matt returned to the Academy campus, Janice felt a delayed prickle of unease. Could a spell for making a large beast drowsy kill a much smaller animal? There was so much she had to learn about this magic business!

The cat was beginning to stir, making low, mournful noises, by the time they got to the door of Janice's room. She inserted the key as Matt took hold of the bag's zipper. Both of them shared a brief, lunatic grin.

"Show time!" he whispered.

Janice opened the door. Matt yanked the zipper down and tossed the bag in.

As she pulled the door shut, a quite gratifying uproar broke out inside the room. Squawks, yowls, and the crashes of toppling furniture filtered through the door.

Janice went for the lock. "That should be enough." As the door swung open, she heard Cosmo's voice rasp a familiar syllable. It sounded like the brief Word Janice had learned to summon the small fire elemental.

A second later, a somewhat singed alley cat came barreling out, caterwauling its unhappiness.

"Oh, Matt . . ." Cosmo's raucous voice made a horrible contrast to the honeyed tone he was using. "Would you mind coming in here?"

Matt froze, as if he hoped by absolute stillness to escape detection.

"Come on, kiddo. If you think I can't read someone's aura through a wooden door—" Cosmo paused, then went on. "No, on second thought, don't come in. I can wait to get mine back—and you can wait and worry. Somewhere, sometime, you'll be outside and notice there's a shadow over you—and then the Fecal Bombardiers will strike. It won't just be me—I've got lots of friends, full of poop."

Cosmo's next words seemed to have ice on them. "And tell your friend there with you—she won't have to worry about hearing my voice. Ever again."

The parrot was as good as his word, maintaining a frozen silence in Janice's company. When he flew off on his bathroom breaks, he was gone longer and longer.

That was just fine with Janice. Maybe an eagle might nail Cosmo while he was out on poop patrol.

She scowled. More likely, he'd call down a lightning bolt and fry the eagle. Ten days of the two-week trial period had passed when Professor D'Estaing threw his curveball. The spell-casting class was breaking up, but the professor called Jan to the lecture podium.

"You're absolved from the assignment I gave the others." The professor's perfect features maintained their usual poker-faced expression. Jan wondered what it would take to stir some emotion in those flat gray eyes.

It took her a moment to realize that D'Estaing was holding out a small book. "One must be more observant, Ms. Redding."

Flushing, Jan clumsily took the book. It was bound in some faintly scaly hide, rougher than alligator.

It took a moment for her to realize what it was. Dragonskin. This had to be a particularly valuable grimoire.

"I've marked the spell I selected for your project," D'Estaing went on. It's called 'Invocation for an Unknown Spirit.' You'll find it similar to the procedure we used to contact and bind the small elementals we now call with single-syllable Words. However, you'll be going for a larger, more powerful quarry."

D'Estaing's tone didn't change as he went on. If anything, it became more offhand. "There is, of course, a certain danger in dealing with unknown beings. But it should be negligible, given your training and the presence of a familiar."

The professor's handsome face remained implacably placid, but to Janice it seemed to radiate insufferable superiority. Maybe that was why she couldn't bring herself to open her mouth and tell him that, for all practical purposes, she had no familiar.

Janice took two days to prepare for the spell. There was a long, complicated chant to be assimilated, and she spent considerable time getting the best available materials to assemble her wards.

The night before the making should have been spent in perfect rest, but Janice couldn't sleep. She rose early, set out feed and water for Cosmo, and waited, trying not to show too much tension. Finally, the bird pushed out through the hinged parrot door set in the window, and Janice was alone. Her first move was to bar the entrances to the room. Lately, Cosmo had disappeared for a couple of hours, but Janice wanted to make sure she was undisturbed.

Then she began erecting the first set of wards, surrounding herself and her desk. Simple strips of Velcro stuck to the rug were all that was needed. With a few chants, Janice felt the prickling on her skin that signified power at use. She'd already drawn the curtains before beginning, but now the room seemed to go even more shadowy, sealed off by the arcane barriers she raised.

The low noises of the dormitory also receded to near-silence. An explosion might impinge on Janice's consciousness enough to distract her, but anything less emphatic in the outside world would escape her notice.

Janice cleared her throat. Now came the more exacting job, building the wards that would contain whatever she invoked. Since she had no idea what attributes this creature might have, the defenses couldn't be tailored. She'd have to come up with the best general-purpose wards she could devise.

With string, colored chalks, and candles, she set to work.

By the time Janice finished, a trickle of sweat ran down her back—a shockingly physical sensation after her workings on the nonmaterial planes. She sank back in her desk chair, stretching. The wards were as sturdy as she could make them. Janice's breathing slowed as she monitored herself. The dragonskin book had advised using a familiar's reserves to power the wards. But Janice figured she had more than enough juice to press on.

The thought of juice reminded her of the drink and snacks she had left on one end of the desk. She forced herself to eat and drink a little, in spite of the nervous jumpiness of her stomach. Better a touch of nausea at the beginning of the spell than exhausted resources at the end.

Snack finished, Janice settled herself back in the chair, although she knew from experience, she'd be hunched over the desk before she was through. In the middle of her desk sat a silly-looking plastic troll—a toy she'd dragged around from her days as a little kid. That would be her focus, surrounded by all her elaborate defenses.

Janice picked up the book and turned to the page with the spell. It was, of course, written by hand in a crabbed script. The art of deciphering this sort of thing was one of the odder introductory courses at Sorcerer's Academy.

The tightly packed lines had included English, foreign words, and some syllable collections which seemed to be nonsense-rhymes. Janice had carefully researched them all for correct pronunciations. Now she started the chant. This was not something Janice could simply memorize. Reading the whole spell silently affected part of the working. The book recommended dividing the chant between mage and familiar. She'd had to content herself with mastering the trickiest bits. After all, the whole thing would be in front of her, in off-green ink and yellowish parchment.

Holding the book in both hands, Janice began the chant,

skin prickling with gathering power. The deeper she continued, the stronger the feeling became—more like pins-and-needles than static electricity.

This is one heavy-duty spell, the thought crept across her consciousness, only to be banished. The words must be everything now. They seemed to resist as she tried to enunciate them. Even the English phrases came out like tongue twisters.

More sweat gathered at the back of Janice's neck, on her forehead, as she plowed onward. The sections she'd assimilated went a little more easily. She droned away through one of those bits. Then came another of the less familiar passages.

Janice reached the middle of a seemingly interminable list of unfamiliar names when the bead of sweat reached her eyelashes and fell. For a split second, the greenish letters blurred. Janice's voice stumbled as she blinked and went on. Had she missed a line?

Two? She couldn't be sure. And she couldn't go back to check. Interrupted spells usually had unpleasant consequences for their would-be casters.

Besides, she could feel the spell working. She had a flickering metaphysical image—herself, casting a glowing net through immeasurable deeps, the mesh coming in contact with something, drawing around it . . . Then the contact began to manifest on the physical plane. Although her attention was all on the book in her hands, Janice was peripherally aware of . . . changes.

Her sweaty skin now grew clammy as the air around her became chill.

Guess I don't have a fire elemental by the tail, she thought.

The muscles of her jaw began to hurt from the steady enunciating.

No. She daren't lose her concentration. Not in the middle of the Binding.

Another metaphysical image—net meshes snapping.

Janice desperately chanted on into growing coldness. She

could see her breath. A disgusting coppery taste filled her mouth, and her nose seemed to be running.

She went to turn the page on the book, and her thumb stuck to the page. This wasn't just sweat. What could it be—some trace of glue or gum embedded in the sheet's surface? Janice pulled free to find she'd left a perfectly defined thumbprint on the parchment—in dull red.

Blood red.

Luckily, she was in another memorized section. Janice looked at her hands. Tiny reddish pinpoints gleamed on the skin—blood welling up through her pores. She swallowed hard, recognizing the taste in her mouth. She'd encountered it once before—in a skating accident where she'd lost three baby teeth.

Whatever she'd got hold of apparently liked blood, could call it out of her—and didn't even seem to be inconvenienced by the wards that were supposed to enclose it.

Despairing, Jan fumbled ahead through the pages. The thaumaturge-author had included an emergency Banishment spell. Would it be sufficient to rout the Presence that was now in the room?

More to the point, could Janice cast the spell before whatever It was caused some kind of hemorrhage?

Trying to ignore the coating on her tongue, Janice plunged into the new chant. But faint sounds began to impinge on her consciousness.

Not now, she thought. *Can't be distracted.*

But the intrusions continued, growing louder and louder. Dimly, she heard a raucous voice utter a multisyllabic Word.

Light flooded the room as the window blew in. The crushing pressure on Janice diminished as the alien Presence in the room was distracted in its turn.

Cosmo came flying through the wrecked window, wings flapping as if he were fighting a gale. The parrot's squawking voice was chanting . . . chanting the same Banishment spell Janice was trying to read aloud.

She joined in, and the numbing cold abruptly receded.

The disgusting seepage in her mouth and nose stopped. Janice's voice emerged as a husking rasp.

Yet she and Cosmo seemed to harmonize perfectly.

The Presence briefly surged, trying to reestablish itself. But it recoiled from their combined chant.

Janice realized there were no more words on the page. And the Presence, whatever It had been, was gone.

She stared blearily at Cosmo, who fluttered in the air before her. Apparently, he'd been talking, but she hadn't heard.

"Not about to lose another partner, especially to stupidity," the parrot squawked, coming in for a landing on top of the dragonskin book. "The only thing stupider than tackling that spell alone was assigning it in the first place. The damned thing is wonky."

Jan was wholeheartedly willing to agree, but no words came out. The world began going fuzzily gray around the edges, then the top of the desk was mysteriously coming up at her face.

She heard the beating of wings and one furious squawk as everything went black.

Student Profile Notes:

I am assured Ms. Redding will make a full recovery after this mishap, and may receive a discoverer's credit for the creature she accidentally invoked. Appended is the Lauderdale Grimoire, with bloody thumbprints still marking the crucial passages. Lauderdale's Incantation has long been known to produce erratic, even fatal, results. Ms. Redding's experience with the chant should help pinpoint the source of the danger.

Professor D'Estaing has received a reprimand for presenting a first-year student with so hazardous an assignment. I was not swayed by his argument that "wastage of Talent," as he so colorfully put it, should best occur in training rather than in practice.

A more satisfying outcome of this incident is the establishment of a strong mage-familiar bond between Ms. Redding and Cosmogenes, son of Hermia. While initial relations with parrot familiars can be contentious—

"Like some of the incredibly stupid stunts you pulled in our first year together?" a voice squawked in Dean Kerwin's ear.

He turned from the computer screen to direct a withering glare at Hermia, the red-breasted female parrot perched on his shoulder.

"Stow it, worm-breath," the Dean growled.

SLEEPWORK

Laura Anne Gilman

Ignoring well-meaning advice from her family and friends, Laura Anne Gilman took the plunge and submitted—and sold!—her first short story in 1994. Since then, she has written or co-written four media tie-in novels, while her short fiction has or will soon appear in the magazines *Horror Garage*, *Realms of Fantasy*, *Flesh & Blood* and *Dreams of Decadence*, and the anthologies *Familiars*, *The Night Has Teeth*, and *ReVisions*, among many others. She is also the author of a number of non-fiction books for teenagers, and co-edited the anthologies *Other-Were: Stories of Transformation* and *Treachery & Treason*. She lives in New Jersey with her husband Peter, and cat Pandora. More details can be found at http://www.sff.net/people.lauraanne.gilman

M R. Wentworth was full of it.
Jay shoved his hands into his pockets and stared at the path in front of him. All right, that wasn't quite fair. It was too early in the semester to tell if Wentworth was full of crap. He strongly suspected the teacher was full of crap. Which was a different thing, and a completely valid statement.

For one thing, he had them call him mister, even though

he was a doctor. Well, a psychiatrist, anyway. Jay figured if you were going to go to medical school, and earn all those letters after your name, you should use them, even if you were teaching Dream Div 101 instead of pshrinking wealthy nutcases. Understanding a dream portent could be useful, yeah, but what self-respecting sorcerer wasted all their time poking around in someone's dreams? Especially somewhere like here; Sorcerer U was so well-protected you couldn't even have a bad dream without triggering all sorts of wards, and getting called in for a session with Wentworth or one of his staff anyway.

Still, you had to admire a guy who let you do your homework while you were sleeping. No paperwork, no staying up all night to get everything done, no grading—good deal all around.

Jay took a cautious step onto the pathway, slightly reassured when the gold-flecked stones underfoot crunched solidly. The way they had been shimmering a second before, he hadn't been sure they would support his weight. And since there was nothing around them except some kind of pearly fog . . .

"Follow the path that appears, and find what lurks inside your own dream psyche. Until you do that, you will be unable to aid others with their own."

Jay snorted, striding along the path with casual confidence now. He was totally in sync with his own mind, thanks anyway. Get through this course with a solid B—no need to sweat it for an A—and they'd turn him loose on the real stuff. The training they'd been promising him since he was five, and first levitated his sister Julie out of her crib. The Jormunganders had a history of weirdness: talent popped up every couple of generations, so nobody freaked too much. In fact, his great-something grandmother had been the Queen's Sorcerer back in Norway. But everyone since then had been more focused on being Respectable Citizens. Jay had always known that wasn't for him. He just wished learning to use the magic that was his genetic inheritance wasn't as much—or more—work as regular school.

Suddenly he stopped. The fog was thicker than it had been before.

Something's not right.

He'd learned to trust that voice, the one in the back of his head that went with the goose bumps on his arms, and the hairline trigger of unease in his spine. It had been with him since puberty, and kept him from making some seriously boneheaded moves.

"This is my dream. My mind. I determine what happens here."

The words that looked so silly on the page felt even sillier when he said them, forming the words one syllable at a time, feeling them in his mouth the way they had been taught. But the fog seemed to shimmer and thin a little as the echoes of his voice faded. He nodded once, satisfied, and started on again. All he had to do was walk the path, and it would take him back around, and he'd wake up in his bed in the morning. How Wentworth was going to check on who did their sleepwork or not wasn't his problem. He'd done it, and—

Watch it!

He jerked his upper body out of the way just as a silvery, sharp-edged something whizzed past him at Mach 3.

"What the hell?"

He turned his body, every nerve alert, ready to jump aside again. "Not good, not good . . ." The whole point of the sleepwork exercise was to not get distracted. By anything. The fog swirled, and just inside he could see the swirls and shapes of his own imagination forming and re-forming. Dreams, nightmares, wishes and fears, they were all out there. According to Wentworth, anyway. It was a psychological manifestation of his own psyche, quote endquote. They were supposed to create a path out of their own concentration, the same way you kept from drifting off into daydreams in class. "Assuming you do," Wentworth had said, a wave of nervous giggles sweeping the class. They were supposed to walk across the void without getting sidetracked by anything, good or bad. A visualization of his own control over his mind . . .

Right. Control. Get some control. "This is my dream. I determine what happens here."

The words didn't have the same solid feel in his mouth this time, and he could sense, even as he pronounced them, that it wasn't working. He risked a look backward, trying to gauge the distance back to where he had started, but the fog was curling across the path, obscuring it. He could risk it . . .

If you're a coward . . . are you a coward?

The voice seemed louder in here. Mocking. Jay set his jaw, and walked forward again. Everything that happened here was under his own control. They wouldn't give assignments that were dangerous. Not to freshmen, anyway.

Right?

"Right," he said out loud. "Hey!" he shouted out into the mist, knowing he sounded like the stupidest kind of street tough even as he did it. "Come on, then! I'm ready for you!"

There was a faraway noise, like something crashing, like cellophane ripping. Jay swallowed. Hard. "Um . . ."

Idiot. You just let it in.

As a dark, curling tendril came out of the mist, reaching toward him, Jay couldn't disagree with the voice's assessment of his I.Q. The tendril hesitated, moving slowly, like a fish floating in water, then darted forward out of the mist, grabbing him around the waist and jerking him forward. Jay yelped as he felt his feet lift up off the path, and without thinking about it struck downward with his left hand. The Swiss Army knife that appeared in his fist stabbed blade-first into the tendril, making a pale slice in the—flesh?—that oozed like swamp mud. Jay gagged a little from the smell, but stabbed again, harder this time.

The tendril dropped him, and he landed on his butt on the path, gasping for breath. It withdrew into the mist, obviously injured, and Jay scuttled back until he felt the other edge of the path under his hands. Where was that knife? He reached out for it, and felt it form again under his fingers. Duh. Dream-fight, use dreamed weapons. A sword would be better—

And the blade stretched out, less of a sword than a two-foot-long Swiss Army knife. The only trouble was, no magical sword-wielding instinct kicked in to tell him how to use it.

It's your dream, you tell it what to do. Honestly, sometimes I don't know why I bother . . .

Jay stared at the blade, willing it to shrink down to a more manageable length. It ended up looking like a bread knife. A deadly, wicked-looking bread knife. Shifting to a more comfortable crouch, he waited, his heart still beating frantically in his chest, for the thing to come out at him again. His back felt horribly unprotected, and he imagined a solid stone wall at his back, foot deep and six feet high. Risking a look up, he saw something that almost resembled what he had wanted, covering him, and not much more.

Good enough. It would have to do. He was so going to have a talk with Wentworth, when this was over. Easy assignment, my a—

The fog was split by a face the size of Jay's torso, narrow and yellow-skinned, three black, lidless eyes starting at him with an intelligent malice. He'd seen that look once before, in the eyes of a kid in seventh grade who had wanted Jay's lunch money.

Jay had given it to him, then and every day for the rest of the month, until he had convinced his mom that he really wanted to brown-bag it. It wasn't worth fighting over.

What did this creature want?

Its circular mouth opened, showing three rows of sharp white teeth, like a shark's. *"Give way."* Its voice was serpentine, hissing even without a single ess sound in its words. At the same time, Jay felt it tap-tapping all around him, tendrils searching for a weakness, a crack.

"You're already in my brain," he told it, holding the blade between them as though he knew how to use it. "Give way how?"

"Give way," it repeated, and behind the head a picture formed out of the mist, of a tall gate, and taller walls . . .

The front gate of the Academy.

Jay might have been a slacker, but he wasn't dumb. He had listened to the speeches at Orientation, had read the paperwork they had him sign before he was allowed onto school grounds that first day in September. The first commandment was Thou Shalt Not Let Unauthorized Beings In. And he might not know Professor Reynard's personal guest list, but he was pretty damn sure this thing wasn't on it.

The word took a few minutes to get past his throat, but it finally made it: "No."

The face lunged, and Jay yelped, the blade dipping as he scrambled out of the way. But his fingers tightened on the plastic red handle before it could drop entirely, some instinct bringing his arm up, elbows locked, making a sweeping cut into the space where the creature's chest might have been.

Well done! The voice said, managing to sound surprised and vindicated all at once.

"A little help would be nice," Jay replied, pulling the knife back and going into a crouch again as the creature turned, craning its long, snakelike neck to look for him. Its eyes looked pissed, now.

All you had to do was ask.

Jay swung with the knife again, but the creature's start of surprise wasn't from the metal that missed it by a good foot. Jay scrambled out of the way again, a frantic palm-down gesture with his hand expanding the pathway several feet in either direction, just in case, and saw a large red fox hanging onto the back of the creature's skull by its teeth.

"Gross."

Like you were doing so much better?

"Good point." Jay saw something that wasn't there coming out of the corner of his eye, and ducked and slashed in one impossible move. The tendril recoiled, then slapped him across the head, knocking him down to the path. His vision swam, and a hand raised to the side of his head came away bloodied.

Fight it!

"I'm trying," Jay said in disgust.

Not that way, you moron. I swear, sometimes I want to disown this entire family branch. It's manifesting in your dream. Stop it! Otherwise it'll take over completely, and be

*able to use you to get what it wants. Trust me. And you don't
want it to get what it wants.*

Unbidden, a vision appeared like a wide-screen TV in his
head: the walls of the school buildings cracking open, the
tendrils of this thing oozing through, carrying a wave of
something worse on its back . . . students collapsing, blood
running from their noses, eyes, and ears, teachers trying to
fight back, caught unawares because the threat came not
from outside but from within . . . from within him.

No!

Dropping the knife, Jay pulled in on himself, arms
around his knees, and stared at the beast. The fox was doing
enough damage, pulling bits of yellowing flesh off with its
teeth, that the thing seemed willing to leave Jay alone for the
moment while it dealt with this smaller, more immediately
dangerous foe. The only problem was, Jay didn't have a clue
what he was supposed to do.

All right, think. It's nasty, but dumb. This isn't the master, it's just . . . an advance guard. The master's that blackness stuff, and it's not here yet . . . don't panic. You can still
stop it. Maybe. *Think!* It knocked, you responded, you invited it in. The silvery thing was its doing? Maybe. But that
didn't hurt you—it was dreamstuff. This thing . . . what did
the fox say? That it was manifesting in my dream. It's taking over my brain? It's solid now, getting more real. And
when it's totally real . . .

Don't think about that. Think about getting rid of it. Wash
it out of your brain. That's it!

Closing his eyes and concentrating, trying to ignore the
thing lurking over him, he tried to remember exactly what
was on the page in the textbook he had been reading before
he went to sleep. The incantation that made sure he went
into a REM sleep right away, and the one that set him on the
dream path . . . but what was on the next page? He had
skimmed it, not really paying attention . . . something for
next class, about cleansing a mind of bad dreams . . .

For the first time in his life, Jay wished he'd been born
with overachiever genes. Being a couple of classes ahead in

his reading would really come in handy right now. Come on, Jormungander; *remember* . . .

There was a faint tickle in the back of his head, like something was moving in there, and the words seemed to form of their own volition:

"Dream of water's running deep. Dream of cleansing, safety keep."

It sounded stupid. But the thing you learned, pretty fast, was that almost every spell sounded stupid when you just listened to the words. It was what was underneath that was important. He shaped the words within himself as he spoke them, tasting them in his mouth, feeling their weight deep in his chest. The dream-fox disappeared from his awareness as he focused all his attention on the thing that was even now reaching one disgusting tendril toward him.

"Dream of earth's solid hold. Dream of cleansing, safety told.

Dream of fire's warming heat. Dream of cleansing, safety meet.

Dream of air's moving clean. Dream of cleansing, safety seen . . ."

Every word of the spell built, like pressure in his throat, until it was a solid, almost-sentient thing. Jay had worked spells before—everyone had, even though freshmen weren't supposed to without permission. But those had been cantrips, small things. Charms to distract attention, or make food taste better. This shouldn't have been that much more powerful—but it was. He didn't have time to wonder why; as he spoke the last word, he raised the energy up, hurling it toward the back of the thing which was about to slam the fox's limp body down off the pathway. It hit, expanding with a reassuring silver-blue glow until it encased the creature's head and neck, spreading down to the extended tendril-arms. The fox, dropped, twitched once, and was still.

Please, let this work! I think if I die here I really will die. I don't want to die!

The last thought slipped out, an anguish Jay immediately found humiliating.

"Jormungander?"

Disbelief, followed hotly by concern, an unfamiliar mental touch that quickly transferred into a flow of familiar visuals: graying hair, well-groomed nails, heavy silver watch, soft chuckle, crease of a frown over cool, intelligent eyes.

"Professor Reynard!" He meant to send it the same way the query came, mind-to-mind, but discovered when his voice cracked on the last syllable that he had shouted it out loud. The feeling of contact faded, making him wonder if he had hallucinated the feel of the school's master. No time to freak about it now: the spell had checked the creature, but showed no sign of dispelling it. The thing was too well-entrenched in his dream now. And it was looking at him like he was next on its to-do list.

Pulling himself up, ignoring the creaking in his back and knees that suggested he was going to hurt a lot when—if—he woke up, Jay reached for the abandoned knife. Like something out of a *Star Wars* movie, it flew into his hand, handle-first, he noted with a detached relief. All he needed to make this night complete was to slice open his palm like a bagel-butcher . . .

"Come on, then. Leave the fox alone and come pick on something a little closer to your own size."

The thing hung back, almost like it was sizing him up, and Jay started to get pissed off. He was not supposed to be dealing with this. He was a freshman, for Pete's sake! This was not in the class syllabus, and it sure as hell hadn't been in any of the brochures!

"Come on, you useless piece of mud! You got me, fine, but I'm not going to let you use me to get anyone else. Not if I have to stay in here with you for the rest of my life!"

With a roar that slammed into Jay's head like a sumo wrestler hitting the mat, the thing rushed him. He bent his knees and leaned forward, trying to remember everything he ever picked up about getting hit playing tag football. With any luck, the thing would run right onto the blade and die.

The next thing he knew, he was on his side, and the sharp pain over his lungs was suggesting he'd broken more than one rib. A snarl and a yip sounded nearby, and he managed to look up to see the fox, somehow still alive, scrabbling at the thing's elongated neck.

"I am not getting shown up by a figment of my own imagination," he whispered, the pain too intense to speak louder. Reaching out, he grabbed the blade, then squinted at it and felt stupid. The sword shimmered, then re-formed into a small, deadly looking gun exactly like the ones he had seen on TV. Then he frowned, looking more closely at his creation. He could create what he had seen, apparently, but not what he hadn't. The gun was solid—he had no clue what went on inside. The sword returned, and he lunged.

The yellow flesh, he discovered, tasted like Play-Doh. It had been disgusting when he ate a piece when he was a little kid, and it was even more so now. But biting, at the time, had seemed like a good idea.

Only if you have the teeth for it. The fox rushed again from the other side, red tail straight out behind it. *Go for where the ears would be. I think it's sensitive there.*

Jay swung the blade again, the muscles between his shoulder blades shrieking in agony. It had been an hour, a lifetime, a second since the fight had begun, and he didn't think it would . . . ever . . . end.

Time slowed, the blows rising and falling like moving through a heavy gel, then there was a popping noise, and time sped up again.

But there was another player in the game. Another human, an older man, dressed in slacks and shirtsleeves that somehow glinted like metal . . . like armor.

"Professor Reynard!"

"Behind me, young Jay," the school's master commanded. His sword was a huge thing, double-handled, dark and battered and more than capable of taking on any number of monsters.

Jay grabbed the fox with one gore-streaked hand, and scooted-slid down the path behind the warrior-mage.

To the rest of the world, Professor Reynard was a well-respected academic who had taken on the job of maintaining and running the institution his ancestor had founded, a fundraiser and problem-solver who made his Ivy League equivalents look like pikers. To the student body, he was He Who Must Not Be Backtalked—respected and liked, but never ever underestimated.

To Jay, watching him thwack and slice at the creature, forcing it backward inch by inch until it teetered on the edge of the path, Reynard was something close to a god. The fox stirred at that thought, and Jay stroked the top of its head in absentminded apology, never taking his eyes off the two figures in front of him.

The words were garbled—Jay could almost swear that he understood, but his brain wouldn't wrap around it.

Don't listen. You're not ready for this yet.

Reynard's sword dipped down, and Jay wanted to yell a warning—the thing would attack! But instead the thing dropped its long neck as though in surrender, and shuffled backward another step, falling off the path and disappearing into the dark swirling mists that seemed to draw away from it even as they swallowed it up.

Reynard turned then, the shadow of armor melting away, his sword revealing itself to be nothing more than the glossy black fountain pen no one ever saw him without. He capped it, and replaced it in his shirt pocket. Jay scrambled to his feet, realizing after he had done so that his hands were empty: the fox was gone.

"Sir! I—what *was* that thing? It almost killed me!"

"Yes." Professor Reynard had a look on his face that took Jay a minute to recognize: anger. "Yes, it almost did. With your permission?" Jay nodded, confused, as Reynard's eyes got kind of hazy. Jay could almost *feel* the older man's sharp-honed mind touching his, scanning what had happened, then reaching out through the mists—*well, duh, this is your dream, of course you can feel it*—and the sudden jolt of connection as he reached another person. The sense of connection went away, and Jay stood there, waiting, only occasionally casting nervous glances back into the mists.

Then Professor Reynard was back there with him, eyes clear and alert. "Only you, Jormungander, could so muck up a simple first-semester exercise in control—well, you and Matthew."

Jay grinned. Compared to Matt, he was a pure-driven saint of good behavior.

"I have asked Mr. Wentworth to check on the others in your class . . . even with your ill-advised invitation, nothing should have been able to breach our walls." Reynard looked even more tired than before, the lines in his face sagging, making him look like an oversized basset hound for a split second. "Are you going to be all right?"

"Oh, yeah. Peachy."

Reynard grinned briefly at that, then became serious again. "Go on, then. It should be all right now for you to finish the assignment. It may be a little boring, sidestepping daydreams, but that's a risk you're going to have to take. Just don't invite anyone in this time, okay?"

"Nobody who doesn't already live inside," Jay promised solemnly.

Reynard nodded, then stepped off the path into the mist, and faded.

"Nicely worded," a voice said from behind and off to the right. Jay turned.

"You were the fox."

The redheaded man standing there shrugged. "My physical body's a little . . . tied up right now. So I like to spend a lot of time in dreamspace. You gave me the shape. It's not one I've used before, but I like it."

"You helped me. Why?"

The man showed sharp white teeth in a wicked grin. "Maybe next time I won't," he said. A fox sat where he had stood, winked one small black eye, and trotted off into the mist, in the opposite direction from the one Reynard had taken.

Suddenly, the thought of listening to *that* for the rest of his life was more than a little unnerving. Jay might be slow on the uptake, but he got there eventually. A shapeshifting redheaded entity that could only travel in dreams, and made comments about disowning the entire Jormungander clan?

The implications of having a demigod of dubious morality living in your head, especially when family legend claimed that said demigod was your long-long-long-longer-ago ancestor, was probably covered somewhere in those papers he had signed when he was accepted to the Academy. He was going to have to check when he woke up.

"It's going to be a *long* four years."

Loki's high-pitched fox's yelp laughed back out of the mists in agreement.

LICENSE TO STEAL

by Mel Odom

Mel Odom is an Oklahoma-based author who has written nearly a hundred novels that span the spectrum from science fiction to gaming to young adult to mystery. Among his recent books are the well-reviewed fantasy novel, *The Rover*, several books in the *Buffy the Vampire Slayer* and *Sabrina the Teenage Witch* series, and the novelizations for the films *Vertical Limit*, *Tomb Raider*, and *Blade*.

I was standing on the street by the Inferno, one of the neon-lit nightclubs on the main drag in Tucson, Arizona, when I saw the mark I wanted. Turned out, I should have left him alone. But I tended to obsess about things, and once I got it in my head that I knew what I was doing, I stuck with it. Sometimes that worked in my favor. But not always. It didn't that night.

The night was a bad one, the kind when the wind came straight in off the desert, the kind that was so cold I realized straight away that selling the jacket I'd swiped at the soccer fields last week hadn't been a good idea. But, hey, the day I sold it the temperature was in the seventies and Burger Bob's was having a two-for-one special for lunch and I didn't have to bring a friend. I was also broke because the pickings had been thin, but a quick trip to Harry's Prawn Shop with the coat had put me back in the chips for a couple days.

Harry's is actually a pawnshop, but the guy that made Harry the sign made a mistake. Harry went ahead and took the sign, along with a hefty discount, and now had a shop nobody could forget. After selling the coat to Harry, I'd eaten good, but now I was freezing. My life was pretty much one or the other. Oh, yeah, I got rained on a lot, too. Hardship was nothing new to me, but it was annoying—especially since I knew I was so clever and only needed a decent break every now and again to stay even with the world. I mean, that wasn't so much to ask for.

The guy I wanted parked his dark green Lexus in front of the Inferno and got out with a folded bill ready for the parking valet. The valet reached for the money, but the guy closed his hand over the valet's, leaned in close, and said, "This is my car. I like it a lot. As long as you remember that, we're good. Got it?"

The valet nodded, and I could tell the grip the guy had on his fingers hurt. I mean, really hurt, not the kind of hurt a guy wore when he was shilling change off the straights on the street.

"Yes, sir," the valet said. "Got it."

The guy smiled. "Terrific." He let the valet's hand go and strode toward the club's entrance.

Strode wasn't one of the words I used much. I'd read the term in a couple of books at the library in Albuquerque, New Mexico, when I was stuck there one winter. The tourist trade had drawn me there and an arts festival I'd heard about in the news, figuring where there were tourists there were pockets to pick. I hadn't counted on getting busted by the local police department and getting locked up in juvie. Of course, as soon as night fell, I was out of there and back on the road again. Reading wasn't something I particularly liked to do, but libraries were warm and I could sleep in one part of the day every day while I waited on night to fall. But this guy *strode*.

He was tall and rangy, like a good baseball pitcher, and he had the moves like a guy always looking for the next thing to happen. I knew he'd be hard to catch unawares, and that made him dangerous and a challenge. I liked both, but that wasn't a good thing in the profession I'd chosen.

Or maybe I should say, the profession that had chosen me. I called it a profession, maybe so what I did would sound better to me because I made it a practice never to take something from somebody I felt couldn't afford the loss.

The guy was probably in his late twenties, just this side of being old, a few inches over six feet and slender. His slicked-back black hair fit him like a helmet and he was clean-shaven. He wore wraparound blue mirror sunglasses and an expensive dark suit that was probably Italian.

Tony Tentoes, the kid who trained me, told me Italian suits were the best. I got my training in bus stations in Albuquerque when Tony Tentoes and me were swiping suitcases and pawning suits and whatever else we found inside them.

After I kind of claimed the guy walking into the Inferno that night as my own, I felt better. Standing around hustling chump change outside a place like Inferno wasn't smart. For one, most of the people going into the club carried plastic, not cold hard cash. And for another, the security people posted outside the building aren't exactly chummy with panhandlers buzzing their crowds. And third, the Tucson PD had a bunch of newbies on the night shift who loved rousting street kids.

I had a good feeling about this guy. He had come out with the folding money just fine, and I figured I could boost his wallet and be on my way. If everything worked out, I thought maybe I could even rent a room for the night and sleep in an honest-to-God bed for the first time in a couple of weeks instead of one of the flops that the street kids had set up around the city. That rented bed couldn't be at a Holiday Inn because I was only fourteen and didn't have any real ID—unless they checked my police record, but there were a few places in town that could be had on the cheap for a guy traveling cash and carry.

I snapped the lapels on my shirt collar up and went after the guy. I knew it was going to take more than attitude—and probably more than a bribe—to get me past the entrance. I was fourteen, hardly old enough to be admitted into a place like the Inferno.

But I had something else, something that had drawn me all the way to Sedona a couple of times even though I didn't know what it was then. I had magic. I knew a few people that had magic, and that was one of the reasons I'd gone to Sedona those times. These days, Sedona attracted people with magic, but only those that believed and even most of them on the sly. Even folks not doing anything really wrong have got to feel like they're getting away with something some of the time. And I knew about Sedona. Or, at least I thought I did until that night.

See, while I was busy reading books with characters who strode in them, I was also reading about the Academy of Advanced Study, which is located in Sedona. The instructors who worked at the Academy taught people about magic. From some of the people I'd talked to over the last couple years, I'd also learned that the Academy was called Sorcerer's U.

Knowing what I'd learned on my own—using my natural talents, just as Tony Tentoes had told me—I felt that being taught to do what I did in school would be a waste of time. And instructors had this habit of trying to teach you what you were supposed to do with the things you learned rather than let you do what you wanted to. Rules, rules, and more rules.

You also had to learn a lot of crap I didn't want to know. If I wanted to know something, I read about it in the library or talked to people who knew. If I needed to know about something, it would generally cause a problem in my life. Like when I had to start learning about security systems. Doors and locks couldn't hold me out, but I'd gotten busted a couple times because of motion detectors and pressure sensitive flooring. But overall, I'd had enough of school two years ago when I left home at the age of twelve.

I walked toward the Inferno, but I ducked around the alley at the corner. The alley was long and narrow, sandwiched in between the nightclub and a Mexican restaurant. Thinking about enchiladas and sopapillas made my stomach growl, and I swear the rumbling was loud enough to scare the cats working the dumpsters out back of the club. I figured I could spend part of my ill-gotten gains on a meal at the restaurant that night if I could be in and out of the Inferno before closing time.

Provided the guy I intended to rip off didn't hang around the club looking for me.

At the back of the Inferno I found the rear entrance, a heavy metal security door set into the brick wall. No matter how well done a security door was, I always found a way through, and I usually did it through magic.

One of the things I'd come to understand from talking to the street people in the different cities I'd lived in during the last two years was that magic came to a person in one of two ways. The first way—and the way that most people found it—was by learning magic through books and instruction. The other way was like I did it: a kind of stumbling process where you found out one thing about yourself that was really weird, then figured out all the other weird things that went with the ability.

Me? My special magical power involved breaking into places. That ability fit my current profession quite nicely.

When you think of a magician, probably you think of the guy who put on the show back in grade school. The guy I watched back then was pretty lame, but for a dollar—and it wasn't even mine to begin with—I got out of class for an hour. Those school magicians either make with the mumbo jumbo words—kind of a nudge, nudge, wink, wink thing—or they don't say anything at all and just wave their wands around.

I had to concentrate to do my magic. Most magic people I know had to concentrate to do their stuff. Some of the older

street people I've known that can do magic say you have to
enter a trance state, sorta like self-hypnosis. Me? I think
maybe they've been attending too many AA meetings for
the free soup and sandwiches.

When I "ghosted," as I called it, I reached into my brain
and pushed until I felt a click. The first time I did it, I just
wanted to turn invisible. My mom's life was a mess ever
since my dad, who was a trucker, ran off with somebody my
mom and me never met. After my dad disappeared, Mom
started dating and didn't care too much for herself. I ended
up with a succession of new stepdads till I decided I'd had
enough. See, a lot of these new stepdads liked the idea of
bossing a kid around—even one that kept to himself like I
did. I didn't have friends at school, and I sure didn't need to
make friends with the stepdads. But that didn't stop them
from trying to take the stepdad job seriously.

Luther wasn't the first stepdad to hit me, but he was the
first that enjoyed the job. Big-time. He'd explain to my
mom that the bruises or the busted lip was just his way of
trying to "toughen" me up so I could play sports. Me, I was
never much into sports. Too much team stuff.

I spend a lot of money on video games, and my nickname
Wil-o-Wisp—which I broke down to WOW because most
game consoles only allow three letters to be saved to memory—was on most machines in the arcades whenever I was
in town. It was kind of funny, because in some arcades in
some cities I was kind of a local legend.

My mom named me William, after my grandfather, but I
went by Wil because it suited me. Kind of a rebellious thing.
My mom used to tell people when I said, "I Wil," that was
just me introducing myself. Actually, "I will," got to be a
motto of mine. The bad thing was, most of the stuff I got rebellious about was stuff no grown-up wanted me to do or
wanted to deal with.

I got in a lot of trouble in school. That wasn't a biggie
with me, because all I had to do to get into real trouble was
go home. Detention meant not going home till later, and
sometimes Mom and whatever stepdad was there would be

gone by then. The way I thought of the situation, school was
probably just as happy to get rid of me as I was to get rid of
school.

One night, Luther had put away most of a twelve-pack
and I knew things were going to get downright ugly. Mom
was working her second job of the day. She managed to stay
employed somewhere—cleaning houses, waiting on tables,
that sort of thing—whenever there was a new stepdad in the
house, but the stepdads seemed to just kind of work their
way through one six-pack after another and complain about
how the right sort of work wasn't going on at the time.

So Luther started haranguing me—that's another word I
found in a book at the library and decided I liked—one
night, and things got out of hand. I figured maybe he was
drunk enough that I could get around him and get out the
door. I made for the door all right, but he hadn't been as far
gone as I'd thought. He caught me and started walloping me
good.

That was when I wanted to be invisible. More than anything else in the world I wanted to be invisible then. Instead,
I felt that click in my brain and Luther's punches and slaps
passed right through me like I wasn't there. I stood there and
watched his fists and hands pass through me like I was fog.

That happening like that freaked me out. But me standing there and not being touched freaked Luther out even
more. I'd always been sharp, hardly ever missed an opportunity—although I'd tried to take advantage of some oppor-
tunities that I'd had no business even getting next to—so I
jumped on the chance to really put the screws to Luther.

I started accusing him of killing me, told him I was my
own ghost come back to haunt him for killing me. Luther
used to sit in front of the television with hijacked cable he
got from the apartment next door—see, he used to hook up
cable in the house; and getting cable in the house till the
company found out was the only good thing he did—and
watch horror movies. Night after night, he'd sit in that leaning recliner with a cold one and a bag of microwaved pop-

corn. Luther didn't have any trouble believing I was a ghost, and he knew he wasn't so wasted he was imagining things.

After that night, Luther left me alone, and, found another girlfriend a couple days later. Usually, Mom would be upset with me each time a new stepdad left, like it was my fault somehow, but I think she was tired of Luther, too. With him in the house, there was never any popcorn and the recliner—the only piece of living room furniture we had—was never empty. I mean, the guy must have had cast-iron kidneys. All that, and a winning disposition.

I had experimented with "ghosting" till I could do it every time. Provided I had time to concentrate. I didn't think about that ability being some kind of magic spell. At least, not then.

But standing there in that alley outside Inferno's that night, I knew I was working magic. I felt the familiar click in my brain and lifted my arm. My hand passed through the metal door. When other kids asked me what it felt like, all I could compare it to was shoving your finger into Jell-O. It was cold and there was some resistance, but you knew you were going to poke a hole in the Jell-O. I mean, come on—it was Jell-O.

The different kinds of stuff I walked through—metal, wood, plastic, and even water a few times—felt different. Some were tougher to get through, and some were colder than others, but I went through them all. The only dangerous difference was that I needed air. I could walk through water, but only as long as I could hold my breath. I could also fall through the earth, which is a really creepy feeling and took a lot more concentration than I usually had or even wanted to give.

Once I knew my arm would pass through, I stuck my head through the door. After I knew no one was standing in front of the door, I went on through. I got lucky, because no one saw me stepping through the door. Although I was basically intangible, I wasn't invisible. Man, if I could ever get those two together, I'd be unstoppable. I *clicked* back into the flesh-and-blood world and felt the music vibrating into me at once.

The Inferno was the typical club scene. The building held three bars and lots of female servers that looked like they'd stepped out of, and were wearing clothes from, Victoria's Secret. The bartenders were guys' dressed in tuxedo pants and looked like they'd just come from Gold's Gym. On the other hand, the bouncers looked like trolls in black club T-shirts with SECURITY written on the chest and back.

Volcanic eruptions kept going off on the walls, which were juiced with projection screens that ran from floor to ceiling. The scenes of pouring lava and erupting lava and bubbling lava made it seem like the club had been set in the interior of a volcano.

The dance floor was huge, filled with bodies gyrating to the basso thump of techno-pop pumping from truly awesome speakers. I kept moving, knowing with my small size and grungy clothes that I was going to draw the attention of a security guy any minute. My heart was thumping nearly as hard and as fast as the backbeat.

Then I spotted my guy, the guy who'd driven the dark green Lexus. He was standing near one of the bars, laying the mack on a couple of pretty fly girls in miniskirts who looked like they were eating it up. I figured once they saw the Lexus, they'd be his. He kept flashing the key chain, and they kept seeing the stylized symbol.

Seeing the guy like that, knowing he was getting by in his life on flash, I figured I owed it to the world to bring him down a notch or two by relieving him of his wallet. I got close and timed the sonic booms that crashed out of the surround sound when the volcanic eruptions touched off, then "bumped" into him.

I hit him just hard enough to get his attention and spill the drink he dangled nonchalantly in one hand. When he turned around with an angry look on his face and twin reflections of me on his mirrored sunglasses, I bumped him again, making it look like I'd been staggered by the guy behind me.

"Sorry," I said, and made a show of grabbing his glass so

he wouldn't spill it on both of us. While his mind was on his drink and on not acting like he needed me to help steady him, I ran my other hand inside his jacket and boosted his wallet. I felt it, smooth and leathery against my fingers, and it was mine in a heartbeat.

"Watch where you're going," the guy snarled.

I should have known when he snarled, you know. I mean, I should have known what he was. Not many kinds of people can pull off a full-blown snarl that can make you want to wet your pants. But that guy did. Me? I slipped his wallet down inside my pants and tried to walk away.

"What are you doing in here, kid?" the guy demanded.

"Partying," I said.

His eyes squinted and he stared me up and down. "You don't look old enough to be in here."

"That's what the guy at the door said until I showed him my ID," I said. I put on a show of being irritated, then turned and got out of there, retreating behind the line of people quitting the dance floor.

I was almost to the door, already *clicked* into "ghost" mode when I heard the guy screaming curses behind me. I didn't turn to look; I knew it was him even before I recognized his voice. My concentration started slipping—and me with one arm already shoved through the door!—and I threw myself forward.

I already told you that I had to concentrate to "ghost," but maybe you didn't understand that I had to keep concentrating to stay like that. Part of how the magic works, I guess. Once I started learning how to "ghost" and started experimenting with it, I found out that if I didn't keep concentrating, whatever I was trying to pass through would shove me out, like squeezing the red part out of a pimento. In the beginning, I had nightmares about getting cut in half by being trapped midway between something, or being frozen forever in a really thick wall. Sometimes I still did.

Over half of my body was through the club's back door, so when my concentration broke and I was shoved out of the door, I was shoved out into the alley. I tripped over my own feet and fell, managing to skin my chin on the asphalt and scaring a dozen cats to death.

I pushed myself to my feet, my heart pounding in my throat. Reaching down to my pants, I fisted the stolen wallet and started toward the alley mouth at a dead run. With the security door locked up tight behind me, I figured I had a minute or two head start at least before he got the door open because I'd noticed the door wasn't equipped with a fire crash bar.

Metal shrieked behind me.

I turned and looked behind me just in time to see the metal security door ripped from the frame. The guy strode out of the nightclub holding the heavy door in one hand, something I knew even a WWF wrestler couldn't do, and this guy wasn't nearly as big as Hulk Hogan or Goldberg.

I never missed a step, just kept on running.

But the guy tossed the security door aside like it was a disposable burger carton and came after me faster than anything human could have. That's when it hit me that the guy wasn't human. See, after I found out that magic works but not everybody can work spells, I also found out that supernatural creatures—at least, some of them—were real, too. I still hadn't seen a dragon or a unicorn, but I'd seen other things.

I knew what the guy was, and I should have known before we got to the alley. But I'd been concentrating on getting his wallet.

He covered the distance between us in three long strides even though I'd run like a madman. I helped him out by tripping over an orange-and-white tabby cat with green eyes and a missing ear. Even as I was falling, the guy was so fast that he caught me by my shirt collar before I could hit the ground.

He yanked me up and plastered me against the alley wall. My breath exploded from my lungs at the impact and spots filled my vision. I reached for the magic and wanted to "ghost" so bad I could taste it.

I never got the chance.

The guy looked down at me, holding me by my shirt collar like I was a kitten. I saw myself twice in his mirrored sunglasses. "So you're the kid," he said, letting me know I'd definitely overstayed my welcome in Tucson, and that he'd heard about the two other times I'd gotten caught "ghosting" through things. "I got somebody I want you to meet."

I started to speak, I even gasped out that I'd give the wallet back.

But he squeezed my throat and I couldn't even breathe.

"I don't think so, kid," he said. "Now that I got you, you ain't about to get away."

Darkness nibbled at the edges of my vision and started creeping in. I thought I was dead.

Then he grinned and I saw his fangs. I realized that I'd been caught by a vampire just about the time everything went black.

I woke up later feeling like somebody had buried a hatchet in my skull. Only darkness greeted me. I reached for my neck, feeling for the two holes I felt certain would be there. I figured I'd probably passed out from oxygen deprivation before the vampire had bled me dry. My fingertips only found smooth skin.

"Jacques didn't bite you, little thief," a woman's voice said.

Cloaked in the darkness around me, I jerked and nearly fell. But it wasn't just because I tripped over my own feet. My head also felt like a helium balloon barely attached to my shoulders.

"How do you do your magic, little thief?" the woman asked.

I squinted my eyes against the darkness, but it wasn't any use. I couldn't see the woman. However, I smelled her perfume.

Without warning, someone hit me in the face. As woozy as I was feeling anyway, I hardly felt any pain, but I dropped to my knees. Before I could get a hand out, I fell forward and my face crashed against the floor.

Now, I wouldn't have ever said I was the sharpest tool in the shed, but I figured if I at least stayed down, I wouldn't get knocked down again. It didn't sound like much, but I thought it was the brightest plan I'd had in a long time. While I was down there, I concentrated, reaching for that click in my brain that would let me "ghost" out of there.

I couldn't.

"Trying to use your magic isn't going to help you, little thief," the woman mocked.

I turned my head, realizing her voice was coming from another direction and that she was walking around me.

"You're a natural magician," she told me, "not a skilled one. The spell I've got on you keeps you from using your power while you're in this place."

"Where'm I?" I asked, trying to ignore the fact that my voice was slurred, but I was really afraid of getting an answer. If I learned too much, I just knew I was going to be dead. I didn't know why I wasn't already vampire kibble.

"Alive," she said. "For now. Jacques, turn on the light, please."

Abruptly, a halogen lantern shone into my eyes. Stabbing pain filled my head. Before I could stop myself, I threw up, shuddering and shaking. I don't know if it was the light or the spell the woman used. Although I knew magic could be used to cause sickness in others, no one had never targeted me like that.

Shielding my eyes with a hand, discovering only then that they'd been tied together. "What's going on?" I felt like my mouth had been filled with peanut butter.

"I'd heard of you, little thief. The phantasm that can walk through walls." The woman stepped into the light.

She was tall and beautiful, with an exotic accent that matched her dark good looks. She wore a long dark-red dress that fit her like a glove, and she could have given any of the women in the Inferno a run for their money in a Miss America or Victoria's Secret fan fave contest. A fur wrap covered her shoulders.

And I could feel the magic radiating off her. The strong

sensation was like an electric current. Some magic users, I'm told, can sense magic in others. Sometimes I could. With her, though, there might as well have been a flashing neon sign.

Jacques the vampire stepped into the light as well. He folded his arms across his chest, grinned at me, and stared at me from behind the mirror lenses.

I waited, barely curbing all the questions that ran through my mind. First and foremost was why either of them would be interested in me. But since they knew about me, it wasn't too hard to figure.

"I have a job for you, little thief," the woman said. She smoothed her hands over her hips and emerald fire glinted in her dark eyes.

"No way," I said. "I'm retired. Losing my touch. Or maybe you hadn't noticed." With all the history I had with my mom's boyfriends, I'd developed something of a smart mouth. Usually, though, a snappy comeback only earned me more trouble. But since I was in trouble anyway, I wanted to get my licks in as soon and as often as I could.

"You can retire," the woman said. "But not until after this job."

I started to say something, but I didn't know what, so I just shut up and listened. Jacques the vampire looked disappointed. Maybe he'd had dibs on me if I didn't play ball.

"Have you heard of the Academy for Advanced Study in Sedona?" the woman asked. "I believe the students call it Sorcerer U."

"Sure," I said. Nearly everybody into magic had heard of the Academy.

"They have a number of unique things there," the woman said. "One of them belongs to me. I want it back."

"Maybe you should ask," I said.

The woman frowned at me, then glanced at Jacques.

The vampire shrugged. "The reward was for finding him," Jacques said. "It didn't say anything about making sure he wasn't an idiot."

The woman looked back at me and shook her head.

"Please don't play the simpleton, little thief. I find the act boring, and if I believed you, Jacques would be chewing the marrow from your bones by now."

Jacques grinned as if the thought was particularly agreeable to him.

"Sure," I said. "I'd be happy to get it back for you." But all the while, I was planning on pulling a vanishing act as soon as 1 got out of the woman's sight.

Before I could congratulate myself for being so clever, the woman stepped forward and plucked a hair from my head. She said some words I couldn't understand and drew some mystic symbols in the air. I knew the symbols were mystical because they each glowed for a minute after she finished drawing them.

"How familiar are you with magic, little thief?" she asked, pulling my hair straight in her fingers.

"Enough," I said, even though I knew I wasn't or I could have countered her spell and escaped.

"With this hair," she told me in a deadly, quiet voice, "I can find you anywhere on this world, and in quite a few of the realms that overlap this one. You can run, as they say, little thief, but you can't hide. Not from me."

She smiled, and I totally believed her.

"I can't believe you dragged me into this," Harry complained.

I looked at him sitting in the limousine seat on the other side of me. I'd been told to find someone to pose as my parent. Sadly true, Harry was the best someone I could come up with. Folding my arms over my chest, knowing I'd heard him say the same thing dozens of times during the limo ride from Tucson to Sedona, I glared at him.

"I don't owe you anything," Harry protested again. Jacques had volunteered Harry after I'd suggested him. Harry was a short fat man. As a pawnbroker, he was always looking to cut a deal—just like the deal he made with the sign painter who'd come up with Harry's Prawn Shop. His toupee didn't fit his round face and head very well and looked like he'd scalped a bear to get it.

"If you'd paid me more for the coat I brought in, neither one of us would be here now," I said, knowing what I was saying was true and that Harry was in large part to blame for what I was going through. However, Harry was about the only adult I knew who didn't fall into the concerned parent role automatically when dealing with me.

The concerned parent came in one of two flavors. Either they wanted to take me in and parent me, which I'd had enough of, thank you very much, or they wanted to lock me up in juvie till I became an adult, which was not a prospect I was looking forward to.

"You stole that coat," Harry said, his plump face florid from all the drinks he'd had from the limo bar during the drive. "I gave you a fair price for stolen merchandise. I could lose my license."

I wasn't even sure if Harry had a license.

"Stupid kid," Harry said, uncapping another drink. "See if I ever buy stolen goods from you." He upended the bottle.

I hoped he wouldn't be drunk by the time we reached Sorcerer's U. Normally he wore an undershirt held in place by the tie-dyed suspenders that kept his dungarees up over his rolling stomach. Tonight, though, Jacques the vampire had gotten him a tuxedo. I figured that if Harry were still able to walk by the time we reached the private school, we'd both be doing good.

The Academy for Advanced Study sat near the center of Sedona on flat land under the wide-open night sky. Buildings flanked the school, but Sorcerer's U wasn't crowded. Several buildings made up the school, all of them Spanish-styled, built of adobe bricks and covered by red tile roofs.

The limo driver pulled up to the entrance near the high, whitewashed wall that fronted the Academy, then hurried back to let us out.

I stepped from the luxury car feeling tense and nervous. From the stories I'd heard, Sorcerer's U was guarded by a ton of protective spells and wardings. The mystery woman—I hadn't learned her name, and Jacques hadn't exactly been chatty—felt certain that I'd be able to get by a lot of the spells and wardings with my magic. She'd said something about my skill being localized and nondisruptive, none of which I had understood, but she thought it was a rare occurrence.

During the last three days while preparations had been made to take advantage of the Academy for Advanced Study's Open House night, I'd tried to escape. Jacques tracked me down in minutes, somehow guided by the hair of mine that the woman still had. Getting caught hadn't been fun. I'd spent a full day in a small cell with no food or water. Knowing I could have "ghosted" out of the cell had made it even worse. Or maybe it was just the thought of Jacques tracking me down a second time if I tried it.

Harry joined me on the walk in front of the school. "Man," he said, gazing around. "There must be some doin's going on at this place." Then he clapped on his top hat and we followed a red-suited usher toward the double doors of the main entrance.

A couple of greeters, a guy and a girl about my age, met us at the door, explaining to us that they were students at the Academy. HI! I'M JANICE took Harry by the arm and led him back to the banquet table. That made me happy, because food meant Harry wouldn't be quite as wobbly when the tour of the school grounds commenced at seven. We were fashionably early.

Janice was kind of stocky and had a Hispanic look despite the mass of curly yellow-brown hair piled on her head. She also had a New York accent and tended to talk kind of high and mighty, which was entirely lost on Harry, especially after he'd targeted the banquet table.

HI! I'M BARRY tried talking to me about the school and passing out literature. Evidently, the Open House event was a yearly thing so that prospective parents could see where their kids and their money were going.

Me, I was impressed by the place. It was simple but elegant. I thought about all the street stories I'd heard about the Academy, about how the school was supposed to have been started by a bruja, a Spanish witch, back in the 1840s. Of course, it took another forty years for the idea of such a school to catch on, and they hadn't gone looking for students. The only kids that attended Sorcerer's U were there by invitation. A millionaire named William Bryan Reynard, who had also happened to be a sorcerer, founded it at this location.

We passed one fat redheaded kid I could have sworn I'd seen in a couple of movies. He was walking around with a battered silk hat, saying, "Hey. Want to see me pull a rabbit out of my hat?" Then he'd pull a whole zoo out of the hat except a rabbit, and cackle like a lunatic because he thought it was so hilarious.

Other kids showed their parents and anyone else interested the magic spells they'd learned, as well as projects. There were a lot of illusions, fireball creation, blowing winds, and shape-changing going on.

I had to admit, the school looked good to me when I thought about all those nights ahead of me spent sleeping in alleys. Because I'd figured I wasn't going to steal another thing after I got out of the mess I was in.

"So," I said to Barry as he handed me a cup of punch, "is there any truth to the rumor that the bruja that started this place still walks the halls at night?"

"Doña Rafaela de Leon?" Barry shot me an irritated look, then shook his head. He wore his dark hair pulled back in a ponytail and I thought maybe he was of Navajo descent because there was a rez near Sedona. "That's just a story. You know, to frighten the new kids with. Tradition."

"Sure," I said. "So do you like it here?"

Barry shrugged. "I miss the waves, bro. I grew up in Los Angeles, but I lived on a surfboard."

Someone caught Barry's attention and he went away, but not before I palmed his name badge—because the mystery lady told me they were all magically encoded somehow with security spells—and got directions to the nearest bathroom.

Actually, I already knew where the bathroom was. I knew the whole layout of the school. The mystery woman and Jacques the vampire had made certain of that before they sent me to the Open House. I knew where the room was that had the glass ball the mystery woman wanted.

So I left Harry there annihilating the banquet table and made my way to the bathroom. Like the rest of the school, the bathroom was rustic and spiffy all at once. I didn't spend much time there, just clipped on HI! I'M BARRY, made the *click* in my brain, and "ghosted."

I walked through walls easily enough, but took care to keep my bearings. The buildings didn't quite match up with what the mystery woman and Jacques the vampire had told me, but they'd told me to expect that as well. Sorcerer's U had a whole lot of spells and wardings on it, and sometimes rooms from other worlds and dimensions overlapped ours. Or maybe rooms in our world overlapped other dimensions and worlds. Whichever it was, I just hoped I didn't get lost.

Seven minutes later—for some reason I timed the whole thing like I was in a James Bond movie, which should have told me things were going to go badly because they always do for 007 when he's on a tight deadline—I reached the room I was looking for. The only real deadlines I faced were the end of Open House at eight-thirty and Harry eating Sorcerer's U out of house and home sometime before then.

Eight-thirty was eight-thirty, but Harry was a question mark. The man could eat. I'd never seen him in the pawnshop without food.

The room I'd searched for and found was a small one, looking like a museum wing that had been shut off from the rest of the school. Judging from the resistance I'd encountered walking through the wall, I guessed that the room was heavily protected by spells because it sure wasn't the wood and plaster or fatigue that had slowed me down. I'd considered not going through and telling Jacques and his mistress that I hadn't been able to do it, except that I figured if she could find me so easily, she'd probably know when I was lying, too.

I hurried down the stacks and racks and tables of weapons, paintings, and all kinds of stuff I didn't have a clue about. At the end of one of the tables, I found the crystal ball the mystery woman had sent me for.

The ball was about as big as a cantaloupe and clear as a glass of spring water. A three-toed bird's claw with black talons made a perch for the crystal ball, clutching the ball in a death grip. Deep inside the crystal ball was a statue of an old Asian woman in a shawl standing beneath a tree filled with owls. The bottom of the crystal ball was covered with snow, and I got the impression the scene was winter and the old woman had a hard life. I felt sorry for her.

But I didn't hesitate. I moved in for the kill, shoving away old books, a battle-ax, and vials of powders and potions. The sooner I had what I came for, the sooner I was out the door and away from the mystery woman and her pet vampire. But when I put my hands on the crystal ball, I was zapped so hard by electricity that I got knocked from my feet.

Groggy, my head spinning, I got back to my feet.

Get the crystal ball! the mystery woman screamed into my head.

See, not only did she know where I was all of the time, she could also tell what I was thinking. "I am," I growled, my hands numb from the electric surge.

Do it now!

I eyed the crystal ball. "Got any suggestions?"

The mystery woman cursed at me and told me to get to it.

I took off my suit coat—Harry wasn't the only one fashionably attired—and wrapped it around the crystal ball. Feeling kind of pleased and choosing to view my success as an omen, I turned around.

"What do you think you're doing with that?" A man stood between me and the wall I'd come through only moments ago.

I recognized David Reynard, descendant of the founder of the Academy for Advanced Study, from the pictures in the literature I'd been given earlier and the news articles I'd read. The HI! I'M DAVID REYNARD badge he wore helped give it away. He was tall and solid looking, definitely not a guy to jerk around. His eyes blazed a little.

I felt as if ants were crawling all over me, and I knew it was because of the power he wielded. I tried to speak, but my voice locked up in my throat.

Run! the woman thundered inside my head.

And I tried. I really did. But my legs wouldn't move and my feet felt as though they'd been set in concrete. Besides that, if Reynard was as good with a spell as I'd heard, I knew I'd probably be brain-fried before I reached the wall. And I have to tell you, my concentration wasn't doing very well either. I wouldn't have been able to "ghost" through the wall.

Without warning, a blue dot appeared in the air behind Reynard. As I watched over Reynard's shoulder, the dot elongated into an oval portal that Jacques the vampire stepped through. He was carrying an old-fashioned shotgun and was lifting it to his shoulder when his foot touched the floor of the room.

Alarm klaxons rang as though Armageddon had descended.

David Reynard didn't take his attention from me, and I guess maybe he figured that it was me that set the alarms off finally.

Jacques raised the shotgun as two huge Golems stepped out of the portal behind him. Both Golems stood ten feet tall, and it had probably been hard squeezing through that small portal.

Made of earth and rock, they had barely distinguishable humanoid features. Earthen Golems were incredibly stupid; I knew because I'd seen them around. Usually sorcerers summoned Golems, but sometimes they just formed on their own like mushrooms. I knew the mystery woman had sent these Golems.

I watched, dry mouthed in horror as David Reynard stepped toward me and Jacques took a bead on him. Then the woman in the crystal ball I held in my hands looked up at me. The owls in the tree shook their wings.

"Choose your destiny, Wil Tucker," the old woman in the shawl ordered.

I felt the magic moving around me. Probably the whole Academy was shutting down. Even with my "ghosting" power I was betting I might not make it out of the building without getting caught. And I figured Jacques and the earthen Golems wouldn't let me use the portal the mystery woman had opened up inside the room. I guessed that she used me, used the link between me and her made by that hair of mine she had, to target the location of the room to open the portal. Otherwise she'd have done it before.

"Choose," the woman in the crystal ball said.

There was no choice. I dropped the crystal ball and lunged for Reynard, who tried to backpedal away from me. But I was too quick for him. I knocked Reynard down, and the shotgun boomed about the same time a load of buckshot cut the air where Reynard had been standing and totally decimated a quartz statue of a turkey. I still haven't found out what the turkey had to do with anything.

I was lying atop Reynard, knowing I was only about a heartbeat ahead of being killed by the Golems closing in on us. Reynard spoke and gestured, and magic shimmered through the air. Mystic symbols burned into the earthen Golems.

As I watched, the Golems dried out as though they were being microwaved. They both took one more step, then crumbled in an avalanche of dust and dirt clods, tumbling and skittering across the floor and raining down over us.

By then I was moving, too scared to just lie there, watching as Jacques reached into his pocket for another shell. I didn't know why he didn't attack Reynard, who was having a coughing fit from dust inhalation, up close and personal, but maybe Reynard had wards protecting him from vampires.

Jacques thumped the shell into the shotgun about the time I took up a jagged piece of wood that had been the pedestal the quartz turkey had stood on. Still in motion, I fisted the wood and started for the vampire.

Smiling, Jacques turned toward me with the shotgun. I knew he wouldn't hesitate, and I was all out of running room.

"Don't falter, boy," a woman's voice said, and I recognized it as the old woman in the shawl. "You can do this. You're strong."

I felt the *click* in my brain as I "ghosted," and saw the muzzle blast flame. The buckshot passed through me as if I were nothing; then I plunged the wood toward Jacques as I reentered the real world. The shotgun barrel burned my cheek and I felt the shock of the wood plunging into Jacques' chest, going through his dead heart.

Jacques had time for one scream, then he burst into dust and broken bones that rattled when they hit the floor.

You foul, despicable brat! the mystery woman screamed at me through the psychic connection. *I'll get you for this! I promise you that! No one betrays me!*

Fearfully, I looked up at the blue oval, halfway expecting the mystery woman to step through it and blast me with a lightning bolt or a fireball, or resurrect Jacques and sic him on me.

Instead, Reynard got to his feet and inscribed mystic symbols that shredded the portal in flashes of purple and yellow flames. That was about the time school security broke the door down and entered the room in a rush.

After that, things got kind of crazy.

I really figured I was headed back to juvie, and the thought was depressing. Been there, done that, really glad to have "ghosting" powers. But juvie always takes all your stuff.

Surprisingly, Reynard—

[Note: Mr. Tucker, since this paper is going to be accepted as part of your schoolwork, I'd appreciate it if you didn't refer to faculty or the head of the Academy in such familiar terms. Professor Nagata]

[Well, excuse me. I'm not changing the whole paper. He became Professor Reynard after I accepted the scholarship. Wil Tucker]

—offered me a scholarship to the Academy. He also took great pains pointing out that I would be safe there—and incidentally, the Academy might not be safe as long as we didn't know who the mystery woman that sent me was. That has become objective number one. After I square up all my class work, of course.

Objective number two is the crystal ball with the old woman and the owls in it. Sorcerer's U has become a repository of all kinds of magical items over the years, and most of them were put there because they were dangerous. Nobody knew the old woman in the crystal ball could speak, and she hasn't spoken since. But he feels that since she chose to make contact through me, I'm probably the best guy for the job of finding out the crystal ball's story.

I pointed out to him that the crystal ball was obviously of great importance to the mystery woman, and probably dangerous for me to be poking around. He said he'd think about it and get back to me. The next day, the crystal ball's history got assigned to me as a class project, which I think absolutely bites.

[Note: Mr. Tucker, while this is a personal document and Headmaster Reynard has allowed it to be presented in both your school file and as homework, I think it would behoove you to refrain from such caustic commentary. And don't think that I haven't noticed you've not referred to Professor Reynard as Professor Reynard since my earlier comment. You're overusing the pronoun without a definite subject even though Professor Reynard is the only man you've talked about in this section. I will count off if this isn't corrected in the final paper. Professor Nagata]

So here I am in Sorcerer's U when I wondered about the place and never thought I'd get here. Not exactly the land of chuckles. Also, I don't fit in the way most of the other students fit in. Tough. I'm me. For now, I'll stay here and I'll work on that stupid crystal ball till I figure the mystery

woman is no longer interested in me. Or until I've had it up
to my ears with homework. Then we'll see.

[Note: Is this a threat, Mr. Tucker? Because if it is, you're
going to be dropped a whole letter grade on the assignment.
Professor Nagata]

[Wow, if you can drop my score a whole letter grade, I
must have done okay. Go ahead and drop it. I'll just add it
back in and know what I really got on the paper. That ad-
justment will snowball, of course, because I'll have to adjust
the nine weeks' grade and the semester grade. Wil Tucker]

CHASING TIME

by ElizaBeth Gilligan

ElizaBeth Gilligan is a happily married mom of two teens and the Keeper of the Vast Menagerie—eight cats, one dog, frogs, newts, and over a hundred guinea pigs (daughter's homeschool genetics project). She has been writing ever since she figured out how a pencil worked. Her mother reports that ElizaBeth declared as early as the age of two that she was going to "make books" when she grew up. Her first and second short stories appeared in DAW anthologies. As a novelist, she aspired to one day find a place in the DAW family and, to her great delight, April 2003 saw the release of her first book, *Magic's Silken Snare*, in the *Silken Magic* series by DAW.

When she's not writing or working on one of her various projects, she leads an on-line research group for writers and hangs out at sff.people.lace.

BARRY Silverhorse sat in a meditative posture. Janice Redding knelt behind him and frowned. Her fingers palpated Barry's scalp.

Matt Johnson dropped onto the slope next to them. Neither of his friends paid much attention to his arrival. He rolled onto his belly, pulled up a blade of grass, and began to chew on it.

"Are you two serious?" he asked after several minutes.

Janice rolled her dark eyes. "*Some* of us want to pass our classes."

Matt clutched his throat, flipped onto his back, and faked an ugly death, complete with convulsions. After a moment, he sat up, rubbing the grass from his hair. "Guys, didn't anybody tell you? *This* is a sorcerer's academy and we're *already* sorcerers. No matter what, Reynard can't take that away from us."

"Well," Barry said, "some of us want to understand and control our powers."

"Oh, you're not still on that, are you?" Matt sighed.

"What're you talking about?" Janice asked, looking from one boy to the other.

"Nothing," Barry said quickly. He glowered at Matt. "So, what's the big deal? Why aren't you studying?"

"Because I found something more interesting."

"Something more interesting than phrenology?" Janice asked, pretending to be shocked. She shoved a curling lock of yellow-brown hair back behind her ear. "So, spill it, Johnson. You've got our attention . . . or is that all you wanted?"

Matt made a face at her. "C'mon, Barry, you've got to see what I found."

"What about me?" Janice asked as the boys scrabbled to their feet.

"You can come if you want to," Matt said. Despite his attempt to hide it, his voice betrayed his reluctance.

"'Fraid a girl might show you up?" she asked. She scooped her books into her bag and hurried after them. "So?" she gasped, slightly breathless, "Where are we going?"

"You gotta see this horse—" Matt said, as he led them through the maze of adobe academic buildings.

"This is about a *horse*?" Barry said, stopping. "C'mon, Janice, let's go to the library. At least we won't have to hear him. Mrs. Grundy's Silence spell will take care of that!"

"Aw, guys!" Matt ran ahead of them. "If it were just any old horse, I wouldn't blame you, but you gotta see this to believe it!"

"Is it a unicorn?" Janice asked.

"Pegasus?" Barry asked simultaneously.

Matt just shook his head. "Give me five minutes, guys. You won't regret it."

Janice hesitated, looking at Barry to see what he thought. He shrugged. The decision was hers. "You've got two minutes, Johnson, and if it isn't worth interrupting my studies, I'll . . . I'll—"

Barry stepped in. "I'll levitate a ton of fertilizer from the stables to your bed."

"Yeah. Make sure that he's in it first."

"You'll only regret this if you don't come," Matt said. "Besides, you've got to see the weird old lady, too."

"What old lady?" Barry asked.

"Maybe a returning instructor?" Janice said.

Both boys turned to look at her.

"Don't you remember? In Orientation, Professor Reynard said sometimes teachers would come and go without notice."

"Is there *anything* you don't remember?" Matt asked.

"Not really," Janice replied. She shoved her dusty curls behind her ears. "Unlike some people, I pay attention."

Matt snorted and headed off, leaving the others to follow him.

Janice and Barry caught up as he rounded the Health Center, the hub for the medical needs at the Sorcerer's Academy and educational facility for studying the magical, healing arts. Matt slowed from a jog to a semi-sedate walk as he circumnavigated the pit where Professor Sanchez prepared for her Monday Archaeology class.

Supposedly, Professor Sanchez was a *bruja* with roots in the community. She was a small woman with glossy black hair and penetrating dark eyes, who looked like she could pose for one of the "great and beautiful lady" portraits in Sedona's art galleries. At the moment, a straw hat covered her hair and gloves encased her elegant hands. She stood up on the top platform just as Matt passed by.

"Good morning, students."

One did not ignore the Academy's professors. They all stopped in an ungainly clump.

"Good morning, Professor Sanchez," Janice said.

The professor eyed them thoughtfully. "What are the three of you up to?"

"Up to?" Barry repeated, suddenly looking very guilty.

Matt shook his head. "Just a little experimentation with dowsing, ma'am," he said. He pulled a forked stick from his back pocket and held it up.

"You'll forgive me, I know," the professor said as she prowled the catwalk that staged the different levels of her Archaeology lab, "but your dowsing rod looks suspiciously like a slingshot."

Matt nodded. "Yes'm. We were attempting to meet your challenge to use what we have at hand rather than getting fancy tools that do half the job for us."

"Mmm," Professor Sanchez said. She stared straight into Matt's eyes. "I find students are usually up to no good when they quote my lessons back to me. You wouldn't be trying to leave the compound, would you?"

"No, ma'am!" The three of them spoke as one.

"Proceed, then, but bear in mind that I'll be checking on you," the professor said. She moved farther into her diggings, only her hat visible. Just as Janice opened her mouth to protest, Sanchez called up, "That goes double for you, *Señorita* Redding."

The three of them hurried off, following Matt's lead. They looped around the Mathematics Building—one of their least favorite subjects, despite Professor Hertz's insistence that it was impossible to undertake higher spellwork without a complete understanding of Mathematics—and the Alchemy Lab to the perimeter wall and south toward the westernmost part of campus and the stables.

Janice looked at the back of the barn and the surrounding

paddocks. "You know there's a quicker way here, don't you?"

Matt stuck out his tongue at her and crouched down. Barry hunkered down behind Matt, who wove his head back and forth like a rattler looking to strike. "She's not there."

"Who are you looking for?" Janice asked.

Matt turned and looked slowly up. He sighed and rose to his feet as well. "There was this old circus wagon here earlier."

"A circus wagon?" Barry asked. He stood. "You dragged us all this way for a circus wagon? And this horse you want us to see? Like there would *ever* be a circus—I mean a normal one, not like when Sheila Fitzgerald burned down the Alchemy Lab—on this campus?"

"I never said it was a whole circus," Matt said. He shoved his fists into his pockets and scanned the yard. His eyes narrowed as he focused in on something. "There it is, over there!" He pointed to the farthest corner of the stable.

Barry and Janice followed his gaze. Wedged between mounds of straw, they could just make out a corner of yellow wall and red-tiled roof.

"But we're not supposed to go there," Janice said. "Don't you guys remember Professor Reynard's speech?"

"Who cares? Come on!" Matt took off through the open area between the paddocks, dodging from shadow to shadow. He ran along the barn's length, his head ducked below the line of windows. He looked back and waved an arm, beckoning them on.

"Did you see how he ran across that field? What's with all the spy stuff?" Janice asked. "Does he think somebody's watching?"

Barry shrugged.

"Is this a guy thing, or is there a memo I didn't see?"

"I didn't get the memo either. After you?"

Janice laughed. She covered her mouth when Matt started pantomiming for her to be quiet. She wriggled her brows at Barry and tiptoed across the barnyard only to collapse in a gale of giggles at Matt's feet. Barry closed the distance and helped Matt get Janice standing again.

With Janice's giggles finally contained, Matt led them around the barn. He stopped and pointed to an odd-looking horse grazing less than twenty feet away from them, just outside the door of the brightly painted circus wagon. The air around it shimmered in the sunlight. The scent of magic rolling off the beast was almost palpable.

"Have you ever seen a horse like that?" Matt whispered.

"My experience with horses is limited," Barry said. Despite his irritation, he could not look away from the radiant gray sheen of the animal's coat. The horse's black mane and tail glinted in the bright daylight. "But, no, I haven't. Most horses don't look like they'd glow in the dark."

"I may've grown up in the city, boys, but if there's one thing girls like, it's horses. I've read tons of books and I've never seen one like that," Janice said. She squatted down, staring at the horse. "Not even in fairy tales."

"What kind of horse is it, do you think? It's sure not one of the school string," Barry said, jerking his thumb at the Academy horses, all of them entirely mundane.

Matt shook his head.

"Probably some type of cob," Janice said. "At least as far as its breeding goes."

The boys looked at her.

"You can see from its thick bone structure that it's bred for work," she pointed out. "Cobs were used to draw carriages back when everybody used carriages. They're stocky animals with nice, high gaits."

Barry turned to Matt, looking for confirmation.

"Don't ask me—she clearly knows more about this than I do. It's a funny-colored horse. And there's something strange about it. There we come to the end of my knowledge."

Janice pulled her backpack in front of her and began burrowing through it.

"What are you doing?" Matt asked nervously.

She pulled a bag of apple slices from the pack, and

smiled. "I'm going to make friends. Besides, she's lost her tether."

"Wait—!" Barry said.

"Do you think that's a good idea?" Matt said.

They were talking to Janice's back. Without stealth or caution, she sauntered over to the horse, clucking her tongue to draw its attention.

The horse whickered; its head came up, ears pricking toward Janice. Its black tail swished. Lazily, its eyes drooping in the heat of the gathering day, the horse ambled over and reached for the apple bits in Janice's outstretched hands.

"What're you feeding my horse, *Señorita*?"

Janice turned, and pulled her hand away.

An old woman stood on the steps of the wagon. Sharp-eyed, she wore black from head to toe. Her gray hair was tied back with a black-and-gold scarf knotted at the nape of her neck. When she came down the steps, shades of dark blue, green, and purple swirled throughout her skirt. Massed bangles of gold and silver adorned both her wrists almost to the elbow, and silver hoops hung from her ears.

"Uh, bits of apple. I'm . . . I'm sorry," Janice stuttered. "I should have asked permission." She looked toward the barn where the boys had been hiding. They were gone. She fumed. "I just saw your horse loose. It's new, isn't it? I mean, on the compound. I mean, I haven't seen you before and . . ." She fell silent. "I'm sorry," she mumbled again.

"She doesn't need a fence to know where she belongs." The crone came down the last steps. "Don't tease my Meg with that handful of apple. Give it to her or don't."

The silver horse butted Janice in the back. "Of . . . of course," Janice said.

The horse, Meg, butted her again, nickering happily when Janice held out her hand and offered the apple slices. The mare lipped them up gently. Janice stroked the horse's nose, noting the telltale black "eel-stripe" down her back and across her withers. "So, she *is* a dun."

The old woman laughed softly and reached up to scritch

the mare behind the right ear. "You know something about horses, do you?"

"A little. Not as much as I'd like to. I mean, I've never actually owned a horse of my own." Janice smiled. She liked this old woman, who looked like the *abuelitas* she'd seen in New York. They smelled of home-baked bread and cookies . . . and sometimes erasers, from helping the *niños* with their homework. This old woman, though, was a *bruja*. She smelled of herbs, horse, and magic. Janice closed her eyes and breathed in the aroma. Before coming to Sorcerer U, she had never thought that magic had a smell, though of course some experiments did have noxious side effects. The Alchemy Lab, for instance, always reeked.

"I am Madame Roushka."

Janice's eyes popped open. Oops, manners . . . She felt her face warming as she blushed. "Janice Rosa Redding, *Señora*."

The *bruja* nodded. "So, did you come all this way just to feed my old Meg an apple?"

"No, ma'am . . . well, yes . . . sort of . . ."

The old woman gave the horse a firm pat on the neck. The mare turned and walked away, tail swishing amiably as she went back to her grazing. "Come, you will have tea with me."

"But—"

"You have homework to do, yes? And your friends to find," the *bruja* said. She climbed up the three stairs to her caravan. "You need fuel for such work."

"Exactly," Janice said. She frowned. "Wait a minute . . . my friends?"

"Yes, the young boys who left you to your fate, abandoning you to an unknown magical being."

"You knew about them?" Janice asked, surprised.

The *bruja* laughed. "Come. Have tea with me and leave them to stew in their own juices. It is early yet and there is all of tomorrow before classes begin again on Monday."

Intrigued, Janice climbed the steps and entered the wagon. She expected to find a living space not much better

than the apartments some of her friends and their families
lived in back home—there were closets at the Academy bigger than some of those apartments. Inside the little wagon,
however, everything seemed much more roomy than she anticipated. The ceiling was fairly low, but the living space
was comfortable and cozy.

Madame Roushka indicated that Janice should sit on a
low-slung divan of behemoth proportions. She sat and accepted a glass of iced tea from her hostess.

Madame Roushka took her place, cross-legged, on a
cushion on the floor. She was remarkably limber for a
woman who had to be at least in her fifties, judging by her
appearance. The woman drank deeply from her own glass,
then leaned forward, brushed aside a dangling scarf on a
tabletop and keyed in a "Save All" command on the laptop
it had hidden.

"So, now we shall talk, hmmm?" Madame Roushka said.
She set aside her glass and took Janice's free right hand in
hers. She turned it this way and that. "You are a 'southpaw'?
Your left hand is dominant, yes?"

"Yes. You're reading my palm?" Janice leaned forward to
watch the old woman inspect her hand. "We haven't covered
Palmistry in Basic Divination yet."

Madame Roushka's brows rose. "No? I always taught it
first."

"You used to be an instructor here?"

"Indeed. But you should know that already. Professor
Reynard—like his father before him—has always been very
strict about who is permitted into the compound." Madame
Roushka's tongue peeked between her lips as she concentrated on Janice's hand. "You seem a bright girl. Your hand
speaks of great potential, so tell me, what is the key to Divination?"

"Observation, according to my professor."

"Good. Now tell me what that means."

Janice sat back, confused. "I don't understand."

"When you make your observations, what is it that you
are considering?"

"It depends what kind of divination you're doing. If you're reading phrenology, then you must carefully study and analyze the bumps and grooves—"

"Phrenology! Phah!" Madame Roushka exclaimed, waving her hand dismissively. "A child's game, a parlor trick at the very best. The only bump or groove that might convey anything to the reader is if the querant has been hit in the head!"

Janice giggled. "That's what it seemed like to me, too. All I observed for sure was that the guys like getting their scalps rubbed."

"Then, perhaps, my young friend, this is the answer to your professor's questions," Madame Roushka said. She quirked an eyebrow. "Who is your instructor?"

"Professor Edwards."

"I retract that advice. Professor Edwards and I have had our disagreements on the matter," Madame Roushka said. "But that is not what brought you to my little *vardo*."

"*Vardo*, ma'am?"

"My home . . ." Madame Roushka gestured at their surroundings.

"Are . . . are you with a circus?" Janice asked.

"Psh," Madame Roushka snorted. "No circus. I am Romani . . . that would be 'Gypsy' to the uninformed . . . and I am not a performer. I read palms, it is true, and I have my other talents, but I am *not* a Showman."

Janice noted the distinctions Madame Roushka made and filed them away. "So, do you live here all year round?"

"Here, I presume, is the *vardo*? Yes, *Señorita*, I live here always," Madame Roushka replied. She leaned forward, her dark eyes glistening, "Though the ground my home is rooted to varies. But is that truly what you wanted to ask? What brought you and your young friends to my humble home? And when they ran away, why did you not run, too? Why is that? Answer my questions and I'll answer one of yours."

"It's not like I'm brave or anything," Janice murmured, though she was still steamed at Barry and Matt for just ditching her. On the other hand, she was enjoying herself now, and they were off shaking in fear somewhere. Boy, was she going to rib them about this! "We came because we could see the magic. We wondered what it was. It shimmered around your horse. Her name's Meg, right?"

"Careful, pet. Less scrupulous entities would take advantage of you and make that your question."

"What do you mean by 'less scrupulous entities?'"

"Since I am a professor and I am here to instruct, I will not count that as your question either," Madame Roushka said. "You have been taught by now, I am sure, that there are other intelligent beings than humans, beings capable of controlling magic? Some of these creatures will seize upon any opportunity to thwart you. You, however, are not interested in lectures about elementals, jinn, and suchlike, I would guess. Your question was to be about Meg, I presume?"

"Maybe." Janice said. "I've always loved horses. Some girls go all goofy over musicians and actors and stuff. I guess I've seen too many stars and not enough horses." She grinned. "I know horses don't mind if you don't look like some sort of sick supermodel who hasn't eaten in a year and—"

Madame Roushka held up her right hand, waggling her forefinger in Janice's direction. "You need not explain, my dear, I understand completely. So that is what you find in a horse? Understanding, hmm?"

Janice nodded. She hadn't really ever thought much about it before this, but it summed up her fascination for horses.

"I like all horses. But Meg is something special. Even my not-so-reliable friend Matt could see it."

"You *are* a perceptive young thing, aren't you?" Madame Roushka said. She rose from her cross-legged position without pause or aid. "Come."

Madame spoke simply and motioned for Janice to follow her down the stairs and out of the wagon. She clicked her tongue and the mare came to Madame immediately, whickering and bumping her head into her mistress' midriff. She nosed the *bruja*'s skirts, snorting happily when the old woman brushed back the forelock of her mane and scratched the solid white star on her forehead.

The marking was far more than the elongated white diamond shape one expected to see on a horse. The hair on Meg's glittering gray face swirled in such a way that the star looked more like a pentagram than a diamond. And its boundaries changed and shifted even as Janice watched.

"Way cool!" Janice breathed.

Madame Roushka smiled. "Her kind is rare indeed. There aren't many like my Meg."

"Her kind? Is she like a unicorn or Pegasus or something?"

Madame Roushka turned her attention to scratching behind Meg's ears. "It depends upon who you ask. Meg is a horse, a *real* horse. The creatures you name are purely magical creatures that are horselike in nature. Meg is not a magical creature at all, but rather a horse capable of magic. Only a very rare horse is capable of that."

"Meg can work magic?" Janice asked, astonished at the concept of an animal incapable of speech, without the faculties of a greater intellect, who might be able to cast spells.

Madame Roushka laughed softly, rubbing the horse's face. "In her own way, yes. She is capable of wanting to please, or being disagreeable. Her desires are decisions, you understand, acts of simple will. Combine her will with her magical heritage and—*voilà!*—you have magic."

"You keep talking about her 'kind.' What 'kind' is that?" Janice asked.

"You noticed it yourself. If her coat were mostly tan or blonde, she would be a dun. No?"

Janice nodded. She leaned her head comfortably against the large horse's warm, muscular neck.

"Her kind is sometimes called Gray Dun or, for the more imaginative, Silverhorse."

"Silverhorse?" Janice looked up, surprised. "That's the name of one of—" She stopped. She was annoyed, but didn't particularly want to get Barry or even Matt in trouble.

"Yes, that's right, it's the family name of some of the

local tribes . . . among the Diné, I think," Madame Roushka said. "very observant, *chica*." She reached out and stroked Janice's curls just as if she were a horse. "Now, my Meg and a very few of her kindred, they are called 'Tick Tock Duns.' Can you guess why?"

Janice shook her head.

"There you are!"

Both Madame Roushka and Janice turned at the sound of Professor Sanchez's voice.

The young professor strode toward them, followed by Barry and Matt. Janice sighed. As usual, the teacher looked like a million bucks. She always did. If only Professor Sanchez weren't so nice, then Janet could have hated her in earnest. No one deserved to look that pretty in dirty work clothes that would have made Janice look as though she'd gone mud wrestling after donning Salvation Army retreads.

Matt, thinking himself out of the line of Professor Sanchez's sight—and not yet the focus of Madame Roushka's attention—began pantomiming some sort of elaborate excuse for running like a scared sheep at the first sign of trouble. Professor Sanchez turned and said something to him, catching him in mid-contortion. He froze under her unexpected attention, looking wide-eyed, slack-jawed, and remarkably silly.

Where was a camera when she needed one? Janice smothered a giggle. Oh, well, even without a picture, she could tease him about this for weeks. Matt shrugged awkwardly and blushed. Barry seemed to have found something interesting to look at in the sky.

Professor Sanchez removed her work gloves, shoving them into her hip pocket, and reached for Madame Roushka's outstretched hands. "The Fates have brought us together again, Madame! I am so pleased to see you. David did not mention your return at last evening's staff meeting or I would have come sooner!" She kissed both of Madame's cheeks.

Madame Roushka returned the greeting. "I arrived late.

As you know, I always prefer to keep the *when* of my arrival something of a mystery."

"And no one does it better." Sanchez turned her attention to the boys and Janice. "I'm sorry these students have disturbed you. They're first years, you know. They've got," and she fixed the teens with a stern look so that they wouldn't miss the point she was about to make, "no business being anywhere near the stables without an instructor or upperclassman to accompany them."

Uh-oh. Busted . . . Janice and the boys looked at one another. What punishment were they likely to get? Detention? Probation? Turned into newts? Worse?

"Our young friend here, *la chica bonita*," Madame Roushka patted Janice's shoulder, "has been no bother at all. She was my guest for tea."

"How unprecedented." Professor Sanchez's brows rose in astonishment. "And the boys?"

Madame Roushka looked them both over. "I am afraid that I am unacquainted with either of them."

"Then they didn't bother you, after all," Professor Sanchez gave Matt and Barry a look that said all too clearly that they had not completely evaded trouble. Her gaze fell on Janice. "Despite the invitation that the boys failed to mention, *Señorita* Redding, you are a first-year student as well. Other first years are not suitable escorts for you to venture onto this portion of the school grounds. If you had mentioned your appointment when we spoke earlier, I'd have escorted you myself."

So much for getting out of trouble! Janice thought. *Now what?*

"I think it's time to leave," Professor Sanchez said. "Say good-bye, Janice."

Madame Roushka patted her shoulder. "We will see one another quite soon, I predict."

"Come along," Professor Sanchez said.

Janice made her farewells to Madame Roushka and followed the teacher along with Matt and Barry.

"I'm very disappointed in you three," Professor Sanchez

said as they walked back to the main part of the campus. "You know the Rules. I thought you understood the reason for them." They followed the teacher into the Sociology Building and down the main hall. Professor Sanchez opened a door labeled in gold lettering with her name, flicked on the lights to her office, and motioned the three of them in. "By all rights, I really should report you all to Professor Reynard. This has been a serious breach of the Rules."

Janice sighed in relief. So Sanchez wouldn't be telling Professor Reynard. They might have hope for life beyond this afternoon. Maybe they weren't destined to spend the rest of the academic year as newts—or worse.

The professor's voice sounded pinched and irritable—a far cry from her normal elegant speech. "I do not understand how the three of you—among our very best students this year—could fail to comprehend the necessity for obeying the Rules. This is no ordinary campus. We regularly receive visitors, and some of them are highly . . . volatile . . . in nature. We need to keep track of where our more vulnerable—"

"You don't mean Madame Roushka is dangerous?" Janice said.

"Of course she's dangerous." Professor Sanchez leaned across her desk. "You don't get to be a tenured member of *this* faculty if you aren't. Am I understood?"

Janice nodded, and so did the boys. But Janice was having a hard time wrapping her head around the concept of Madame Roushka as some kind of threat. She seemed like such a nice old lady.

"Yeah, you can just feel how powerful she is. Barry and me were scared to fits when she came out of her—" Matt began. He met Professor Sanchez's unblinking gaze and realized his mistake. He tried, Janice noted, to make himself smaller. It didn't work.

"So you abandoned a classmate, and left her alone to face what you perceived to be a serious threat?" Professor Sanchez's expression darkened like the sky did, right before a tornado hit. "How long did you wait before summoning my help?"

Barry stared at the floor, silent.

"Not long enough," Matt muttered.

That was the wrong answer.

And the storm broke loose.

Ultimately, Professor Sanchez assigned all three of them to read reports written about first-year students who had broken Academy Rules. The Librarian, Mrs. Grundy, was assigned to supervise their research. After their reading was finished, each of the three of them had to write a thousand-word essay on the merits of observing the Rules, essays that would be published in the campus paper. Then they each had to spend a week working with the janitor, Mr. Humphries, cleaning the Potions Laboratory.

After reading the first few reports, Janice decided that she'd rather stroll through Central Park alone at midnight than roam the off-limits areas of campus. A simple mugging seemed a lot more comfortable than being turned into a nebulous specter incapable of communication (at least until the professors worked a counterspell), or having invisible skin, or being turned into a giant centipede, or dealing with any number of misplaced appendages. Janice had a headache just from thinking about what it would feel like if her face changed places with her foot. Multiplied by a hundred if she got changed into a centipede first—well, it didn't sound good. And those were mild disasters that Rule-breaking kids had survived! She hadn't even started on the *really* dreadful stuff in the archives.

She pushed aside the papers. The boys looked pale. She started to whisper, failed to make a sound, then remembered the Silence spell was in effect. She tore off a sheet of paper, scribbled a note, and slid it across the table to Matt.

This is all your fault!

He had the nerve to look like his feelings were hurt! Matt used the ruse of stretching to look for the librarian, and then, when the coast was clear, he sent a note back to her. *I wasn't*

*the one who went into that old woman's wagon! You could
have vanished without a trace. We had to do something!*

Barry shook his head and leaned down over the binder of
reports as if determined to ignore them both. It was just like
him, Janice thought. He was too afraid someone might
prove his people's suspicion that all sorcerers were bad. He
seemed desperate sometimes to prove the obvious—that he
was just a kid with some interesting powers and enough
smarts to know he needed to learn to control them before the
powers controlled him.

*We shouldn't have gone there in the first place! You
dragged us out to see the horse. I merely carried things to
their logical conclusion once we saw it,* Janice scribbled
back.

Matt rolled his eyes. *I just wanted you to see something.
You decided to feed the stupid horse, then go into that crazy
lady's wagon!*

Mrs. Grundy's Silence spell didn't seem to bother Matt
much, but then he liked dramatics. Janice ached to take this
outside where she could give him an earful!

You dragged us out there! Janice craned her neck, even
turned in her seat to be sure the librarian wasn't watching
them. She balled the paper, mouthed a spell, and blew the
dazzling ash into Matt's face. In the air, she etched glowing
symbols. *Madame Roushka is not crazy! And Meg isn't stupid!*

Matt stared at her as if she were insane and waved a dis-
pell over her sigil. On paper, he scribbled. *You're as crazy
she is, and who is 'Meg'?*

The horse, stupid!

Matt glared at her. *Well, how was I supposed to know?
Could've learned a lot if you hadn't run off!*

Barry grabbed the paper and Matt's pen, giving a smile in
the direction of the plump and graying Mrs. Grundy who,
returning from the stacks, stopped to look in on them.

"Gruesome reading, isn't it?" she said.

The three nodded. It was pointless replying in words.
Nothing they uttered would break through the Silence spell.

"The three of you should consider yourselves very lucky," Mrs. Grundy continued. She pushed her tortoiseshell eyeglasses up her nose with a long crooked forefinger. "You fell into good hands on your little adventure. That's not always the case, you know. Not all danger comes from supernatural forces, and neither is everything safe that appears safe. The reverse is true as . . ."

She looked as though some idea had occurred to her in a forceful manner. Without further word, she took a pen and notebook from her pocket. She wandered away in the general direction of her desk.

Matt took only a moment for relief, then scribbled another note. *You say we could have found out stuff if we hadn't run. Okay, what did you find out?*

Madame Roushka said Meg was a special kind of gray dun.

While Matt read, Janice wrote a note for Barry. *She said horses like that were also called "Silverhorse," just like your people. I think there may be a connection . . .*

Matt read Barry's note, too. He whistled soundlessly and wrote: *Cool!*

Janice pulled the paper back and wrote: *She called Meg a "Tick Tock Dun."*

The boys frowned. Barry jotted: *What's a Tick Tock Dun? Should we look it up?*

Matt's head bumped up and down so vigorously that he looked like a toy Chihuahua in a rear window of a car.

Maybe the library has something about the breed. Madame Roushka stopped talking when you guys showed up.

Matt looked disbelieving. *Maybe she was pulling your leg. Who ever heard of a Tick Tock Dun?*

Janice grabbed the paper. *This is the Academy, Brainiac. There's lots of stuff here we've never heard of before.*

Barry nodded and grinned.

Matt crumpled the note and threw it. It ricocheted off Janice's shoulder into the metal trash can behind her.

In magical neon, the words *He shoots! He scores!* appeared over the can. They looked at each other, amused, even if the Silence spell made it impossible to giggle. After some wild hand gestures, they established that none of them were responsible for the joke. The author of that prank was apparently another student with too much time on his hands.

Barry turned the paper over and wrote. *We're in the perfect place to find out if that old lady lied.* He pointed to the racks of books.

Anything's better than reading these, Matt agreed, pointing at the reports on the table in front of them. *I've had just about enough of students crashing and burning—usually in full Technicolor.*

Yeah, it's a wonder anybody sends their kids to SU. Professor Reynard must have some kind of deal to keep this stuff out of the papers! Janice scrawled.

Setting aside the Rule-breaking reports, they began a surreptitious search for books on magical animals. They found shelves and shelves of bestiaries, none of which mentioned anything so tame as a horse. Finally, after delving through a profusion of books with fantastically drawn manticores, phoenixes, rocs, questing beasts, sea monsters, dragons, and unicorns, Janice ran across a small volume full of familiar animals, including a slate-gray image of an ordinary-looking horse. She slapped the book in exultation, drawing the boys' attention.

After a brief struggle to position themselves so they could all see the proper page, Janice and the boys read about "The Gray Dun/Silverhorse." They found nothing about the glittering aura of magic around the animal they had all witnessed, or the magical properties of the beast, much less any reference to a "Tick Tock Dun."

Matt and Barry sat back.

Frustrated, Janice stared at the book. To have come so close and struck out! She closed the book in disgust. Then it hit her. *The book was full of nothing but familiar animals!* She sat up and dragged the book back. There was no place in *this* library, much less the Academy at large, for an ele-

mentary book on ordinary animals. Such a volume was
much too simple for even the youngest of students here.

So why was it in this library?

She stared at the title: *The Magical Nature of Earthly
Fauna.* She supposed that could mean "magical" in the same
way Walt Disney used the word when he referred to his
"Magic Kingdom," but she doubted it. She opened the book
at random.

Staring back at her was a thin, wolfish animal. The Coyote. Its eyes sparkled. Was that glitter an effect of the light?

Janice looked closer. The eyes refracted light like the
beast was alive! She thought hard. Magic was in the book!
She knew it! But how to access it?

Excitement gave her the jitters. But self-control was
everything—or so her professors insisted. She took a breath.

Aha! What was that first spell she'd been taught in Orientation class? The spell every sorcerer needed to know if he
faced a mundane or magical challenge? She would un-
doubtedly learn stronger spells in the future, but that basic
spell should work on this book, placed here where anyone in
the school might run across it.

She reached into her pocket and pulled out some lint.
Something mundane to anchor the spell was a necessary
component to cast it. She rubbed the book with the lint and
mouthed the words of the spell.

Reveal your true nature!

The Magical Nature of Earthly Fauna glimmered, like
the flash of a lightning bug. It gave off a puff of smoke.
Janice felt power surge and eddy around her hands.

She smiled. The boys paid close attention, leaning forward. Barry shifted in his chair to be sure no one was watching them.

Janice thumbed through the pages featuring horses, past
the graceful White Mare, the demonic-looking Nightmare,
and stopped at the page featuring the Gray Dun. A horse, an
oddly normal-looking horse, stared back at her.

Just as she was about to take full advantage of Mrs.
Grundy's Silence spell to let loose with language likely to

turn the air blue, she spotted the difference. The horse in the book, the Gray Dun, stared back at *her.* Upon its forehead blazed a white star that became a swirling pentagram. Just like Meg's.

Janice stroked the star thoughtfully.

To the right of the horse, new words began to appear. All three of them leaned close to read about "The Tick Tock Dun."

Born of a Gray Dun on the final day of February, in a Leap Year, is the Tick Tock Dun. Usually female because of the feminine association with monthly cycles, the Tick Tock Dun is capable of controlled travel through Time. The sorcerer who possesses such a beast must train her carefully lest the mare be lost on the first occasion of such an errant trip through time, or the owner . . .

The three stared at one another in amazement. Janice leaned closer over the book to read every detail about the time-traveling horse. Including the printed instructions on just how to make it work . . .

So engrossed were they in their research, the blinking of the library lights took them completely by surprise . . . off, on, off, for the count of ten, and then on again. It was almost closing time!

Matt spotted the librarian and closed the book. Janice shoved it to the end of the table and the three of them picked up their forgotten reports.

Mrs. Grundy stood at the end of the table. "Professor Sanchez must have put the fear of the Unknown into you three. You're the first lot who actually stayed until closing!"

"Oh, we're not the first to have to do this?" Janice said, surprised when she could hear her own voice. She stacked all of the reports they'd read into one pile.

"C'mon, guys, it's Pizza Night!" Matt announced. He grabbed his belongings and led the charge to the dining hall.

Anywhere that the faculty and full student body of Sorcerer U gathered buzzed with enough excess magical energy to cause solar flares—so the dining hall was carefully sealed, glowing with so many wards and protective sigils that ordinary light seemed redundant.

Even with the guardian spells in place, Janice paused in the doorway to get her bearings. The world tended to tip and tilt when she entered the dining hall. She breathed in the smells of pepperoni, cheese, marinara sauce, and yeasty baking bread.

Janice had mixed feelings about Pizza Night. Bountiful slices of any type of pizza made her all the more self-conscious about her weight. It was tough to watch others there chow down on triple-meat-triple-cheese heaven without a care in the world while she nibbled at the single slice of the plainest veggie thin crust she could find sitting on her own plate. She breathed in the room's aroma deeply—no calories in that.

Janice sighed. She would never convince herself that she didn't love Pizza Night. The food aside, every student's studies were set aside in favor of games, movies, and general merriment on that night.

Matt elbowed her arm. "C'mon, Barry's saved us a seat in the corner where we can talk."

"I was going to eat with—" She stood on tippy-toe, looking for friends. Cassie and Silva waved for her to join them.

"We have to decide what we're going to do."

Janice hoped he didn't mean what she thought he meant. "What are you talking about?"

"Do you want to read any more of those reports?" Matt shuddered, looking queasy.

Janice knew how he felt. She suddenly wasn't all that hungry either.

"Well?" Matt demanded.

"No, I mean, of course not, but—"

"Not here!" Matt looked this way and that, turning once more into Double-Oh-Trouble.

"You're just going to get me in more hot water, aren't you?"

Matt looked wounded. "I'm trying to get us all *out* of the doghouse."

Janice sighed and nodded in agreement. She gave a re-
luctant wave to Cassie and Silva before following Matt,
stopping long enough to grab a drink and a slice.

Barry had wrangled a table underneath the TV. It was deserted there, with most of the students opting to sit somewhere else in the huge hall where they could actually see the
screen.

Janice chose the deepest corner of the booth. Most students sat with friends and dorm mates. Dating was gently
discouraged, both because it tended to be a distraction for
the students involved and their friends and classmates as
well, and because, at a sorcerer's academy, nasty breakups
took on new shades of ugly.

"What's this great plan you've dreamed up?" Janice
asked.

Matt took a quick look around. "I say we take advantage
of having a Tick Tock Dun on the campus."

"Meaning what, exactly?" Janice asked. She felt an anxious tingle in her stomach.

"Meaning, we use the horse to travel back in time . . .
say, to last night. We write ourselves notes telling us what
not to do today in case our memory gets wiped or anything."

"So, we go and do again the exact thing that got us in
trouble the last time we did it, only more so? Just when do
you propose to pursue this brilliant idea?"

"Tonight," Barry said.

"Now," Matt added.

"Now?" Janice squeaked.

"Sure," Matt nodded. "It's Saturday night, the curfew
isn't in effect yet and everyone's having fun."

"But the faculty is watching."

"Not that closely. C'mon, we can do this! Really—it
makes the whole thing go away! All we have to do is go
back one night."

"Madame Roushka only arrived last night. We can't go
back to before when she and Meg got here, can we?" Janice
asked.

"Man, she's right," Barry said. "Have you thought this through? We could get into lots of trouble."

"Listen, guys, sometimes you just have to act and pick up the pieces afterward."

"And just how many pieces are you proposing that we end up in?" Janice retorted. "I read those reports today—it could get messy."

"C'mon, it's all of us or none of us," Matt said. He punched Barry in the shoulder. "You up for it?"

Barry hesitated, then nodded reluctantly. "If we write those editorials, man, we're dead. We'll be laughed off campus."

"That leaves you. It's two to one," Matt said to Janice. He squared his narrow shoulders and tried to look intimidating. "You in?"

"No."

"What do you mean 'no'?" Matt said. "Why not?"

"Because we don't know enough to pull this off and because Meg belongs to Madame Roushka. We have no business messing with her."

"The book said that to travel forward in time, we need to turn the horse clockwise. To go back in time we turn her counterclockwise. How dangerous could it be?"

"That's what those other kids in those reports probably said," Barry observed.

"Oh, man, not you, too!" Matt said.

"There's so much that we don't know—" Barry began.

"And, at this rate, we'll never learn!" Matt folded his arms over his chest. "Okay, if that's the way you want it to be. What movie are they showing tonight?"

"Really?" Janice asked, surprised. "You'll cave?"

"Yeah. I hope, at least, the film's something really good."

"A Jackie Chan flick," Barry said.

"Cool," Matt said. "Find us primo seats and I'll be right back."

"Where are you going?" Janice asked suspiciously.

"Geez, Janice, can't a guy visit the head?"

Janice felt like her blush went from her toes clear up through her hairline.

Then it was time for the movie to start. Everyone pulled tables out of the way and pushed the chairs around to form a theater. Professor Reynard waited for the room to quiet down before waving a remote control like a wand. The light dimmed and the feature of the evening began.

As Jackie Chan clung to a street sign, holding on against impossible odds, Barry squirmed. Janice hissed in his ear. "What's your problem?"

"Matt."

Janice closed her eyes. She felt like an idiot. She couldn't make out the time on her wristwatch, but Jackie Chan had already defied the bad guys at least four times. Matt had given them the slip!

"Let's go. Me first, and then you," Barry said.

"Why you first?"

"So I can check the bathroom. I mean, he might have been telling the truth. You saw how much of that pizza he inhaled. It could have consequences . . ."

It made sense. Janice leaned back in the plastic dining room chair. Barry rose, hitched his pants up by the belt loops and squeezed down the row. Some of the kids made a fuss. Janice figured she'd better make her exit out the other side.

When the time came, Janice inched her way down the other aisle, whispering apologies. She unexpectedly encountered Cassie and Silva.

Cassie grabbed her hand. "Coming to join us now? I was watching you over there with Matt and Barry. What's up?"

"Nothing," Janice whispered with as much emphasis as she dared. Around them, everyone laughed as Jackie Chan removed the steering wheel of the car he was handcuffed to. "Uh . . . I really gotta pee."

"Don't forget to come back, huh?" Silva said. "I want to hear all about this 'nothing.'"

Janice rolled her eyes. "Right. See you in a few!"

As she rounded the corner, Barry grabbed her. "He's gone."

"Should we tell?" Janice asked. "No. We can't tell. We'll all only be in worse trouble."

"Why would we be in worse trouble if we didn't do anything?" Barry asked. He muttered an oath. "We're gonna get it no matter what we do. Sanchez got madder about us leaving you than she did about us being in the wrong place and your being mixed up with what's-her-name."

Janice was too angry with Matt to correct Barry. "C'mon. We'd better get down to the stables before he leaves without us."

The night was cold. Janice ran, hoping that the exercise would warm her up. They took the shortcut to the stables, the straight route Matt had avoided that morning. They kept a constant watch for faculty members or older classmates and still managed to reach the stables in record time.

They reached Madame Roushka's little site just as Matt vaulted onto Meg's back. In the moonlight, the Silverhorse gleamed like treasure, and bucked like fury.

Matt hung on to Meg's mane for dear life.

"Matthew Johnson, get off that horse!" Janice ordered.

"Yeah, like how? Through the air and onto my rump?" he replied, distracted by the need to hang on for dear life.

Janice approached Meg, speaking softly, and grabbed her halter. Meg gave another halfhearted buck, then stood stock still in the center of Madame Roushka's campsite. Janice scratched her between the ears.

Matt laughed. "That was easy! Are you coming or not?" Janice and Barry climbed on behind him. Matt tapped the mare in the side, and she spun to the left—counterclockwise.

A whirlwind of magic swept over and through them. A cloud of gray swirled around them . . . above their heads and beneath their feet. A giant vacuum sucked Janice's breath away. She hung onto Meg's mane for all she was worth, fearing unimaginable horrors if she let go. The smell of magic—this time a rancid and unsettling scent—rose with the wind and filled her lungs. Something slimy and snake-like winnowed through the ooze whipping against her legs, arms, and face. Janice decided then and there that she didn't like time traveling. The next time, she would leave it to the experts!

Janice coughed. She choked.

A wall, as hard as ice, hit her and knocked her down, and put paid to her poor, mistreated stomach. If this sort of hurling were an Olympic sport, Janice would have taken the gold.

Finally it was over. Janice fell to her side and stared up into the sky, a beautiful starlit desert sky. She struggled to sit up.

Barry was beside her, on his knees. He managed to look worse than she felt.

Matt lay next to them with his face in the sand. Janice kicked his leg to see if he was alive. The world around her tilted this way and that. Matt groaned. Good. He was alive— the better to suffer with them. He'd gotten them into this. He was darned well going to be conscious enough to share the pain.

Janice became aware of Meg standing over them . . . and two pairs of human feet beside her. Adult feet. Important looking feet. She looked up. The feet led to twentieth century clothes—sort of—and then to the stern faces of Madame Roushka and Professor Sanchez. Janice kicked Matt again, harder.

"What happened?" Matt groaned. He was immediately sick.

Janice took it back. She didn't want to see him sick. No, really, she didn't. Her own stomach couldn't take it.

Madame Roushka knelt down and handed Janice a cool, damp towel. "Don't you mean 'When happened?'" she asked.

"Fine. When?" Matt said weakly. "Did we pull it off?"

"Yes, you actually managed to travel through time," Professor Sanchez said. "We've pulled the story of your last couple of days from your memories."

"So when are we?" Janice asked. She wondered if she could get away with kicking Matt again.

"It is Friday night," Madame Roushka said. "I don't believe we've met yet officially."

"Get to your feet. You'll need a night in the infirmary," Professor Sanchez said.

"But . . . but how did you know? . . . I mean, why are you here?" Matt asked.

Professor Sanchez crossed her arms.

"How did you know where . . . er . . . when to find us?" Barry asked.

"My Meg is a lovely mare. In fact, I think she has more sense than you do." Madame Roushka patted Meg's side. "She dropped you off right at my feet. I made my own inferences and called for help. Your professors here have filled me in on who you might be."

Janice managed to get to her feet, but her legs were awfully unsteady. "You gotta find a way of getting The Club or Lowjack for your horse, Madame Roushka. Though, as tempting a mount as she looks, she's no fun at all to ride."

"The same thought had occurred to me—in fact, that's my Protection spell you're suffering from," Madame Roushka said. "I doubt you'll try to ride her without my permission again, hmmm?"

"What—what happens to us now?" Matt asked.

Professor Sanchez eyed him. "Well, your friends came after you to stop your foolishness. From what you remember of tomorrow, I think there's been enough suffering to go around." When she saw Matt relaxing, she added, "That is, there's been enough suffering for *them*."

Janice almost felt sorry for Matt. He looked horrible.

"What'll happen to me?"

Professor Sanchez couldn't help but smile. "You'll find out soon enough—all in good time . . ."

A SALTY SITUATION

by Robert Sheckley

Robert Sheckley vaulted to the front ranks of science fiction writers in the 1950s with his prodigious output of short, witty stories that explored the human condition in a variety of earthly and unearthly settings. His best tales have been collected in *Untouched by Human Hands*, *Pilgrimage to Earth*, and the comprehensive *Collected Short Stories of Robert Sheckley*. His novels include the futuristic tales *The Status Civilization*, *Mindswap*, and *Immortality Delivered*, which was filmed as *Freejack*. He has also written the crime novels *Calibre .50* and *Time Limit*. Elio Petri's cult film *The Tenth Victim* is based on Sheckley's story "The Seventh Victim."

BORIS had a favorite spot he liked to go to when life became difficult for him. This was one of those times. When his afternoon class in Astral Projection was over, he walked down the Academy's main road, past the low adobe buildings with their red tile roofs that gave the place the air of a sleepy old-world Spanish colonial addition to the redstone buildings of nearby Sedona, Arizona.

He was a tall fourteen-year-old with regular, blunt features and a shock of yellow hair, inherited from his Russian parents. He walked with a teenager's slouch, his hands jammed into the pockets of his khaki trousers, scuffling his Doc Martens—a gift from Bill Froelich, his roommate at the Academy.

He wished he had Bill here to talk now. Bill, with his cool East Coast ways, always had a calming effect on Boris' excitable nature. But Bill was gone. He had left in the morning, immediately after his Pyromancy 101 class, to fly back to the Boston area for a long weekend with his parents and sisters. He had promised to bring Boris back a salamander—a genuine fire-starter. Bill's family kept several in their walled back garden. Boris was looking forward to playing with it. It would be a treat, but right now it didn't make up for his friend being gone.

His other friend, Barry Silverhorse, was on his way to his grandfather's hogan not far from Sedona. Barry would have to answer charges of sorcery—no small matter in a traditional Diné (Navajo) society. But Barry only used sorcery to fight sorcerers, and he had a letter to that effect, written by David Reynard, head of the Sorcerer's U—or rather, according to its official letterhead, the Academy for Advanced Study.

Barry would be all right. And Boris could most likely go home with Barry another time and see for himself what traditional Navajos were like. But not now, not this time. Boris was alone on a four-day weekend. And he didn't even have classes to occupy him. Not until next week.

Boris was a gregarious, outspoken boy. He didn't like being alone. He enjoyed being in a crowd.

He could go into Sedona, and look at the tourists looking at the sights. But he had done that several times during the school year, hadn't found it very amusing, and didn't want to do it again now. So now he was going to his favorite spot—a little fountain out in the desert, a fountain with water piped in from the Academy. The ground around the fountain was paved, and there was a low stone wall to one side, and a single bench chiseled out of Sonoran stone. The wind whistled overhead, lizards scuttled through the sand

and rocks, and Boris always had a sense of rare peace in that place.

Boris walked along, his backpack heavy on his back. No wonder, for it contained several of his class books, a psychic detector, a multitool pocketknife, and several other items he liked to have with him.

This visit to the fountain was going to be different, however. As he approached his destination, he saw that someone was already there, sitting on his bench. A small person with smooth black hair and a tanned oval face. As he got closer, he saw it was a girl.

If there had been any way to retreat without embarrassment, Boris would have done so. He still wasn't sure how he felt about girls. Some of them were very attractive, of course—but they were mysterious creatures, and he didn't understand how their minds worked.

No help for it. He continued walking, planning on saying hello, exchanging a few words, and returning to the Academy. Just as if he'd planned to do that from the start. Maybe he'd come back again at sundown, when the girl would likely be gone.

But now he slouched up to the fountain and nodded at the girl. She looked like one of the students at the Academy. In fact, he thought she was maybe in his Egyptian Spells course, a quiet girl with straight black hair cut in bangs across her forehead, who sat in the back of one of his classes and never said much.

"Hi," Boris said, as he sat down on the ground and leaned against the low stone wall.

"Hi," she said. "You're in my class with Professor Baxter."

"Yeah," Boris said. "I'm Boris Korzinsky. I don't get much out of that Egyptian stuff."

"It's not too practical," she said. "Most of it doesn't work these days. Greek magic is better. But you have to take the Egyptian first. I'm Yael Golan."

Boris nodded. "I'm from Jersey City."

"I'm from Ashdod," Yael said. "That's in Israel."

"I've heard of the place," Boris said. "I was born in Russia—near St. Petersburg. But I was pretty small when my parents sent me to the States."

"They sent you?"

"To live with my Uncle Vladimir in New Jersey. I won this scholarship. To here. My parents wanted it for me, but they didn't want to leave Russia."

"You were brought up by your uncle?"

"He had a wife then. Dora Mae. She was an American."

"With a name like that, I would think so," Yael said, and they both laughed.

"Anyhow, I guess we're both American now," Yael said. "And we're both stuck here for the weekend."

"Where would you go," Boris asked, "If you could go anywhere now? Israel?"

"I'd go to Paris," Yael said. "I flew to America from Paris. I loved it."

"I've heard it's nice."

She gave him a look that seemed to say that "nice" was insufficient for Paris. But she didn't try to put him down.

"Paris is something," she said after a moment. "I'm going there next holiday."

"Your folks flying you there?"

She shook her head. "My parents are dead. I was raised by the kibbutz. But they're not going to fly me to Paris. I'm going to make the money myself."

"How you going to do that? Wait tables at night in Sedona?"

She shook her head. "No way. I've got some plans."

Boris knew it was time to get moving. But he was intrigued. "Plans like what?"

Suddenly she seemed embarrassed. "Never mind."

"No, really, tell me, maybe it's something I could do, too."

She looked at him for a long moment. He was struck by how light-colored her eyes were, in contrast with her black hair and tanned skin. A pale blue. She was sort of pretty, in a quiet way. She had small features and full lips. He didn't think she was wearing any makeup.

"Well," she said, "I plan to work at what I'm good at. Magic."

"How can you do that? Doesn't the school forbid it? Who's going to hire a fourteen-year-old?"

"It's not the school's business. Any magic I do would be far out of their jurisdiction. And you're right—up to a point. Nobody around here will hire me," she said. "Maybe nobody in the States. Or on Earth. But Earth isn't the only place."

"It's not?"

"Ever hear of the counter-Earths?"

"I've heard of them, sure. We studied some of them in my Introduction to Ultimate Realities Class. But to get to them, you need Access."

She nodded. "I've got Access."

He stared at her, impressed in spite of his wish to appear otherwise. Access, also known as Spiritual Transport, was one of those ancient magical powers so unusual that they seemed mythical. If you had Access, you could, by your own will, go in bodily form to lands and places that still couldn't be located scientifically. Samuel Taylor Coleridge was believed to have had a moment of Access when he wrote "Xanadu." The knight at arms in Keats' poem "La Belle Dame Sans Merci" must have had Access. In more modern times there was Caspar Hauser and others who gave evidence of being able to go to lands beyond human ken. More prosaically, every age had a few individuals with the Accessing Ability. Yael was claiming it as her own.

"Don't stare at me so," Yael said. "I didn't do anything to get it. My guardians had me up in Ein Hof studying Cabala. I hated it. They even had me make a Golem once. I didn't like that either."

"So you've got what Charles Fort called a Special Talent," Boris said.

"I suppose so. I only know I can do it, and there's money

to be made and work to be done out there. Especially in the counter-Earths."

"Could you bring someone with you?" Boris asked.

"I don't know. I never tried."

"Well, if you could . . . Look, Yael, this Access is something big, very big. You're right, if you could go to a counter-Earth, you could really do something fabulous. If."

"What do you mean, if?"

"If you had the kind of personality that could do it."

"What makes you think I don't have one? I assure you, I want very much to work magic for a living."

"Sure you do, and so do I. And so does everybody else. But can you sell yourself? Can you find the jobs, and do what it takes to complete them, and bring the money back despite maybe people trying to stop you?"

"I can find jobs," Yael said. "I've already found one."

"And have you taken it?"

"Not yet. I want to be sure it's okay. I'm still . . . thinking about it."

"How long have you been doing that?"

She looked away from him. "About six months."

"Six months!" said Boris. "Jeez, what have you been thinking about?"

"Well," she said, "the pay is very good, but I'm not sure about this job. There's something weird about it . . ." Her voice trailed off. "I'd never want to do anything bad with my magic . . ."

Boris said, "Are you not sure you can handle it?"

She made a very slight nod.

"Why don't you tell me about it? Where did you hear about it?"

"I saw it on the Alternative Bulletin board."

"What's that?" Boris asked.

"A bulletin board from the counter-Earths for jobs involving Magic. I copied it out." She opened her small purse and took out a piece of paper. She read, "'The Salt Machine on Earth 341-01 is in disrepair. Evil Magical interference suspected. Very good pay for the man or woman who can fix it.' It was signed, Lengues, counselor in charge of salt production."

"That sounds straightforward enough," Boris said. "What makes you think it's weird? Or wrong? It's just a machine. A mechanic should be able to fix that."

"But not if there's evil magical interference," Yael said. "And I'm not much good with machinery."

"But magic is what we do," Boris said. "Come on, Yael, take me there with you. I'm good at this stuff. And I make a great front man. Anything magical they come up with, we can handle."

"But we're only in our first year here at the Academy."

"A lot of the stuff coming up in the next years is just detail work on what we've already learned. We've learned the basis of magic already. What do you say? I'm bored, and I could use a gig!"

"I suppose we could have a go at it," Yael said doubtfully.

"Great!" Boris said. "Let's go there and check it out."

"You mean now?"

"Yes. Right now. We've got this whole weekend ahead of us. Let's go right now."

Yael sat silently for a long time, with her chin resting in the palm of one hand. Boris could imagine what was going on in her mind. He figured she was a pretty shy girl in spite of her magical talent. She had lived for a long time without parents. Somehow she hadn't picked up a lot of confidence.

Suddenly she made up her mind. She stood up and reached out her hand. Boris stood up and clasped it. Her eyes rolled back in her head. Boris wondered if she was fainting. But it wasn't like that at all. He felt an indescribable movement in her hand. It seemed to be vibrating. And as he looked around, the colors of the desert were changing. They were shifting toward purple. He blinked, and they went to black. He blinked again, and there was light. And now they were somewhere else.

*   *   *

They were standing in a stone courtyard. A sign on one of its walls read, "Area for Access Travelers." Ahead of them was a wooden door.

"How'd you find this place?" Boris asked.

"This is where Access brought me. But I never stayed before."

"We'll stay this time," Boris said, with more confidence than he felt. "This time we'll learn the problem and solve it and get paid. Then you can go to Paris."

"And where will you go?" Yael asked.

"I haven't decided yet. Here comes someone."

The door at the end of the courtyard opened. A tall man wearing a crimson cloak came out. The cloak was lined with blue fur. The man was middle-aged, had a long nose, and a supercilious air. His movements were languid.

"I suppose you've come about the salt machine?" he inquired. "I am Lengues, Counselor for Salt in His Majesty's Realm."

"That's right," Boris said. "What's the matter with the salt machine?"

"It will no longer produce salt."

"May we see it?"

"I suppose so," Lengues said. "It's my duty to show it to any parties likely to effect repairs. Especially magical repairs. But frankly, you two don't look likely to me. You're very young, for one thing."

"Where we come from," Boris said, "the young do all the inventive work."

"I might not like where you come from," Lengues said. "Come this way."

He led them through the gate and into a very large building of wood and stone. They went down a corridor to another door. Lengues opened it and gestured. "There it is."

In front of them was an open framework machine some twelve feet square, composed of flywheels and pistons of bronze, with connections of leather tubing, and bright wire attached to armatures of quartz. A small, bald old man sat on a bench beside the machine. He had been dozing, but he woke up and got to his feet when they came in.

"Good afternoon, Schmuel," Lengues said.

"Good afternoon, my lord."

"Crank up the salt machine. Show these people how it works."

Schmuel turned a crank set in the machine's side. As he turned it, Boris and Yael could hear a melody being sung in a thin, ghostly voice.

"What's that?" Yael asked.

Lengues said, "It's the song of the machine. Much nicer than the sound of metal rubbing against metal, don't you think? Over here is the output stage." He led them around to the back of the machine. There was a wide-mouthed chute. From it trickled a grayish-green substance.

"What is that?" Boris asked.

"We've had it analyzed," Lengues said. "You may stop now, Schmuel. It is water."

"Unsalted?"

"Of course, unsalted. Young man, this machine, when it is working properly, produces an unending stream of salt, enough to supply the whole kingdom. Lack of it has put the place into a panic."

"Why don't you use some other source?" Yael asked.

"There is no other source. Nowhere on the planet is salt found in large quantities. It simply does not occur here. It is one of the anomalies of this counter-Earth 341-01. We have almost everything you have on your real Earth, except for naturally occurring salt."

"We have a lack of mist, too," Schmuel put in. "Plenty of fog, but no mist."

"That's enough, Schmuel. We don't want them to learn all our secrets."

Boris opened his backpack and took out the psychic tester. He pointed it at the machine and took a reading. Nothing. Of course, it didn't have the range of a professional machine. But there had to be a problem in there somewhere. The machine's open framework made it possible for Boris to slip between flywheels and piston rods, and penetrate to the heart of the machine. The dial on the tester twitched. He ran it along one of the supporting girders. The machine twitched again.

"Yael," he called out, "tell me what you make of this."

Yael squeezed in beside him. She read the dial of the tester, took it out of Boris' hands, and poked it deeper into the machine. The dial turned madly.

"It's that blue part," she said.

"Are you sure?"

"Of course I'm sure. Let's take it out."

With her slighter build, Yael was able to reach the blue part, undo the bronze screws that held it in place, and lift it out. It was about the size of an orange.

With the part isolated, Boris was able to take several different readings. He found unmistakable magical interference of the darkest sort.

"Yael," he said, "can you pick up a directional reading?"

She nodded. "It's not far away."

Boris straightened up and turned to the part. He turned it over in his hands, studying it. It seemed amazing to him that a machine with such tiny orifices could put out a quantity of anything. Studying it closely, he could see the tiny crossed lines on the inside that were evidence of magical interference.

"Come on," he said, "let's get out of this machine."

Outside, in front of the machine, Boris said to Yael, "Listen, we can do this. Let's make our deal with Lengues now. Cash on the barrelhead, or its equivalent in goods we can sell on Earth."

Yael looked uncertain, but finally nodded. Boris walked up to Lengues, who was sitting at a little table eating what looked like a sherbet.

"We can do this," Boris said. "But we want to get paid first."

"Payment after completion."

"No, payment first," Boris said. "We may have to buy

supplies, even replace this part. Come on, payment in advance is the usual way."

"Well," Lengues grumbled, "I suppose I can pay half in advance, half on completion. You've got to have an incentive to get the job done, though. You must put up a forfeit."

"What forfeit? And what sort of an advance are we talking about?"

"About the advance . . ." Lengues reached into an inner pocket in his cloak and withdrew a small velvet sack. He opened it and poured out half a dozen blue-white diamonds into Boris' hand.

"I believe these are valuable where you come from," Lengues remarked. "We have more of them here than we know what to do with."

Boris looked at Yael. She walked over, taking a loupe out of her purse. "I learned to appraise diamonds in the kibbutz," she said. She examined the diamonds. "These are very good," she said after a while.

"Okay," said Boris. "We'll do it."

"But about that forfeit . . ." Lengues said.

"What would you suggest?"

"We will need your partner's detention here against the success of the mission. She has Access. We remove that Access until the job is complete, or my advance returned."

"Hey, wait a minute!" Yael said.

"It's just a formality," Boris explained. "We've practically got this thing licked already. If worse comes to worst, we can return the diamonds. But I think we can do it! We'll be finished in no time—and you can go to Paris for the next school break!"

They agreed to the forfeit, Yael reluctantly. Lengues attached a thin, intricately woven metal bracelet around Yael's wrist. The bracelet couldn't be taken off. It would prevent her from using her Accessing ability until Lengues removed it.

"I don't like this," she whispered to Boris.

"Not to worry. We've as good as got this thing licked. Let me use your loupe."

Screwing the loupe into his eye, Boris turned the part in his hand, looking for any signs of anomaly. On one flange he found tiny engraved writing. It read, "This is a genuine part made by Alistair of the Castle. No substitutes are permitted. Attempts to insert a substitute will result in destruction of the machine and death to the perpetrator." It was signed, Alistair of the Castle, Wizard First class and Maker of Magical Objects.

"That's just great," Yael said, when Boris explained this. "What do we do now?"

"I guess we'd better not try any substitutes. We'll go to where this Alistair is, find the talisman he's using to hex the salt, and counteract the magic."

"He's a full wizard," Yael pointed out.

"Sure, but a counter-Earth wizard. That probably doesn't amount to much. And we probably know a lot of magics he doesn't. Anyhow, we'll be in and out before he knows what's going on."

"How do you know that? I have doubts about this whole thing," Yael said.

"Oh, come on," Boris said. "We're here, so let's do this and get out with the loot."

So they went to Alistair's castle. They couldn't proceed there by magic—no magical transportation was allowed in counter-Earth 341-01. Lengues provided them with a bullock and a cart, and a map. It wasn't far, he said. But even a short distance is long when you go at the slow, lumbering speed of a bullock. They both fumed at the delay, and finally Boris tried a magical speed enhancement called Presto on the bullock. This didn't do much—magical speed enhancements were over-rated, especially when used on a bullock— but it did let them proceed at the speed of a trotting horse.

It was early evening when they got through the surrounding hills and approached Alistair's castle. It was a classically spooky building, silhouetted starkly against the evening sky, with walls and battlements and belfries. The building rose to a single small room on top of the pyramidal structure. They tied the bullock to a tree, hidden from the view of the castle.

"I'll bet that room is where he keeps the talisman," Boris said. "We'll have to go through the whole palace to get to it."

"It's growing dark," Yael said.

"Is that my fault?" Boris asked.

"It's just that dark magic is always more potent at night. And I'm pretty sure that Alistair likes dark magic."

"Let's hurry, then. We still have at least an hour of daylight."

After crossing the bridge over the moat, they found a small door to one side of the massive wood-and-iron main doors, which were guarded by a dropped portcullis. The side door was unlocked.

"This is probably the one he uses when he has to go shopping," Boris said. "Saves having to haul up that heavy portcullis." He opened it and they walked inside.

The corridor they found themselves in was long and twisty, and lit at intervals by tall torches.

"If he's away, why did he leave the torches on?" Yael asked.

"Probably likes to have a light on when he comes home," Boris said. He was growing a little tired of Yael's dour commentaries.

They walked down corridors paved with flagstone, and then up long flights of stairs, guided by the psychic tester. On the second floor there were bats. On the third floor there were small flying dragons with red-and-green iridescent scales, who attacked them, singly at first, then in droves. Yael had a charm against magical and mythological creatures, and they both huddled behind its field. For a while, it looked as if the dragons might overwhelm it. Finally, Boris found an old sword in the hand of one of the mailed statues that lined the staircases, and he swatted the things away until they reached the third floor. Here the dragons abandoned their attack.

Now there was an eerie silence. The torches were spaced farther apart, and they walked in darkness much of the time. They turned a corner and faced another staircase. But before Boris could put a foot on it, Yael pushed him violently out of the way.

"Hey! What's the big idea! This is no time for games . . ."

Boris fell silent as he saw that Yael had pushed him out of the way of a thin winged dagger, which had buried itself into the wainscoting not far from his head.

"Thanks!"

The dagger was twitching, trying to pull itself out of the wood. It succeeded, looped in the air and came at Boris again. Boris made a gesture he had recently learned in Magical Gestures Workshop at the Academy, and the dagger fell to the floor.

Boris picked it up. "We might be able to use this," he said, and handed the dagger to Yael. She slipped it into her purse.

The fourth floor was the final one. Here they encountered a disconcerting silence, and a sense that hidden eyes were watching them.

The psychic tester pointed them toward a ladder that led directly to the final room. Boris mounted, followed by Yael. The darkness became more intense. It was a comfort to feel Yael's hand on his shoulder as he climbed.

By touch, Boris knew when he was in the room. He left the ladder and cautiously took a few steps. He felt Yael's hand tighten on his shoulder. He was amazed at how strong this thin little girl was. Her grip soon became crushing. Boris could feel his shoulder bones nearly being wrenched out of their sockets.

"Hey, easy," he said.

"What are you talking about?" Yael asked. Her voice came from across the room.

The hand shifted its grip. It was around his throat. It was squeezing, hard. Boris grabbed the hand and found it terminated at the wrist. It was just a hand, nothing more, but it was squeezing the life out of him. He sank to the floor, still trying to pull the hand away. But the pressure was relentless, and still growing. Boris felt himself blanking out, sinking to the floor.

Then, suddenly, the pressure stopped. The hand released its grip and curled in on itself. It took Boris a moment to realize what had happened. Yael had taken out the dagger and stabbed the hand with surprising strength. The point had penetrated the hand at its back, and bitten in deep.

Now she took a small object out of her purse. It burst into a lurid yellow-white light, releasing a cloud of protective incense. By its powerful glow, Boris could see the hand trying to twist itself inside out to grasp the dagger with its fingers, and finally expiring, collapsing like a speared spider.

"Where did you get that?" Boris asked. "And what is it?"

"A Fairy Light. Magical Science Class experiment. Dark magics can't stand it. Didn't you make one?"

"I made a Voice Thrower," Boris said. "Come on, let's find that talisman."

By the glow of the light, they saw a tall dais in the room, and on that dais, under a glass cover, was a sheet of tarnished lead with indescribable writing cut into it.

"That's got to be it!" Boris cried.

Boris looked around. Only Yael there. Feeling vaguely guilty—he had been brought up not to destroy things—he swung the heavy plastic base of the psychic tester at the case. The glass shattered. Boris took off his jacket, wrapped it around his hand, reached in and took out the talisman.

"We got it," he said to Yael. "Now let's get out of here."

They left the room in a state of extreme trepidation. Boris was convinced they had gotten away with the talisman too easily. Where was the wizard Alistair? Was it possible he didn't know what was going on here? Or did he know, and was holding back his attack, biding his time—until when?

But no attack came. The dagger room had no point. Below that, the dragons that had infested the corridors must have been out to lunch, because there was no sign of them. All the corridors were suspiciously still and devoid of any danger, or indeed, movement of any sort except their own.

And so they came out of the castle by the same door they had entered, crossed back over the moat, and returned to where they had tied the bullock. Mounting, they rode—at a leisurely pace, even with the aid of Presto—back to the courtyard where they had begun.

Lengues was there waiting for them, making an effort to suppress his impatience to know the results of their expedition.

"So what happened?" he asked.

"We brought back the talisman that controls the salt machine. This is it. And when we cancel it out, we can fix the machine."

"And what about Alistair?"

Boris gave an exaggerated shrug. Lengues raised both eyebrows, but asked no further questions.

"Let's do what is necessary now," Lengues said. "The people need salt."

They proceeded to the room where the salt machine was located.

Boris and Yael both walked up to the machine. Boris reached in with the talisman in his hand. It wasn't difficult for him to mold the soft lead to the salt machine unit.

He looked at Yael. She leaned in, too, and they both chanted Words of Power they had learned in class, but in very low voices because they didn't want Lengues to pick them up.

The salt machine began to hum and shake. A thin trickle of a white substance began to come out of one of the nozzles.

Lengues tasted it. "Salt!"

"We're okay, then," Boris said. "Release us and pay us off."

"Just a moment," Lengues said. "Something funny is

going on with the machine. Schmuel, are you turning the handle?"

"Not me, boss," Schmuel said.

Boris saw that the thin trickle of salt had been replaced by a steady stream of salt, and then by gouts and geysers of salt, blowing out of every hole, orifice and injection device the machine had, as well as blowing salt out of its exhaust pipes. The salt was piling up on the floor. Soon a mound of it threatened to drown the salt machine itself. But Lengues called for workers with shovels, and they arrived promptly and managed to keep down the rising salt tide.

Suddenly there was an explosion from within the machine, and the metal talisman came shooting out. It hung in the air, turned and stretched, grew thinner and longer and wider, and finally took the shape of a man.

"The Wizard Alistair!" Lengues cried. "But I thought you said it was a talisman."

"Great ones like me," the Wizard Alistair said, "act as their own talisman. Lengues, you aren't playing according to the rules. You're supposed to pay me off when I cause trouble, not send in the midgets! You'll regret this!"

Lengues cried, "I had no idea these young people were going to make unauthorized use . . ."

"I'll deal with you later," the wizard said. "It's that fiendish little boy I want. You there!" and he pointed at Boris.

Boris cowered back, and Yael cowered with him. The Wizard Alistair was a huge and imposing sight, and frightening in his anger. He launched himself at Boris. Yael crumpled to the floor. Boris found the Wizard's long, wiry fingers around his neck, tightening. He reacted instinctively, with a head butt. Caught by surprise, Alistair fell backward. Yael threw her purse at the wizard. Something in it burned the wizard, but he soon put out the fire.

Now Boris was getting angry, and losing his usual deference toward adults. Especially adults who seemed to be up to no good. What right did this wizard, on a whim and for a payoff, have to stop the salt production this world depended on? And what right did he have to get angry once his silly ban on the salt machine had been violated?

Boris summoned up Words of Power he had learned at the beginning of the term and spat them at the wizard. The hands loosened for a moment, then tightened again as the wizard threw off the Words of Power with his own spells.

Boris writhed and squirmed. He could feel the life being choked out of him. He was dimly aware of Yael there. She was sitting in a kneeling position. Her eyes were closed. Her lips were moving . . .

And a mound of dust on the floor began to lift and turn. It became a miniature tornado, attracting other bits of dust to itself, and then scraps of paper, pieces of wood, loose coins, a flying bird . . . And it grew into a man, a large awkward looking man with a face of clay and hands like splintery sticks. The creature heaved itself to its feet and began to lurch toward Alistair.

"What is that?" Alistair cried.

"It is a Golem!" Boris shouted. "A genuine Jewish earth-born Golem, and its coming after you!"

Alistair turned toward the Golem just as the creature crashed into him. Spells like electric fire, flung by Alistair, rippled down the Golem's gray skin and brown clothing, and dissipated harmlessly. Boris added his remaining cubic centimeters of power to the attack, and the wizard turned, began to move away, dwindling into a thin stream of smoke, then disappearing.

When Boris recovered his senses, he said to Lengues, "We'd like our release and our pay, please."

"At once!" said Lengues. He seemed to be considerably shaken by the incident.

"And we'll leave the Golem here, in case that wizard comes back," Yael told him. "It should prevent further trouble."

Less than an hour later, Boris and Yael were back at the Academy.

It had been late afternoon when they left, but from the direction of the sun, Boris could tell it was just past dawn now. A few students were strolling to early morning classes. He asked a passing student, "Excuse me, what day is it?"

"Monday."

"You're kidding!"

"Nah. Why kid about something so stupid?" The student walked off.

"If it's Monday, I've got to run," Boris said to Yael. "I've got class with Professor Reynard this morning. Meet me at the cafeteria at noon, okay? I have something I want to talk to you about."

"What is it?" Yael asked.

"I want to talk to you about us going out together on other jobs. We make a great team. I think we did some good back there in that place. Maybe we could do more good. Not to mention the possible rewards! You'll have a great time in Paris. Maybe I could go with you. What do you think?"

"We'll talk about it over lunch," Yael said. She smiled and ran off toward her dorm.

Boris proceeded to class. He was thinking this was the first he could remember seeing Yael smile.

FIELD TRIP

by Jody Lynn Nye

Jody Lynn Nye lists her main career activity as "spoiling cats." She lives northwest of Chicago with two of the above and her husband, author and packager Bill Fawcett. She has written twenty-two books, including four contemporary fantasies, three SF novels, four novels in collaboration with Anne McCaffrey, including *The Ship Who Won*, a humorous anthology about mothers, *Don't Forget Your Spacesuit, Dear!*, and over sixty short stories. Her latest books are *The Grand Tour*, third in her new fantasy epic series, *The Dreamland*, and *Applied Mythology*, an omnibus of the *Mythology 101* series.

WHAT do you mean, you do not have your permission slip, Benjamin ben-Adan?" Professor Nagata demanded. The tanned teenager before her looked as though he wanted to dig the toe of his shoe into the rough planks in the deck of the wooden sailing ship, but Matt and Barry knew that the Israeli student would rather be torn apart by demons than show shame. The Oriental Sorcery teacher, elegant as always in close-fitting black with a loose jacket of scarlet silk tied at her waist, returned his expressionless gaze.

"I'm sorry, Professor," Ben said, his back straight as an arrow. "I forgot it." His twin sister Shoshanna lounged by the ship's wheelhouse with her friends, giggling at her brother's discomfiture. She never forgot anything. The two made faces at one another, and Barry was impressed once again by how much the siblings looked alike, with their sharp profiles, high cheekbones, and distinctive noses, except that Ben was built on sturdy lines, whereas Shoshanna had a great figure with a small waist.

"As for you, Ms bat-Adan," Nagata said, raising her voice, "I've told you and your friends again and again to wear ordinary clothes in public. What if another ship comes within eyesight? Why are you overstressing the protective spells around us?"

"Sorry, Professor!" The three girls quickly shed the robes covered with neon-color constellations. "They were just for fun." Nagata nodded at them sharply, then turned back to Ben.

"Well. Now, about that slip . . ."

"Abba and Emah aren't home, Professor. They're at a conference in Kansas."

"Really." Nagata reached into her sleeve. Barry watched carefully. The Canadian teacher was always surprising him with what those silk sleeves held. The long, slim hand emerged holding a white bird. A carrier pigeon! Barry gawked. The girls giggled. Popping the capsule off the bird's leg, Nagata scribbled a quick note. She threw the bird into the air and watched as it vanished with a flash of light.

Within moments, another bird appeared from the clear blue sky, this one with black-barred feathers. It alighted on Nagata's wrist. She unfolded two papers from the capsule. Barry recognized one as the missing permission letter. The ink on the parents' signatures was still shiny and wet. The other paper must have been personal; Nagata handed it to Ben, who read it and turned scarlet. Quickly he shoved the note into his pocket and glared defiance at everyone who was staring. His parents were frustrated with his poor memory, but they loved him.

All the first-year students from the Academy were on a daylong expedition by ship that had left directly from Sedona. Barry still couldn't believe he was standing on deck in the middle of the ocean. About breakfast time someone had noticed a pole sticking up out of the ornamental pool in the garden in the very midst of the Academy buildings. Within minutes a ship rose up higher than a house, water dripping from its shining white sails and rope rigging. Even Matt, who said he knew something about ships, couldn't figure out how old it was. Its wooden sides were varnished and painted in blue, scarlet, and gold like a Spanish galleon, but at the top of the wheelhouse was a very modern-looking radar antenna. The moment the students had filed on board, the ship sank back into the pool. Some of the students still hadn't recovered from seeing the water closing over their heads.

Within a couple of minutes they'd emerged from the depths in the shelter of an island, surprising gulls and terns as they surfaced. Someone had said it was San Clemente Island, which meant they were out in the Pacific Ocean. They'd gone hundreds of miles in the blink of an eye. Barry knew from the tales the Diné told around the campfires that there were underground passages and waterways used only by spirits and shamans. In a way he felt there was something wrong that they were using a sacred path to go on a *field trip*. Professor Nagata had looked at him very sternly and pointed out that learning was sacred, and the spirits understood that students needed to be educated to treat the ancient ways with respect. He had to let it go at that, but he was nervous. What if there were other things traveling the old ways behind them? The girls who put on store-bought sorcerers' robes he thought were both silly and irresponsible, mocking the ancients.

Barry was one of the few who were not insanely delighted by the recent rash of magic-themed motion pictures. Too many ignorant people would see them, then try to trifle with what they did not understand. The others, especially Janice, told him he was crazy. He ought to be glad that magic was getting good P.R. for once. What if the day came when the *brujos* at the Academy had to come forward to save the world? Surely he didn't want the magicless hordes throwing rocks at them, or worse? It was a shame, because he loved movies, and the special effects were great.

Three of the instructors were accompanying them on the outing: Nagata, Ruta Diamondbrow, the Ojibwa botany professor, and Professor Edwards.

Of the last, Barry could only see a pair of pants and the heels of expensive boots. Edwards was hanging over the side of the ship, the victim of a queasy stomach.

"I thought that legend stuff about wizards not being able to cross water was all crap," Matt said, tilting his head toward the ailing Professor of Comparative Enchantments.

"He's not the only one who's sick," Barry said, glancing behind him. He felt great sympathy for the older man. He had a pocket full of ginger tablets and one in his mouth. He hoped the supply would last until he got home. He was a desert boy, by nature and nurture. Being completely surrounded by water freaked him out. Once the coast had disappeared behind him, leaving only clear blue sky and green-black water, he started to feel disoriented. He even lost track of time, but constantly looking down at his watch was adding to his case of *mal de mer*. "Janice, you all right?"

"No," Janice moaned. She straightened up from leaning over the opposite side of the boat. "I'm sick. I wish I'd never gotten on this stupid boat in the first place." Barry offered her a ginger tablet. She popped it in her mouth with a defiant expression.

"And miss out on a genuine magical adventure?" Matt asked, with a twinkle in his eye.

"It's all right for you. I bet your family has a big fancy boat."

"My uncle's got one," Matt admitted. "He takes us out on it all summer. But I'd go anyway. It just sounded interesting to me."

"I'm with you," Barry said. "Ms. Diamondbrow says

there's a lot of magical plants for us to study. She wants to get cuttings for the Experimental Lab."

"How's she expect to get *plants?*" Matt asked. "That'd mean someone'll have to get right down into the water."

"What's the idea anyhow?" Janice asked. "Nagata was pretty mysterious about this trip, like she didn't want us to know too much in advance."

"I want you to use your own powers of observation," the Oriental Sorcery professor said, unexpectedly overhearing them as the wind caught their words and threw them to her. "This is a test. Many of you feel like fish out of water—how appropriate a metaphor that is—but that is good. It means you'll be watching all the time, and not rely upon what I told you. You miss so much that way. *Trust.*"

"How far are we going?" asked Amanda Warren. Barry grinned. He had a soft spot for the thin, intense girl who was as unselfconscious as a child of six. She always wanted to *know.* Her burning curiosity went well with her natural talent, which was clairvoyance.

"Why not find out for us? Use your scrying mirror," Nagata advised her. At once, Amanda rooted in the huge backpack she always carried with her. The girl must have every divining tool known to mankind, from a deck of Italian cards to a Magic 8-Ball.

"I don't like this," Janice said. "Not telling us anything is more than treating us like babies. It's dangerous."

Barry shook his head. "They're doing everything they can to protect us. I can feel the wards around the ship. Can't you?"

"Gift wrap," Janice said shortly. "If I wanted the world to know I was carrying around a bunch of baby sorcerers, I'd put the biggest, nastiest guard spells on them that you ever saw. We're wearing neon lights for anyone to see who can. Haven't the teachers been telling us for weeks that we've got to be careful now that our powers are starting to wake up? This is when the evil powers can kidnap us, before we've had enough training to protect ourselves. This is when we're useful pawns. I don't like being vulnerable."

"It's a test, like Nagata said," Matt said.

"It's a setup," Janice said.

"Who's setting us up?" Matt asked. "Nagata?"

Janice looked mulish. "Maybe. She makes me nervous. She just doesn't look like a teacher. Even a magic teacher."

The Texan shook his head and put on his thickest accent. "Y'all are loonier than a Canadian dollah, girl. Y'all're just jealous 'cause she dresses bettah than yew."

"What?" Janice asked. She looked at Barry. "What did that mean?"

"He said, you're entitled to your point of view," Barry said, eager to make peace, bowling over Matt's protest that that wasn't what he'd said. "Look. Shoshanna's brought her little snake."

"It's not a snake," the Israeli girl corrected him sharply, letting the slip of quicksilver-green flash back and forth between her palms. Shoshanna had incredible talent with living creatures. The teachers said she had all the marks of a natural shaman. She put it back in its miniature aquarium and held it up for the others to see. "It's a sea serpent. I found it in the sea off Eilat."

Matt leaned close. "Looks like a garter snake. We've got thousands of 'em where I live."

Shoshanna ignored him. "I think it's about five months old. The ancient texts say it will grow to be over two hundred man-lengths long."

Janice lifted her eyebrow. "Twelve hundred feet? That little thing?"

"Baby pandas are less than an inch long," Shoshanna pointed out. "He's grown almost three inches since I found him. He calls himself 'Wave-cleaver.' I call him Sid."

"Are you planning to let him go?" inquired Professor Edwards, who'd finally levered himself off the rail. Probably nothing left to throw up, Barry thought sympathetically. His slightly slanted eyes narrowed as he peered at the little creature. "This is not the ocean of his birth."

"Oh, no, sir!" Shoshanna clasped the little glass case to her chest. "I was just going to let him swim alongside the ship. He hasn't been in open water since I got to the Academy. He misses it. He promises to come back."

The teachers exchanged glances. Barry wondered once again what it was they were sailing into. "Very well," Edwards said. "I'll assist him down to the water, if you would like. A simple spell, but it will prevent him from being swept under our hull."

"Thank you," Shoshanna said. But she watched nervously as the slender professor wove a pattern between his hands. Though he'd been at the Academy for some time, it still thrilled and frightened Barry that he could feel the power rising around him. A spell was a process, not a thing—that had been hammered into him from day one. Though he'd been told also that magic was neither good nor evil, it pulled at his consciousness, trying to drive him to do more. He feared that urge might one day force him to do something evil just to make use of his power. It could corrupt a weak mind. That was why his people believed sorcerers to be evil: they had to be strong just to keep the power from running their lives. So many must have failed.

Edwards had incredible control; that Barry could not deny. A net made of nearly invisible filaments of light surrounded the baby sea serpent. suddenly, the tiny creature lifted straight out of the tank in an arc that led over the side. The students all ran to watch it being lowered down the steep sides of the ship into the waves. Edwards wore a faint grin on his face. Shoshanna gasped as the net vanished. For a moment the teens couldn't see the serpent, but then Ben let out a shout and pointed. Sid was following them on the crest of the ship's wake, a quicksilver slice arrowing along on the black-glass waves.

Deep below the surface they could see shadowy shapes looming up to flank Sid.

"Are those whales?" Matt asked, pointing. "Think they'll surface?"

"Not whales, son," Edwards said, with a lifted eyebrow. "Most likely adult serpents. Hope that they do not surface. A full-grown serpent can wrap its coils around the ship and crush it to matchwood before we could explain to it who we are."

Ben peered forward at the horizon. "It's so empty here. Nothing but water."

"Not yet," Mr. Edwards said. "There's still a great deal of air out there."

Almost as soon as he spoke a drizzle began to fall. Barry looked up at the sky. Huge clouds had rolled silently above them, covering half the sky. Most of the students ran for the wheelhouse stairs.

"Where are you going?" Matt shouted. "It's just a little rain!"

Thunder drowned him out as the rain started to fall harder. The deck began to roll under their feet. Barry grabbed his arm. "We had better get under cover!"

The girls in the stairwell shrieked as he tried to pass them.

"The inside is full!" said Ilora Banwe, a tall girl from Mali. "The boys won't let us down there to the bottom floor."

"That's belowdeck," Janice corrected them, trying to insinuate herself between them. "Come on, push in a little. We're getting soaked!"

"No!" the girls cried.

"Don't make me use a Shrink spell on you," Janice threatened them. "You know how it got out of hand the last time."

"Don't you dare think of using magic on us," Ilora said, her eyes flashing. "I'll curse you back to your ancestors!"

"I'm getting wet!"

"So what? It won't kill you!"

"Stop it," Barry said, pulling his friends away and looking for a sheltered spot on deck. "What if the teachers hear you?"

"They're not listening," Janice said, yanking her arm free. "Look at Nagata. She's *dancing* in the rain."

So it seemed to be. The Oriental Sorcery professor had her arms outstretched and her head thrown back. Her short hair and red jacket were plastered against her, and her eyes were closed, but she swayed back and forth and twirled in little circles.

"What's she doing?" Matt demanded. Janice growled, her curly hair matted into an unlovely mass like a Brillo pad.

"I don't care. I just want to get in out of the rain. Salt water's horrible for my hair. I'll have to condition it to death to get it to lie down again."

"Over here!" called Ben's voice. Barry looked around. An arm snaked out from beneath the white canvas covering a lifeboat and beckoned. The edge of the cloth lifted. The three friends crept inside. The sheeting formed a cozy little tent, though the daunting presence of the lifeboat loomed above them.

"It's out of the rain," Shoshanna explained, making room for the three newcomers. "We noticed it when we came aboard. When you live where we do, you scope out a safe place wherever you go. I just hope Sid is all right."

"Probably having the time of his life," Matt said reassuringly. "You don't get many waves in a tank. I bet he's slaloming down those breakers like a rollerblader."

"Hang on," Ben said, clinging to a rope as the ship leaped like a horse taking a fence. Janice closed her eyes, her skin as green as the sea. "My God, where are we going? What's the matter with you?"

Barry didn't answer for a moment. His body felt like a banana being peeled, but the sensation went deeper than his skin. He was stripped naked to the world—but not the visible world.

"The wards are gone," he said. "Can you feel it? They've dropped the wards."

"Why?" Janice asked, her eyes wide with alarm, her seasickness forgotten. "Why would they do that?"

"Come out!" Nagata's voice demanded over the howl of the storm. "Come out now! This is your lesson. Are you afraid? Are you cowards?"

Barry saw the challenge light fire in the eyes of his companions and knew it burned in his, too. He had never felt so vulnerable, far away from terra firma or any landmarks at all, but if Nagata said this was a test of some kind, he was going to prove he was equal to it. "Come on," he said, crawling toward the canvas flap. "We'll be the first out on deck."

The sky above them was black, but an eerie light illumined the ship. Edwards no longer looked ill. Instead he seemed to be listening for something in the distance. The sails had been loosened. They were wrapped by the wind against the masts. The very sea drove the ship onward. Diamondbrow held on to the tiller, her strong hands holding it steady though the ship leaped and bounded.

"We must be open to the experience!" Nagata announced. She looked like a spirit, the bones of her face stark in the pale green light, her arms thrown wide.

Suddenly, Ben pointed out at the waves. "Look! The horizon is *rising!*"

"That's impossible," Matt argued.

"You're crazy," Janice said. "The ship is sinking. We're all going to die. Start bailing out one of these boats." She grabbed the fire bucket off a hook and started scooping water out of the boat under which they had been sheltering.

But the sky continued to shrink from a hemisphere to a steadily decreasing disk over their heads. Water poured up around the hull. The students who had refused to come above deck into the storm were forced up out of the hold by the rising waves. A few were screaming. Others were crying.

"This is a spell I know to keep from drowning," Ben shouted. "Take a handful of water and pour it into your other palm, saying . . ."

"Do nothing!" Edwards bellowed, roused suddenly from his listening posture. "Trust us! Show respect, and all will be well!"

The ship was in a goldfish bowl of dark seawater now. The students clung to whatever they could to keep from being swept off their feet as waves washed the deck. Barry sprang to the top of the wheelhouse and pulled Janice up, while Matt boosted the ben-Adan twins from below. Janice was spitting seawater as tears ran down her face.

A huge roar shook the boat. Barry looked away from the people he was helping, up into the largest face he had ever seen.

Out of the very walls of the whirlpool, out of the deep green water of the ocean, a being had manifested itself. Waterspouts formed its arms and legs. A swashing expanse of water formed its body. Its head tilted over the ship. Waves curled and crested around the top and rear like wild, white hair. Barry was taken by surprise. The being had *features*. He could see eyes, a nose, a mouth, even ears.

"Behold!" Nagata cried, throwing her hands toward the creature. "The element of water!"

Its clear, blue-green eyes, round as marbles, stared down at them, and eyebrows made of foam lowered. It picked up the ship in one great hand like a titanic scallop shell. The ship began to spin like a top.

"Its palms are whirlpools," Ben said, his face gray under its tan. The great face went by again and again. To their alarm, the mouth opened wide and drew closer and closer. "It's going to swallow us!"

"It's only curious," Nagata said, her eyes brimming with amusement. She was the only person on board whose face wasn't green. "We dare to enter its domain. It will not harm you."

"I hate this!" Janice cried. She put her fingertips together and touched them to her forehead. "Spirits of the world, hear me!" The Oriental Sorcery professor took her hands and pulled them apart, breaking her concentration. Janice glared at her.

"Stop that! Calm yourself," Nagata commanded all of them. "Be easy. No spells! This part will be over in a moment."

It was the hardest thing Barry had ever done, watching as the great mouth engulfed them. Water swelled around them, pouring up over their shoulders, over their heads. Suddenly unable to stand the thought of drowning, he panicked. He gasped, kicking off the deck, seeking the fast-disappearing bubble of blue that was all that remained of the sky. Something grabbed his foot. He flailed at it, but it pulled him down. Nagata grasped his shoulders and held on to him as the sea closed over their heads. It grew darker and darker until the only lights were tiny bubbles of yellow coming from the lanterns hanging off the roof of the wheelhouse. She held up a warning finger, keeping it in his face until the hull of the ship bumped against the bottom, casting up a cloud of sand. Barry felt as though his lungs were about to burst. Then Nagata spoke, her voice sounding as if it came from a long way off.

"Breathe," she said. "Everyone! Breathe!"

Barry stared at her, but he couldn't help it. Black spots were swimming in front of his eyes. His lungs let go of their own accord. Bubbles exploded out of his mouth. He watched them go, wondering how long he had to live. Involuntarily, his midsection expanded, forcing him to inhale water.

It didn't hurt. He blew out the first "breath" and cautiously tried another. It felt . . . normal. He looked around him. Everyone else was experimenting with inhaling and exhaling water. Matt caught his gaze and laughed. It was a weird, bubbly sound, and made Barry laugh, too. Shoshanna and Ben seemed to adapt the quickest. They helped the teachers orient the others.

"Isn't this wonderful?" Shoshanna asked. "I have never been so far down. My rebreather will only take me to two hundred feet. We must be a mile down. Do you scuba dive?"

"No," Barry said. "The only place I've ever swum is in a pool. I've never really been in the sea."

"I have," Matt said, "But only shallow dives. Too bad it's so dark. I didn't think it would be dark down here."

"It is interesting," Nagata observed, coming into the small circle of light, her short black hair floating out around her head, "that nearly all of you live near the sea, but you are seldom in it."

"We go out all summer," Matt protested.

"You are on it, not in it. What do you know of water?" Nagata waved a dismissive hand. "Now you will learn."

She swept a hand around her. At first the students thought it was dark, but as their eyes grew used to their surroundings, they saw bright dots floating all around them.

"Photoplankton," said Ilora, realizing that they now really were in deep water.

"Some of them. Others are water spirits. They are always around you, but you do not see them because the element of fire holds sway over light in the upper atmosphere."

"The first thing you must learn," Edwards said, "is that elementals are not trustworthy, as we understand trust. They do not deal in the same realms as we do. It is a pillar of existence, true only to its nature. Water is life. Without it, life as we know it does not exist. You cannot control it. That is, you cannot control it all. You can manipulate small amounts. Even causing a wave to rise, or calling a storm, is a small measure of all the water that exists. The elemental represents all of it. You must learn to respect it, know what it can do—and what it cannot. Air is formlessness. Water is formlessness plus gravity. Yet, within its depths you do not perceive gravity in the same way as you do in air. The second thing you must understand is that for today we are under the protection of the elemental. That is why you can breathe. You are free to explore this place as much as you choose, but if you are blocked from touching anything or going anywhere, respect those limits. We enjoy a precarious truce. A misstep on your parts could cost us all our lives. Do you understand me?"

The teens nodded, causing their hair to bob in the water like so much seaweed.

"Good. Go on, now." Edwards waved a hand. "See what there is to see."

A school of glowing fish erupted in their midst, obscuring their vision. When it cleared, Barry found himself floating close to the sandy bottom among sculpted black corals and pale-colored rocks that made him feel as though he was at the bottom of an aquarium. The overhead was far more intense than that around them. He squinted up at it for a moment, then lowered his dazzled eyes to his friends.

"Where are we?" he asked.

Janice reached into her pocket for the pendulum she carried for simple divination. She swung it over her palm. The heavy plumb at the bottom was only a little hampered by the water. "Same place," she said. "I think our eyes have been adapted. Look at me." Barry stepped close, moving in slow motion because of the current's drag on his clothing. "Yes. Your pupils are the size of dimes."

"So are yours," Barry replied.

"Amazing," Matt said. "You're right. There's the ship. It looks like a wreck just sittin' there."

With their enhanced vision the brightly painted ship seemed almost garish. Flitting in and out of its portholes were translucent fish outlined in light almost too bright to look at; some with eyes, others blind. In the distance they could see other shapes, some tiny, others huge. The way the water bent light, Barry couldn't identify any of them.

"We should be cold," Janice said, "but it's warm down here. Almost hot. Look at Ben!"

The Israeli student was hovering near a cluster of neon-purple squid. He was using a light-producing spell to flash patterns of luminescence at the squid. Rather than fleeing from him, they were semaphoring back.

"I think he's getting through to them," Matt said. "I wonder what he's saying."

"I wonder if he knows," Janice said skeptically.

"Ah! You three," Professor Diamondbrow beckoned them over. She was a small, muscular woman with dark hair and bright brown eyes. "Come and help me. I'm gathering plants for the Botany Lab."

She showed them how to walk on the sea floor. Getting around required a step halfway between a flutterkick and a stride. It took a while before the three were confident in this method of locomotion. Soon they were flitting all over, tumbling over one another's heads and chasing the fish to and fro through the waving ribbonlike plants growing amid the coral. The fish almost smiled over their shoulders, taunting the students into swimming faster.

"I was so scared when we were coming down here," Janice admitted, "but now I'm having a great time. When I was a kid, the only places we went to on field trips were museums and things."

"Don't let your guard down," Diamondbrow said, shaking her head so that her short hair flowed around her. "Just because it doesn't look dangerous doesn't mean it isn't."

"I know," Janice said, with a defiant look at her friends.

"Hey, look over here," Matt said, scoot-swimming ahead. "There's a clam the size of a Volkswagen down there!" He gestured to the others and disappeared over a rock mass. Almost as abruptly he shot upward into view again.

"What happened?" Barry asked.

"I ran into a wall," Matt said, sheepishly. "Something pushed me back before I could touch the clam. It's got a magical barrier of its own."

"Let me see," Diamondbrow said, flicking her feet so that she left the ground. Barry followed, enjoying the sensation of weightlessness as he floated on his belly or his back, or sitting with his legs crossed. It was as good as flying, which he'd never yet been able to do outside of his dreams.

He had no trouble spotting the clam. Its ridged shell was as gigantic as Matt had said. It stood temptingly halfway open. Diamondbrow approached very slowly. Barry, too, was attracted to it. He wanted to see what was inside. Before he realized it, he was swimming toward it, hand out, but he never reached it. Something invisible was in the way. He felt ahead of him. The water was rubbery. The harder he pushed, the harder it pushed back.

"That is a no-go," Diamondbrow said. "Water doesn't want you to disturb the clam. Don't touch anything you're not invited to. Don't worry. There are plenty of other things to see."

"I'd almost expect to see mermaids swimmin' around," Matt drawled, floating on his back.

"Maybe another time, if we prove worthy," the teacher

said with a smile. "This is the learning experience we are allowed at present. We're being observed."

"You mean mermaids really exist?" Janice asked.

"In a way," Diamondbrow said, but refused to give them more details. At her direction, they dug up spiny or wavy plants and bound the roots using a simple spell to contain nutrition and the right temperature water around them. Barry swam after Diamondbrow, carrying the bag full of plants. He turned over the fronds with interest, looking forward to examining them in Botany class, even as components for potions in the Experimental Lab.

"What about this one?" he asked the teacher, putting out his hand to touch a mass of cup-shaped leaves. Thick clusters reached toward him, caressing his fingers and curling into his palm. Diamondbrow smiled.

"I think we may safely take that one. It wants to go with us." She dug out the pseudobulb, and chanted the binding spell.

A dog-sized mass of light flew by, followed by a narrow streak of bright green at eye-level, closely pursued by Shoshanna.

"Oh, sorry!" she said, fluttering to a halt after nearly kicking Barry in the head. "Sid and I were following that glowing jellyfish. It's going to show us the cracks in the seabed."

"It talked to you?" Barry asked, amazed.

"Not at first," Shoshanna said, her cheeks red with excitement. "It talked to Sid, but gradually I could understand it. It's so . . . alien." The tiny sea serpent came to whiz around its protector's head. "All right. I was just stopping to tell my friends . . . Would you like to come, too?" she asked the other teens. They looked at the teacher for permission.

"Go ahead," Diamondbrow said. "Just be back at the boat by the time we're ready to leave."

Barry glanced up at the blinding sea overhead. He thought he saw shapes moving, but it hurt too much to stare. "Are those other sea serpents around?" he asked Shoshanna.

"Yes," she said. "And other things. Sid is afraid of them.

And if he's afraid, there's no way I'm going to try to find out what they are."

The tiny serpent darted ahead, then came zipping back to round up the humans when they moved too slowly. Shoshanna was always talking to it, laughing when it spoke to her, though Barry could hear nothing of their exchanges.

"You look like you're really enjoying this," he said.

"I am," the Israeli girl admitted. "For the first time Sid and I are in the same element. I think I understand him better. I've promised him I'll let him have more freedom, but he told me he's grateful that I've given him a safer life. Few of his eggmates will have survived. The sea is merciless."

"Life on land is merciless, too," Janice reminded them.

Barry chuckled, and the others glanced at him. "You know, for a moment this felt like no big deal. We're just walking around, looking at plants and a few fish. I was disappointed there weren't more exotic creatures down here, like mermaids or a kraken. Then it struck me: we ought to be crushed like eggshells at these depths. And we're breathing water. We're experiencing a dozen miracles, and I was taking them for granted."

"You're spoiled," Janice said, grinning. "The wonders of the world are handed to you on a platter, and you want more."

"So many of the animals are white down here," Matt commented, as they swam-walked behind Sid. The heat was increasing steadily the farther they got from the ship.

"Light never reaches them," Janice said.

"What about those?" Matt asked, pointing to a cluster of startlingly red pipes sticking out of the sea floor where bubbles rose.

"I read about these," Shoshanna said, excitedly "Tube worms! They're one of the many life-forms that live where it is hot here in the dark."

To the teens' surprise, the water was actually boiling around them. Janice did a cooling spell to protect them as they took a closer look. Tiny white crabs, eyeless and translucent, hunting for prey among the ruby-colored tubes, skittered away out of reach.

"I wonder if we can bring back one of these reeds for Diamondbrow," Matt said. "She'd really like it."

"They're not plants," Janice said. "They're primitive animals. Don't touch."

But Matt refused to listen. He got tossed backward several times before giving in.

"They're really pretty," he said, running a speculative eye over them. "There's got to be a way."

"Don't bother," Janice said. "Water doesn't want you to take any, so forget about them."

Barry's head snapped up as he heard a shrill whistle. "They must be calling us back."

"I hate to leave," Shoshanna said, sticking out a finger to stir the water near Sid. The baby serpent seemed to take it as a caress, and performed a figure eight of delight. She shoved off to follow Barry back into cooler water, her pet tagging along. Janice let the protective spell drop. The water around them seemed to warm up.

Matt hurtled along behind, kicking hard to catch up. "What's the hurry?"

"I don't know," Barry said, "but Edwards is herding everyone onto the ship."

The enigmatic professor caught sight of them. "The truce is at an end for now," he said. "Make haste. We must get back to the surface."

Even Nagata looked upset as she swam aboard. "Everyone hold on to something," she said. "Water is capricious. When you notice its mood change, you must be prepared to move."

The light around them died abruptly. Everyone cried out a protest.

"Silence!" Edwards called out. One by one the lanterns lit, but the ship was already moving upward.

As they rose, they felt the protection of Water drop away from them. The teachers hastened to replace it with wards of their own making, which felt feeble and insufficient after the overwhelming presence of the elemental. Edwards' hands were raised toward the sails, and he chanted words of power in an unknown language. Bubbles began to pour out of the deck, surrounding him and billowing outward until they filled a globe with the ship at its center. Barry gasped for a moment as his lungs filled with air. As water was squeezed out of the protective area he settled to the deck. He felt bittersweet regret at no longer being able to defy gravity. His hair and his clothes were dry. Edwards let his arms drop. His head was bowed with weariness. Barry jumped to help him sit down.

"That was amazing," he said to Edwards. "Can we do that spell ourselves? I'd like to go back there one day."

"When you are a much more advanced magician," Edwards explained, taking deep breaths to restore himself. He patted Barry on the knee. "You are halfway there, though. You have a great deal of power, and the wisdom of your ancestors is at your command. Put them together, and there will be nowhere on Earth in its many layers that you cannot go."

"Wow."

Like a cork popping up, the ship exploded onto the surface of the water. Diamondbrow went to the tiller, and turned them to face toward the lowering sun. Edwards continued chanting, filling the sails with a swift-moving westerly.

"That was awesome," Matt said. "I can't wait to do it again."

Janice started to reply, when the prow crested a wave and dropped into a trough. Her face went pale. "I can't wait to get back to the Academy," she said. "I wasn't sick while we were down there, but the second we hit the air, it all came back." The ship rolled again. "Ooh. That was a hard one. I guess I got used to the mild currents underwater."

Barry looked around in alarm. "That was rougher than when we were on our way out," he said. "It's almost as bad as when the elemental swallowed us."

Almost as if it was reading his mind, the water began to

roil around the hull. The teens stared down, not believing it was happening again.

"I thought it was all over," Janice said. "Why is it following us?"

The water reared up in great crests, threatening to swamp the decks. All the students hurried to find something to cling to. A great head reared itself above water, but it wasn't the formless mass of the elemental, but a serpentine head with huge, slit-pupiled eyes. The students screamed and flinched back. To their horror, another giant, fanged face appeared on the other side of the ship.

"Steer clear!" shouted Edwards. Grimly, Diamondbrow grasped the wheel and wrenched it to the left. He drew twin spheres of fire from the center of his body and flung them at the serpents. Roaring, they dove beneath the surface. The ship rocked wildly, but it was moving toward the east. "Hurry! I will lay a spell of speed upon us, but it will take time!"

"What's happening?" Shoshanna cried as Nagata made her way on deck. This time even the Oriental Sorcery professor was pale.

"Something has gone wrong," she said, her lips tight with strain. "We are lost. The elemental has sent the giant serpents after us. We are no longer under its protection. We will drown."

"What?" Barry exclaimed. "Why?"

"Be calm, be calm," Edwards called. "We are not dead yet. We'll all do our best to get everyone home again."

"Can we talk to them?" Ben asked.

"Not when they're this angry," Edwards said. "We need speed. I want everyone to help us outrun the waves. Together now: 'lo winds, fair winds, blow, winds, blow. Fill the sail, speed, not gale, blow, winds, blow.' It's ancient, but it works. One day when we're less frantic I'll teach you the tune. Do you have it? Together now!" He led the students in the old chant, slowly, but rapidly increasing the tempo. The ship began to pick up speed. The heaving waves began to drop behind them.

Nagata paced up and down. "How could we have angered the elemental? It was ready to dismiss us." She rounded upon Ms. Diamondbrow. "Ruta, did you take something from it?"

The Botany professor looked horrified. "No! I only took plants that were offered to me. Anything I wanted that I was not allowed whipped out of my reach. I got the message: Another time, when Water is feeling generous. I would *never . . .*"

"I know, I know."

Nagata sat down on the deck. With a force of will that Barry knew he wouldn't be capable of under similar strained conditions, she went into a meditative trance, fingers joined at the tips, hands resting on her folded knees. In a moment she rose, her face grim.

"Did someone take anything that was not offered? Anyone? Speak now! Our lives depend on it!"

Matt raised his hand sheepishly. "I . . . it was me. I thought those tube-worm pipes were pretty." He pulled a length of the red cylinder from his pocket. "Nothing was living in it. It was empty when I picked it up. I had to fight to break it off, but I didn't realize it would get so mad. Can't I just throw it back?"

At that moment the huge face of a serpent rose out of the water before them. The ship sloshed up against its neck. The serpent struck again and again, trying to close its jaws on the prow.

"Shall we summon the element of air to help us?" Ilora asked, desperately clinging to the cabin door frame. "Or earth?"

"Do you want to add a hurricane to the tidal wave?" Janice asked, angrily. "Or earthquakes? No way." She was furious with Matt, who couldn't manage to meet her eyes. "Did you think it wouldn't notice? It was all around us. Didn't you see the faces? The eyes?"

"That's not helping," Barry said. "We have to do something."

"Oh, sure," Janice said. "Reason with angry sea serpents. Go ahead."

An idea struck Barry so hard his mouth dropped open. "I can't," he said, "but I bet Shoshanna can."

The ship leaped and rocked, but they managed to hand their way around the sodden deck without falling overboard. They found the Israeli girl and her brother huddled underneath the lifeboat. Shoshanna was clutching the aquarium to her.

"Shoshanna, we need your help!" Barry said, then realized to his horror that the aquarium was empty. "Where's Sid?"

"I've lost him," she said, tears running down her face. "We had to board so quickly I didn't have a chance to retrieve him. I've been Calling him."

"Have you found him?" Barry asked.

She nodded. "He can't keep up. He's miles behind us. I'm afraid we're going to die, and he'll be left alone in a strange ocean."

"Angels protect us," Ben chanted, his eyes closed. "Michael, Raphael, Gabriel, Uriel, intercede for us. Grant us the power to save our lives. Oh, God, I've forgotten the rest of the prayer!"

"Intercession is what we need," Barry said. "Shoshanna, can you talk to Sid?"

"Yes," Shoshanna said.

"Tell him we're running away from his big cousins. They're his species. Can he persuade them to leave us in peace?"

"He's only a baby," she wailed. "He's afraid."

"He's our only chance," Barry said. "He's their little brother. Surely they will listen to him. You treat him well, don't you?"

The girl's blue-green eyes flashed fire. "Of course! I love him."

"Then if he loves you, too, he will tell them. It may be the only chance we have to get home."

"They might eat him!"

Barry threw up his hands. "If he can't help us, we'll all be eaten. Tell him . . ." he glanced at his friend, who was red to the ears, "tell him Matt is very sorry he took a piece of pipe. He will give it back. Tell them to tell their master it will never happen again. We send our respects."

Shoshanna nodded and closed her eyes to concentrate. Suddenly, her eyes flew open, and a strange, otherwordly expression was on her face, her shaman's talent manifesting itself. "I can hear them! I can hear all of them! Aaah!" She shrieked just before the boat seemed to sustain a terrible impact. Barry and Matt were thrown violently against the rails. "One of them is biting the ship. It is afraid of the light. *Who is throwing the light at them?*"

"Offensive spells," Janice said, tightly. "The teachers are defending us."

"I'd better go stop them," Matt said, edging out from under the canvas.

"No, let me," Barry said.

Matt straightened his shoulders. "All this is my fault. I'll go."

Barry moved aside to let him out. He and Janice watched their friend hand himself awkwardly across the tossing deck. Matt lost his footing, and struck the boards with a bang. Janice shouted as the Texan slithered toward the edge of the deck. He flailed around until he caught hold of a hatch cover, steadied himself, then made his way to his feet. As the ship tossed the other way, he ran to hug the wheelhouse and edge himself around to the other side.

"It's Professor Nagata," Matt shouted, over the crashing waves. "Stop it, ma'am! We're trying to communicate with them!"

One more blaze of light flashed over the top of the wheelhouse, making the serpents recoil, but then it was over. Shoshanna muttered to herself, her eyes staring at nothing. The serpents waited. Matt drew back his arm and threw the piece of red coral. It arced high over his head, and dropped into the water, directly between the sea monsters.

Suddenly, they straightened up, as though they were listening to something. Four gigantic slit-pupiled eyes turned until they seemed to look directly toward Barry and the rest who were hidden underneath the lifeboat. Then, the serpents dropped down into the sea. The waves closed over their heads. The ship rocked violently one more time, then wavered to an upright keel on a perfectly calm sea.

"It's over," Barry said. "Whew!"

"Good idea on your part," Janice said. She looked at Shoshanna, who was still chanting. "How'd you know it would work?"

"I didn't," he said. "I just hoped. But what chance did we have?"

"One slight, little chance," Janice said. "Named Sid. Come on. Let's see if Edwards can help get him back aboard." She smiled at Barry, Ben, and his sister. "That was some teamwork," she said. "I wonder if you'll help me out with just one more little task when we get back to Sedona. I can't do it alone."

"Anything," Ben said. His sister nodded.

"Of course," Barry said, curiously.

"Good," Janice said, swiping at her matted locks in annoyance. "I want you to help me throw Matt in the fountain. I mean, just look at my hair! *Twice* in one day!"

PARENTHETICAL PREFERENCE

by Von Jocks

Von Jocks believes in many forms of sorcery and enchantment, and most especially in the magic of stories. She has written them since she was five years old, although it took another twenty-five years before she started publishing. She now writes historical romances as Yvonne Jocks, paranormal romances as Evelyn Vaughn, and fantasy short stories as "Von" Jocks. She has also edited and contributed to two forthcoming anthologies about witches—*Witches' Brew* and *Words of the Witches*. When not exploring fictional dimensions, Von lives in central Texas with her cats, her TV, and too many ants. She teaches community college English to support her writing habit, or vice versa, and only wishes research papers could be this much fun. Feel free to write her at PO Box 6, Euless TX 76039, e-mail her at Yvaughn@aol.com, or check out her web site—www.yvonnejocks.homestead.com

TO judge by the groans coming from Professor West-brook's Freshman English class, you'd think the students were victims of a nasty gastrointestinal virus. Or

maybe, this being the Academy for Advanced Study—aka
Sorcerer U—a nastier, gastrointestinal *curse*. But the situation was much, much worse.

They'd gotten their research papers back.

Cassi stared in silent dismay at what had been her ten-
page, laser-printed, double-spaced offering. Actually, she
was staring at the big, red "D+" scrawled across its proper-
MLA-format cover page. Had she dared voice her pain in
even a small whimper, she would. She never got Ds.

Even in *normal* high school, she'd never gotten Ds!

From the mix of gasps, groans, and angry snorts around
her—not to mention one poltergeisty binder flying into the
chalkboard and a shared, group aura in angry shades of
red—her classmates weren't down with it either.

"This *sucks!*" protested Janice Redding, from the seat beside Cassi's. If anybody was going to argue with their staid,
bespectacled teacher it would be Janice. Janice, with her
yellow-brown hair, olive-toned skin, and New York background, wasn't afraid of anything.

"Really, Ms. Redding?" challenged Professor Westbrook,
and took off his wire-framed glasses to polish them on a
handkerchief. He'd warned the students on the first day of
class that they couldn't scare him either. Not just because
he'd fought more demons in his time than they could clas-
sify, but because they'd never met his wife. "Develop your
argument. What specifically do you mean by *it,* and how
does *it* suck?"

While she listened, Cassi looked back down at her once-
beautiful paper, so neat and organized and comfortably *contained,* with its parenthetical references and block
quotations and extensive works-cited page. She thought she
had plenty of support, especially for the topic she'd drawn.

"It sucks," supported Janice, "because I didn't move my
butt out to B.F.N. Arizona to do stupid, mundane busy work,
that's why."

To judge by the murmurs of agreement throughout the
classroom, and the purply power tinges Cassi saw zapping
amid the room's already negative shared energy, Janice

wasn't alone. The reason they were here—the reason they were *all* here—was magic. Classes like Intro to Divination, or Comparative Enchantments, or even P.E.—Psychic Education—were the draw at Sorcerer U. It was the M.I.T. of Magical Arts.

Cassi smiled to herself. The Juliard of JuJu.

The Sorbonne of Sorcer—

Professor Westbrook interrupted her thoughts with a sniff. "You were reminded at orientation that the Academy for Advanced Study, while an unusual high school, is a high school still. That means some English, Math, and Science."

"Yeah." Janice pointed at him with her whole hand, fingers arched like he was her homey. "But our Math class is Numerology, and our Science class is Alchemy."

"And your English class is research papers, at which none of you excelled," finished Professor Westbrook, unmoved. "So for the rest of the period, why don't you all get into study groups and summon up a clue as to where you are, on the whole, lacking?"

Study groups?

Other students stood and began to yank their desks into clusters, grouping mostly by shared interests or friendships—both of which left Cassi out. She watched them with a sinking feeling, wishing her ability to see energy could in any way help her here. At least separating them into groups effectively dispelled the nasty shared aura which—without the unity of so many upset adolescents facing a common enemy—faded into little pockets of indistinct, storm-cloud grays. Oh, the energy stayed blacker over the group of ceremonial Goths. And it shimmered silvery blue over the Wiccan contingent by the window, where four young ladies had joined hands to form an impromptu healing circle. But mostly, it powered down on its own.

Cassi glanced toward where Professor Westbrook sat, ignoring the lot of them—his shields, as a teacher, kept her from reading *him*. Then she peeked over her shoulder at the handful of students squaring off their desks near her corner. Those four didn't seem to have any one, obvious tradition.

Janice Redding slumped back in her desk, projecting a tough attitude that her aura didn't wholly support. *She's hurt,* thought Cassi, surprised. *She thought she would do better on this assignment, too.*

The dark-in-more-ways-than-one Barry Silverhorse folded gracefully into his own desk, black eyes troubled with their own rebellious business. Cassi hadn't been able to read much off the city-Indian's aura since school started. Whether that was his doing or hers, she wasn't sure.

She didn't *have* to read Matt Johnson's aura. Anything you needed to know about Matt, you could see on his open face, his blue eyes, and his wide grin. He and dark-skinned, black-haired Ashanti, sitting beside each other, were like altar statues for day and night. Cassi envied Ashanti, both for her friendship with Matt *and* for her sparkling clear aura. Even at fifteen, a year older than most of the freshmen at Sorcerer U, nothing seemed to faze Ashanti Equiano. Not even a horrible grade in English.

But maybe that was because Ashanti was French, and it didn't carry as much weight to her?

It carried tremendous weight for Cassi—and now she was expected to be social, too? Didn't Professor Westbrook *understand?* The other students might not get her silence, but at least they were learning not to expect . . .

Then Matt glanced quickly around the faces of his group in silent question and turned toward her. "Pull your chair closer, Cassi. Let's make it a magic five."

She could have melted with gratitude as she hurried to comply. At that moment, her aura was probably summer-sunshine-sky blue.

Like Matt's eyes.

"So, then, class," continued Matt, as if he'd done nothing generous at all. He adopted a nasally voice that was dead-on for Professor Westbrook. It was not a magic trick. "Where are we, on the whole, lacking?"

Janice said, "It sucks that we weren't able to choose our topics."

"Alors," noted Ashanti. "Technically, we *did* choose

them." She had a thick accent, so that her "we" sounded like *ve* and her "them" sounded like *zem*.

Not that Cassi was in any position to complain.

Janice said, "We picked them out of a *bowl*—that's chance, not choice. What the hell do I care about some guy from the past making stupid predictions about the future?"

"Who was your author?" asked Matt. "Nostradamus?"

"Some English putz." She actually looked at the front of her paper which—Cassi noticed—had no title page. "Herbert George Wells."

Barry groaned. "You got H. G. Wells? You lucky dog. That is so unfair!"

"Why? Who did you get?" Janice tried to snatch Barry's essay off his desk, but he slid it even more quickly away from her.

"Some stupid poet."

"I am researching Shakespeare," admitted Ashanti, with a Gallic shake of her head. *"Tres Anglais."*

Matt grinned. "I drew Tolkien."

"You butthead," protested Barry, clearly even more jealous than he'd been of Wells.

"Some of us are just blessed with good fortune." Matt grinned, spreading his hands. "Good fortune and, sadly, D-minus grades. How 'bout you, Cassi?"

Uh-oh. Had he not noticed . . . ?

But instead of staring at her, as if he expected her to actually talk about it, Matt just reached for her paper, which she quickly showed him.

He blinked at it. "Who's Eleanor Porter?"

She turned to the first page and pointed at Porter's most famous book title, and he winced. "You're full of it!"

Cassi shrugged. She wished she were.

"What is it, already?" demanded Janice, almost climbing over her own desk to get a look. Then she pretended to choke. *"Polly*-freakin'-*ANNA?"*

Cassi nodded.

"You poor kid!" Which was a funny thing for Janice to say, since Cassi thought the New Yorker was younger than her by several months. "Do you think maybe Westbrook is a few kings short of a minor arcana?"

"Who is Pollyanna?" asked Ashanti, confused.

Barry said, "It's a kid book, right? About some idiot girl who sees good in everything?"

She's not an idiot girl, thought Cassi, in defense of the main character. *Just . . . optimistic.* It had been a comforting story to read, actually. Alone in her dorm room. Listening to snatches of the other girls' CDs, computer games, and conversations. Always conversations.

But she couldn't defend cheerful little Pollyanna out loud, so she just shrugged again. Besides, it had been a lousy choice for *this* assignment.

In fact . . .

Janice glared at Professor Westbrook, across the room, maybe doubting his sanity. Matt wheedled Barry into confessing that his author was William Butler Yeats. And Cassi dug into her backpack and pulled out the original assignment sheet. Since Matt seemed to have taken charge—whether he'd meant to or not—she put the paper in front of him, like an offering.

"Oh. Good idea. Let's start with the basics." And he read their original instructions out loud.

"You will draw slips of paper, each revealing the name of a famous author. Using comprehensive research, prove that this author was or was not a magic user in his/her own right."

Unlike Shakespeare or Tolkien or even Wells, the author of *Pollyanna* wrote no fantasy or sorcery at all, just a lonely little girl who ran around making friends and playing a "glad" game to feel better about her tragic life. Unlike Barry's famous poet, Eleanor Hodgman Porter hadn't even been involved in any magical societies. The woman had been a wholly mundane, church-going New Englander. Of course, Cassi's paper had concluded that Porter was no magic user. What other possibility was there?

But a D? Even a D-plus?

Janice made a disgusted noise. "We may have to use

magic ourselves, just to figure out what Westbrook even wanted."

Which is when Matt started to laugh. It was a happy, friendly sound.

He understands, thought Cassi, straightening hopefully as she watched his aura brighten. *Whatever it is, he understands.*

"Did I say something funny?" demanded Janice, jutting out her chin with a bit of gangsta-style head action.

Matt—being Matt—took no offense. "It says 'comprehensive research,'" he repeated.

They all stared at him. They knew that much.

"What if Professor Westbrook meant for us to use magic all along?"

They continued to stare. But Cassi could almost see the bursts of light over their heads as they each, almost simultaneously, caught on.

The group between them and the windows heard them, and the next thing Cassi knew, the illumination of their shared understanding was starting to fill the room, like a daisy chain of psychic sparklers.

"Well bless-ed *be!*" exclaimed one of the Wiccans.

"But how?" demanded Ashanti, and looked toward where their teacher had begun to deign to notice them again. "How are we to do this?"

Professor Westbrook folded his arms, leaned back against his desk, and looked bored. His entire posture said, *You tell me.*

It was one of the Goths, bouncing in a very un-Goth fashion, who raised her hand and called, "By trying their spells out?"

"My author didn't write stories with spells," protested her boyfriend—at least, Cassi assumed from their matching T-shirts and nose-rings that he was her boyfriend. Their energy neither confirmed nor denied.

"Well mine *did,*" the girl argued back, and their auras began to lodge protests against each other.

"Maybe we could do a seance and ask the writer," suggested a cute redhead who always sat up front—she looked more like a cheerleading captain or class president than a magic user.

"Or we could look for traces of signature magic in their words," added a skinny guy with braces.

Their teacher shrugged amenably, seeming to accept all possibilities. "For the purposes of this project, and considering this school's history, *nobody* does magic alone," he warned them, and glanced toward the back corner. "Brett, that goes double for you and Christopher Marlowe. Also, I want to remind you of the school rules regarding manipulative magic, destructive magic, violations of privacy, firecode safety, etc. You've all got a week's extension. Any questions?"

Janice scowled—but Cassi could see subtle signs that she, like the others, felt relieved. "Why didn't you just tell us that's what you wanted from the start?"

"Because if you never think to use magic unless you're instructed to, you'll end up pretty poor sorcerers," answered their teacher. "Anything else?"

Cassi found it interesting that he used the half-joking term sorcerer, instead of magic user or mage. *He knows our nickname for the school*, she thought.

And Professor Westbrook thought back at her, *Duh.*

It wasn't like the other freshmen at Sorcerer U were ignoring Cassi, much less shunning her. Magic ability and social acceptance didn't always mix, so more of the students than not had spent time on the receiving end of snobbery. Besides, the Academy hosted students from all over the world. Around here, an inability to accept diversity would be a bigger handicap than silence. But even those students who made an extra effort to include her seemed to do it as much out of charity as interest. What with their inability to chat about anything like bands or movies or whatever, those fleeting attempts at friendships hadn't exactly stuck.

Especially when they learned her real secret.

Cassi had thought she was used to being alone—but

she'd always lived at home, in Georgia, before now. She'd at least had her family. Now . . .

What if coming to the Academy for Advanced Study had been a mistake?

Over the last month, more and more of the new students had been forging bonds that, through nobody's fault, didn't include the silent blonde. Cassi hadn't realized how lonely she'd gotten until the opportunity to hang with people as cool as Matt, Janice, Barry, and Ashanti for the weekend had her redoing her nail color three times. Only as she started a third coat—Passion Plum—did she stop and consider how sad this was.

They weren't her *friends,* after all. They were just her study group.

She put the lid back on her nail polish, even though she'd only done one hand, and the nails on her other hand were still Daisy Dazzle, a glittery yellow. The group had spent yesterday afternoon doing new research and coming up with ideas to test the magic of the others' chosen authors—but not Cassi' s. Cassi's author clearly wasn't magic anyway. Of course, Cassi may have helped research, but she hadn't contributed a hell of a lot to the brainstorming session, so maybe that was karmic fairness. For today, they'd agreed to split a cab to and from Sedona's shopping district to get the supplies they still needed for Ashanti's and Janice's projects.

At least Cassi could maybe carry stuff.

Anyway, she should probably worry more about the others realizing that she was so backward, she'd never ridden in a cab before than anybody noticing her nail color.

Feeling especially un-Pollyannalike, Cassi grabbed her Muppet backpack and headed out of her dormitory room to meet the others. She could hear pockets of conversation from some of the other rooms.

". . . told him, don't you dare try that love-spell crap on me, and he said . . ."

". . . no. *No!* You are so full of it. She didn't really believe that would *work,* did she . . . ?"

". . . you think? You aren't just saying that, are you? Because I thought Libras . . ."

There were so many ugly ducklings finding out they were swans, around here. That should seem like a *good* thing.

Cassi hurried.

Nobody *did* notice her nail color, when she reached the ironwork front gates set into a long, adobe wall. But that was probably because Matt was talking funny. Not his usual, goofy-but-charming funny, either. Garbled-funny. And he looked uncharacteristically annoyed about it.

"We weren't supposed to do magic alone," accused Janice, glowering at him, while Cassi walked up.

Matt protested something that sounded like gibberish. Gibberish with a whole lot of vowels and weird punctuation marks like foreign languages used—umlauts and accent circumflexes . . . or accents circumflex. And stuff. Either way, it seemed especially weird that Cassi still understood him.

She knew what he'd said was, *I wasn't alone, I had Ashanti with me.*

She'd also heard the *duh* in Professor Westbrook's look, earlier that day in the classroom. As her mama so often said, she was just wired differently than most girls.

"He was not alone," said Ashanti, her own words English—if heavily accented English. "I was with him. He did not want to try forging a ring, and had a better idea how to prove that Monsieur Tolkien knew magic."

"I get it," said Barry, nodding slowly. "The wizard Gandalf in *Lord of the Rings* does his spells in Elvish, doesn't he?"

Matt nodded and said something that meant, *Exactly.* But it took four words.

Cassi felt just as glad they wouldn't be forging any rings, considering how that had turned out for some of the inhabitants of Middle Earth. But *Elvish?*

Ashanti said, "We thought if we got his project out of the way, it would leave more time this weekend for everyone else's."

Janice made a disgusted noise.

Barry said, "So have you tried doing any spells in Elvish to see if it really works?"

Matt said what might have been two words, complete with a tilde, but meant something along the lines of having been so startled that he couldn't speak human anymore—much less English—he hadn't thought to try doing a spell.

Barry stared at him and said, "Uh . . . yeah. Whatever."

Janice had more to say than that, and poked Matt in the chest for effect. Several times. "Way to go, Johnson. What good are you to us if you can't even talk right?"

Cassi caught her breath before she could stop herself.

Matt narrowed his eyes in a way that didn't need translation. It still took Janice several beats to realize what she'd said. To Cassi's relief, she didn't automatically start offering gushing apologies. She just said a gruff, "I didn't mean you, Cassi."

But she blushed a little under her olive complexion, like maybe she would have offered gushing apologies if she thought it would do any good.

Cassi tried a fleeting smile, to say that she didn't mind. Then she noticed that Matt, glancing back toward Barry, shrugged in answer to the Navajo's original question. The blond-haired Texan then turned to point at a spiky cluster of yucca, by the adobe wall.

Even as he drew breath to speak whatever spell he might have tried, Cassi surprised everyone by covering his mouth with her hand.

The hand with the Daisy Dazzle nails.

Matt's blue eyes widened at her over it in dancing curiosity. He asked a question, which tickled. Muffled Elvish sounded a lot like regular Elvish.

What he asked was, *What's wrong?*

Cassi parted her lips—then closed them and swallowed, frustrated. She didn't want to resort to using the little notebook she had to carry everywhere, to *write* him her caution to be careful. But if speaking Elvish really did increase his magical abilities, he should attempt something very, very small first.

She, of all people, should know.

His mouth felt really weird under her bare palm, so she snatched her hand away, flushing. She made do with pointing at the yucca, then lifting her arms over her head, like an explosion. Or a *tah-dah* gesture. One of the many problems with not talking.

To her relief, Matt seemed to understand. He said, *I wasn't going to blow it up, just start a little fire.*

She quirked an eyebrow at him, cynical, and he shrugged a concession that maybe this wasn't the best place to start even a small fire—much less a mistakenly large one.

Then his blue eyes widened and he asked, in surprised Elvish, *You understand me?*

She nodded.

He looked relieved. *Great! Then you can . . .*

She shook her head before he even managed all the glottal stops that apparently went into the Elvish term for *translate*. Having her for a translator would be like having a visually challenged Seeing Eye dog.

"That Teletubby BS is really starting to piss me off," warned Janice about his Elvish, turning to wave for the cab that had turned down the street in their direction. She'd telephoned for them to be picked up—this was not like a big city, where a person could just hail an empty cab as it drove by.

Or so Cassi assumed it worked in big cities.

Matt said something like, *It's no picnic on this end, either.* Or maybe *It's no buffet from this side.* Or maybe . . .

Well, Cassi got the gist, anyhow, and sent him a sympathetic look.

"Can we just get this done with?" demanded Barry, as the cab pulled up to the curb by them.

"We love your company, too, Silverhorse," warned Janice, circling to the passenger side.

Barry faced her over the hood of the yellow sedan. "I didn't mean it that way and you know it, Redding."

"Yeah? Well how *did* you mean it?"

Ashanti said, "I believe I will sit in back with Matt and

Cassi." Matt wholeheartedly agreed with her in Elvish, leaving *Silverhorse* and *Redding* to join up for shotgun.

Perhaps there were times when silence wasn't so bad.

"I do not think," warned Ashanti as they headed down the produce aisle of the Sedona MegalaMart, "that the store was made for this." Despite that, the front of every shopping cart boasted the sign, *Anything You Could Ever Want to Buy.* "Is our shopping list not extreme?"

Other shoppers were already giving them funny looks, probably more because of their age—and number—than their purchases. The contents of the large bags they already carried, from Gerri's Gems and Sprig-and-Twig Herbs down the street, might surprise even those locals used to Sedona's more New-Agey elements.

Personally, Cassi felt more uncertain about the combo supermarket/discount warehouse than she had about the magic shops. She'd never been shopping in a store this big without her mom. Even without her speech issues, she would not have admitted that to the others.

"What, extreme?" challenged Janice. "It's for school, isn't it? That freakin' footnote business is extreme. Hacking up real newts and frogs instead of using substitutions—*that* would be extreme. Whipping up a potion?" She blew her lips outward. "That's nothing."

Footnotes? Cassi cocked her head and wished she could comment. Matt raised a hand, tried—*our essays didn't need footnotes, just that parenthetical reference stuff*—but, of course, it came out all vowelly again, and Janice just glared at him.

"If you don't stop that . . ." she warned.

He spread his arms in a gesture of frustrated helplessness. Or a tah-dah. But probably the first. Then he slanted his blue gaze at Cassi, as he'd been doing more and more while they shopped, and she nodded agreement. An English nerd, she knew research-paper rules like other students at Sorcerer U knew their own Books of Shadows. Footnotes seemed to have gone out of style before any of them were born.

Her own kind of time travel, Matt added softly. Since Janice's research topic was H. G. Wells—her project involved an alleged time machine—Cassi smiled delighted agreement. It was fun to have an inside joke, especially with Matt.

Barry, on the other hand, followed paces behind them, shoulders slumped, as if pretending he didn't know them at all. Or maybe he was just deep in thought.

Cassi still couldn't read Barry.

They were carrying notes from herbals and a popular paperback spell book, to translate the ingredients from the famous witches' potion in *MacBeth*. To make herself useful, Cassi went to a nearby carrel of fresh flowers and chose a stem of daisies in crinkly green tissue.

Daisies looked like eyes, after all. That was important. Eye of newt, though . . .

Ashanti said, "But I do not want 'a charm of powerful trouble'!"

Matt—to whom Cassi had loaned her hated little notebook—scribbled, *So change the words.* It turned out he could at least *write* in English.

Ashanti shrugged, looking both French and helpless that way. "Change them to what?"

"What's the original spell?" asked Janice, looking over the store's selection of potted ivy—aka Lizard's Leg.

By now, Ashanti could quote it. Eyes of newt, wool of bats, blind-worms' stings, blah blah blah. A vegetarian, Cassi had been relieved to learn that everything on the list was actually a plant. Wings and arms and hands were leaves; toes were roots, etc.

Holly leaves even *looked* like bat wings.

But even with substitutions, they needed the chant—and who wanted toil and trouble to double, double? They'd have to substitute there, too.

Trochaic tetrameter, Cassi decided firmly.

It was when she had those kinds of thoughts that she almost welcomed the fact that she couldn't just blurt them out. How nerdy could she get?

Then again, the rhythm of Shakespeare's spell—DOUble

DOUble TOIL and TROUble—were classic magic. All they
had to do was come up with a charm that used the same beat.

She tried beating the rhythm out on the handle of the
shopping cart, to explain that, but the others just looked at
her strangely, so she quickly stopped, embarrassed.

She hated being looked at strangely.

It didn't even help when she gave up, took her hated little notebook back from Matt, and scribbled the words:
trochaic tetrameter.

Janice said, "Oh, my God, Matt's spell is contagious."

When Matt laughed out loud, it was, to Cassi's surprise,
at Janice. Then Ashanti started softly clapping out the
rhythm with her dark hands. Cassi hesitated, then started in
on the shopping cart again. ONE two, ONE two . . .

"It is the beat of the words," Ashanti explained, catching
on quickly—maybe because so many poetic terms weren't
English at all. "She means that if we imitate the beat, we can
change the words, yes?"

To Cassi's delight, Barry—with a slow grin—began to
stomp out the rhythm right there in the MegalaMart produce
aisle. He danced mainly with his boots, holding his body
erect, like at some Navajo powwow. STOMP-stomp,
STOMP-stomp, STOMP-stomp, STOMP, stomp.

Ashanti began to clap again. Cassi joined in on the shopping cart, more confidently. Matt began to pat his jeans' leg,
to keep time.

"Oh!" Janice seemed nowhere near as put out by this as
she'd been by Matt's Elvish. "The rhythm the words make."

Ashanti nodded. "'*Double Double*—"

Cassi and Janice both pressed hands over the black girl's
mouth, and only then recognized mutual understanding in
each other's gaze. Ashanti's deep, dark eyes widened.

They'd just been raising energy with the drumming, after
all. And between the bags from the other stores, and the
plants and flowers they'd been collecting here, they had
most of the Wyrd Sisters' famous ingredients on them.

Except for the blind-worm's sting. For the life of them,
nobody had been able to figure out blind-worm's sting yet.

Everyone breathed out a sigh of relief.

When Cassi and Janice both moved their hands from Ashanti's mouth, Janice said, "Hey, tight nails."

Thank you. It's Passion Plum. Cassi made do with smiling.

Barry continued to dance in a slow, strong circle. Now the shoppers *really* gave them funny looks.

For the first time in years, Cassi didn't mind.

Heading down from the dorm rooms toward the basement entrance, her Muppet backpack weighed down with crystals and books, Cassi actually smiled or waved through open doors at other girls on her hall. As if she belonged. As if she were one of them.

Maybe it was inevitable that life bring her back down, and hard.

When she remembered that she'd left her copy of the *MLA Handbook for Writers of Research Papers* back in her room, she rolled her eyes at herself, doubled back—and heard it.

"—feel sorry for her, is all," said Moira Pearson's voice from her room. And even though Cassi had nothing more than instinct to warn her, she slowed down anyway.

She'd felt this prickly, stomach-turning sense of self-consciousness so often, since her childhood, that she should probably name it and consider it an imaginary friend. Except that it was no friend to her.

She had no friends. And sure enough—

"It was nice of them to let her in their group and all," continued her classmate. "But what use is she? Really, how good a magic user can she be anyway? Don't you need to be able to talk to do magic?"

Only in role-playing games, thought Cassi numbly, fully stopping before anybody in the room could see her eavesdropping.

Some kind of bag rustled—candy, or maybe chips—and Stefani Harris said, "I heard that she's *able* to speak, she just *doesn't.* Do you think it's her way of getting attention?"

"Poor Janice and Ashanti," mourned Moira.

"Poor Matt and Barry!" corrected Stefani, with a giggle. Cassi wasn't the only one who thought Matt and Barry were awfully cute.

Too cute to think that they were spending time with her out of any reason but pity.

She backed up slowly, away from the open room with its conversing roommates as they began to dish about other good-looking boys in class—and to laugh about some of the supposed losers. Cassi had never been able to dish about anyone. By the time she was old enough to know boys were even different, she'd . . .

Well, she'd learned better.

Still, maybe because the last few days had been so much fun, she felt this particular slight more painfully than she usually did. Her breathing was strangled, her eyes stinging. Poor group, being stuck with her. If she had any pride, she would drop off her supplies and leave them to themselves.

Maybe she should even leave Sorcerer U. A few months ago, she'd thought it might be her only hope, but what had changed?

Maybe she had no hope.

She turned, so that she could walk faster. Then her walk became a blind run. She ran until she reached the basement stairs, where she stopped to desperately compose herself.

She had one consolation anyway, she thought, wiping away tears. At least other people's words had the power to do damage, too.

That, at least, wasn't just her.

"Better, better / higher letter / Improve the grade, or you'll upset her."

As Cassi crept down the metal stairs, more apprehensive about her study group than any scare-the-freshmen legends about the Academy's basement, Ashanti looked up from the rhyme she'd just read. "Cassi! You are here, *bien.* This is not right, is it?"

Matt, sitting on the concrete floor and leaning back

against a cardboard box with a spiral notebook on his lap, made an insulted noise.

"But why would I call myself *her*?" demanded Ashanti, turning to him. "Is this an Americanism?"

"No," said Janice from where she and Barry were huddled over the alleged time machine, which a sophomore had admitted was hidden down here. "It's not an Americanism."

The time machine was the only reason they'd agreed to finalize their magical attempts in the basement. They wouldn't have, otherwise, even if they *didn't* believe the rumors about the Academy's basement.

Rumors about monsters. And other dimensions. And monsters from other dimensions.

Even Janice wasn't sure how old the machine they'd found under a canvas tarp really was. Apparently English teachers had been assigning this particular research paper for years, and someone always drew H. G. Wells. Students had been passing this machine down from one class to the next for longer than they'd kept records.

Short of summoning Martians, how else were they going to prove the author's capabilities? Matt's experiment with the Elvish had them rethinking any attempt to turn someone invisible.

Looking down from the stairs at the machine, Cassi was surprised to feel some of her hurt from Moira and Stefani's comments drain away from her. Part of it was that the energies in the basement—what she could read without making an intrusive effort—seemed surprisingly welcoming, despite those comments. And part was sheer fascination.

Like the description in Wells' novel—*The Time Machine*, of course not *The Island of Doctor Moreau*—this mechanism was large, with white levers and a long leather saddle as a seat. Pieces of it seemed to really be made out of nickel, out of bone if not ivory, even out of rock crystal. The whole contraption was supposedly powered by quartz rods, so the group's last task before taking it for a test drive was to glue quartz crystals to those curved rods, using a silicon adhesive, as their power source.

Nobody even had a driving permit, much less a license. Luckily, there was no minimum age for time-travel.

Their plan was to visit W. B. Yeats and ask him, flat out, if he was a magic user. That would be enough to prove both Janice's and Barry's papers. Then if Matt could just do some unusual magic in Elvish, and they could find blind-worms' sting for Ashanti—not to mention coming up with a decent chant—they'd be taken care of, too.

Unlike the other students' research topics, Cassi's author was clearly not a magic user. None of them knew how to prove that, though. As she hesitated on the stairs, that one fact allowed her to reconsider just dropping off the supplies and running away. She might not be a great help, but at least she wasn't distracting them with work on her project.

Matt tore another offering from his spiral notebook, bits of paper wafting to the floor, and handed Ashanti another offering.

She read, "*Kind, kind/leave pain behind/by this chant my grade I'll bind.*" And of all people, she looked her uncertainty at Cassi.

Relaxing a little more into their group dynamics, Cassi shook her head.

"Can't do spells on teachers," Barry reminded them as he glued crystals. "Besides, how can you get a better grade by proving that it works, if your only proof is the better grade?"

Not that Barry was completely objective. He seemed uncomfortable about doing spells, himself—one reason they were using Janice's project to prove his own paper's premise.

Cassi softly clapped her hands. CLAP clap, CLAP clap.

"And it's not tetramic trochamameter," translated Janice. Sort of.

Matt took the paper back from Ashanti, crumpled it into a ball, and arched it into the shadows behind him. It vanished in a way that could have been due to more than darkness.

The freshmen turned quickly back to their projects, pretending not to notice. Janice even looked up at Cassi, still on the stairs, grinned, and said, "Do you have to be invited in or something?"

"That's vampires," Barry reminded her as Cassi made herself take a step closer, then another one. Then, before she knew it, she was in the basement, too. Moments later, she was helping glue crystals.

She didn't need to be able to talk to do that.

Ashanti took Matt's next suggestion, read it, and said, "I'm not saying this."

So Matt reclaimed it from her and handed it to Barry, who read it and made a face. But he let the others in on the joke by reciting, "*Barry, Barry/Way too wary/Learn that magic isn't scary.*"

Only then did he crumple the rhyme and drill it at Matt's head. "Yeah. Real funny."

Matt laughed in Elvish.

"There," announced Janice, slowly drawing her hand away from where she'd been holding the last piece of crystal to its appropriate bar. "As soon as it dries, I'll oil it— Wells' time traveler talks about oiling the crystals—and we'll see if this really works."

They all stared at the machine, seemingly unsure whether to hope for it to work or not.

"We aren't going to accidentally kill our grandparents and erase our own existence, are we?" asked Barry. "'Cause that would suck."

"Maybe we can erase Professor Westbrook's existence," said Janice, and Matt chided her in Elvish. Something about her being full of crap. Or poop. Or manure. The word sounded less insulting in Elvish, though.

"Keep it up, Tinky Winky," Janice warned him.

He rolled his eyes at Cassi and—with lots of vowels and more umlauts, asked how she stood it. He'd been speaking Elvish for a good two days, now. It showed no sign of wearing off.

She looked back at him and thought, *It's better than the alternative.*

But nobody among the study group seemed to be particularly good at mind reading. Besides, she wasn't sure there was enough paper in his notebook, even college-ruled, for a true explanation.

Would they be her friends if they knew? Would they stay her friends if she never told them?

But that assumed they were already her friends. And as Professor Westbrook would say, she couldn't exactly develop that argument. Then again, Pollyanna would think the best of them.

Cassi wasn't sure that was a good thing.

When Janice pronounced that the glue was dry, then oiled the crystals as instructed, everyone—not only Cassi—fell silent. They'd all done magic at home, and in the controlled environments of their classrooms now that they'd gotten accepted to the Academy. But this was big stuff. This could affect their futures in more ways than grades.

Then again, the future was indistinct, even without trying to fit five teenagers into the single saddle of an iffy time machine.

Stories about college students stuffing themselves into phone booths had nothing on this, Cassi decided, wedged between Matt and Barry, someone's elbow in her side, someone's foot digging into her calf. But then, they were Sorcerer U students. In their world—

Janice pulled the white lever.

—anything might be possible. Maybe even . . . friends.

The world seemed to reel around her, and she held tighter to Matt. She felt as though she were falling—from Ashanti's cry, she wasn't alone. The basement around them got hazy.

The door above them opened, and several students came in backward and very quickly. They hurried down the steps—still backward—and walked right through the group in the time machine before turning around and skittering, still backward, back up and out.

Janice moaned something that sounded like, "Ohhhhh!"

The room grew fainter around them, then vanished. Light strobed across them, bright then dark, faster and faster, like the passing of days—months—years. A strange murmur filled Cassi's ears. Confusion wrapped itself around her mind, and she gave in to the simple reassurance of the others being with her. At least if they all died a grisly death, it would be together.

But then, slowly, the confusion receded from her, and she realized that whatever motion she'd sensed had stopped now.

She saw that they no longer sat in the basement of Sorcerer U, but in the middle of a large, round room.

A very large, very round room.

A room lit with candles, lined with shelves and draperies, and filled with dozens of chanting, black-robed men.

Janice whispered, "Oops."

The chants wavered only a little as these faceless men seemed to stare from the darkness of their cowls at the visitors who had magically arrived in their midst. More impressive, though, was their energy.

Cassi could feel their power, could see it as roiling cyclones of purple and black and blue and scarlet churning through the air around them, circling them like guard animals. All of it seemed to be directed by three tall figures closest to the chalked circle which, she belatedly realized, enclosed them and the time machine both.

The air over the circle fluxed and glittered, and Cassi knew without testing it that they were trapped inside. Not that she would have tried testing it.

The chanting continued, sending flashes of lightning crackling through the gathering storm of energy. The temple's hangings were etched with magical symbols. Tall, ornate shelves held the strangest looking supplies—casks and bottles and locked boxes—many of which practically screamed their inanimate power, their need to be used. A large symbol hung over everything, a circle divided into five quarters, enclosing what looked like a Star of David, which itself enclosed a crucified human figure. Over that was a name, and despite it being written in what looked like Latin, it was so powerful that Cassi could hear it, like an echoing shout.

Hermetic Order of the Golden Dawn.

They'd just time traveled into the middle of one of the most powerful groups of ceremonial magicians in history!

Of the three head wizards—all of whom wore a badge that looked kind of like a red rose on top of a golden, equal-armed cross—one on the side stepped forward. He drew back his hood, revealing a dark face that was, had to be—

Aleister Crowley?

Not a magic user anybody wanted to screw with.

He pointed at them, and in the charged atmosphere of this room, this careful circle of magic, Cassi suspected she wasn't the only one watching the blackness of his magic roil off of him and toward them. He said something in Latin—but if she could understand Elvish, she could understand this.

It had something to do with calling them demons and trapping their immortal souls to do his bidding.

Another of the leaders snapped at him to stop, his own hood falling back, but Crowley—aka the Beast—did not listen.

Janice, Barry, Ashanti, even Matt sat in silent horror. And in horror, Cassi finally spoke.

"Oh, God . . ." she whispered.

She hadn't put any forethought in it—but neither was she taking Anyone's name in vain. God's sudden appearance above them, blindingly bright, complete with the harmony of trumpets and organs and a million faithful voices, provided the perfect distraction.

But then, how could S/He not?

In that moment, Janice pulled the white lever again—and everything in the middle of the secret society's inner sanctum began to reel, to fall, to rush into fast-forward.

The world around them grew faint, once again.

Just before it completely vanished, and confusion wrapped itself around her again, Cassi heard one short, accented word in Elvish.

It loosely translated into *Blind-worm's sting*.

Then they were back in the basement, falling out of their

saddle onto the concrete floor, the crystals that had powered their journey shadowed and smoking.

"That was . . ." said Janice—and sat up specifically to make the sign of the cross. "And Crowley, too? Talk about your extremes!"

"I saw Yeats there, too," insisted Barry, his voice shaking a bit. "He was the one arguing with Crowley. I can put that in my paper . . . if I can just figure out a way to put it on my works-cited page."

"But, guys, that was . . ." Janice still hadn't finished that particular sentence.

Ashanti said, "What is this?" That's because Matt had just handed her a small, ornately carved jar, carefully stoppered and filled with some strange-looking herb.

"Blind-worm's sting," he answered—then laughed in pure delight at having spoken English. "Hey! God must have cured me!"

"It was!" agreed Janice. "God. Wasn't it?"

She asked it of Cassi—who carefully just nodded. Now they knew she could talk, after all. Now they knew how dangerous that was, and they would get angry with her, storm away.

Instead they piled on top of her for a group hug.

". . . for a charm of perfect pizza," finished Professor Westbrook, reading from Ashanti's paper. "Anyone familiar with the witches' chant from *Macbeth* should recognize that the trochaic tetrameter is strong throughout the spell and, despite some creative rhymes, Ms. Equiano did keep the basic scheme of couplets. She managed all the ingredients— for the charm, not necessarily the pizza—which is particularly rare. And apparently the pizza that then arrived was as perfect as anybody in the study group had ever tasted, so the magic worked. All of this neatly supports her thesis that William Shakespeare either was a magic user, or had some interesting sources. Good job, Ms. Equiano."

And he handed Ashanti her nine-page, laser-printed, double-spaced, proper-MLA-formatted essay. Cassi should know, since she'd helped proofread for everyone in the group.

What good was it for them to have a friend who was an English nerd, without a little formatting help now and then?

After murmuring a quick, *"Merci,"* Ashanti tipped the essay so that the others, craning their necks, could see. As if Cassi wouldn't have known from either Professor Westbrook's praise or her silvery-blue aura.

She'd gotten an A.

Matt had gotten an A, too. Janice and Barry had gotten A-minuses. Only a few pockets of gray or red marked where someone fell short of their expectations. Overall, the class's energy had improved considerably from the previous week—except for the eddies of uncertainty from students who hadn't seen their grades yet.

Like Cassi.

She began to get that sick-to-her-stomach feeling as Professor Westbrook went on to explain why Brett's paper on Christopher Marlowe's *Dr. Faustus* had only gotten a B—and to remind everyone to please make sure to visit Brett in the infirmary until he was able to return to his studies.

It made sense that the rest of Cassi's study group would get A's. They'd done interesting magic and written good papers . . . well, decent papers which she and Matt had managed to help polish into good papers, especially when they converted Janice's old-fashioned footnotes to parenthetical references. But none of that had helped Cassi with *Pollyanna*. She'd done no more magic than to explore the secrets of learning and friendship and, more often in the last few days than she could ever have divined, the power of being glad.

Besides, she'd changed her mind about her essay's thesis at the last minute, and had to redo the whole thing.

Janice, across the aisle, caught her gaze and gave her a surreptitious thumbs up. At moments like that, Cassi couldn't help but feel that maybe there were more important things in life—and Sorcerer U—than English grades.

When Matt suddenly tickled her from behind, she

jumped, swallowed back a silent giggle, and knew it for sure. Especially when she saw that the tickle had only been part of a stealth operation to toss a note onto her lap.

It read, *You worry too much.*

She'd learned, over the weekend, that Matt and Ashanti weren't, like, dating or anything. Matt was just a really friendly guy.

More and more to be glad about.

"Now this one," said Professor Westbrook, "is particularly intriguing. Cassandra Jones was given the unenviable assignment of investigating Eleanor Hodgman Porter."

The class stared at either him or Cassi with a complete lack of recognition. Even the group energy went still with confusion.

"Ms. Porter wrote hundreds of stories for magazines and newspapers, and several best-selling books," Professor Westbrook continued, his tone somehow implying that they'd should've known this. "You'd know her for a children's book called *Pollyanna*."

Now the class reacted much like Cassi's original study group had; laughter mixed with exclamations like "No way!" and "Get out!"

In light of their disbelief—easy to see in the room's energy—Cassi found herself questioning her essay's conclusion even more desperately.

"Contrary to popular belief—" Westbrook drilled Janice with a *look*, when he said that, "—I did not add that name to the pot merely to torture innocent students. I was hoping that someone particularly adept at magic would choose it, and indeed, she did."

Cassi felt herself go all hot and prickly, even before Matt poked her in the back. Did he mean *her?*

"I'll read you a passage," the teacher continued, and she felt even hotter. What if nobody believed her? What if she'd completely embarrassed herself?

"'*In conclusion, both Mrs. Porter and her heroine were magic users of the best kind,*' read Professor Westbrook—and drilled the class with a glare before even those students revving up for a burst of laughter could make a sound. His glare was a powerful thing. *"If magic really is the ability to change one's reality by changing one's perception of that reality, then Pollyanna casts spells throughout the book. Eleanor H. Porter's magic proves even stronger because, by creating such a long-lived character, she has taught this magical ability to countless children long past her own life's span, and continues to do so. Despite* Pollyanna's *reputation for foolish optimism, we shouldn't overlook the very real power of either the book, its several movie adaptations, or the many 'glad' clubs that were formed during the height of its popularity."*

Cassi stole a peek at the class's group energy, and it didn't frighten her. It hovered gently, still but not stagnant, as almost everyone listened to Professor Westbrook's voice.

To her own words.

"Pollyanna, like so many other books that have imprinted themselves on our world, reminds us that words contain immense power and stories even more. Therefore the most mundane of novelists can become the best kind of magic user—even Eleanor Hodgman Porter.'"

He handed Cassi back her paper.

It was an A-plus.

Cassi thought the best part was tipping it so that Janice and the others could see, and watching their auras brighten to match her own.

Only Stefani Harris—who had gotten a C on her report—voiced an objection. "That's kind of lame, isn't it? I mean, if that's true, then everything is magic."

Cassi blinked, stunned to see a tinge of green around Stefani's desk, brightest around her head, like a halo, where people's auras were easiest to see. Was she *jealous*?

Of her?

Professor Westbrook quirked an eyebrow at Cassi. "Go ahead, Ms. Jones," he encouraged. "We teachers are here for a reason."

"You tell her," agreed Janice loyally.

"Don't worry so much," agreed Matt. And they, more

than anyone but her mother, now knew what they were asking of her.

So Cassi took a chance. She cleared her throat. She swallowed. Then she looked at Moira and said, "Everything is magic. Especially writing."

Almost immediately, everyone's pens and pencils then reared up and started slithering off people's desks. They darted all over the room, Bics and Papermates and #2 pencils, many of them apparently to join the rapidly emptying boxes of chalk up front. Students screamed; many began to run for the door. This time, it wasn't a reaction to their grades. Or a pop quiz.

It had happened again. Cassi stared at the chaos around her in horror. Even at Sorcerer U, it had happened!

Now she had to decide whether to stay silent, or try saying something else to fix things—a tactic which often just made things worse.

To her relief, Professor Westbrook just winked at her and mouthed, *I've got this one.* And he set about trying to capture a piece of chalk long enough to start writing a counter incantation on the blackboard. "Class dismissed," he called, to those students who hadn't yet fled.

One of the witches had recaptured her Tigger pen and was petting it into bouncy-pouncy submission with one finger. A Goth had opened one of the windows, to aid in the other writing instruments' escape, shouting something about liberation.

When Cassi turned slowly to face her study group—her friends—they were laughing. But not at her.

"God, you're fun," snorted Janice.

A multicolored gel pen undulated across the toe of Cassi's shoe. She kicked it gently away from her and joined in the group's shared smile. And their shared energy. It was part hers now.

Maybe she was in the right school after all.

FINAL EXAM

by Josepha Sherman

THE room was featureless, with walls of plain adobe, reddish brown in the near-darkness. There were neither windows nor doors, but none who sat there heeded that. None of the figures could be seen clearly, as though each wore its own shadows. And all listened without motion to the one who stood before them, featureless as the others in shadow.

"They have been tested."

A whisper from another shadow: "They have passed their tests. What now? What now?"

The main shadow rose, looming over all. "Why, what else? We simply watch for now. Next year's class will be here soon enough. Then we shall try again."

Kristen Britain

GREEN RIDER

As Karigan G'ladheon, on the run from school, makes her way through the deep forest, a galloping horse plunges out of the brush, its rider impaled by two black arrows. With his dying breath, he tells her he is a Green Rider, one of the king's special messengers. Giving her his green coat with its symbolic brooch of office, he makes Karigan swear to deliver the message he was carrying. Pursued by unknown assassins, following a path only the horse seems to know, Karigan finds herself thrust into in a world of danger and complex magic....   0-88677-858-1

FIRST RIDER'S CALL

With evil forces once again at large in the kingdom and with the messenger service depleted and weakened, can Karigan reach through the walls of time to get help from the First Rider, a woman dead for a millennium?   0-7564-0209-3

To Order Call: 1-800-788-6262